Brave Kingdom

Brave Kingdom

Frances Murray

ST. MARTIN'S PRESS
NEW YORK, NEW YORK

8315123

Library of Congress Cataloging in Publication Data

Murray, Frances.
    Brave kingdom.

    I. Title.
PR6063.U738B7   1983   823'.914   83-9756
ISBN 0-312-09503-1

First published in Great Britain by Hodder and Stoughton Ltd.

First U.S. Edition

10 9 8 7 6 5 4 3 2 1

This novel is dedicated to my friends in the Staff Room of the Ladies' College, Guernsey and in particular to Margaret Surridge, Elaine Berry and Anne Forsyth who were so helpful in providing me with material about old New Zealand. Teaching has its frustrations but they are compensated by the friends one makes.

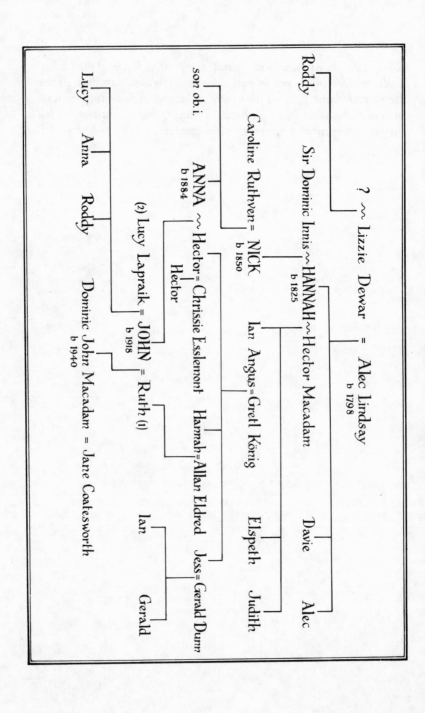

Contents

OVERTURE

1

Festival time in Edinburgh means little enough to the people of that city, if you are to believe them. They grumble at the crowds between them and the bar, at the risen prices; they sneer at the souvenir junk which appears like an annual fungus in the shop-windows and bustle their way to work along Princes Street with an impatient and pitying glance at those strolling along the broad pavements with nothing to do but stare about them. It is their pride to deny that they have ever taken advantage of the wealth of talent strewn before them, year after year. They attend the Tattoo once in a while, stare scornfully at the weirder manifestations of the Fringe, providing such spectacle is street theatre and thus free, but few of them pay to attend the concerts, the exhibitions, the plays and the films. They leave them to the 'visitors', a comprehensive word covering all sorts and conditions of incomers from the earnest Japanese to the pot-smoking eccentrics camping in elderly Bedford vans around the outskirts. It even covers the Glasgow *cognoscenti*, there in force and ineffably conscious that while Edinburgh has the name, grim, grimy Glasgow has the game. Like the ancient Athenians, the modern Athenians say 'nothing too much' and the Festival is too much. They endure it rather than enjoy it. If once in a while the waves of excitement and enthusiasm spread far enough to include them, it is an occasion indeed. Secretly, however, they savour the world's attention, regard the banners and the bunting which bedizen the ancient city with grudging appreciation and look up at the battlements of the castle, dramatised by light against the throbbing summer darkness, with a sense of possession so deep that it is akin to passion. That sight and the festive city glittering around the dour rock below can take a newcomer by the throat and silence comment. There above is beauty, that combining of natural grandeur and human endeavour which epitomises what men call art. Even the taxi-loads which stream

11

to and fro along Princes Street around half-past seven, aware of unaccustomed finery and half-digested early dinners, not to mention the vast cost of the tickets they finger so anxiously, even these pause to peer up at the splendour which dominates the city.

John Macadam and his wife, Lucy, were not exceptions: as their taxi turned west into Princes Street from St. David Street they drew in their breath and leaned forward to stare.

"There," Lucy said. "That's worth twelve thousand miles and a Moss Bros monkey suit, isn't it?"

John grunted derisively but went on looking until the taxi halted for the lights. They were in the middle of a long line of taxis all blinking their intention to turn down Lothian Road. The driver sighed, lit a cigarette and let his engine idle.

"Big do on at the Lyceum tonight," he commented. "This is my third trip down here in an hour."

"We won't be late?" Lucy asked anxiously.

"Got twenty minutes," said the driver.

The lights changed and they dawdled down Lothian Road in slow procession, passing and then being passed by people who had decided to walk in all the panoply of evening dress looking strange among the shorts and shirts and skimpy, summery clothes of those out to enjoy Edinburgh after dark.

"Concert at the Younger Hall too," the driver volunteered. "Worse'n Piccadilly Circus at rush hour this time of night."

"Quicker to walk," John muttered.

"The Festival must be a difficult time for you," Lucy remarked quickly.

"Aye," agreed the driver, "but there's money about and folk ready to spend it."

He nosed expertly into a gap and brought the shabby front of the Lyceum into view. Across the *porte-cochère* were emblazoned the words WORLD PREMIERE and they could see a glittering chattering crowd seeping inside.

"Took yon fella down here an hour since," the driver told them and jerked his head at the world-famous name on the bill-boards. "Over the moon, he was. Full of it. Says it's the greatest thing since sliced bread."

John felt Lucy take his hand and squeeze it.

"They're all like that, singers. Either over the moon or sick as a parrot because of some joker writing in the paper."

He swung suddenly to the left.

"You see a lot of them this time of the year. And they talk. Anyone'll do as long as they can bend your ear. Don't stop to think opera isn't everyone's cuppa . . . but you get all sorts in this job. Here you are then. Near as I can get you. There's Royalty expected . . . can't get up to the doors for the Fuzz."

John and Lucy climbed out looking about them as if they were not quite sure they had come to the right place. The driver watched them and wondered. Not the usual opera goers, that was for sure. Didn't have the patter. He told John the fare and watched Lucy settle her shawl about her shoulders. She must be about sixty, he reckoned, and that dress was home-made. She'd been pretty, though, in a quiet sort of style. He wondered what part they came from for both were as weatherbeaten as cowboys. John fumbled in his pocket to find money and the driver turned his attention to him. Proper man-mountain that one, six foot three or four if he was an inch and if he got through the evening without bursting out of that hire-job he'd be lucky. He pocketed a hefty tip and grinned over at Lucy.

"Enjoy yourself," he said, "but rather you than me."

He drove off and John looked after him muttering and easing the tight stiff collar of his shirt. Lucy was looking about her like a child at Woolworth's window. He took her by the arm and marched her towards the doors.

"You're supposed to let me take your arm," she complained, "not march me off like a criminal."

"If I lost hold of you you'd never make it."

"Well, just remember I'm wearing high heels for the first time since we left here."

"Gawd," John said. "I hope he appreciates what we've done for him."

Once inside they went to the box office, pushing with difficulty through the crowd chattering their way to the auditorium. John bent down to speak through the gap in the glass.

"Sold out," said the girl, shaking her head with practised regret. "I'm dreadfully sorry, sir, but there's not a seat to be had, not anywhere, and a waiting list as long as your arm."

John looked uncomfortable, coloured and murmured something. It had an effect which seemed magical. The harrassed girl looked up and beamed.

"Oh, you *did* get here! We were all so hoping you would. I have your tickets here, right here. Wait, I'll come with you . . . show you . . ."

She nodded to someone to come and take her place and deal with the hopeful queue which had formed behind them and then emerged from the door, holding out her hand.

"Oh, such a pleasure to meet you both. We've been on tenterhooks, you know. Mr. Macadam was just on the phone a moment ago to ask if you'd come. Mavis's phoning backstage. He'll be so thrilled. All that distance. This way."

She beamed again, her delight in their presence real and warming; then shepherded them through a curtained arch and along a narrow sloping corridor.

"I hope it wasn't too dreadful a journey. I mean to say, a strike just at that point. They do it on purpose, I always say. I took your cable in to rehearsal and I just wish you could have seen his face."

She opened a little door which made Lucy think of *Alice in Wonderland* and the light and noise of the auditorium washed over them.

"We kept this box for you and believe me it wasn't easy. Everyone, but everyone's coming tonight. Marvellous. There's drinks over there, and two special souvenir programmes. Oh, and a note from Mr. Macadam."

They surveyed the box with awe. It was a large one with four chairs disposed behind a plush-covered balustrade.

"What a night this must be for you," their guide declared breathily. "How proud you must be."

Beyond, they could see the auditorium already packed solid. The audience were chattering and exclaiming and pointing each other out. There was a sense of self-congratulation in the air; this was the place to be, this evening would be something to remember. The light glinted off jewellery, shining, newly-coiffed hair and white shirt fronts. Through the hum came the notes of the orchestra tuning up, like the first flames of a bonfire, leaping and dying.

"That's the most exciting noise I know," their guide

14

exclaimed and then looked abashed. "I must love you and leave you. It's all go out front, tonight. I hope you've got everything you want. Bye, lovely to meet you, see you after, I hope. Oh, it's going to rock them . . . everybody says so, even the stage-crew and they couldn't care less as a rule. It's out of this world!"

She closed the door on her enthusiasm and left them to themselves. John gave Lucy a hunted look and pulled a chair back into a more obscure corner.

"Like being in a glass case," he grumbled.

"No one's going to look at us," said Lucy serenely and leaned over the balustrade, looking about her with frank curiosity and pleasure. "Just think, all this for Nick, our Nick. What does he say in his note?"

John was fumbling for his glasses.

"He says, so far as I can make out, that it's marvellous to have us here, this night of all nights, and he'll come round at the end. He's got a surprise for us and hopes we'll think it was worth making the journey for. His love to us both, now and ever."

Lucy turned round, her eyes wide.

"I wonder what sort of surprise," she speculated, "public or private."

"What do you mean?"

"Music or matrimony, I suppose."

John grunted and folded the letter neatly back into the envelope.

"Didn't think he'd ever marry. He's never lacked for company, God knows, and the young don't seem to think it's as important as once they did. Do you want him to?"

"I'm not sure. Yes, I think I do. He's getting to the stage where he needs a . . . I was going to say a home but a home wouldn't be much use to him hurtling round the globe like a satellite."

"If this is a success he may want to do more composing and less conducting. You can't compose hurtling round the globe, as you put it."

"He's managed so far."

"He said most of this was written when he was at Bennachie last Easter," John said thoughtfully.

15

"Anyway," Lucy declared, "he ought to have children. 'Now is the time that face should form another . . .' "

John shook his head at her and grinned.

"Haven't you got enough grandchildren, woman?"

"You can't have too many."

"The way the world's going I sometimes wonder what will happen to the tribe we've begotten between us," John reflected rather grimly. "There are times like Christmas when I feel like Isaac . . ."

"As long as it's not like Ishmael."

"Oh, no," he assured her, "for me this is the wilderness, not Bennachie."

The lights dimmed slightly and Lucy picked up one of the programmes.

"It'll be starting in a moment and I haven't the faintest idea what it's all about."

John took the one she handed him. On the cover was a design of profiles in silhouette superimposed upon the wheel and tower of a pithead hoist. Across this in jagged red lettering were the words THE GRESFORD PIT. At the bottom in fat black type it said, 'A new opera composed and conducted by Dominic Macadam'. Inside the cast list read like a *Who's Who* of the operatic world. At the very back was a full-page portrait photograph of Dominic Macadam. His father stared at it and smiled a little.

"Now he's getting older he looks more and more like that picture of Hannah in the sitting room," he murmured.

'Born in New Zealand of Scottish descent . . .' began the potted biography on the facing page. John let the programme drop to his knee and looked out towards the red and gold of the curtain, wondering of what interest it could be to this audience that Nick was born in New Zealand. Did they know by instinct that musical ability was only a part of the story? How many thousands of musicians as fine as Nick had never gone beyond singing in the choir or whistling behind the plough? There had to be more than that. He looked down again at the bland concise wording. It was, he supposed, a ritual gesture to appease this universal sense of the vast immanent forces within every living creature. To think of the web of ancestry which resulted in a single personality was like looking at the stars on a

16

frosty night, except one was looking inwards and not outwards; it was a humbling experience.

The audience began to applaud; the leader of the orchestra
was coming in. She bowed and took her seat. The clapping
died and the hum of conversation died with it. Heads craned to
look at the little door through which she had come. A tall, lean
figure emerged, dark-haired and pale-faced. The applause
started again, swelling and swelling as Dominic Macadam
came to the centre of the orchestra and turned about to acknowledge his reception. He looked to his right and grinned at
their box as if there was no one else in the theatre at all. Lucy
waved and then, overcome by embarrassment, bent her head.
The rest of the audience clapped and stared and craned and
wondered. The house lights faded. Dominic Macadam turned
round, tapped his baton and the first ominous chords of the
overture rolled out.

John could not rid himself of this sense of looking inwards
into infinite distances. With one part of his mind he listened to
the laying down of the theme, appreciating the skill which
made so much of a simple motif, but with another he began to
wonder in which part of the web of ancestry the story of
Dominic Macadam, musician, could have begun to take shape.
At which point had the threads begun to twist into his pattern?
Perhaps it had begun with Hannah, with Hannah Lindsay, the
blacksmith's daughter in the Kirkton of Langmuir, a century
and a half before this World Première. Her brother Alec had
been a fine singer before the Lord, if all accounts were accurate,
and her grandfather had been welcome with his fiddle at
bridals throughout three parishes. That same fiddle was
hanging on the wall of the sitting room of Bennachie to this
day. But Hannah had brought more with her than the music,
much more . . .

HANNAH'S STORY

2

The Reverend Donald McLagan drained his glass and set it down on the table among the wreckage of Lizzie Lindsay's funeral feast: from a professional experience of such occasions he had decided that the widower's provision was only just the hither side of parsimony. There was no ham, no beef, only sweet stuff; no port wine, just tea and a single bottle of whisky among near twenty menfolk. Better things might have been expected of Alec Lindsay who, so rumour said, had a bonny penny salted away. He was a skilled smith, never short of work, and had a useful holding of pasture land where he fattened beasts for the market: and Lizzie, God rest her, had brought him a goodish bit. How much no one knew but that didn't stop folk speculating. Nothing ever stopped that, thought the Minister cynically, not even death: he would wager that of those black-clad figures pacing respectfully behind Lizzie Lindsay's coffin, most had wondered not for the first or for the last time who had fathered her first bairn. Lizzie herself had never let on, nor had her people, and if Lindsay knew, it wasn't a subject which anyone in their senses would care to broach with him. And now the lad had gone, no one knew where, and there were plenty to say Alec Lindsay had driven him away which was a poor way to keep the bargain made all those years ago. And there were more to say that it was Roderick's going, and never a word from him to say where, which had killed his mother, and never mind the late-come bairn which lay beside her in the coffin. McLagan was inclined to agree with them: he knew that death had come as a release to Lizzie Lindsay. She had sinned, poor creature (as who had not, he thought uncomfortably) but she had paid a heavy penalty marrying a coarse creature like Lindsay.

At this point, when the rest of the funeral guests had departed, he usually offered a short prayer for the easing of grief but there seemed little need for it on this occasion.

21

"Aye, Lindsay," he said, "I'll be off."

Lindsay rose and nodded: he was not a large man but he was broad and heavy in the shoulders and had huge scarred smith's hands. His grasp was more painful than friendly. The Minister turned to the daughter, silent and pale in the corner, her two younger brothers glowering on either side. There could be no doubt of their paternity, reflected the Minister, it was stamped upon them. Hannah there was another matter.

"As long as you've Hannah you'll not have lost Lizzie," he observed, "if she isn't her very likeness."

"Aye," Alec agreed unenthusiastically.

Hannah looked at her father and a flicker of some emotion passed over her face. She was a tall slender girl with a long, rather colourless face and delicate features. Her hair was very dark, scraped back unbecomingly into a heavy bun; a few tendrils which had escaped indicated that it might wave, even curl, if it were given the opportunity. Her eyes were grey-blue, large and well-shaped. The Minister saw the shadows beneath them and reflected that Lizzie had one genuine mourner. Lindsay showed not even the conventional signs of grief and doubtless felt none. The boys looked bewildered and sulky rather than griefstricken. McLagan patted them on the head, which made them flinch. In the Kirkton of Langmuir the Minister was also the Dominie and he had a heavy hand for those who neglected their catechism or miscopied their text. Alec and Davie were more used to clouts on the lug than pats on the head. Lindsay turned to the other remaining guest, Dougal Lapraik.

"You'll get the Minister the length of Braeside, Dougal?" he suggested.

Dougal, packed tightly into funeral blacks which seemed to belong to a much smaller man, shook his head as far as his collar would allow and went even redder in the face.

"I was wanting a word, Mr. Lindsay," he said uneasily. "I'll not keep you long."

He looked apologetically at the Minister. McLagan understood well enough what he was at. Dougal and Hannah had been promised four months. They had not yet bespoken his services but in the normal way of things they would be married before the New Year, earlier if they anticipated the ceremony as so many did. But there was no sign of that, nor like to be. Lizzie was dead and the harvest almost upon them, there would be little time for fornication, thought the Minister, even were there more inclination for it than he could detect in Hannah. He wondered a bit at Dougal's choice. His own taste was for a cosier creature, someone warmer and less remote. Perhaps when his own poor Sarah had followed Lizzie to the kirkyard he might . . . he pulled guiltily away from such reflections, trying to suppress the images in his mind. Sarah had been ailing a long while and he was a man who found it difficult to discipline the flesh. He cleared his throat portentously and took his leave.

Alec Lindsay closed the front door behind him with an impatient thrust. It was unused except for weddings and funerals and moved with noisy reluctance. Back in the parlour he found the boys gobbling scones and jam.

"Are you clean out of your head?" he grumbled to Hannah, "letting them eat in their good clothes? D'you think I'm made of money? Away, you two. Up the stair and shift into your old duds."

The boys clattered upstairs and Hannah began to gather up the cups and glasses.

"Well, Dougal?"

Lindsay slumped into the carved chair, unbuttoning his waistcoat and loosening the black stock round his throat.

"Take off they boots, Hannah," he ordered. "They're ower tight on me."

Hannah knelt at his feet and began to undo the laces, tight-knotted with the smirr of rain which had accompanied the funeral.

"Speak up, man. What's amiss?" he said impatiently.

"I'm to take Netherbiggin from the term," Dougal informed him. "I was at the Big House yesterday and signed the lease."

"Do you tell me that," observed Alec.

"Aye."

There was a brief silence.

"I was wondering, could I ask Mr. McLagan would he cry us in the Kirk next Sunday?" Dougal blurted out.

"With her mother scarce cold . . . 'tisna decent," declared

23

Lindsay and pushed Hannah with his boot. "D'ye mean to take all day?"

"They're tight with the wet," she muttered and looked down again.

Lindsay turned his small bright eyes upon Dougal.

"Why the haste?" he asked sarcastically. "You've bided your time till now. Have ye bairned her?"

"I have not!" said Dougal roughly.

"Well for her."

Lindsay clenched his huge fist and held it under Hannah's nose.

"Fine she kens what she'd get. Not that it's likely, mind . . . too touch-me-not is our Hannah, as I don't doubt you've discovered . . ."

Dougal flushed angrily.

"Oh, aye, you can colour up, my young bubbly-jock, but it'd take a better man than you to stop me saying what I think. Why d'ye want the banns cried this instant minute?"

"Because I'm to go into Netherbiggin . . ."

"For God's sake, I'll be quicker myself!"

Lindsay sent Hannah sprawling with an impatient thrust of his boot and bent to undo his own laces. Dougal made a strangled, inarticulate noise and moved to help her up.

"I doubt you'll be needing her tocher to stock the place," observed Lindsay slyly.

Dougal helped Hannah to her feet before he replied.

"I'll not deny it."

"Then," said Lindsay, "you'll need to look elsewhere."

There was a moment of silence.

"How . . . elsewhere?" asked Dougal.

Lindsay kicked off one boot.

"Someplace else," he said. "You'll not be getting a penny with Hannah, not a penny piece."

The two young people stared at him, unbelieving.

"But we agreed . . ." Dougal protested at last. "Three hundred pound. I'd your word on it."

"Nothing on paper," said Lindsay, "and never a witness."

"It's not your money," Hannah cried angrily, "it's from my mother. She told me so."

"Her will says you get it when you marry a man I approve. Oh, yes it does. I saw to that."

He eased off the other boot and grinned at them maliciously.

"And as long as I need a woman-body in this house I'll not approve of any man that comes sniffing after Hannah."

Hannah had gone very pale.

"Oh, dearie, dearie me," Lindsay said with mock concern, "will Dougal no have ye without a tocher, lass? Och, but it's an ill world."

Hannah looked across at Dougal but he wouldn't meet her eyes. She turned on her father.

"Do you mean what you say?" she demanded.

"I mean it, depend on that. Why should I pay out money for a housekeeper when I've got you?"

She stared at him for a moment, her eyes narrowed in hatred.

"May you roast in Hell!" she cried out and looked at Dougal who was punishing the brim of his hat. "And what will you do?"

"Damn it, lass, I need that money," he said sullenly. "I counted on it. Without it I'm done. I can't want beasts, not on Netherbiggin."

"More fool you," jeered Lindsay. "Never count money till it's in the hand."

Hannah suddenly whisked round in a flurry of black skirts and ran out.

"That's ill done, Lindsay, real ill done," Dougal said angrily. "Without I'd the money promised I'd not have taken on the place."

"Och, never fash yourself for a puckle silver, Dougal. There's Farmyre's lass panting for a man like a bitch on heat . . . and Farmyre is a warm man, Dougie, a far warmer man nor me."

"His Chrissie's ten year older nor me," Dougal protested.

"Then he'll pay the more to be rid of her. More than you'd have got with Hannah. Just think on that, no the ten year."

Dougal glowered and said nothing.

"And think on another thing," Lindsay went on. "Chrissie's mebbe old, aye, and plain as porridge but she'll be grateful, oh aye, she'll be grateful, and that'll make her warm and willing.

25

She'll not make you unwelcome at your own table and in your own bed. She'll make a cosier armful than ever Hannah will. That one's her mother's daughter right enough. You mark my words."

Dougal stared, startled by the venom in Lindsay's voice.

"And what if she is a bit older," Lindsay went on, "just you wait a wee. Like enough you'll bury her while you're still young and then you can pick out a lass more to your mind. Just you think on that."

Dougal flushed.

"I'm no proud of my part in this," he ground out, "but my lease is signed and I haven't a stiver to pay a penalty. But there's one thing pleases me fine, Lindsay. I'll never be kin to you. I'd as soon be kin to a stinking brock. As there's a God above, Lindsay, I hope I see you get your comeuppance!"

"Comeuppance! I've had my comeuppance!" Lindsay bellowed and came to his feet. "Wasn't I married on her mother these twenty year?"

"Aye, you were. And well paid for it," Dougal shouted back, flown with anger and contempt. "All the Kirkton kens that. And they ken why. You were paid to father another man's bairn, Alec Lindsay. And I might ha' kenned you'd break your bargain with me for God kens you broke your bargain with Lizzie's folk. You set about to drive Roddy away as sure as I stand here!"

Lindsay's face was purple.

"Out!" he bellowed. "Out of here afore I break your neck!"

"I'm no feared of you," said Dougal contemptuously, "all you're fit for is beating wee laddies and kicking lassies. But I'd sooner muck out the pigs with my bare hands than file them striking you!"

He spat at Lindsay's feet and strode heavily away, slamming the back door till the whole smiddy echoed. Upstairs, Hannah stood at her bedroom window and watched him out of sight. Her face was expressionless.

"Where've ye got to, ye fushionless bitch?" called her father from below. "Are they crocks to wash themselves?"

Hannah turned away from the window and tied an apron over her black skirt. Her room was under the roof, small and sparsely furnished; a narrow bed with a patchwork quilt, a chest of drawers, a chair, a table and a tiny mirror on the wall. At the foot of the bed stood a heavy wooden chest. Hannah stared down at it for a moment then bent and lifted the lid. It was almost full: there was linen, carefully embroidered with elaborate 'L's, there were blankets and tablecloths and in one corner a smaller wooden box. Hannah lifted the paper and straw which covered the contents, revealing the delicately fluted china cups which nestled in the straw.

"Hannah!" bellowed Lindsay.

She fingered one of the cups, replaced the cover and shut the chest.

"My hope chest," she murmured aloud and then laughed. "Some hopes."

It was winter and bitter cold outside so that the acrid smelling warmth of the smiddy was welcome. Hannah brought in a napkin-covered basket and laid it on a bench.

"Your mid-yokin'," she said.

Davie turned round from the object he was filing and smiled at his sister. Four years had changed him from a sullen hobbledehoy into a powerful young man taller than his father and with the same skill and strength in his hands.

"Is father no back yet?" he enquired.

"No," Hannah said and settled herself on the bench. "The dear knows what he's at in the town, for I don't."

"You've a look on your face like the cat at the cream-pot," said her brother apprehensively. "What have *you* been at?"

"I was up at the Big House," she said. "I saw the factor and Alec's to go to the Mains as third horseman after the New Year."

Davie whistled.

"What'll father say to that?" he asked.

"Plenty to me," Hannah said indifferently, "but nothing to the Laird and that's what matters. There's too much custom comes here from the Big House."

"And Alec?"

"Oh, he's fine pleased. He's to have a good pair, pure-bred Clydesdale, and he was on at me about them for an hour after."

"He's the dead spit of Granpa Dewar, Alec," observed Davie, "he fair dotes on horses."

"Aye, and I'll tell you another thing if you'll keep it to yourself. Granpa Dewar's got an eye to Alec to take on Overlangmuir when he's past it. Uncle Andrew'll never make a farmer."

Davie swallowed a mouthful of scalding tea.

"Why not send Alec to Granpa now?"

"He'll learn more at the Mains," Hannah said decisively, "and he'll need to do as he's telled . . . no bad thing for our Alec. And if he was at Granpa's, father'd be everlasting fetching him away to mess with our stirks and pigs here. He'll not do that to the Laird. And in a year or so Alec'll not have to heed father any more than you do."

"I heed him," Davie protested, smiling.

"When it suits you," said Hannah shrewdly. "If you want to gang your own gait, you do. And he keeps his mouth shut for fine he kens you could dump him in there if you'd a mind to it."

She jerked her head at the horse trough. Davie laughed.

"Now, would I do sic a thing?"

"Mebbe no, but you could and that's what counts with father. And you've a sure hand with all the Laird's machines. You'll fare well enough, Davie, whatever you decide . . . and now Alec's provided for."

There was a short silence as Davie, not a fast thinker, pondered the implications of that remark.

"I called in at Netherbiggin on my road home," Hannah told him. "She's to name the new bairn for me . . . Hannah Christine."

She chuckled at the idea.

"You're a saint, right enough, Hannah," Davie said. "Other lassies in your shoes wouldn't go next or nigh the place, let alone helping yon great thowless creature. Do you never think it might have been you in her room?"

"Aye, I do, and I think I'd have made a better fist of it," said Hannah and laughed. "But these days it's no great matter. Times I think I'd a lucky escape. Poor Chrissie, three laddies in four year and this one the only girl."

There was a rattling of hooves and wheels outside and a familiar voice swore ill-temperedly at the horse.

"Father," said Davie.

"Aye. And in a rare taking by the sound of it," returned Hannah and went to the doorway. "Mercy on us!"

Hannah's exclamation brought Davie to her side in the smiddy entrance. He was in time to see his father lift down from the cart a young woman, heavily pregnant and dressed in shabby finery; a worn velvet gown lavishly trimmed with grimy lace, a bonnet with a broken feather and a braided plum coloured cloak with the braid hanging off in loops and a tear in the hem. Her hair was sandy-red and hung out of the bonnet in great tangles, greasy and uncombed.

"Who in the name can that be?" Davie muttered.

"I'd not care to enquire too close," Hannah replied.

Alec Lindsay turned about and saw them staring. His face was dull red.

"Davie! Hannah! Come here!" he bellowed.

They went forward slowly, taking in the newcomer's heavy belly and her sullen unwashed face.

"A right trollop," muttered Davie under his breath. "The old goat . . ."

Hannah said nothing but her expression was grimly amused.

"This is Minnie," said Lindsay and jerked his thumb at her. "She's your new good-mother. We was married yesterday."

"Not a day too soon," observed Hannah. "Good day to you, mistress."

Minnie looked around her, at the smiddy, the outbuildings, the dungheap in the corner with its complement of hens, the rambling old house; then she looked her stepchildren up and down.

"In the name o' the wee man!" she exclaimed shrilly, "ye didna say they was older nor me. And ye didna say I was to bide in a midden!"

"Less of your lip," growled Lindsay. "Hannah'll take you round the place. Davie, I've a load of bar. Give's a hand with them."

Minnie and Hannah stared at one another.

"Best come with me," said Hannah at last, "I'll show you where you can wash yourself and then you can see over the house."

"First I'll see the place and then I'll tell you what we'll do,"

Minnie returned aggressively. "I'm mistress here now and you'd best mind that. I'll no play second fiddle to any old maid."

"Do you tell me that," said Hannah gently. "Well, better an old maid, to my mind, than a slummocky trollop. There's well-water and good yellow soap in the scullery there before you'll set foot in the house."

She grasped Minnie's arm and marched her across the yard while Davie and his father watched open-mouthed and dismayed. Minnie struggled and howled abuse.

"Davie!" called Hannah calmly as Minnie wriggled and shrieked. "There's linen airing in the kitchen. Fetch me a towel, a clean shift and a petticoat. And a blanket from the press in the good room."

She dragged her screeching stepmother into the scullery and shut the door. Davie clattered the armful of iron bars he was lifting back into the cart and with an apprehensive glance at his father hurried into the kitchen. When he came out laden with linen, Lindsay was standing undecidedly outside the scullery door. The noise which was coming from that small dank apartment passed belief. Minnie was shrieking and swearing, using the lurid vocabulary of the Glasgow back streets. Every now and again the noise was diminished as if by the forcible application of a wet cloth to the face. Davie, his eyes wide and his face unnaturally solemn, knocked on the door. After a moment it opened and Minnie's clothes were hurled into the courtyard.

"Bury them in the midden," Hannah instructed. "They're alive."

Davie looked doubtfully at the tawdry bundle while a furious tirade emerged from the scullery. Alec Lindsay's mouth dropped open and he scratched uneasily at his belly. The bonnet followed the clothes and blew across the yard to where the mare was waiting to be unharnessed. She put a large muddy hoof on it. Davie advanced to the door with his armful.

"Hang them over the mangle," Hannah instructed impatiently. "I can't leave this Devil's daughter or she'll be up and away."

Davie hesitated on the threshold, peeped in, retreated fast and looked at his father.

"Father, I canna go in there! She's mother-naked in the wash-tub!"

"Towel!" Hannah demanded above the din. Lindsay grabbed the linen from Davie and went in. He was greeted by a blast of reproach and abuse.

". . . if I'd kenned you'd a bultin' borrow-cow to a daughter I'd never a let you put the ring on ma finger, ye lyin' old bastard. Will ye stand there and see her scrub the skin aff of me and me eight months gone?"

The tirade ended in a bubbling shriek as her head was doused by a jugful of cold water.

Outside Davie and his father looked at one another.

"What way did ye not tell us this was in the wind?" asked Davie reproachfully.

"I didna ken myself," snapped Lindsay. "Her mother put the law on me, the old cow."

"Hannah won't like it," warned Davie.

"Hannah can make a kirk or a mill o't," blustered Lindsay. "It's my house and I'll bring who I want in it."

"Fetch me a comb, Davie," called Hannah, "and the long-nebbed scissors from my work-box."

Davie turned and made for the kitchen, closing his ears to the wails of angry protest which followed this ominous request.

"It will grow again," said Hannah inexorably, "and the faster for being clean. Never you mind the bairn, the sooner it gets used with washing the better, and you hold your ill tongue, nobody was ever the worse of soap and water."

3

Two months after Minnie's bath Alec Lindsay knocked on the door of the Manse. The Minister opened it himself.

"Aye, so it's you, Lindsay. Come your ways in. You'll be wanting the new bairn baptised, I dare say. What's her name to be?"

"Euphame," returned Lindsay and scowled at the thought of his mother-in-law whose name it was. "Euphame, Alexandrina, Jessamine."

McLagan smiled slightly.

"Come inbye." He indicated the door of his study. "I'll need to write them all down. Man, it's a fell mouthful."

"Aye," Lindsay agreed dourly, "and she's sickly forbye. Such an expense to put on a stone if she doesna live."

He cleared some books off a chair and sat down while the Minister found a piece of paper, then a pen and then a knife to mend it. His desk was covered with paper from which dirty glasses and cups were emerging like rocks at low tide. Lindsay remarked other signs of domestic disorder. The hearth was dirty and the fire choked with the ash of several days; dust lay everywhere.

"Mistress Duthie's away, I hear," he observed.

"She's got a daughter sick in Motherwell," sighed the Minister. "Agnes went off to see to the bairns."

And she probably wouldn't come back, reflected the Minister sourly; the girl wasn't likely to recover and there were four children as well as their feckless father. He sighed again. The prospect of finding another housekeeper, the fifth since the death of his wife, was daunting. What he really wanted was another wife and was it not for the fact that he was reluctant to relinquish the little innkeeper's widow in Falkirk he would have tried to find one long since. Sarah had been dead nearly three years. Housekeepers were demanding creatures and hard to find, even harder to keep.

"What you're needing, Minister, is a wife," said Lindsay, echoing his own thoughts. "Housekeepers are kittle cattle."

"Aye," McLagan agreed. "I've given the matter a deal of thought but good wives are scarce."

And who should know that better than Alec Lindsay, he thought maliciously, whose new-wedded wife was rumoured to have been in hot pursuit of poor Davie within days of her lying-in. Davie had resolved the situation by moving out to lodge with the Logies and, if the gossip was true, he'd soon be asked to cry the banns in a hurry for Sarah Logie and Davie. Moreover, he had heard, as who had not, of Minnie Lindsay's bath. He smiled sardonically at his visitor.

"Matrimony's a serious step," he said, "especially for a Minister."

"Imphm," grunted Lindsay. "What would you be looking for, Minister, supposing you were on the hunt for a wife? A widow-woman, mebbe, or would you rather look for a younger piece?"

McLagan stiffened at this enquiry and Lindsay leaned back in his chair and assumed an unconvincingly casual air.

"I dare say you'd be looking for a bit of money with her," he went on, "it's aye handy."

"I might," agreed McLagan suspiciously.

"Well," said Lindsay, "there's three hundred pounds goes with my Hannah."

McLagan gaped. He had heard from Dougal Lapraik just what Lindsay had done after Lizzie Lindsay's death to keep Hannah and her domestic accomplishments at the smiddy. By all accounts, the new Mistress Lindsay was unlikely to rival her stepdaughter as a housewife.

"Hannah?" he said incredulously. Hannah's father went a dull red.

"Aye," he said. "Hannah."

"Why?"

"Why not?" blustered Lindsay. "High time she was married. She's four and twenty and not improving with age."

"She could have been Mistress Lapraik these four years," observed McLagan drily, "and a far better match. I'm twice her age and more."

Lindsay glowered at him.

"The smiddy's worse than Donnybrook Fair," he blurted out. "The wife's aye at me to be rid of Hannah, and Hannah's got a tongue on her like a wasp's arse, because she's provoked, you understand, and she's aye at the coarse remarks till Minnie's fit to be tied. I tell you, Minister, there's no living with the pair of them. Minnie'll come screeching into the smiddy when I've folk in, even the Laird, and she'll lay tongue to Hannah till I dinna ken where to look. I'm fair sick o' being the speak of the countryside. And dinner-times, merciful God, half the time the air's full of soup or sowans or crocks. One of them's got to be on her way or there'll be murder done and I'll not hang for either of them. Three hundred pound, Minister, a chest of linen and stuff, her mother's dresser and a fine silver teapot. She's respectable, trust me for that, and she can stretch a shilling as far as most and further than some. Just what you're after."

The Minister recovered his breath.

"And what's Hannah after?" he demanded. "Does she know what you're at? I don't see her being handed over like a spare beast."

"Hannah will do as I tell her," announced Lindsay. "Well?"

McLagan rose and kicked at the clogged-up fire.

"I'm away too old for her," he said, and she's too skinny and cross-grained for me, he added to himself.

"Three hundred and fifty and a good milking cow," Lindsay replied at once.

"I still think . . ." McLagan began but was interrupted.

"Four hundred's my last offer," declared Lindsay. "She's real spry about the house, ye ken. She can cook and make butter and milk and sew and knit and I don't know what all. And she can hold her tongue for days together, when she's not provoked . . ."

The Minister was irresistibly reminded of Mungo the auctioneer praising a doubtful beast at the Tuesday mart.

"And what provokes her?" he enquired.

"Minnie," said Lindsay bitterly.

McLagan wrote down the names of the baby on a slip of paper and slipped it into the Bible at the reading for next Sunday. He needed time to think. Hannah might not be the cosy, uncritical armful he had in mind but there was no denying Lindsay's was a good offer.

34

"Mind," said Lindsay, "if you're not quick off the mark it's all off."

"If Hannah is agreeable," the Minister began huffily, "we might . . ."

"Just you cry the banns next Sabbath," Lindsay told him and got to his feet. "I'll answer for Hannah."

He spat on his huge hand and thrust it out.

"It's a bargain, then?"

McLagan ignored the gesture.

"We are not at Falkirk Tryst, Lindsay," he rebuked. "I shall speak to her."

"Marry the Minister!" Hannah exclaimed an hour or so later.

"You can marry him or go to service," her father told her. "I'll not have my house turned into a battlefield."

"I've no wish to stay and see it become a midden," she retorted. "Will you part with my tocher then?"

"Aye. I'm to put another hundred to it, and Bonnie forbye."

"My, my, but Minnie must be leading you a life of it," Hannah jeered. "To think you'll part with good money to be rid of me. But I'd not have Bonnie, she's never thrown a heifer yet. *If* I agree to this . . .*if* . . . I'll have Maggie."

Lindsay glared at her.

"Maggie then. Damn it, woman, I've made a good match for you. You might say a thank you."

"Haivers," said Hannah scornfully, "you've suited yourself, as always. You call a widow-man who could be my father a good match?"

"A man of the cloth . . . a minister . . ."

Hannah laughed in his face.

"Oh, aye. Most respectable, except that there's a bairn at the Mill that's the living spit of him and another west the country there that he pays for by the week. Oh, most respectable . . . he's bedded half the women in the parish *and* has a slut in keeping in Falkirk. A man of the cloth, oh, aye, a rare bargain."

"You'll be mistress at the Manse," Lindsay reminded her, "and folk'll look up to you. Isn't that worth a thank you?"

"If that's what you want, thank you," said Hannah ironically. "But never think I believe you did all this for me."

"He'll be up for his supper the morn's night."

"Then you'd best see yon trollop washes herself and minds her language," Hannah suggested scornfully, "or she'll affront us all."

"Ach!" spat Lindsay in disgust and made for the door.

"And you'd best watch the pair of them or they'll be bedded while you wait!"

With this parting shot she went upstairs. Once by herself she considered the proposition more seriously. She had little liking and no respect for McLagan and was sure he had as little for her, but she was determined to leave the smiddy and there were few alternatives open to her. To marry the Minister would be no bed of roses but it would be a sight better than living with Minnie or going into service. It would be hard to be a servant in somebody else's house. That she might marry someone more to her taste than the Minister she did not even consider. At twenty-four she was on the shelf. No one would look her way and there was no one she wanted to look her way. She raised the lid of the long neglected hope chest and pondered the 'L's embroidered on the linen.

"It'll not hurt him to sleep on sheets marked 'L'," she said to herself. "From what I hear he doesn't sleep in his own bed often enough to notice."

Four months later the Kirkton had become accustomed to the idea that Hannah was to marry the Minister and the banns had been called twice. One cold afternoon she decided to go down to the Manse and measure the parlour windows for new curtains. There was a length of rose-patterned chintz in her chest which might cheer that grim chamber. A light powdering of snow lay over the frozen fields and the air was clear and sharp. The smiddy lay outside the Kirkton near the main road to Falkirk overlooking the strath where the Kirkton straggled along a burn. It spread before Hannah like a map with the squat, grey kirk at its centre. There was another figure in this bleak landscape, toiling up the hill towards her. It was Tam the Post, smothered in comforters and mittens under his grey

36

plaid and his bag thumping at his side. He paused at the sight of her and blew on his fingers.

"A snell day, mistress."

From his bleary eye and wavering grin Hannah deduced that he had made a number of attempts to keep out the cold.

"So you're to be married on the Minister, mistress," he observed and a mournful drop gathered on the end of his nose. "I wish you happy, lass . . . aye."

To judge by his expression, Tam's hopes did not keep pace with his wishes. Hannah thanked him with a nod.

"I'm on my way to the smiddy," he announced and scrabbled in his bag. "You could save me a cold walk, mistress. There's a letter for your good-mother."

"I'll take it," Hannah offered, rather surprised, for Minnie could not read. Tam handed it over and shuffled off down the lane to Netherbiggin.

Hannah examined the letter in her hand. It was a fat packet, grimy and dog-eared, covered with various superscriptions: it was addressed to Mistress Lindsay at the Smiddy of Kirkton but it had been a long time on the way. In fact it had left New Zealand more than a month before Minnie had become Mistress Lindsay. Hannah felt her heart beat faster and she examined the writing closely. It was the clear, well-formed hand learned under Mr. McLagan's supervision at the Kirkton School. It was not unlike her own writing.

"Roddy!" she exclaimed under her breath. "It's from Roddy, it must be . . ."

Without hesitation she opened the packet and unfolded the half-dozen closely written sheets inside to look at the end. The signature was plain, '. . . your loving son, Roddy.' Hannah stared at it for a long moment, then folded it up very deliberately, put it in her pocket and set off back up the hill.

Once back at the smiddy she paused in the kitchen and listened carefully to gauge the whereabouts of Minnie and the baby. They seemed to be upstairs. Hannah ran up and found the door of her bedroom ajar. The baby was lying on her bed and Minnie was rooting about in the chest at the foot of it. Hannah stood in the door for a moment and swallowed hard.

"Take your clarty fingers out of my gear," she ordered

quietly, "and take the bairn off my bed and shift her napkin, she stinks to high heaven."

Minnie started upright and dropped the lid of the chest with a bang which set the baby crying again.

"I've a right to see what you're making away with," she whined. "There's better stuff here than there is downbye. What way can you have all that and me just a wheen rags and crocks?"

"You've no right next or nigh my room," Hannah declared. "Out!"

Minnie stood her ground.

"It's my house and all that's in it," she shouted. "And for a start I'll have back that teapot and they bonnie cups."

"They're mine from my mother," Hannah informed her, "and I'll see them in flinders before you'll have them. Out!"

"I'll not be ordered out a room in my own house!" yelled Minnie.

"After a week Thursday it'll be your own to do as you please with. I'll not be here to see you make a midden of it, thank the Lord. In the meantime you can be off and take Euphame with you. And leave my chemise behind. I can see it in your pocket."

She swooped on Minnie and pulled the garment out from under the soiled apron. Minnie glared at her and Hannah laughed suddenly.

"The dear only knows why you'd thieve that. It wouldn't look at you."

She held it up. It was no more than a handful of fine white cambric, embroidered in white and patently far too small for the buxom girl opposite.

"Hae it! You'll need that more nor me!" Minnie spat out. "From what I hear the Minister'll no bother ye much, ye skinny bitch!"

She stalked out of the room with her baby. Hannah looked down at the stain of urine on her coverlet, her face twisted with distaste. She stripped it off, rolled it in a bundle and hurled it into a corner with the chemise.

The first part of the letter made her weep, for it begged to hear from home and referred to other letters unanswered and, as Hannah knew, unread. He told his story once more and she

38

read it, the letters dancing and blurring because of the tears in her eyes. Roddy had had a bitter hard time of it alone in the world as young as he was and no stolid ox of a laddie like Davie. He'd walked to Glasgow and found a job there carrying baskets in Candleriggs market, and lost it to a bigger lad after four backbreaking days. Months of near-starvation, begging, holding horses and running errands ended when a ship's officer wanted a cabin boy in a hurry and took him aboard a brig bound for Australia. It was a rough hard life aboard but he was fed in a fashion. In Sydney the ship had picked up a cargo for Dunedin and, once there, he had jumped ship and found a job with a carter taking supplies up-country. There his luck had changed: the letter became eloquent in praise of one Hector Macadam, runholder of Bennachie, who had taken him on.

". . . I've been here five year. It's a big holding. Land's not that dear and there's plenty to be had, not like the North Island. But it's no that easy to stock. Prices here would make our Mungo stare, twenty-five shilling and more for a ewe. We could run three or four hundred more but will need to wait till next year's clip and mebbe longer than that if wool prices don't improve. But we'll get them one day, never fear.

"One day I meant to come home and show you all what I was good for. I know now I'll never do that. I'm not the kind to make a fortune and I don't want to come home. I'm fine pleased with life here now my health is better . . ."

Hannah frowned. Roddy had been slight but healthy enough.

". . . nothing ails me now but that I miss you and Hannah and it grieves me that I may never see you again. Hannah would say that is because I'm missing our creature comforts for we have no women on Bennachie. I've learned to wash and bake and cook in a very couthy fashion so that you'd laugh to see me pin out the linen with a mouthful of pegs or make scones as good as Hannah's. But it's Hector that's a dab hand at the breadmaking . . ."

At the end of the letter he lapsed once more into the short uneasy sentences in which he tried to tell his dead mother how sorry he was to have grieved her by leaving secretly as he had done and Hannah wept again because her mother could never read it. At last she wiped her cheeks, folded the letter, put it at the very bottom of the chest and piled the rumpled linen on top. She sat on the lid and stared out of the window as if there was a message for her in the pattern of trees leafless against the sky.

Hannah's wedding day dawned stormily. A north-easterly wind howled round the houses of the Kirkton, splattering the windows with sleet. Gradually the sky paled to reveal the racing ragged clouds and one or two windows showed yellow in the gloom but the smiddy remained obstinately unlit. In the half-light Dougal Lapraik turned the new trap which was his Chrissie's pride off the Falkirk road. As he passed the smiddy door he smiled to himself under the folds of his muffler and the smile broadened into a chuckle. His mare mistook the sound for encouragement, picked up her feet and trotted briskly towards the Netherbiggin stable. He was unhitching the weary beast when the kitchen window was thrust up and his wife leaned out.

"Where in the world have you been, Dougal Lapraik? It's seven past and nothing done outbye and us bidden to a bridal."

"A wee errand, just," said Dougal stolidly.

"What kind of an errand to take you out the house at two in the morning?"

Dougal didn't reply at once.

"Och, just a wee job for a friend," he said at last.

"What friend?" Chrissie demanded, but he led the mare into her stable without saying any more. "When you've done milking," she called after him, "I've your Sabbath suit laid ready. But make haste."

Dougal backed the mare into her box and chuckled with the malicious glee of someone who knows something no one else does. He sat down on the cornbin and laughed till the heavy plough horses stamped and snorted with unease.

Some hours later as the Kirkton worthies arrayed in their Sabbath finery began to converge on the smiddy for her wedding, Hannah was signalling for a cab outside Queen Street Station in the city of Glasgow. A porter stood beside her, half-concealed behind a barrow which was piled with the wooden chest from her bedroom, corded and labelled, an ancient cow-hide trunk with a domed lid fastened by thick straps, a small but elegant chest-of-drawers wrapped in sacking like a baby in a shawl and atop of all a bulging basket-case, carefully tied with twine. The cab-driver eyed all this with dismay and then climbed down to help the porter load it on to his cab. He opened the door for Hannah who was doing her best to look as if she appeared in Glasgow in her best clothes at least twice a week.

"Where to, mistress?"

"The Broomielaw," said Hannah. "I want . . ."

She consulted a scrap of newspaper held ready in the palm of her glove.

"I'm wanting a Mr. D. S. Mitchell, passage agent."

"Aye, I ken whaur he's at."

Mr. Mitchell's office was in two rooms up three flights of stairs. The first was filled with newspapers and piles of yellowing dockets with an ancient clerk scratching slowly away at a ledger, knee-deep in the clutter. The windows overlooked the river and the ships nestling up to one another along the stone quay, their masts and spars crossing and re-crossing each other in an intricate design. Mitchell himself lurked in the second office. He was a bird-like man, very thin and bald, who picked over the papers on his desk like a chicken on a dung-heap.

"Dunedin," he said rather mournfully, "Dunedin. Now, if it had been Auckland, or Sydney . . ."

"It's near Dunedin I'm wanting to go," Hannah said, wanting to go to the window and see whether the cabbie was still there with all her traps.

"Well," he said doubtfully, "there's *Polyxena*. But she's sailing this afternoon. She's a clipper, Stewart and Robieson."

He glanced at a dog-eared almanac.

"She'll take the tide downriver about midday. There she is."

He indicated *Polyxena* lying outside the cluster of ships at the quay. There was a bustle on her decks which spoke plainly of imminent departure; rolls of canvas were being hauled about and long spars being swayed up the masts.

"This afternoon!" Hannah exclaimed.

Mr. Mitchell cocked his head on one side.

"Too soon?" he enquired.

41

"No, no," she assured him, "that's just what I was after. It was just that I didn't expect to find just what I was after. Things never are that easy."

"Ah, but there mayn't be any berths on her," Mitchell reminded her. "How many travelling?"

"Just the one. Me."

"You don't mean to tell me," said Mitchell incredulously, "that you're to travel alone? In a clipper ship all the way to Australia?"

"New Zealand," corrected Hannah.

"The feck of the passengers leave at Melbourne. Haven't you heard? They've found gold out there. At a place they cry Ballarat or the like of that."

He drew in his breath between his teeth and shook his head.

"No daughter o' mine would be let travel in one o' they ships. Dearie me, dearie, dearie me," he reproved, "but they're a rough lot, right enough. The raff and scaff, just all going out to make fortunes and none too scrupulous how they do it."

"Never mind that," said Hannah. "Will there be a berth?"

"I can't tell, not this near sailing time. You'll need to ask at the office," he said and pulled out a battered silver watch. "And you'd best make haste. It's just two hours to high water."

"Is it far? I've a cab waiting."

"No far. Ann Street, tell him."

Stewart and Robieson's office was larger and tidier than Mr. Mitchell's but very much gloomier. The clerk behind the guichet looked harassed at her request but begged her in refined accents to take a seat while he made enquiries; Hannah, too restless to obey, wandered round the dingy room looking at a series of engravings which embellished the walls. These depicted maritime scenes unlikely to inspire confidence in the company's clients. There were ships dismasted, ships struggling up from under mountainous seas, ships heeling at impossible angles. Hannah's eyes widened as she went from one to the other.

"Mr. Fintry will see you in one minute, ma'am," the clerk's voice announced from the guichet and then he added in much more natural tones: "Enough to make ye spew, aren't they? See them and ye've nae need tae gang tae sea!"

"I never saw the sea," Hannah admitted.

"Neither did yon artist felly."

"I never even saw a ship till this morning."

"Is that a fact? Well, if you're for New Zealand you'll see a sight more of ships than you'll want to. It's sixteen weeks and more to Dunedin if the luck's with you and never a sight of land till you fetch Cape Otway. You'd not get me aboard one of they clippers, not if you paid me to go, not for all the gold ever mined."

Hannah, only half-attending, was looking at one dramatic scene in which a desperate figure, hair blowing over his face, his clothes torn to shreds and his eyes rolling heavenward, was tying an equally bedraggled female to the stump of a mast. It was entitled, *The Last Resort*. She peered at it, trying to make out other details of shipboard life but a breaker towering menacingly above the figures obscured most of the rest of the vessel. A bell tinkled in the inner office.

"You may go up now, ma'am," said the clerk in his professional voice, "through to the right and two flights up."

Two flights up was better lit and more luxurious; the chairs were covered with leather rather than horsehair and in place of the engravings were highly coloured oil paintings of various craft fixed in waves of vivid blue as opaque and immovable as ribbed sand. Another high-collared clerk stood at a high desk and peered at her through pince-nez.

"If you would oblige me with your requirements, ma'am?"

"I want a passage to Dunedin, if you please."

"Cabin?"

"If possible. But I'll take whatever berth is available. Whatever is left."

The clerk looked up in bewilderment.

"What have we left? I don't think I . . ."

"On the *Poli* . . . something, sailing today."

"Today! You mean the *Polyxena*. No . . . no . . . I don't think we have . . ."

He consulted a massive book and shook his head.

"No," he said finally. "Not a suitable berth to be had. These gold finds," he added, "have been very good for business."

Hannah's heart sank.

"When will there be another ship?" she asked.

"There'll be plenty sailing every day from Liverpool . . . London too," he said, "but there's a great demand for berths, specially on the fast clippers."

He shrugged and Hannah tried to decide what to do. Lodgings in Glasgow would eat away at her resources and there was always the chance that her father might find her. Liverpool and London seemed as far away and as strange as Dunedin itself.

"There is the *Philip Hanley*," said the clerk, "sailing on the seventeenth of next month, if you care to wait. New ship, well found, excellent cooking and washing facilities, piano in the saloon, cow kept aboard for fresh milk, the very finest of provisions . . ."

He looked enquiringly, his pen poised.

It was just at this moment, some forty miles to the east, that Alec Lindsay realised that his daughter had left home. A search in the house conducted by Minnie, extended to the steading by Davie and then to the Kirkton by young Alec, had proved unsuccessful. Minnie reported in a loud whisper that 'a' her gear was gone.' Lindsay, mewed up in the parlour with the wedding guests and now getting increasingly restive, reported this circumstance to the bridegroom in an angry whisper.

"She'll have been called away, surely," McLagan whispered back, unable to believe himself jilted. "A bairn, mebbe. She'll have left a message for certain."

"I tell you her gear's all away," Lindsay hissed. "Her clothes and the linen and the crocks and all that. Even the rosewood chest. And there's no message."

McLagan caught the enquiring and interested eye of his fellow minister, come from the next parish to perform the ceremony. He smiled confidently at him and drew Lindsay aside.

"Are you trying to tell me she's run off? Without a by-your-leave?"

"I doubt that's just what she's done," said Lindsay.

"Who was the man?" demanded McLagan, forgetting to whisper.

Dougal, sitting beside his Chrissie, had observed the exchange and he smiled blissfully. The other guests were raising eyebrows at one another.

"It was me," declared Dougal. "I took her to Falkirk station for the early train this morning."

The reaction to this speech was all he could have hoped. He restrained his glee for the sake of the buttons on his waistcoat. Lindsay and the Minister turned on him, gaping. Chrissie gave a little shriek and put her hand over her mouth.

"I was to tell you," Dougal went on stolidly, "that she'll not be back. She's away to join Roddy."

"Where?" bellowed Lindsay. "I'll have her hide for this, if I hang for it!"

Dougal stared at him as placidly as one of his own stirks.

"I didna think to ask. Canada mebbe, or Australia . . ."

"And why, may I ask," Lindsay growled menacingly, "when you kenned fine that she'd gone did ye no say?"

Dougal got out of his chair. He was a bigger man than Lindsay and a lot younger and he was hoping very much that Lindsay would try to hit him, waistcoat buttons or no waistcoat buttons.

"I telled ye once, Alec Lindsay, that I'd like fine for to see you get your comeuppance," he reminded the older man contemptuously, "and now, by God, I have."

Lindsay's face went purple and he clenched his great fists. McLagan and his friends came forward hastily and caught hold of him: he shook them off as if they were flies and advanced on the waiting Dougal who was beginning to rumble with laughter. There was a concerted and undignified scramble to the door by the rest of the guests. The parlour of the smiddy was a confined space for a brawl.

"Here!" Minnie shrilled suddenly, "where's she got the money for the fare?"

This observation halted Lindsay in his tracks; he swayed back on his heels and looked appalled.

"The Devil!" he muttered. "I had it in the house. I was going to give it to the Minister after the wedding."

"Had what?" demanded the Minister.

"Hannah's tocher, ye gomeril. Four hunder pounds in gold sovereigns . . ."

He turned on Dougal.

"Did ye give her any siller?"

"I offered," Dougal admitted proudly, "but she said she'd plenty."

Lindsay gave a deep groan and trampled his way upstairs where he could be heard opening and shutting cupboards and drawers violently and swearing. Minnie and McLagan stared upwards as if expecting a divine revelation while the rest of the guests followed Dougal's example and began to laugh, discreetly at first and then louder and louder. There was a despairing bellow from above.

"The bitch . . . the damned blackhearted bitch . . . she's away with it. Four hunder pounds in gold sovereigns and every penny I made at the mart on Wednesday! I'll have the law on her!"

4

Hannah had drawn breath to ask the clerk to reserve her a berth on the *Philip Hanley* when a man and a woman came into the office, obviously in the middle of an argument.

"I won't go without *someone*," the woman was saying. "Who is going to look after Lucy?"

"Lucy is nearly ten years old," said the man in an undertone, conscious, as his companion was not, of an audience. "Surely, for once, you can make shift to look after her yourself. You'll have nothing else to do."

"And when I'm sick?" she returned. "You know I'm always sick. Who's to look after her then? Not to mention me. Not you, that's certain!"

She gave a tinkle of unamused laughter and went on, "I tell you again, I must have someone. If you can't find a suitable person I simply will not come. Lucy and I will have to come by a later boat. And that . . ." she sat down on a chair and looked at him with a defiant smirk, ". . . is my last word on the matter."

She tossed her head and flicked irritably at her flounced skirts. Mr. Fintry abandoned Hannah without scruple.

"Captain Innis, Mrs. Innis . . . good day to you. May I be of some assistance?"

Captain Innis turned away from his wife, his face flushed with anger and embarrassment.

"We're in something of a scrape," he admitted. "My wife's maid has cleared off this morning to be married and now she won't be coming. We've a mountain of baggage down there ready to go aboard *Polyxena* and there's no time to go off hunting for a nursemaid all over Glasgow. And if we did find one she wouldn't want to come halfway round the world at an hour's notice."

Mr. Fintry shook his head over this predicament.

"I suppose there might be a suitable female among the

passengers in the steerage," he suggested doubtfully, "but these days we don't carry many . . . er . . . respectable females. The gold finds, you know."

"As if I would have someone like that," protested Mrs. Innis petulantly.

Captain Innis's lips tightened.

"You must see it's quite impossible," Mrs. Innis went on and Hannah, standing quietly in her corner, thought she could detect a note of satisfaction in the light, quick speech. "You'll have to book a passage for Lucy and me and some really suitable female on the next sailing or the one after that."

"I don't like the idea of your coming all that way un-escorted," protested her husband.

Mrs. Innis shrugged and succeeded in looking both provo-cative and mulish.

"Perhaps you would rather Lucy and I didn't come at all," she suggested and her husband looked at her angrily and uncertainly.

"You know very well I want you to come but I can't conjure another Maxwell out of thin air within an hour of going aboard," he told her tensely. "Don't be so unreasonable."

"I will not stir without a maid," said his wife smugly and smoothed her fine kid gloves. "You are the unreasonable one to expect me to."

The gloves were part of a fearful and fashionable outfit singularly unsuited to shipboard living. Mrs. Innis wore a hooped skirt at least four feet across of violet cloth trimmed with black cord and velvet flounces. Over this she had put a fur-trimmed paletot and a violet velvet hat with a curling feather calculated to succumb to the mildest sea breeze. Up until her entrance Hannah had felt pleased enough with the prune-coloured silk which she had intended for her wedding gown and the serviceable brown serge cloak which she had stitched herself. Mrs. Innis made her feel dowdy and, in an obscure way, resentful. It was unfair and ugly to place her husband in such a predicament before total strangers. Mr. Fintry was intent upon his desk, rustling importantly at papers as if he did not hear the altercation. Innis glared at his wife and made an impatient movement towards the door, almost bumping into Hannah.

"Come," he said firmly, "this is no place to air our differences. Time we were going aboard."

He held the door open and Mrs. Innis rose sulkily.

"Don't order me about as if I was one of your soldiers," she said tossing her head, "and unless you find me a maid I mean to go back to Wetherpark . . ."

She threw him a look which dared him to contradict.

" . . . and I mean to take Lucy with me!"

She went out smiling derisively at her husband. He looked after her, his lips pressed into a thin line, and then turned to Mr. Fintry.

"If you should hear of a suitable person," he said, "I'd be much obliged if you'd send her aboard at the Tail of the Bank, but even if you don't we'll . . ."

He laid some stress on the 'we'.

" . . . we'll be aboard in an hour."

"I'll make enquiries, Captain," agreed Mr. Fintry, "but time is very . . ."

An idea struck him. It was the same idea which had occurred to Hannah some little time earlier. He looked across at her with his eyebrows raised in an agony of interrogation. She nodded emphatically. Innis missed this exchange because he was halfway out of the room.

"Captain Innis . . . sir . . ."

He turned about in surprise.

"This young lady," said Mr. Fintry, scrabbling through his papers to find her name, "Miss Lindsay . . . she is very anxious to obtain a passage in *Polyxena*. I think she might consider . . ."

Captain Innis looked at Hannah for the first time. It was a very direct very blue regard. It seemed to Hannah that he was slightly startled. She was conscious of an unaccustomed sensation and found a little voice in her mind saying, 'My, but you're a bonnie lad.' The tremble in her legs she put down to anxiety that he should think her suitable for the post.

"Might you?" asked the Captain. "Have you done this kind of work?"

"I've kept house since I was twelve year old," said Hannah rather gruffly, "and I've brought up both my wee brothers. I can make and mend and wash and iron . . ."

"Splendid," interrupted the Captain, "splendid. I can't believe my luck."

He smiled at her and she bent her head for fear she should smile back. A thought struck him.

"My wife will require certain duties . . ." he said vaguely, "her hair and clothes and suchlike, I'm not perfectly sure what . . ."

"What I don't know I'll never be younger to learn," Hannah assured him. "There'll be no grand parties and balls aboard the boat, I daresay."

"No," he agreed rather doubtfully. "I should explain that she doesn't enjoy the best of health. She has a weak stomach and she has trouble with her nerves . . ."

Mrs. Innis had not appeared frail to Hannah, indeed her fine plump figure and high colour had suggested health so robust as to be almost ungenteel and her readiness to argue in public had not suggested nervous debility so much as a determination to get her own way. However, Hannah was desperate to secure the post.

"I'd be a sight better sicknurse than a maid," she blurted out very conscious of his eyes on her. "I nursed my mother till she died."

A faintly amused expression on his face suggested that this was, perhaps, not the happiest of commendations.

"We must hope that the sea voyage improves her health. But I expect Lucy will be your main care. You'll have to share a cabin with her. You don't object?"

"I was prepared to travel steerage if I could go no other way," Hannah told him. "A cabin will be luxury."

"You're ready to go immediately?"

"My baggage is below. I've nothing to stay for."

She remembered the waiting cabman with a slight start and wondered how much he would be wanting for waiting around half the morning. Captain Innis smiled with relief and she was conscious again of the strange effect his smile had upon her insides. A scrap of the *Song of Solomon* swam into her mind, '. . . and my reins were moved for him.' She realised to her horror she was blushing.

"Well," he said, "in that case, I can't think of anything else except to say thank you for coming to our rescue."

"Hadn't I better have a word with your wife," Hannah suggested.

"Lord, yes, I suppose you should. Quickly!"

He grabbed her by the hand and hauled her downstairs at a run. They were in time to see Hannah's cab disappearing into Jamaica Street. There was no sign of Mrs. Innis but just inside the door was a pile of luggage; two metal trunks, two leather hat-boxes and a huge brassbound wooden chest, all of which owned in fresh white letters that Captain Dominic Innis of the 65th Regiment was their proprietor. Beside them lay Hannah's luggage. Hannah stole a glance at her new employer and was not surprised to see him look thunderous.

"It seems that Mrs. Innis has decided not to wait," he said calmly enough.

"It's my cab she's taken," observed Hannah. "She'll have my fare to pay as well as her own."

"I've no doubt both will figure on my reckoning at McLean's Hotel," he said bitterly and pulled at his chin. "Look, I'll ask them here to find a hand-barrow and send you aboard right away with all this. We'll have to come aboard by the tender first thing in the morning. She'll be lying at the Tail of the Bank tonight."

Hannah let that pass: the habits of ships were a closed book to her and this was no time to enquire into them.

"Are you sure your wife will agree to employ me?" she demanded. "I'm a pig in a poke when all's said."

He looked amused and uncertain.

"Hardly that," he demurred. "But perhaps you have a testimonial I could show her?"

Hannah shook her head.

"I've never been in service. I was at home."

"Have you a letter of introduction from your Minister?"

Hannah suppressed a nervous giggle at that idea and shook her head again.

"I didn't think to ask him," she admitted, which was true enough.

"Why are you so anxious to go to New Zealand?"

"To join my brother."

"What does he do?"

"He's a farmer . . . a sheep farmer. I have a letter from him, but it's not to me, it's to my mother."

He looked at her rather helplessly.

"Tell her I'm a blacksmith's daughter, a countrywoman, clean, sober, respectable and just twenty-four. My name's Hannah Lindsay."

"You're not married?"

"No," said Hannah.

"Or likely to be? Maxwell's young man chased after her to Glasgow and carried her off."

"No," Hannah declared firmly. "I'd a close call I don't deny, but there'll be no one chasing after me."

He looked amused and Hannah felt herself blush again.

"I have the feeling that there's a tale to be told," he said, "but time enough for that when we're aboard. Did you leave the wretched man standing at the altar?"

Hannah, her cheeks scarlet, said nothing.

In the tiny cabin on *Polyxena* Hannah shifted her position on the hard bunk mattress. Four hundred sovereigns in a neat moneybelt round her waist made it difficult to sleep. She abandoned the attempt and lay staring into the darkness while the ship, anchored and waiting for the tide off Cowal, lurched uneasily. It was only then at the end of an exhausting day that she began to have qualms. The strange noises and smells of the ship brought home to her what kind of a venture she had undertaken. She was embarked upon a voyage to the uttermost ends of the earth and might never see her own land again. A weeping farewell she had made for it had rained all the afternoon as *Polyxena* worked her way downriver and she could see nothing but the gleaming muddy banks of Clyde. Not that she had watched them for long because the ship was still preparing for the voyage and the decks were cluttered with stores and baggage and busy with the crew trying to stow them before the ship reached the livelier waters of the firth. She was conscious of a chilly sinking in her midriff and knew she was afraid. 'What if Roddy's dead or gone away . . . what will I do? I must be off my head. I could be snug in the Manse, this night, with a home of my own . . . folk to look up to me . . .' She had a sudden mental picture of Donald McLagan, flabby, elderly

and watery-eyed, his waistcoat stained with ash and the food
he dropped as he ate. His hands were small and white and soft
and she shuddered at the thought of them on her body. Even
without Roddy's letter, she decided, she could never have
married him. She did not link this decision to her encounter
with Innis.

As she tossed to and fro with the ship's motion, she wondered
briefly what had happened at the smiddy and wished she could
have been a fly on the wall. Dougal was plainly looking forward
to his part in it. Her father would be ill-advised to wreak his
ill-temper on Dougal, or Minnie. Minnie could give as good
as she got. *Polyxena* dipped and rolled in the swell and she
contemplated the long hazardous voyage ahead with a return
of the chilly sensation. 'Roddy did,' she reproached herself,
'hundreds of folk have done it. Why should you be feart?
Lucky to be aboard, that's what . . .'

From the deck below she could hear the passengers in the
steerage. They sounded in good spirits, though admittedly
they could well come out of bottles. She had seen them troop
aboard, laughing and joking, with their bundles and boxes.
What good fortune it was to have a cabin rather than to be
lying this night in one of those huge crowded communal
apartments she had glimpsed, with no more privacy than
could be provided by a sacking curtain around the bunks.
While she was wondering what Lucy, her charge, would be
like and how they would spend their time she fell asleep.

She was wakened by a tap-tap on the door and jumped out
of the bunk, uncertain for a few seconds where she could be.
She had lain down in her clothes and felt frowsy and uncomfortable with a pain in her side where the moneybelt had cut
into her. Outside the narrow door was a lascar steward wearing
a white jacket much too large for him.

"Tender coming, missee," he told her and grinned showing
his gleaming white teeth. "In half an hour they arrive. You
want wash-water? Yes?"

Hannah nodded, too taken aback to reply. She had never
before encountered a foreigner of any kind, unless one were to
count the English which most Scots were quite ready to do.
She knew there were people with coloured skins; she had
prayed to lighten their darkness (uncertain whether this was to

change their colour or to provide them with lamps); she had contributed to missions for their conversion but they had been less real to her than the characters of *Pilgrim's Progress*.

"I come," said the little lascar. "Water all hot and ready. Tea too. My name Elias, missee. You want anything you ask Elias. I fetch."

"Thank you," said Hannah faintly. "Thank you . . . I would like some tea."

The steward touched his breast and forehead in a strange gesture and trotted away into the gloom of the companionway while Hannah prepared herself and the cabins in her charge for the arrival of her employers. She felt unaccountably cheered by Elias.

She watched the arrival of the tender from her porthole in the dreary half-light of the winter morning. The rotund shape of the little steamboat came fussing alongside like a harassed duck, its paddles churning, and she heard the shouts and orders as the companionway was lowered. Before long there were voices to be heard and she went to open the door into the main cabin. This was a little bigger than the one allocated to Lucy and herself but was a good deal less than luxurious. Captain Innis was standing there, looking worried, his head slightly on one side to clear the deckbeams. Beside him was a fair, plump little girl. By Hannah's austere standards she was overdressed in fur-trimmed blue velvet with a white fur muff and white kid boots. Her face was as white as her muff and stained with tears and her hair straggled in damp, straight rats tails from under her fur bonnet. She looked uncertainly and rather inimically at Hannah whose hands itched for a comb and a washcloth. Innis looked equally wind-blown and his manner was flustered. Behind him in the doorway was a red-coated soldier laden with yet more baggage.

"Miss Lindsay . . ." His voice held relief. "This is my daughter, Lucy. I'm afraid she has been ill coming over in the steamer."

Tears rolled down the child's face and she wiped them away with the heel of her hand.

"Never heed," Hannah said comfortingly. "You'll soon feel better. I've hot water ready inbye."

"Lucy," Captain Innis coaxed, "this is Miss Lindsay . . . she's going to look after you."

"Hannah will do me fine," Hannah interrupted. "There's some tea and a bite of toast on the table there for you and Mrs. Innis. You come with me, Lucy, lass."

The child nodded and went through the connecting door to the smaller cabin. Her father looked unsmilingly at Hannah.

"Mrs. Innis won't be coming," he informed her. "I would be glad of a word with you later."

The 'word' was not particularly enlightening. When she returned to the cabin Innis looked anxious and ill-at-ease and the tea and toast were untouched.

"Is Lucy all right?"

"I put her to bed," Hannah told him. "She seemed a wee bit overwrought. She's sleeping now."

Lucy had cried herself to sleep.

"Is she very upset? Did she call for her mother?"

"No," Hannah said repressively: she hadn't made much of Lucy's blurred outpourings except that she didn't want to go on a horrid boat. Innis stood with his back to her, staring out of the porthole.

"Mrs. Innis won't be coming with us. She . . . she dislikes sea voyages."

He said this defiantly, then turned and looked at her. Lucy said nothing. A distaste for the sea hardly accounted for Lucy's presence without her mother. Captain Innis frowned and cleared his throat.

"I have decided that you and Lucy shall come in here. I'll use your cabin. This one will be more comfortable for two."

He looked about it.

"You'll have to stay below a good deal, especially during the first part of the voyage. The weather may not be very agreeable. I'll send Brett in to move my belongings. I'll be in the saloon if you need me."

He went out, tripping over the high coaming. Brett when he arrived was more informative.

"Kicked over the traces *she* has," he confided. "Did a midnight flit, the Boots told me. Dare say I know who to an' all."

Hannah tidied away a pile of Lucy's clothes into a locker.

"It's no business of mine . . . or yours," she told him primly.

Brett considered her slim disapproving back and shrugged.

"Dare say we're better off without her," he declared. "Always complaining. My oath. No one couldn't please that madam."

Hannah stood up and he placed an experimental arm round her waist. Hannah removed it as if it had been a dirty apron.

"Ah, well," said Brett. He was already aware of the dearth of females aboard. In the steerage there was one harassed mother with five sons and two daughters of ten and twelve who was going out to Australia to join her husband. Apart from her, there was only a handful of Glasgow whores going to see whether they could make their fortunes at the diggings and happy enough to recoup their fares en route. Among the saloon passengers there were no females at all for many of the cabins were bespoke by officers of the 65th sent out to reinforce the regiment in New Zealand and by various officials despatched by the Colonial Office to the fast-growing colony. There was one Australian returning home with a fat contract in his pocket to supply wool, a large taciturn Highlander called Sutherland but he had no wife with him. The two large second-class cabins were both occupied by people hoping to profit by the gold finds, clerks, merchants and publicans: if they were married their wives were to follow later. Because of this, Hannah was the only respectable unattached female aboard. Brett, as Captain Innis's servant, was conscious of his advantageous position and had high hopes of stealing a march on the rest of the passengers. Hannah's rebuff he did not find unduly discouraging; it was to be a long voyage and a chase might prove entertaining. He sketched a jaunty salute and returned to the forecabin which he shared with two companies going out to join the regiment. There he lost no time in boasting about his opportunities. Hannah would have been surprised at the terms in which he described her. So would McLagan who had sought solace for his wounded pride in the arms of the innkeeper's widow.

5

Lucy woke, cross and tearful.

"Maxwell called me Miss Lucy," she informed Hannah. "So should you."

"Just as you wish," Hannah returned. "And you will call me Miss Lindsay."

"Why?"

"Why not?"

Silence fell.

"I want to go home," Lucy said at last. "I want to go to London with Mama . . ."

She stopped and looked uncomfortably at Hannah who said nothing and looked completely uninterested.

"I don't want to go on a horrid ship with Papa."

"You'll soon get used to the ship," Hannah promised.

"It's horrid and pokey and smelly . . ."

Hannah said nothing but brushed away at the straight, thick fair hair.

"Maxwell put rags in," complained the child. "She made it pretty and curly. Mama told her to."

"Not much use at sea," Hannah said. "The wind and the damp air will take all the curl out. I'll braid it for you."

Lucy jerked her head away and glared.

"I want it curled. I look a perfect fright when it isn't curled."

Hannah grinned involuntarily to hear her mother speaking through the child. Lucy saw the grin in the mirror and lost her temper.

"I want it curled . . . I want it . . . you've *got* to do it!"

"Then want must be your master," Hannah told her calmly. "For I'll not do it."

Lucy flung herself face down on the bunk and howled with rage and temper. Hannah gathered from the incoherent and muffled utterances that Lucy hated every one: Papa, Mama, Hannah (of course) as well as a mysterious Major Weaver . . .

and Grandmama and Grandpapa and a whole muddle of other names. Hannah, her heart torn for the wretched little thing, let her cry till she was quiet and spent.

"There now," she said gently. "You'll feel the better for that, I don't doubt."

Lucy let her face be sponged and her hair plaited, hiccoughing from time to time.

"I don't really hate you," she volunteered after a while. "It's just that everything's so horrid. I like things to go *on* . . ."

Hannah tied a bow on to one of the plaits.

"No one *tells* you," Lucy burst out. "They let awful things happen and don't say why. It's like earthquakes . . ."

She sniffed and Hannah put a clean, dry handkerchief in front of her.

"Nobody tells you anything and when you ask they don't answer or they say never mind, run away, little girls don't want to know about such things. And all the time you know there's something wrong and you don't know what."

She blew her nose miserably.

"Little girls! I *hate* being a girl. Nobody wants girls . . ."

Hannah laughed at this.

"It's true! It *is*. I heard Papa say once to. . . to . . . someone that he wished I was a boy and she agreed with him . . . I heard her. And old Grandfather at Inchbeg, every time he sees me he goes . . ." Lucy gave an exaggerated sigh and mimicked an old man, ". . . sad pity you didn't make a boy of her, Nick . . ."

Hannah made no comment. Lucy went on talking. Gradually it became plain that one Major Weaver had been a frequent visitor to the house while Captain Innis was in Ireland. Lucy did not care for him.

"He asked me how I would like to be *his* little girl," she said disgustedly, "and when I said I wouldn't a bit Mama was cross and sent me upstairs . . ."

Hannah refrained from trying to comfort the bewildered child. There were some things which a few facile words would not erase. Instead, she insisted on Lucy's helping to unpack and arrange the cabin.

"We'll be three months on the way and maybe longer," Hannah said. "No harm in making ourselves as comfortable as possible."

Lucy was delighted; it was like playing at houses.

"Did you have a governess?" Hannah enquired when some schoolbooks came to light.

"Miss Grover," said Lucy. "I liked her. But she told Mama she wasn't going to outlandish parts and she went away. *Everyone* goes away," she added sulkily.

Hannah considered the books. There were copybooks, Scott's *Tales of a Grandfather*, a book of poems which Lucy condemned as dull, a much-thumbed book of simple sums and a Palmer's Geography. Hannah decided that there would be lessons every day. She found slate and slate pencils as well as paper and pens and a stone bottle of ink. Right at the very bottom of the trunk were a number of other books, unbound and carefully covered in brown paper. They were novels. Hannah decided that Miss Grover must have departed on the spur of the moment and abandoned her own personal library. Lucy pounced gleefully on one of them and ceased to help with the unpacking. Hannah took no notice: if this Mr. Currer Bell (of whom she had never heard) could take Lucy's attention from the fact that *Polyxena* was beginning to move in a fashion which reminded Hannah uneasily of the engravings in the shipping company's offices she was welcome to read anything he had written.

Before very long, within a week of *Polyxena*'s putting to sea, Hannah and Lucy had a routine of meals, lessons, exercise and play; they made it a point of honour never to allow weather to interrupt this routine even when the gale they encountered two days out laid the ship over so that their exercise was reduced to a wet and giggling scramble along a life-line. During the gale, lessons had to take place in the angle between the cabinsole and the bulk-head because that was the only place where the slate could be steadied to write on. 'Play' was a convenient term for the hours when Hannah entertained her charge by teaching her to sew and knit and crochet; even darning had its charms for Lucy whose education so far had included drawing and music and even a smattering of French but none of the needlework which country-bred Hannah considered essential.

Slowly, between the two of them, there grew up an undemanding companionship which comforted both. Hannah's impersonal but concentrated attention made the child feel secure: Hannah for her part found that Lucy's dependence restored her own wavering confidence. To look after people was a necessity for Hannah.

Of Lucy's father they saw little. He spent no time in the cabin, but played cards in the cuddy with the few who escaped sea sickness or discussed the situation they were likely to find in the colony when they arrived. Recent news of the Maori wars had been disquieting. He came below only to sleep or to wish Lucy goodnight. Hannah found herself looking forward to these occasions with an intensity which surprised her though Innis had little to say beyond an enquiry after Lucy's welfare. When two days out from the Clyde, she had regretted that Lucy's luggage had not included a few toys he had said little, but when *Polyxena* put into Liverpool to pick up part of her cargo he had appeared that evening with an armful of packages which proved to contain toys and books and above all a splendid doll. She had a body of kid with porcelain hands and feet and her eyes opened and closed. To Hannah's delight she possessed only a calico wrap by way of clothes. To make her a wardrobe was a ploy which would occupy her proud owner for the whole of the voyage. She was named Lady Blanche after Mr. Bell's haughty character because she had a somewhat daunting expression. In the manner of only children, Lucy wove histories about her.

Hannah herself discovered the joys of reading fiction. No novels had come her way before because there were few to be found in the Kirkton. On those few occasions when the good behaviour of his parishioners gravelled him for lack of matter Mr. McLagan was used to denounce all fiction as the work of the devil. During her engagement, Hannah had found out that he did not denounce in ignorance. Behind the respectable, leather-clad divines on the bookshelves in the study lurked a good many of the devil's works, well-thumbed if unbound.

Polyxena boasted a chaplain. Mr. Pellew, an Episcopalian parson, was on his way to take up a living in Canterbury. He had been the incumbent at a fashionable Glasgow church. McLagan had also been used to denounce Episcopalians as Babylonish idolators and Hannah took a certain pleasure in the discovery that, on the whole, he exaggerated. Mr. Pellew lacked horns and a tail, being a kindly short-sighted man well into middle age. He was delighted to lend Hannah pamphlets and cuttings about New Zealand and to help with Lucy's lessons. It was Mr. Pellew who could disperse the difficulties of pronunciation with French verbs and breathe life into the list of Kings and Queens of England. Hannah listened fascinated as the names and numbers became real people. In return, she washed and mended his linen which it sorely needed, for Mr. Pellew was travelling alone, being, as he confided, recently widowed. His venture to the colonies was something he had wished to do when he was young but his dearest Emma had not wished to leave her home. Now, alas, he found himself free. His children were scattered and he had nothing to keep him. To people more knowing than Hannah the red patches on his cheeks and the spirits on his breath early in the day might suggest another reason for his not having achieved preferment at home. She did observe that he took his duties as chaplain lightly; there was a service for the cabin passengers in the cuddy on Sunday mornings but a single visit to the steerage had convinced him that there was little point in trying to snatch brands from the burning there; the Sunday afternoon services on the deck for the steerage passengers were thinly attended.

Soon the weather became warm and the sky blue. The days passed pleasantly, though punctuated with incidents caused by drunkenness among the steerage passengers; with these the Captain, a dour young man, much in the mould of the notorious 'Bully' Forbes, dealt briskly and brutally. One aggressive miner was consigned to the orlop where he contemplated his folly in irons for a week. Another who had been drunk for a week was sobered by dipping him repeatedly into the sea at the end of a rope. All the while, the wind took them steadily south under full sail. Six weeks after leaving the Mersey they crossed the equator and Lucy, from the safety of her father's arms, witnessed the rough antics of King Neptune's Court. Soon after that the wind dropped and *Polyxena*'s progress slowed to a crawl, ghosting over the steely waters with every rag spread. During this time the passengers were able to row off in the ship's boats to fish or to swim.

It was during this time that Hannah, rather to her dismay,

received two proposals of marriage. One was from Brett who had despaired of other tactics. The other was from Mr. Pellew, overcome by a tropical moon, who proposed apologetically and without any real expectation of having his suit well-received. Brett she turned down scornfully but was more gentle with Mr. Pellew.

"I've my brother to find," she explained. "I'd not wish to engage myself till I find all's well with him. Forbye," she added rather uncertainly, "you'll bear in mind we're not of the same way of thinking . . ."

Mr. Pellew had smiled and sighed at this reminder.

"The older I grow, my dear Miss Lindsay, the more I feel that these are artificial barriers but I appreciate you may not feel as I do about either matter."

He did not refer to the matter again. Brett, on the other hand, was much more persistent and when Hannah refused him for the third time he became abusive.

"If you got your eye on your betters, me girl," he said scornfully, "you won't get nowhere. The Captain, he can't marry you . . . wouldn't neither even if he could. Not his sort, you ain't."

"I've no wish to marry anyone," said Hannah.

"Don't you tell me the tale," Brett sneered. "All females is the same. You think you're a cut above me . . . well, you ain't."

"I've told you," said Hannah again, "I've no wish to be married. And even if I had I'd not marry a soldier, not with a fortune in each boot, for I've a better conceit of myself than that, my lad. And even if I did settle on a man who'd be away from me the better part of the time I'd not have you. I expect you've a wife already. You're the kind that must have some female in tow."

Brett called her an unpleasant name, his face reddening. Clearly Hannah had hit home.

"Out of here!" she told him angrily. "The very idea of using such language in front of the bairn . . ."

Brett retreated, grumbling that some women were too uppity for their own good and Hannah looked across at Lucy, expecting her to share her amusement at this episode, but the child was far from amused.

"You'll get married some day, won't you? Then you'll go away too . . ."

Tears sprang into her eyes and she flung her arms around Hannah's waist.

"Lassie, lassie . . . I've told you often and often, I've my brother to look for. I can't stay with you anyway, not once we reach New Zealand."

Lucy burst into a storm of sobs and although Hannah coaxed and petted her she was not to be comforted. At last she fell asleep exhausted, her face in Hannah's lap. Hannah laid her gently in the bunk and as she did so she realised for the first time that the child was extremely hot, her skin was harsh and dry and her breath not sweet. Anxiously she went in search of Mrs. Lennox. As the only two respectable women aboard she and Hannah had joined forces to some extent. Lucy had played with the children and the little girls had attended some of Lucy's lessons.

However, there was no comfort to be had in the steerage. Two of the Lennox boys were obviously very ill, tossing and turning and calling out in the narrow bunk they shared with a third brother. The heat and smell were oppressive.

"It's a fever. Just came on them like a thunderclap. The dear only knows where they were smit," said Mrs. Lennox wearily. "Wee Lucy's likely smit as well."

"There's a doctor aboard," Hannah suggested, "the army surgeon."

"Aye, for all the use that is," sniffed Mrs. Lennox. "I put no faith in them. Feed a cold, hunger a fever, starve a colic and leave the potions alone. It'll pass I reckon."

She wrung out a cloth in sea water and placed it on the forehead of one of the sufferers.

"Keep the fever down the best way you can," she added. "Easy enough with just the one. I'll have the whole family on my hands, I wouldn't wonder."

Hannah left her and hunted out Elias: some minutes later he brought a basin of water, some cloths and, unexpectedly, a lemon and a large pot of tea.

"Tea good for fever," he assured her. "Tea and lemon better than drink water. Water not good now it hot. Missie like, you see."

At first it seemed a mild catching. Like Mrs. Lennox, Hannah thought it would soon pass. However, after two days it was clear that there was an epidemic. In the steerage more than a dozen had sickened and two or three among the soldiers. Lucy was getting no better. Hannah sent a message to Innis. When he came he was shocked by the change in the child's appearance and Brett was sent scurrying for Martin, the army surgeon. He came, unshaven and unkempt, having been up all night in steerage. He examined Lucy who whimpered a little under his touch and complained that her skin ached. Martin sighed and asked Hannah what she was doing for the patient.

"I'm sponging her with vinegar and cold water," she said. "She's having lukewarm tea to drink and lemon-juice and water. Beef broth too when she'll take it."

"Just what I'd recommend," said the surgeon wearily. "I'll send a feverfuge."

"What's the matter with her?" Innis demanded.

"Ship's fever . . . gaol-fever. The same thing that's down there."

Martin jerked his head in the direction of the steerage.

"Is it serious?"

The surgeon glanced at Lucy who was lying with her eyes closed.

"Fairly serious," he agreed grimly and gestured for them to move into the other cabin. He closed the door and added in a low voice, "There's a child dead in the steerage. Died this morning."

"Oh, God," muttered Lucy's father and Hannah wondered unhappily which of the little Lennox boys was dead.

"It's mainly a question of nursing. The fever puts a strain on the heart. Keep her cool and try to stop the fever mounting," the surgeon explained. "Miss Hannah's been doing just the right things already. But she'll need to sleep once in a while. Shall I see if I can find some help among the women aboard?"

"No indeed!" exclaimed Hannah indignantly. "Barring poor Mistress Lennox they're just a parcel of dirty whores. I'd not let them lay a finger on the bairn when she was well, never mind when she's sick. I'll manage fine."

"For heaven's sake, girl, you can't go without sleep. It'll be a long business. How much sleep did you have last night?"

"Enough," Hannah said.

"A doze in the chair with your clothes on, I daresay. No, she's going to need almost constant sponging. Let me find someone . . ."

"No," Innis declared and unbuttoned his coat. "If Hannah says she doesn't want them she's most likely right. I can take my turn. Lucy's my daughter, after all's said."

The surgeon nodded.

"It'll be better than stewing over a tumbler of brandy in the cuddy all day," he observed drily and Innis flushed. "You do just what Miss Hannah tells you and don't argue. She knows what she's about. I'll send Elias with the powders."

He turned to Hannah.

"She'll be far worse before she's better. You understand that?"

She nodded.

"There'll be a crisis in a day or so. You see to it you're ready and rested when it comes. Tell Innis exactly what he must do and then lie down on the bunk and sleep for at least two hours. The powders are a mixture of sage and basil. I've known them help reduce fever but if they don't . . ."

He shrugged.

". . . they'll do no harm and that's more than you can say for most remedies. Rouse her from time to time. Try not to let her fall into a coma."

Hannah nodded again, her heart in her boots.

"Send for me if you're very worried but the truth is that I can do no more for her than you can. No comfort, I know, but the truth is always best in these cases. They need me below."

He left the cabin abruptly. Innis was rolling up his sleeves and he smiled rather ruefully at Hannah.

"Martin's no Harley Street medico," he reassured her, "because he has to deal with soldiers. But he's a good surgeon. His motto is tell the truth unless a lie will help to cure or ease a death."

"I'd rather that," said Hannah. "You can feel the ground under your feet, rough and all as it is."

Innis was surprisingly deft and quick to learn what he had to do but in spite of all their efforts the fever mounted and mounted until Lucy was delirious for much of the time; she called, not for her mother or her grandmother or even for Hannah but for 'Tina . . . Tina . . .' Sometimes she was childishly angry and petulant, sometimes she wailed the name feebly and wept because Tina did not come.

"Who's Tina?" Hannah asked at one point.

"Her nurse," he explained. "She was my own nurse and she looked after Lucy from the day she was born. My wife sent her away last year. Said she needed a governess, not a nurse. They didn't agree, Tina and my wife, never did."

Hannah said nothing. Lucy, as she sometimes did, had picked up the sense of what they were saying and muttered, "I *hate* Mama . . . I want Tina . . . I want her . . . don't go away . . ."

"She seems to have missed her sore," Hannah commented.

"I was away," Innis answered the implied criticism. "I was in Ireland. Tina took my wife to task for playing me false with my superior officer."

Hannah, shocked and surprised, said nothing but dipped her cloth again.

"When I came home Tina had gone. I tried to find out if she was properly provided for but she had died. She was an old woman, you see."

Hannah wrung out the cloth with a certain violence.

"Away you and sleep, Captain," she said prosaically, "there's a tray ready in your cabin."

He didn't move but stood watching her sponge the thin little chest.

"My wife has left me," he said. "She went to Weaver the night before we sailed. I suspect," he went on expressionlessly, "that I have him to thank for this posting. He could hardly have me sent further away. I feel like Uriah the Hittite. But David married Bathsheba. Weaver can't do that."

Hannah drew the sheet over Lucy's chest and began to sponge the flabby little arm. Lucy was no longer plump.

"She left a note instructing me to take Lucy to her mother's. They would collect her when they came back from Paris. She said Weaver was perfectly ready to give her a home . . ."

He swallowed hard and Lucy stirred and whimpered. Hannah wrung out the cloth again as if she had Mrs. Innis between her hands.

"Now I wish I had done that. It doesn't matter where she was to go. At least this wouldn't have happened."

Lucy thrashed about under the cool touch of the cloth.

"Papa . . . where's Papa . . ." she whimpered.

Innis took her hand.

"If I cut my hair," Lucy said anxiously, "I could look like a boy . . ."

Innis stared in bewilderment.

"She thinks you wanted her to be a boy," Hannah explained in an undertone, "she told me once. She heard you say it."

"Did she?" He looked remorseful. "Children are so ready to pick up these things. It was true enough when she was a baby. Not now. I wouldn't be without her. But there's Inchbeg, you see, and the title, and no one to follow my father but me. Oh, God . . . I wish I'd sent her to my father. I did think of it but there was so little time. And it isn't a household for a child; he's old and all the servants are old. My mother died years ago. I truly thought I was doing the best for her, taking her with me. I never thought of this . . ."

"Who knows what's for the best until all's said and done," Hannah tried to comfort him. "You're wearied. Things'll seem better after you've had a bite to eat and a sleep. Away with you."

"You'd think I was Lucy's age," he grumbled but he went.

That night, neither of them slept. Lucy tossed and thrashed about muttering feebly and hoarsely and was hardly to be recalled from her delirium by either of them. The wind dropped again so that the cabin was hot and stuffy and humid and *Polyxena* wallowed in the swell so that it was hard for them to keep their feet. Martin came in twice. The first time he warned them that the crisis was at hand and sent Hannah away to lie down which she did obediently to return to the bunkside as soon as Martin was out of earshot. The second time was some two long hours later when Hannah, alarmed by the change in Lucy's breathing, sent Innis to fetch him. When he came he looked grave and unhappy.

"She's weak," he said, "so very weak . . ."

Twenty minutes later Lucy slipped into complete uncon- sciousness. In half an hour she was dead.

6

Martin closed Lucy's eyes gently and drew up the sheet. There was nothing to be said. Innis was crouched on the deck beside the bunk, his face white and expressionless.

"Best lay her straight," muttered Martin at last. "I'll have to tell the Master. There'll be others to go over with her in the morning. Two men in the port cabin died last night and there's two more Lennoxes like to follow the first."

He glanced at Hannah's stony face.

"It must be soon," he said gently, "in this heat. I'll send Elias down with a composer for him."

They both looked at Innis; Martin nodded at her and left the cabin. Hannah touched Innis gently on the shoulder.

"Captain . . . you'd best lie down."

He rose stiffly, like an old man, and staggered as *Polyxena* dipped in the swell. Hannah led him into the other cabin where he lay on his bunk, staring up at the deck like one stunned.

Hannah straightened the child's body, washed her for the last time and dressed her in her favourite dress. On an impulse she found Lady Blanche, drew on the gown Lucy had laboured to make and then laid the doll in the crook of Lucy's arm before she drew the sheet over the sunken little face. Dawn brought Mr. Pellew from a vigil with Mrs. Lennox, his plump face creased with distress and fatigue. He left Hannah watching beside the bunk while he went into Innis's cabin. Half an hour later he emerged looking perturbed.

"I cannot console him," he said, "he blames himself bitterly. He says he has killed her."

"Aye," Hannah agreed, "he was bound to feel that."

Pellew hovered uncertainly.

"And you, my dear?"

"We did all we could do," Hannah replied. "Bairns go down so fast."

"True . . . true. We are in God's hands and sometimes we must find His ways strange." He paused and pressed his hands

68

together in a curiously distraught gesture. "In an hour," he went on jerkily, "the Master asked me to warn you . . . it must be soon . . . the heat . . . they are waiting outside. . ."

"Best send them inbye," Hannah said wearily and came to her feet. "Does himself wish to see her?"

She jerked her head at the cabin door.

"Better he should not," said Pellew.

"Aye," she assented. "There's a change already. His wee girl's not there."

The burial service was brief, almost perfunctory. Only a few of the passengers appeared at that early hour and Pellew's words were almost inaudible. The Master gave the signal and the canvas-wrapped bundles fell into the oily sea with a splash, vanishing from sight with sickening rapidity. Hannah, beside Innis, could sense his horror and grief almost as if it had been her own and her heart was wrung for him. The Master came to him after the service was over and gruffly offered his regrets: Innis muttered an acknowledgement.

"I must see whether I can help below," Hannah said quietly when the Master and his first Mate had returned to their duties. "I think you should try to sleep."

Innis did not reply but stumbled towards the cuddy. Sutherland, the Australian, caught him by the arm, nodded at Hannah, and led him away.

In the steerage it was like a vision of hell, for the fever had struck at twenty or more of the passengers. The whores had turned nurse and were giving what aid they could. Mrs. Lennox, hollow-cheeked and wild-eyed, was fighting to save her eldest son and her youngest, a baby of eight months. The rest of the family, dumb with bewilderment and fear, were in the charge of the elder sister. Hannah gently enquired about their breakfast and when she was assured they had eaten sent them on deck to play in the shade of the awning which had been rigged amidships.

Surgeon Martin was moving around the crowded, evil-smelling compartment giving advice and encouragement. The passengers who had not succumbed were huddled at one end under the ventilator and many of them were drunk. The air was thick and humid and foul. Hannah swallowed and set her teeth and looked about her to see where her help was most needed. Within two minutes her clothes were as wet as if she had been dipped in hot water.

By midday, in spite of all they could do, both the Lennox boys were dead and their mother had collapsed from grief and exhaustion. While Martin tended her, Hannah laid out the two little creatures as decently as she could and saw them taken away by two crew members, clumsily sympathetic. Maggie the elder girl had crept below again and Hannah left her sitting by her mother holding the water-roughened hand. On deck she found the surviving members of the family playing quietly under the awning with a set of ninepins which was being whittled for them by the ship's carpenter. Hannah took a good look at them and decided they seemed perfectly healthy. Below again, she picked her way through the cluttered starboard cabin till she found Martin, stripped to the waist and gleaming with sweat, as he restrained a delirious miner who demanded to be allowed to bathe in the sea. His friends were standing around showing that mixture of concern and helplessness and fear which is called forth by sudden illness and they parted to let her through.

"What the hell are you doing here?" demanded Martin.

"It's the rest of the Lennox bairns," she explained, "they should be on deck . . . stay there, eat there, sleep there. Down in this hell-hole they'll be smit, sure as death."

"Do as you please," Martin told her. "I'll square it with the Master."

He bent over the babbling patient again and Hannah turned away.

"And you go to your bunk and lie down," he called after her, "or you'll go the way of Mrs. Lennox. If you've had any sleep in the last forty-eight hours it's news to me."

Lucy's box of toys served to content the Lennoxes. Hannah stripped the cabin ruthlessly of Lucy's belongings, barring one or two mementoes which she buried deep in a locker. Elias carried the boxes below and stowed them with the rest of the heavy baggage. When that was done it was close on four in the afternoon and the cabin was as hot as an oven. She asked Elias for a jug of washing water, locked the door, stripped to the skin and washed herself fiercely as if she could wash away the grief and misery of that day. When she had done she could not bear to put her clothes on again. The heat of the sun made the deck over her head almost too hot to touch. Some of the passengers had taken to sleeping in chairs on the deck rather than immure themselves in the tiny baking cabins but Hannah did not wish to face other people. She crept naked under the sheet on her bunk and, too weary even to grieve, slept like one stunned despite the heat and the airlessness and the heaving and knocking of the becalmed vessel.

She woke to pitch darkness. *Polyxena* was under way again for the motion was slow, regular and purposeful and there was the faint sound of wind in the rigging. The ship was like a great sounding box. It was blessedly cool. She lay quietly, remembering. Gradually she realised she could hear something else. On the other side of the bulkhead someone was weeping, a difficult unaccustomed sobbing. Hannah sat up, her heart wrenched by the sound. There was no light in the cabin to find her night gown, nor could she bear to put on the sweat-soaked garments she had taken off. The sound came again. She pulled her sheet from the bunk, wrapped it around her and went softly into Innis's cabin.

It was dimly lit by a ship's lantern turned down very low and she could see Innis kneeling by the side of his bunk, his face in his hands, his whole attitude eloquent of misery.

Afterwards, she was often to wonder whatever possessed her to do what she did, but at the time she gave never a thought to what might happen, just knelt down and put her arms round him as if he had been Davie or Alec or wee Lucy herself. The need to comfort was as overwhelming as a wave of the sea. Innis turned to her and put his head on her breast as simply as if he had been a child. Hannah stroked his hair and reassured him in the same way that she had comforted her brothers after their mother had died. To lie with him later, to let him make love to her and to make love to him in a shy unpractised fashion seemed no more than another way to ease his grief and her own. Later, when he lay sleeping beside her, one arm flung across her waist, she wondered at herself but could not regret what she had done.

At first light she slipped silently out of the bunk and picked

71

up the sheet which lay discarded on the deck. She looked down and saw him sleeping soundly on the rumpled covers and thought defiantly that she had no call to feel shame. Back in her own cabin she washed and dressed hastily and went below to see how Mrs. Lennox fared. She found her asleep too and little Maggie at her side slumped uncomfortably over the wooden side of the bunk. She laid the child gently in the bunk above where her brothers had died. Sleep, she decided, was the best thing for them all. It was a surprise to find Surgeon Martin standing behind her.

"All well here?" he asked. "The children on deck are being spoiled by the crew. I've dared them to come below till I give the word. Elias will see they are fed."

"I'll have an eye to them too."

"And how is Innis?" he asked abruptly. "He was in poor shape when I saw him last night. Burned up with self-condemnation. Poor devil."

"He's sleeping," said Hannah and to her surprise and utter confusion she blushed vividly. The Surgeon saw this, stared and then laughed outright.

"Excellent," he said, dry as biscuit, "the best thing possible. Hannah, you're that rare creature, a good woman . . . not a *good* woman, they're ten a penny and tiresome . . . but a good *woman*. I won't bother my head about him any more. He's in better hands than mine. See he eats breakfast and keep him off the brandy. And you stay out of this pest-hole. You won't be needed here unless I send for you and then you'll be badly needed."

Hannah procured a well-laden tray from Elias and, setting aside a portion for herself, took it into Innis's cabin. She found him shaving, wearing no more than a skimpy towel, and put the tray down on the table. She pegged in the fiddles to hold it safely because the wind had picked up and *Polyxena* was moving briskly.

"Good morning, Captain," she said as she had done every morning for weeks.

Innis turned round mopping at his face. He looked concerned and uncertain.

"The Surgeon says you're to eat a good breakfast," Hannah said, "and here it is. I'll fetch you in a clean shirt."

Very early in the voyage she had taken over the care of Innis's clothes: Brett, she considered, had no more notion of how to care for good linen than fly in the air. While she was kneeling at the chest she was conscious of Innis standing close behind her. He cleared his throat.

"Hannah," he muttered and cleared his throat again. "Hannah . . . about last night . . . I . . ."

"Never heed last night," she said, very matter-of-factly. "Put this on and take your breakfast."

He put his arms obediently into the shirt she held up.

"But Hannah . . ."

"No buts . . . the coffee's getting cold. Here's your under-drawers. I'll fetch your trousers from the kist inbye."

Some of Innis's clothes had had to be left in the larger cabin. When she returned he was standing by the table looking at the tray.

"Have you eaten?" he asked.

"Mine's in there."

"Bring it in. I must talk to you, Hannah. You know I must."

"Very well. If you must . . . but, mind you eat what I've put there."

Almost mechanically Innis ate and drank what she put in front of him.

"Hannah," he exclaimed at last as she refilled his cup. "I don't know what to say . . ."

"Then say nothing," she advised.

"But I . . . I was the first . . . wasn't I?"

"Aye," Hannah agreed. "What of it?"

"If I'd thought . . ." he muttered, "I wouldn't for the world . . ."

"Look," said Hannah, "we didn't plan what happened last night. It just happened and that's all about it. I've no regrets or second thoughts and you needn't have them either, I promise you."

"I've no regrets," said Innis vehemently. "It was the most . . ."

He groped for words, his face scarlet.

". . . it was *generous*," he said at last, "the greatest kindness anyone ever did me. How could I regret it?"

For the second time in an hour Hannah blushed comprehensively; Innis smiled uncertainly at her and she realised that while her behaviour the night before might have arisen out of a passion of grief and pity, the man himself had a powerful attraction for her.

"Away," she protested, incurably truthful. "You're making too much of it. You're a bonnie lad and fine you know it."

To cover her confusion she got up and began to gather the dishes together on the tray. Innis caught her round the waist, pulled her down on his lap and held her tightly.

"There's no saying anything to you, Hannah Lindsay. I must show you . . ."

It was not a gentle embrace. After a minute or two Hannah pulled away from him dishevelled and breathless.

"For pity's sake, man," she protested, "you're under no obligation. . ."

Innis hugged her.

"You've no conceit of yourself, have you?"

Hannah freed herself, her knees trembling and to conceal this went to the mirror to tidy her hair.

"I think as much of myself as most."

"You use none of the tricks," Innis said, "none of the sidelong glances, the meaning looks, the accidental touches . . . not you. 'You're a bonnie lad', you say, and you mean it. Well, Hannah Lindsay, let me tell you something in your own terms. When I saw you in that dingy Glasgow office *I* thought, 'There's a bonnie lass . . .'" he mimicked her gently. "When I knew I'd have to come without Amy I knew I'd best keep my distance from you. Lucy needed everything you could do for her. I couldn't take your attention . . ."

He broke off and turned away.

"It's despicable to be talking like this. It's too soon . . ."

"Better to say what's on your mind," Hannah said. "You won't grieve for her any the less and nor will I. There's no more I can do for the wee soul except make sure you don't poison the memory of her by tormenting yourself for what couldn't be helped. Her death's no fault of yours."

Innis didn't turn round.

"I can't believe that. Nor will Amy . . . or her mother.

74

They'll say if I'd left her with them she'd be alive now. And they'll be right."

"What does it matter what they say?" Hannah demanded. "If your wife had come, Lucy would still have caught the fever. I'm more to blame than you. I let her play with the Lennox children . . ."

"That's nonsense!" Innis interrupted.

"And who's to say if you'd left Lucy with your wife and yon man she wouldn't have been miserably unhappy. Yon Weaver's no the kind to have charge of a bairn."

"How can you know that?"

"I've listened to Lucy talk of him. Forbye, he sounds the same breed as my own father. You said yourself he had you sent on this voyage. Was that true?"

"In a way . . . yes, it was."

"Then *he*'s more to blame than you or me. Much more. He did it to please himself. You meant what you did for the best."

Innis said nothing in reply to this but stared out of the porthole frowning. After an interval, Hannah got to her feet and began to gather the breakfast dishes together.

"I'll be taking these along to the galley," she said.

"You will come back?" Nick said quickly turning round from the porthole.

"I can't go far," she pointed out and he laughed a little.

Martin was standing outside the galley with his sleeves rolled up while Elias was fishing instruments out of a pot of boiling water. The surgeon scowled at her.

"One of the Glasgow whores about whom you were so downright the other day has further complicated matters by electing to give birth," he declared, "and a confoundedly bad job she's making of it."

"Can I help?"

"You? I'd a notion you'd not touch her with a ten-foot pole."

"I said I'd not let her touch Lucy," Hannah returned. "If she needs any help I can give I'll come of course."

"It could be that you've delivered more infants than I have," said Martin slyly. "They're a rare complication of the army surgeon's existence."

"Just the two," Hannah informed him, "and I'll allow they both came easy enough. But I'll do as I'm bid."

"Doubtless," agreed the surgeon. "And you'll not weep and blaspheme in my ears either. Very well. Wash your hands and come along. But I warn you, it's not going to be pleasant . . ."

He was right. It was a prolonged and painful labour. In the steerage where the girl lay there was neither light, nor air nor privacy and she was half-demented with the fever which had brought on the birth. She could do nothing to help herself, screaming with the pain and the fear. Her friends crowded round, staring and exclaiming and offering advice despite all the surgeon's ill-tempered requests for them to take themselves off. After two hours the screaming writhing creature fell into a coma and Martin, streaming with sweat, managed to use his forceps at last and ease the infant into the world.

"A girl," he panted as he worked to free her, "and just as well . . ."

Rapidly he tied off the cord, released the feeble little creature from her mother and handed her to Hannah.

"Take her away. I've my work cut out here. She'll do for the moment."

Hannah washed her gently, almost afraid to touch her, so frail she seemed, and wrapped her in a towel. The women watched her.

"Best give her a name and a blessing," advised one of them, "for sure she'll not be long for this world. Her head's to a point . . . see?"

She dipped a grimy forefinger in the bowl of bathwater and made a cross on the baby's wrinkled forehead.

"Mary, I baptise thee," she said, "in the name of the Father, Son and Holy Ghost . . ."

Martin called out abruptly.

"Hannah, leave it, come quickly!"

Hannah thrust the tiny bundle into the woman's arms and went back to the bunk where Mary's mother lay. Martin had lifted the boards on which she lay as high as he could so that her feet were higher than her head.

"Haemorrhage," he said grimly, "bleeding. Nothing I can do. Either she'll stop of herself, and with the fever on her it's unlikely, or she'll die. Take the weight for me. I'll try to pack her . . ."

A man stepped out of the huddle at the far end of the compartment.

"Let me," he said gruffly and lifted the boards easily, averting his head from the poor creature on them. Hannah turned her attention to tearing a towel into strips for the surgeon.

The hum of talk died and the only sounds to be heard were the faint wailing of the baby and the hush of water along the hull.

"Is there anything I can do?" Hannah asked.

"Pray," said Martin.

Mrs. Lennox swung her legs over the edge of her bunk and came over to them, arms outstretched.

"Give me the wee one," she said. "I've milk yet . . ."

The woman who had baptised the baby handed over the bundle and promptly fell on her knees.

"Hail Mary, full of grace . . ."

"She's going," muttered Martin despairingly.

". . . now and in the hour of our death . . ."

The prayers pattered out, smooth with use and still instinct with supplication while the minutes slipped past and a dreadful pool gathered and spread over the deck planks below the bunk.

"Put her down," said Martin at last. "It's all over."

A long time later, Martin took Hannah by the arm and led her up to the cuddy. *Polyxena* was thrashing along now before a brisk south-easterly and the skies were grey. The saloon passengers had left the deck for the shelter of their cuddy. At the sight of them everyone rose, making horrified exclamations: Martin's shirt was soaked with sweat and hideously blood-boltered and Hannah's once neat grey skirt was stained and dirtied past redemption. She shrank back from the battery of eyes.

"I can't come in here," she protested, "look at me . . . it's not fitting . . ."

Martin took no notice but surveyed the company.

"Where's Innis?" he demanded.

"On the bridge," said one of the men.

"Would you be so good as to fetch him here, Mr. Sutherland," requested Martin and stood back to let him pass through the doors. "And Padre . . ."

Mr. Pellew came forward, his face pale.

"You're needed below," the surgeon said harshly. "There's a child to baptise and the mother to send over the side."

The parson nodded unhappily and Hannah found her voice.

"Mary," she said, "we named her Mary. She was so small and we thought she'd follow her mother. But she's living yet . . ."

"I should have been there," muttered Pellew, "I should have been there, God forgive me . . ."

He hurried out, staggering as the ship nosed into a breaker.

"Your turn to play Samaritan, Nick," Martin greeted him. "Take her below and see she has a brandy . . ."

Innis flushed with anger.

"Damn it all Martin . . ."

"Don't argue," said the surgeon wearily. "Do what I say. And thank you, Hannah. Without you I'd have lost them both."

He slumped into a chair and accepted the glass that Sutherland was holding ready. Innis glowered at him for a moment and then put an arm round Hannah's shoulders and urged her toward the companionway.

"Send Elias with some brandy," he said over his shoulder.

Hannah, clean, comfortable and comforted was asleep when Innis came back to the cuddy in search of Martin. They had a sharp argument. In the end Martin downed his brandy and said bluntly, "Look, it's not what I'd have chosen to do but it was a question of life and death and I needed someone. It was her decision. And when you come down to it, my friend, it's none of your damned business what she does. She's her own woman . . . very much so."

"I brought her on board, she's my responsibility."

Martin looked at him quizzically.

"I doubt if she'd agree with that," he said drily. "Miss Lindsay has a mind of her own."

7

After Mary's mother was slipped overboard at sunset the epidemic ended as suddenly as it had begun. While the calm weather lasted, the Master made the passengers scrub their quarters clean and wash and air their bedding. The baby survived and was adopted by Mrs. Lennox and her family, there being no one aboard who even knew her dead mother's real name, let alone her family circumstances. She had been known as Cowcaddens Kate. Her baggage contained no clues and very little else apart from some tawdry finery and a bracelet of silver and turquoises which, so Elias declared, was Indian work. The Master shrugged over the collection, gave the bracelet to Mrs. Lennox and the clothes to the rest of the women which led to a hideous catfight and which ended only when the washdeck hose was turned on them.

The weather became a little cooler and they picked up a Trade Wind at last which blew them south by east at a steady six to seven knots. Life aboard resumed its monotonous pattern. It was then, not before, that Hannah began to grieve for Lucy as if the child had been her own. She knew with painful clarity what she would have been doing every moment of the day; she slept in the cabin with the gaping empty berth. Her only refuge from that plaintive little ghost was Innis himself and he was ready enough to be so. He abandoned the cuddy for her company. They became friends and companions as well as lovers. He taught her to play cards and she taught him to play draughts. Mr. Sutherland had a fiddle which he played well and some of the passengers formed a choir to sing glees and catches so that there were musical evenings in the cuddy. Innis played the flute and could make the battered old piano in the saloon resound with the accompaniments for songs. During the day he would read aloud to her while she sewed or mended. But most of all they talked: as *Polyxena* made her slow way down into the southern hemisphere there was endless time to talk.

"Tell me," he said one afternoon when Jane Eyre had palled, "what was this close call you had just before we sailed?"

Hannah chuckled and told him how she had come to jilt the Minister and carry off her dowry, all but the cow.

"How did you manage to carry off your baggage?" he asked, laughing, "as I recall, there's quite a pile of it."

"There was a lad, Lapraik, who'd once had a notion of me for all he married some other body and when I asked him would he take me to the Glasgow train he was willing enough. He came by the house just after two in the morning and I had the stuff out in the dairy ready to go down to the Manse, by my way of it. Och, Dougal was willing enough to do my father a backhanded turn . . ."

"Why?"

She told him the tale of the broken engagement.

"So, you could have been married long ago?"

"Aye," she said, "and four bairns round my skirts and all under five. Poor Chrissie. Mind, maybe I'm like my Aunt Jane, she took four years to kindle after she was married though after that it was like shelling peas, one after the other . . ."

She looked up from her sewing and went pink.

". . . and by the same token, Captain, it's the time of the month with me so no use to come chapping at my door this night."

"For someone as forthright as you, my love," said Innis grinning, "you blush charmingly."

"Away with you . . ."

"And my name is Nick," he reminded her.

"Yes, Captain," she agreed.

"My father is Dominic, I am Dominic and my son, if ever I have one, will be Dominic too. I would like a son by you, Hannah . . . in some ways I wish it weren't the time of the month with you."

"No, it wouldn't do," she returned, "just as well I'm like my Aunt Jane. A bonnie pickle we'd be in."

"But it could happen," he persisted. "And if it does . . . as far as I'm concerned you're my wife."

She frowned and put down her sewing.

"But not as far as anyone else is concerned," she replied. "There's the army folk. It wouldn't look well for you."

"I'd leave the army. I'd have done so long ago if it hadn't been for Amy. She couldn't face life in the country, especially the Scottish countryside."

"And by the same token you've a wife already," Hannah reminded him.

"She's left me," he said harshly.

"Suppose she came back to you and begged pardon . . . you'd not turn her away."

"Without a qualm," he declared.

"You say that now but if you were faced with it? You've a soft heart."

"You're more to me after a month than she ever was."

Hannah bent her head over her sewing and didn't answer immediately.

"This ship's like a wee world on its own," she observed at last. "There's nothing here to come between us. It's a simple kind of life, not many people and not much to do. After, it'll be different. Folk'll think it strange you taking up with me and they'll put between us."

"They'll not think it strange when they know you."

"They'll not want to know me."

"That's nonsense," he said angrily. "Don't you want to be with me?"

"Aye, I do," she sighed, "too much for my own good I dare say."

"Well then?"

"You're forgetting why I came. I've Roddy to find."

"We'll find him, I promise you," he urged. "The very first thing I'll do after we land is make enquiries."

"You're going to the North. Roddy's in the South Island."

"What of it? There aren't so many people in the colony to make it impossible. You've got an address."

"From what Mr. Sutherland's been saying you won't have time to do it. You'll have a war to fight."

"Hannah love, what's your hurry? I'll have some leave before too long and we'll go south together. What's a few weeks more? You haven't seen him for more than ten years."

"I don't know. It's just that I'm not easy in my mind . . . not easy at all."

"Why not?" he persisted. "Was it something in that letter?"

Hannah dropped her hands in her lap and looked out of the porthole.

"No, the letter was straightforward enough. But it's because of the letter I'm not easy. I can't explain better than that. But I know I must find him real soon . . ."

After that exchange they didn't talk of what was to happen when they arrived. Innis was confident that in the event he could persuade her to his way of thinking; Hannah knew with certainty what she had to do.

The weather became colder and colder and the passengers looked out the coats and cloaks stowed away since they lost sight of England. The winds fell light and the ship's progress was slow so that gradually the stores began to run low. The last porker was killed and then the last skinny sheep. Meals began to depend drearily on salted meat and dried beans and peas. Private hoards of pickles and jams and other little luxuries dwindled to nothing. The drinking water began to smell. In the steerage the supply of drink ran out and even the gambling schools ceased because there was so little that money could buy. Quarrels arose easily for trivial causes or no cause at all and twice the Master was forced to convene a court and try a man for attempted or threatened murder. When the accused were found guilty he put them below in irons on a diet of ship's biscuit and the stinking water and quarrels ceased. The passengers talked of nothing but food and began to plan in barmecidal detail just what they would eat on their first night ashore. The whores in the steerage found trade brisk as both crew and passengers cast about for distraction.

Seventy-six days out they passed just north of a menacing rocky hump with thick oily smoke blowing away from it.

"Kerguelen," said Mr. Sutherland. "That'll be sealers trying out oil. We've come a touch too far south, I reckon."

The passengers crowded the rail to gaze hungrily at the first land they had seen since Land's End but it was soon no more than a smudge of darker grey on a grey horizon. They saw a ship far to the north and signalled frantically for she was the first they had seen south of the equator but she took no notice and sailed on. Another fortnight passed with light and unpredictable winds until on the morning of the ninetieth day when Hannah and Innis were shivering into their clothes they heard a faint cry high above them and then the muffled thumping of feet running across the deck. Innis looked at Hannah, his eyes bright,

"Land!" he exclaimed, "it must be land . . ."

He ran out of the cabin. Hannah flung on her brown cloak and went more slowly to join the cheering, laughing, embracing throng. She smiled and rejoiced with the rest that the interminable voyage was drawing to a close but in the back of her mind there was a little voice like the slave at a feast saying, 'count the days now and make the most of them'.

From Cape Otway to the narrow, dangerous entrance of Port Phillip Bay was not much more than a good day's run but the tides were strong and ran against them and *Polyxena* had to beat up and down offshore waiting for a pilot to take her through the heads into Melbourne Harbour. Old hands crowded the rail and pointed out the places where less cautious masters had wrecked their ships. Everybody stood on deck drinking in the sight of the flat green coast and the shimmer of blue hills on the far horizon. Everybody but two; Hannah went below to seek out Mr. Sutherland in his usual chair in the cuddy.

"I want to buy some sheep," she announced.

"What?"

"Aye. I want a hundred yearling ewes. You're a sheep man from your talk, I thought you'd be able to advise me."

Sutherland put down his book and stared at her.

"Why in the name do you want a hundred ewes?" he demanded.

"For my brother," and she explained.

"It's right up-country," he warned. "How will you get them there?"

"I'll take them. It won't be the first time I've herded sheep."

"It's a damned long way," he said thoughtfully. "What will Captain Innis have to say to this?"

"He knows this is what I came to do," she told him. "I'll be leaving the ship at Dunedin."

"Well," drawled Sutherland with a faintly amused expression, "I reckon a hundred ewes is a powerful argument when it comes to that point. If you really want them, Miss Lindsay, I'll do what I can. Leave it with me."

Once in Melbourne Harbour the Master dropped anchor in deep water at a considerable distance from the shore and from the other ships lying there. He and Innis posted sentries at every point where a man might try to leave the ship.

"Make your bargains with the shore-boats, gentlemen," he told his passengers. "If I send anyone ashore he'll run and I'll lose him to the diggings. And there isn't a seaman to take his place in the whole of the town."

He pointed to the rank upon rank of masts along the quay-side.

"There's one of the reasons we haven't spoken a ship during the whole of the voyage. The dear knows how long they've been stuck here hunting for a crew or a return cargo. I don't mean to be one of them. I've mail aboard for New Zealand."

Gradually *Polyxena* discharged her cargo of iron bars, cotton cloth and immigrants, boat by boat. Sutherland went ashore in the very first. He had been greeted very respectfully by a number of large taciturn men who came off as soon as *Polyxena* dropped anchor. He refused to take any of Hannah's proffered sovereigns.

"Time enough to pay when I know how much they'll cost," he declared. "But don't worry . . . you'll hear from me."

She had a note from him that night. It began without ceremony:

I've brought you a hundred yearlings, good healthy beasts. There's a mob due to come aboard anyway consigned to the Canterbury Land Company. I've greased the drover in the palm to look out for yours as well. He'll feed and water them and see them ashore at Dunedin. After that it's for you to make the arrangements. He reckons there'll be a wagon of supplies going your way and thinks there'll be a mob with that. He'll find out when he gets there. You owe me £145 and you can pay the purser who'll see me right.

Good luck girl.

E.S.

The sheep came aboard the night before they were due to sail, strange leggy wild-eyed creatures compared to the little shaggy animals Hannah was used to. They didn't go

84

deck-cargo. Winter was on the way and a stormy crossing was to be expected. Instead, they stripped the bunks out of the empty steerage, square pens were erected and the bewildered animals lowered into them, bleating and struggling. The drover was an oldish man, burned almost black by the sun so that his faded blue eyes seemed virtually white.

"Miss Lindsay?" he asked when she approached him. "Them's yourn."

He jerked his thumb at two pens right under the ventilation shaft, just on the spot where little Mary had been born and where her mother had died. The Lennox family had departed for the back-blocks after an emotional farewell.

"Nice mob," added the drover. "Prime beasts. Ought to be when the Baron picked 'em. Dinkum sheep man is the Baron."

Innis was exasperated by this transaction. Not the least cause of this was Hannah's failure to tell him what she meant to do.

"Why not wait?" he demanded. "Aren't there sheep to be had in New Zealand?"

"Only at a price," Hannah said. "They're not easy come by in the South, so Mr. Sutherland told me."

"And what in the name of heaven do you mean to do with them?"

"Take them up-country to Bennachie."

It was some time before he accepted the fact that she meant to do just that. It was an argument which smouldered the whole of the time they were in harbour, poisoning those last days. Innis begged and pleaded for her to come with him to Auckland. He could not believe that she would leave him and poor Hannah, never articulate about her own feelings, simply could not find the words to express the foreboding she had about her brother Roddy or the duty which she felt she owed her mother to find out whether he was well and happy and prosperous. She tried and, when she failed to make him understand, she took refuge in silence.

On the first night of the passage to Dunedin, Innis became enraged by this silence and shook her violently demanding to know whether she felt anything for him at all. She burst into tears of distress, the awkward painful crying of someone unaccustomed to it. Innis, remorseful, took her in his arms and was astonished, even secretly a little shocked by the wildness of her response. Later, when they were lying side by side in the cabin, listening to the sounds of the ship and the faint plaint of the sheep he apologised for making her unhappy.

"I can't marry you . . . I may never be able to marry you. I don't want to lose you and I'm afraid . . ."

"No need to be afraid of that," Hannah told him.

He sighed, looking ahead into an uncertain future.

"Hannah," he whispered a long time later, "are you awake?"

"Mmm."

"You will come to me? Once you've made sure all's well with this brother of yours."

"If you still want me to come," Hannah reassured him, "I'll come."

And that was where they left it. As *Polyxena* drove steadily across the rough Pacific waters towards New Zealand they resumed the easy, loving relationship of the earlier part of the voyage and their imminent parting was not discussed as if they had a mutual unspoken agreement not to spoil their last days together.

Polyxena dropped anchor off Dunedin, a scatter of huts and houses on a green slope, just before dawn on the thirteenth day out from Melbourne. The thunderous sound of the cable rumbling out through the hawsehole woke them both. Innis turned to Hannah and caught her in a hard, desperate embrace.

"You can't go . . . you can't," he muttered into her hair.

"But I must," she whispered.

"Damn you, you'll break my heart. I won't let you go."

"Hearts don't break that easy," Hannah said out of a tight throat. "You'll see . . ."

The passengers for Dunedin were told they were to go ashore at midday with the first boat and Innis sat miserably in the cabin watching Hannah pack up her belongings and put on the brown cloak and the brown silk bonnet in which he had first seen her. Neither of them said very much.

"When will I see you again?" he asked suddenly.

"When I can come, I'll send word," Hannah replied, not looking at him. "And mind on this . . ." she hesitated and came to stand beside him, "folk change and times change. It seems

86

to me that I'll aye put you in mind of your wee Lucy and you might not want that . . ."

"Why shouldn't I?" he cried angrily.

"I wouldn't want to be a burden or an embarrassment to you," she went on as if he hadn't spoken. "Things won't be the same in Auckland. So I'll not come north till I hear again. Or you come for me. That way I'll know for sure I'm welcome . . . no . . . don't start . . ."

She put her hand over his mouth as the protestations bubbled to his lips.

". . . don't say anything. Just mind what I've said."

He grasped her wrists so that she winced and then kissed the palm of her hand and pulled her against him.

"What in hell do you think I am?" he demanded.

"A man," she said very quietly, "a man like other men . . . but one I'm fair set on, Lord knows why."

It wasn't until they were on deck watching the boat being lowered into the water that Innis remembered something. He caught Hannah by the arm and pulled her away from the little group by the ladder.

"Are you . . . have you . . . Hannah, have you any money? I haven't paid you . . . I never thought . . ."

Hannah smiled slightly.

"That's something I'd as soon you forgot. You've paid my passage. I've enough to do me. If I need some to come north, I'll ask you."

"You're sure?"

The moneybelt, now a deal lighter, was snug round her waist.

"Sure as I stand here. I'll be fine, don't you worry."

He looked at her unhappily.

"God . . . I wish I could come with you."

"You're sore needed in the south, by all accounts."

Melbourne had been buzzing with rumours of the Maori uprising.

"You're heading into the bush. What if they're in arms here? When I think what could happen . . ."

"I'll not do anything rash," she soothed him, "not with a flock of sheep at more than a pound each," she added smiling. "I won't let the Maori make a feast of either of us, I promise."

He smiled back uncertainly.

"And there's another thing . . . if there's a child, you'll write as soon as you can?"

She shook her head.

"Now don't trouble yourself on that score. Remember, I'm the very spit of my Aunt Jane."

"I wish you weren't," he said harshly. "I'd feel surer of seeing you again if you were carrying my child."

Hannah swallowed.

"If you really want to see me again," she promised unsteadily, "you shall."

There was an impatient shout from the rail.

"I must go," she said.

From her seat in the stern she could see him standing a little apart, not waving, just watching as the little boat laboured into the landing place. It lay out of sight of the ship in the lee of a little point of land. Just before they turned the point she raised her hand and saw him raise his.

8

Hannah was never to forget that journey up-country. Winter was just beginning and a cold wind blew from the south which searched its way through every stitch she could pile on. The sheep kept their progress slow. Hannah learned to ride in a rough-and-ready fashion and she 'rode herd' on the sheep in order to help pay her passage. She had done this at the suggestion of Maggie Gallaher, a vast smiling Irishwoman whose husband Jem was the carter. She had surged up to Hannah in the tiny wooden building which was dignified with the name of hotel.

"So you're for Bennachie, alannah, and with a mob of sheep and here's myself glad to have you along for 'tis a long day since I'd another girl along the trail so it is."

She had looked Hannah up and down and then shaken her head.

"If you've money enough, girl dear, buy a horse and ride it. Your bum's not best suited to a wagon-seat, the way mine is for me sins . . ."

She twisted her head in its shabby limp sunbonnet to examine her vast rear.

"Sure, didn't the good God design me for sitting half me life on a wooden wagon-seat?"

She had laughed at that in a cosy contralto bellow and ordered a glass of 'the Cratur' from the disapproving barman. From her easy flow of conversation Hannah discovered that Maggie and Jem were childless and between them were building a carrier's business around Dunedin and the tiny little communities which were springing up in the hinterland. Maggie drove the team of oxen which drew the heavy wagon and Jem, who was small and spry and wizened, did everything else. Hannah agreed with them to take her baggage, a load of supplies, flour, oatmeal, dried beans and peas, salt, sugar and bacon, and the ninety-eight ewes which had survived the journey from Melbourne. In return, Hannah agreed to pay ten sovereigns and take her turn at the cooking and washing, such as there was.

"Washing's a darg I've no liking for," Jem admitted, "and my Maggie on a river bank's an open invitation to disaster, so she is."

With Jem's help she had bought a horse: a youngish mare, ugly but sturdy and cheap. Jem spent an hour or two showing her how to ride.

"Folk make a great to-do about riding," he said scornfully, "but the thing is to stay up there in the saddle. And you can't fall off that one . . . gentle as a flower, she is, for all she looks like a circus beast. Pull that to go right, pull this to go left and pull them both if you want to stop. Kick when you want to go and if you're in doubt hold on to anything handy and the devil with elegance. If you do fall, roll up in a ball the way you won't be hurting yourself."

He was pleased with his pupil.

"You'll never ride a-hunting, so you'll not, but if you'll spell me with the mob I'll make it eight sovs, not ten . . ."

The party consisted of thirty skinny wide-horned cattle, nearly three hundred sheep, the ox-wagon, the Gallahers and Hannah. After a few days they were joined by a smiling, silent, Maori youth, Tuomi, whose role seemed to be partly drover and partly scout for he brought news of washed-out fords and other hazards ahead. The wagon was loaded down with winter stores for the dozen or so farms which lay scattered about the headwaters of the Clutha; of these Bennachie lay farthest out to the south-east. Camping gear and stores for the party were carried on packhorses and Hannah, growing accustomed to the saddle, learned to lead one of these. There was no road; a faint trail could be seen at first where wagons had passed, fords across the wide shallow streams had been roughly made, some of the scrub had been cut down and rolled aside. From time to time they passed the black scar of an earlier campfire. Otherwise, they might have been the first people ever to cross these seemingly endless tussock plains.

Sometimes Hannah wondered if it was all a dream. The countryside seemed so familiar and yet the plants, the animals, the birds, the insects were mostly strange, the sounds were different to any she could remember, even the smells. For a fortnight the ground heaved under her feet, reminding her of the *Polyxena* and of Innis. It was part of the dream that she could not fix her mind upon their reunion; it was an event beyond her imagining, like the face of God. She kept carefully within the dream, as dreamers do who don't wish to waken, for to waken would be to find herself in the Kirkton, aging, souring: but the dream, Innis, the new country and the long voyage were so strange that she could barely come to terms with them or with the new self in the dream.

It took them the better part of five weeks; they rested one day in five to ease the beasts which wearied with thrusting their way through the high tussock. At the start of the journey there had been occasional farmsteads where they could shelter and Hannah first began to understand the isolation in which these settlers lived. Maggie was the newsbringer and Hannah listened to the avid exchange of news; hearing of deaths, tragic and bizarre, sickness, accidents, narrow escapes, marriages, births and bankruptcies. With sick dismay she heard Jem repeat his tales of cannibal outrages in the North Island and heard the farmers speculate whether they might have to experience similar things in the South Island. Maggie kept a chest handy filled with things she knew would be welcome and the wives exchanged milk and eggs and lambskins for papers of pins and packets of needles, coarse pottery bowls and mugs, gaily coloured ribbons and tattered books and magazines. One sun-burned, gaunt woman wept openly when she heard Hannah's voice.

"If ye kenned, lassie, whit it means tae hear a voice frae hame. My man's a guid man but he's English."

The homesteads were primitive, mere huts made of sod, or constructed of rough-hewn planks and logs, simple as a doll's house. The floors were beaten earth, the furniture crude, home-made and scanty. Occasionally there would be a treasured piece, a clock or a carved chair or a chest of drawers like her own, brought thousands of miles to grace these comfortless dwellings. All their owners said the same thing; that one day they would rebuild, improve, expand . . . but the land came first. The hospitality was lavish and devoted.

After the first week or so even these isolated farms petered out and there was nothing to be seen but tussock plain and scrub with an occasional patch of bush by the side of the creeks.

"We're making first for Bennachie," Maggie explained. "Them cattle's for Craigie's which is just beyond and we'll be able to manage without you once we've left your mob at Bennachie. And you're afire to be there, are you not, alannah?"

Hannah nodded.

"We've not come this way before," Maggie admitted, " 'twas Hector Macadam himself made this trail, eight, nine years past, and there's not many use it bar himself. I've never been next or nigh the place for he comes into Dunedin for his own bits of stores, so they say, and never a word out of him."

As they climbed, the weather became steadily colder and storms of wind and rain pounced out of the hills to the north-west. Against these, the Gallahers' ragged canvas tent was little protection. The sky was uniformly grey and low until one morning the tent-flap was stiff with frost and when Hannah crept out she caught her breath with awe and surprise for there, along the horizon, their snow-tipped peaks taking on the reddish gold of a frosty sunrise were the mountains; rank upon rank of them as far as the eye could see. Hannah stood staring, the tears standing in her eyes, partly from the cold and partly because of the sheer astounding beauty of the sight. All of a sudden her stomach heaved and she knew she was going to be sick. When it was all over she found Maggie standing nearby with a cloth wrung out in icy water from the stream. Hannah dabbed her face thankfully and then something in Maggie's expression brought home the possibility, the certainty, that she did not, after all, take after her Aunt Jane.

"Sure, I'd a notion it could be that way with you," Maggie said later. "You'd a look about you . . . I cannot say just how it is but I'd know it and envy it the barren great lump that I am."

She sighed and fell silent.

"Will he acknowledge it? The father, I mean . . ." she asked after a long while.

"He will," Hannah said, "but he canna marry me."

"And are you glad of its coming?" Maggie demanded aggressively, "for if you are not I'm no friend of yours and

92

you're none of mine. I'd sell the eyes of my head to be in your shoes, so I would."

"I must be glad," Hannah said, "for it's in my mind it may be all I'll have of him now."

"Ochone . . . is it that way with you? Has he left you, the black heart?"

"No, no, it's a feeling I have, just," Hannah sighed. "Say rather I left him for he was fell anxious I should stay and go on with him to Auckland. But I had promised Roddy in my letter . . . I'd promised I'd come as soon as I could."

"A promise is a promise," said Maggie and shrugged. "And a promise on paper is twice a promise. You did right, alannah."

That night in camp she said suddenly and fiercely.

"They'll point the finger at you up there, girl dear, for they're the narrow kind. They'll sin their own sins behind curtains and call themselves holy. I know them. Let you remember you've friends in Jem and me . . ."

The next day they saw sheep, like tiny white specks along the grey-green slopes of the foothills.

"Bennachie," said Jem. "We'll be there by tomorrow morning."

Hannah stared toward the hills and for the second time on her long journey she felt black afraid. Tomorrow brought snow, tiny stinging particles on an icy wind which blew into their faces, forcing them to peer through half-shut eyes at the way ahead. Maggie's ox-team slowed and shirked and she shouted abuse at them, the cart-whip for once stinging about their flanks. The cattle breaking trail ahead plodded more and more slowly until Jem wheeled his horse suddenly and pointed at a clump of trees.

"We'll camp," he shouted. "This isn't fit for man nor beast."

No one argued. Hannah was struggling to heat a panful of stew over a sulking smoky fire when she heard a hail. When she looked up she saw a huge man on horseback some distance away. He wore a blue Scots bonnet pulled well down on his head and a grey plaid wrapped round him and crusted with snow.

"Macadam?" enquired Gallaher.

"That's me. You'll be Gallaher the carrier. What brings you this way this time of the year?"

"A mob of sheep and some stores . . ."

"None o' mine," Macadam interrupted.

"Fine I know that," said Jem easily. "They're Hannah's bringing."

He indicated Hannah who had risen and was standing beside the fire.

"Your partner's sister, Hannah Lindsay. Hannah, this is Hector Macadam."

Hannah's first impression was one of enormous size. Macadam was more than six feet tall and as broad in the shoulders as her father. His hand was hard and smooth and gripped hers painfully. He was heavily bearded and his dark hair was long. Hannah suddenly heard the voice of Mr. McLagan reading from the story of Jacob, '. . . and Esau was an hairy man . . .'

"Hannah Lindsay!" he was saying, "I can't credit it. I didn't believe you'd come."

"You'd my letter, then?" Hannah asked shyly.

"Aye, six weeks since out of the *Marco Polo*. Roddy was overjoyed, just, but I said to him that it was the sort of thing folks say. It wasn't the kind of journey for a young lass alone and he wasn't to set his heart on your coming. But here you are. It's a damned miracle . . ."

"There's a few loaves and fishes come along with your miracle, Macadam," Jem said and jerked his head at the sheep huddling together against the wind. "There's ninety-eight of them for Bennachie and a good sixth of Maggie's load."

"But it's Miss Lindsay herself I'm best pleased to see," Macadam declared his eyes on her face. "Roddy said to me, 'You don't know Hannah; if she says she'll do a thing, she'll do it if all hell should bar the way . . .' He was right it seems."

"Aye, was he not?" agreed Maggie with a guffaw and then caught Hannah's imploring eye. "Oh, sure, I'm dumb, dumb as a stone."

Macadam accepted a tin bowl of stew and squatted down by the fireside.

"You see," he said slowly, "I'd no way of knowing what he'd said in yon letter of his . . . and no wish to ask him, the way things are . . ."

"The way things are," Hannah repeated. "And what way's that? Save us, but I knew there was something amiss . . . I knew . . ."

"He's awful sick, your Roddy," Macadam told her gently. "I'd the doctor to him two months past but there's nothing to be done. Another six weeks . . . eight mebbe . . . and you'd have been too late, lass."

A fortnight later the voyage, Innis, the journey up-country had faded into a vague half-dream, half-memory. Hannah, moving between the primitive kitchen-place, the wash-tub in the shed by the stream and the tiny one-roomed wooden shelter which Roddy called a whare and in which he stayed alone, found it hard to believe that she had ever known any other life. She baked in the clay oven, learned how to cook over an open fire and how to sweep a floor of beaten earth. Roddy was weak but in little discomfort except for painful stitches in his side which, so he said, were eased by Hannah's repeating the charm which their mother had used. He was a good patient, uncomplaining and obedient; eating and drinking what she brought him, sleeping when she bade him and un-demanding of her company or Macadam's.

Macadam and Hannah entered into an unspoken pact to spend as much time as possible with him. Hannah would ride round the ewes in the home paddocks in the evening, huddled gratefully into Hector's plaid while he sat in the whare. Hector would wash dishes later while Hannah recounted for the twentieth time the tale of Minnie's bath or the jilting of McLagan and darned away at the vast socks which Hector had knitted for himself or knitted more from the harsh homespun wool. Only at night when she lay on a makeshift bed in the kitchen place of the homestead did she remember the child growing inside her or sometimes when she was wakened by alien birdcalls in the early morning she would turn toward the wall half-expecting to find Innis there to reassure her. Then she would weep a little. But the days were too busy for fretting.

She didn't tell Roddy about the child. He could not hope to see it. Nor did she tell Hector, for he was not a man to invite confidences. Before Maggie and Jem had left for the Craigie's farm in the next valley she had scribbled a little stiff letter to Innis:

> . . . I'm needed here. Roddy's not long for this world and I must stay with him. I'll find a way of writing again in the spring. If you've news for me, write care of the Gallahers and they'll find a way to send it me.

Her pen had hesitated over the valediction and, with her heart bursting with longing and affection, she had settled finally for:

> "I am, yours truly, Hannah Lindsay."

This, if not fulsome, had the merit of being exact. About the baby she said nothing at all: a countrywoman, she knew that nine months could be a very long time in which a great many things could happen. Time enough to tell him when the baby was born, she thought. When the Gallahers had gone, she regretted this; he had a right to know, after all, but by then there was nothing to be done for the Gallahers would not pass that way again until spring.

For a month it seemed that Roddy had drawn new life from Hannah's arrival but it was no more than a brief pause in his decline. When she arrived he could still sit up briefly while she made his bed but soon even that exhausted him too much. Four weeks and two days after Hannah arrived she found her brother spitting blood. After that, in spite of all his protests, he moved her bed into the whare. From then on Roddy became weaker. Hector took back most of the tasks which Hannah had taken on, leaving her to care for her brother. Snow covered the hills and Roddy asked to be propped up to see it.

"It's cold," he whispered hoarsely, "and it's death on the sheep but I've aye liked the snow . . . mind on the pair of us playing snowballs coming home from the school?"

He didn't say much after that but lay looking at Hannah and listening to her tales of their childhood together.

The Minister rode up from Inchture, a hard–bitten taciturn man who prayed with directness and brevity. He told Roddy bluntly that there was a place reserved in heaven for him and that Jesus forgave anyone truly repentant of their sins.

"It may not be what Mr. Thomas Burns preaches," he declared, "but it's what I believe. Remember your Pilgrim's Progress? There was great rejoicing when Mr. Greatheart came to the Celestial City. You've borne adversity with courage, laddie, and you'll have your reward."

Hannah, reassured by this comforting and homely speech, went to prepare a meal before the Minister, Mr. McVean, rode the thirty-four miles back to his Manse. In the kitchen-place she found Hector trimming a leg of mutton from the cold-house by the stream and a good clear fire burning ready. He looked up as she came in.

"All well?"

"I like yon man," Hannah said, "and I'd not say that for all the breed," she added defiantly.

"So I've heard," he agreed and smiled at her.

"Roddy asked, would you go up bye," she said.

It occurred to Hannah as she spitted the meat and set it before the fire, that a smile made Hector seem less unapproachable. She wondered what he would have to say when he knew of her condition. Soon he would have to know, her waist was thickening fast.

A week later Roddy died in his sleep without a struggle. Hannah laid him straight, closed his eyes and kissed him goodbye. When she stood back from the bed she was conscious not so much of sorrow but of a black, burning, sour anger against her father who had sown the seeds of the disease. She had heard from Roddy how he had most probably caught it from a fellow-crewman on board ship, but she knew very well that overwork and ill-treatment had weakened him before they drove him away to ship as a sailor. She was still standing there silently calling down retribution on the head of Alec Lindsay when Hector came in and took off his bonnet.

"It's a crying shame!" she burst out, "he loved this place and he'd have done it credit if he'd been spared. It's wrong he should have to die and him not twenty-six year old. There's plenty worse nor him who'll make old bones and the world would be a better place without them."

The hot tears began to run down her face and she mopped at

them with her shawl. Macadam said nothing but put his great arm round her shoulders and turned her to him. Hannah for a moment felt a little less desolate.

McVean came back for the burial and a handful of neighbours rode across with him, the first that Hannah had seen. They buried Roddy a little way from the whare where he had spent his last weeks and because there were no flowers Hannah made a wreath of the alien evergreens. The wind howled round the little group at the graveside and Hannah, looking at the strange faces, wondered suddenly what had become of the handsome college lad who had fathered Roddy. Was he presiding now over some respectable household, ignorant and content to be ignorant of the grief he had caused. With this bitter thought came another which froze the heart in her breast: had she condemned the child she was carrying to a similar fate? Like poor Roddy he would be born without a name of his own or a father of his own.

"Better no father than one like mine!"

She found the funeral party looking at her in dismay and realised that she had cried it out aloud. Overcome, she turned away from the gaping hole where her Roddy lay and stumbled down the hill to the homestead.

When the others had gone Macadam came into the kitchen-place and found Hannah sitting on the creepie-stool and staring into the fire.

"We'll need to have a wee talk," he said gently and produced a piece of paper from the pocket of his shirt. "Your brother left a will. Best you read it."

It was a short document. In a very few lines Roddy declared that he left everything of which he died possessed to his beloved sister Hannah. She read it and handed it back to Hector.

"I doubt he'll not have much, the poor lad," she remarked. "And I would wish that you'd take your choice of what there is for a keepsake. You've done more for him than I have . . . or ever could."

Macadam didn't answer immediately and when he did he looked uncomfortable.

"You don't understand, lass," he said gruffly, "Roddy was my partner . . ."

98

"In a manner of speaking," Hannah interruped, "and it was kind in you to say so but . . . ."

"Half of Bennachie was his."

Hannah stared in bewilderment.

"But he'd never a penny," she cried. "How could it be? Those sheep I brought . . . they were to be his stake . . . they were to give him a start."

"Eighteen months since when he fell ill," Hector went on, "the Minister came over to see him and said he needed an interest in life . . . something to live for. I made over half of the run to him the same day and McVean was witness. I'd neither chick nor child, nor like to have, and he would have had it after me in any event. Forbye, we'd had hard times in the early days, your brother and me, before the flock built up and he was never one to spare himself . . . ."

"No," Hannah agreed sadly, "he was aye one to do everything with all his might. Work or play, it didna matter."

"I thought," Hector continued doggedly, "that this would give him something to live for and if did die . . . well, who should it come to but myself?"

He paused and looked down at his hands.

"I didn't bargain for you, lass," he said almost inaudibly. "Bennachie makes a living for two, more in a good year . . . but I can't buy you out and I can't pay you much of an income, not for a year or two yet and then I'll need the luck."

"But I wouldn't look for . . . I didn't . . . ." Hannah began and he put out a curiously authoritative hand to stop her.

"Wait. I'd best tell you the whole. Roddy'd a bee in his bonnet the way sick folk often have and he told McVean this might bring it about . . . ."

"Bring what about?"

"He wanted us wed."

Hannah stared at him and he looked at her very directly under his heavy brows.

"From the day your letter came he had this in mind. His sister, the best friend he'd had in the old country, and me, the friend he'd made here. It was like a dog's bone with him the way he'd talk about it and I hadn't the heart to tell him it couldn't be."

He paused and pressed his hands together till the knuckles cracked.

"I didn't think you'd come. I thought it was the sort of thing folk say, 'I'll be over to see you one of these days . . .' Then when you did come he was dying and I couldn't make things worse for him. You see, even if you were willing, lass, I can't wed you. I've a wife back in Scotland."

He looked down at the ground.

"You may as well know. I left Edinburgh no more than a flea's lowp ahead of the police."

Hannah stared at him but could find nothing to say.

"I never told Roddy. I never told a soul since I left. But you're due an explanation."

"It's no business o' mine!" cried Hannah.

"But it is. For us to be wed would be the sensible thing. I need someone in the homestead and to help me round the place," Hector told her and raising his head looked her firmly in the eye. "And you, my lass, need a home for your bairn."

Hannah jumped.

"It'll be a relief in a way to tell someone," he went on. "It was this way. I was twenty and a builder just out of my prenticeship . . . a stonemason. There was a big job on up Argyll way. I was new-married and Isa didn't want for me to go but it meant that I'd get a start, a right start and mebbe a business of my own . . . so, away I went. It took longer than I thought. It was a wicked bad summer that year. We were not far off finishing when I'd this letter . . ."

He hesitated, his face twisted with disgust.

"It was from a neighbour, not signed but I knew well enough which good soul it was, and it told me just what my Isa was up to. I tore it up and burned the pieces but it came between me and what I was at so the next day I packed my traps and went home. I reached the house at dinner time the next day and I found them . . ."

He drew a great breath.

"We'd not been married a year . . ."

Hannah did not stir; she saw he was still shaken by the memory of how he had felt that day.

"I took him, mother-naked as he was, and I threw him

down the stair and he broke his neck. I went down after him meaning to bring him outside in the street to make a show of him but he was dead. I couldn't believe it. Isa was screaming and cursing at me and the neighbours gathering in the door-ways like flies and I just ran. I caught the train to Glasgow and shipped out aboard a collier that same day. A year later I fetched up in Australia and thought I was safe. I set up a business as a carrier and was making a fair living till one day I met up with a man I'd known in Edinburgh. He hadn't heard the story but he knew me. I sold my team and came over here."

He raised his head and looked at her.

"I could never tell Roddy this . . ."

"Roddy thought the sun rose and set on you," Hannah told him, "and he'd good reason to think so."

"That was the way I could never tell him. I couldn't tell him he was set on a murderer."

Hannah rose and swung the kettle over the embers of the fire.

"Hardly that," she said calmly. "You didn't set out to kill the creature. If you'd just trounced him out of doors in his bare scud and knocked out a few teeth it would have been a nine day wonder and long forgotten. Your misfortune as well as his that you lived up two pair of stairs."

Macadam stared at her and then chuckled.

"God kens what I expected when I told you yon tale, but it wasna that."

"Well I've a tale of my own," she said.

"I jaloused as much," Hector admitted.

When she had told him he shook his head.

"What's to be done?" he asked.

"I mean to write to Innis as soon as I can," she said. "But I'd be glad if you'll let me bide till I hear or he comes to fetch me. As for Roddy's share of the run, I'll find some way to make it over to you."

"No. You can't do that and I'd not let you if you could. Stay and welcome for as long as you wish. But I warn you, there'll be talk."

"Will it harm you?"

He shook his head.

"I take little to do with my neighbours. I've no wish to have them spier at me where I'm from and the like of that."

"In that case," Hannah decided briskly, "I'll stay a wee while."

Hannah heard from the North Island sooner than she had expected. The first lambs had just begun to arrive when Tuomi appeared in the door one evening. He grinned at her soundlessly and waved a letter. Hannah put a plate of cold mutton before him and took the letter outside to read.

'My dearest,' Innis began, 'I hardly know how to tell you . . .'

His wife had arrived in New Zealand. Amy Innis had sailed on the *Philip Hanley* five weeks after *Polyxena*'s departure.

'She left Weaver inside three weeks,' Innis wrote. 'I haven't come at the rights of the matter yet . . . nor do I care enough to enquire . . .'

Hannah's heart sank as she read on: Amy had returned to her parents' house and they had refused to admit her. New Zealand had become her only refuge. In the circumstances it would be very difficult for Innis to refuse to acknowledge her. There was also the question of Lucy's death.

'. . . she is, of course, very much distressed,' Innis wrote. 'I could not believe you would wish me to be so callous as to refuse her shelter.'

Which was true enough. The letter was long, sincerely affectionate and regretful but its message could not be softened. Hannah could not go to Auckland.

9

When the Maori had settled down to sleep in the chimney corner Hannah went in search of Hector who was tending two sickly lambs in the shed.

"The Gallahers sent Tuomi," she said.

Hector looked up.

"A letter?"

Hannah nodded, her lower lip caught hard between her teeth.

"His wife's come out," she said.

Hector said nothing.

"I could go back to Scotland," she went on. "I've money enough. I could go into service as a housekeeper, wear weeds and a wedding ring. But I'd rather stay. If you'll have me."

Macadam put the lamb he had been feeding back in its nest of straw.

"They'll father your bairn on me," he said bluntly. "I dare say they've done it already for a heavy belly's meat and drink to them. Do you mind?"

"I mind your being blamed for what's no fault of yours."

"My back's broad," he said. "Stay and welcome. The place is half your own when all's said."

"I want to be here," Hannah said, almost as if she hadn't heard him, "not half a world away."

"I'd miss you sore if you went," Macadam said quietly, so quietly she could not be sure what he had said.

Before Tuomi left, Hannah wrote to Innis, a brief, friendly letter with never a hint of the child due at midsummer.

"Have you told him?" Macadam asked, watching her write in the light of the brass lamp.

"No," said Hannah simply. "He'll not be rid of that one in a hurry and I'd not wish to distress him any further. I'm well enough off, thanks to you."

It was after she had sent off the letter that she opened up the kist and brought into use the linen and blankets, the fluted china and the silver which had once been intended to grace the farmhouse of Netherbiggin and later the Manse. Macadam noted this nest-building and smiled to himself. He had a few plans of his own.

Innis wrote again two months later: he suggested that she come to the north and he would set her up in a house in Auckland.

'It isn't what I'd wish,' he wrote, 'but at least I'd know you were well and I could see you sometimes . . .'

He went on to say how much he missed her and how often he thought of her and Hannah felt her throat close as she read it.

"I'd go if I could," she told Macadam later, "but I don't think I could stand the journey, not now . . ."

"And I'd not let you try," he told her. "It's out of the question. Have you told him yet?"

"No," she admitted. "He's got worries enough."

Amy Innis, it appeared, had taken to the bottle.

"When the child's born," she said, "I'll take him north . . ."

". . . or her," Macadam suggested.

"Him," declared Hannah firmly and he chuckled. Her conviction that the baby would be a boy amused Macadam and secretly impressed him. He remembered Roddy talking about her.

'There were times I thought she had the Sight,' Roddy had said once. 'It was uncanny the way she'd know when I was in bother.'

She was nearly eight months along when McVean came again. It was high summer and he arrived while they were sitting outside on the new verandah watching the sky blush into sunset. The Minister tied his horse to the rail and stumped up the wooden steps.

"You're a speak and a disgrace the pair of you," he announced morosely. "The whole neighbourhood's affronted."

Hannah flushed and went inside to swing the kettle over the flame. When she came out Macadam and McVean were glowering at one another; the air was heavy with conflict.

"You're living here in open sin," the Minister was saying. "It's enough to bring a judgement on you."

"I'm willing enough to abide by God's judgement on any actions of mine," growled Macadam. "And your damned nosy congregation can mind their own damned business."

Hannah came between them.

"Don't you dare speak ill of Macadam," she said angrily. "This is none of his; you can ask Maggie Gallaher if you don't believe me. And I'll have you know he's the good Samaritan of this tale . . . none of your Pharisees."

"Then you shouldn't expose him to such gossip," reproved McVean. "Shame on you."

"And shame on you for listening to it," snapped Hannah.

McVean sighed and sat down.

"Let me tell you," Hector said, "I'd have been hard put to it to winter the flock without her. My neighbours so-called are quick enough to condemn me and even quicker to ask me for help at a barn-building or a roof-raising but devil a hair of them did I see when the creek flooded. It was Hannah who was down there and up to her waist in water and how we didn't lose those yowes I'll never know . . . or Hannah her bairn for the matter of that."

"You could give her your name at least," said the Minister quietly, "and that would still their tongues after a while."

"Then I'd give her an empty thing for the name I bear now is not my own and the woman who bears mine is alive still for all I know . . . or care. God damn her for a loose-living bitch!"

"Mind your tongue," reproved McVean. "I'd some notion this was the way of it."

"Then why come here?" demanded Macadam. "Was it just to put her in mind of this ill-natured gossip?"

"No," said the Minister. "It's been on my mind that she's not far from her time now and she'll need a woman body for her lying in and not a soul in the parish ready to come."

Hannah went scarlet.

"I can do without them," she cried. "I've Hector here and if all's well with me I don't need their help. And if all's not well may my death and my son's come between them and their sleep the rest of their days."

"Now, now," soothed the Minister. "There's more to the

Ministry hereabout than prayer meetings and bible classes. I've delivered bairns before I baptised them. Midwives are scarce."

"You'd best mind out lest you get tarred with the same brush," Hannah told him ungratefully, "for that would never do."

He fixed her with an amused blue eye.

"It's my earthly task to snatch brands from the burning and so I shall tell them . . ."

Hannah made a disgusted noise and went indoors where she heard the two men laughing; after a disgruntled moment or two she smiled and drifted, as she so often did on those soft summer days, into a waking dream of showing Innis his son for the first time.

"Roderick Dominic . . ." she murmured to herself.

Roderick Dominic arrived quickly and on the whole unexpectedly on a blazing December day. Hannah rose as she always did at first light, bustled round the house, made a vast dinner and whistled Hector in from the paddocks to eat it.

"Not long now, lass," he said comfortingly while she fanned herself. "Though you're spry enough yet in all conscience."

"I hope he'll let me finish the baking," she said for the dough was rising in a corner and the clay oven was nearly hot.

"Well . . . I'll be in earshot," he promised. "Keep yon whistle handy."

Hannah had just taken the last brownie from the clay oven and was reviewing the ranks of cakes and pies and loaves with a certain satisfaction when the first faint pains began. She put the baking away from the flies in the pantry. This apartment had been the kitchen-place when she had first come to Bennachie and it was made of thick cob which, damp as it was in winter, stayed blessedly cool in summer. The one small window was covered with calico, tacked onto a frame and she had puddled the gaps round the frame with clay from the creek to make it flyproof. She covered the loaves with a cloth and stood savouring the coolness. The new kitchen, light and convenient as it was, could be intolerably hot. As she stood there she felt another pain, not a warning like the first ones but severe enough to make her gasp and cling to the shelves until it was past.

106

When it had left her she closed the door of the pantry with care and went to the room which Macadam had built for her when he built the new kitchen. He had used part pit-sawn timber and part boulders from the bed of the creek. In there she searched for the things which she had put past for the occasion, towels, an ancient blanket scrubbed into respectability and a pile of babyclothes which she had made from her own limited wardrobe and the fine unbleached cotton which Maggie Gallaher had brought in the spring. She stripped her bed and spread the blanket over the straw palliasse. Another pain caught her as she did so, far more severe even than the last and she had to lean against the bedpost. A dragging sensation in her belly warned her that the time was coming very close so she took off her clothes and put on the old nightgown she had set aside. After the next pain, she told herself, she must find the whistle and summon Hector: but the next pain brought the waters streaming down her legs and over the floor and she realised that the baby was not going to wait for Hector or for anybody else. She grabbed the blanket off the bed and crouched down over it as the contractions became intense. In less than a minute the baby's head emerged and then there was another violent contraction and the little shining red creature slithered on to the waiting blanket. At once he began to cry heartily and Hannah had time to hap him in a fold of the blanket before the last contraction brought forth the afterbirth.

Up till that point she had felt perfectly calm, knowing almost instinctively what she must do, but then her head swam and she nearly fell over. It was the baby's crying which cleared her mind. She got up from the floor beside the bed where she had been crouching and sat on the edge, shaking slightly and feeling curiously light as if she might float away. She forced herself to recall the other childbirths she had witnessed and knew what she must do next. Her gown tied with a ribbon at the neck so she plucked at it and pulled it out, looking at her fumbling hand as if it belonged to someone else . . .

The floor she had scrubbed to a fine whiteness was now stained and the irrelevant thought occurred that she should have to plait a rug to cover the mark. Carefully, as if she was made of glass and might break, she knelt down and tied the ribbon tightly round the cord as she had seen Martin do. Roderick Dominic had stopped crying and lay there looking bored and indignant. There were scissors in her workbox, a mile away across the stained floor and into the kitchen and under the window. She wavered to the door, leaned against the doorpost and then holding on to the walls found her way to the window. Macadam had made the box for her and carved an 'H' on the lid. The scissors were in a loop on the lid . . . inside the lid. She had used them to cut Minnie's awful hair . . . long and long ago . . .

When she got back to the bedroom Roderick Dominic was crying again, the tiny perfect hands flailing above the fold of the blanket. She cut the cord and held her breath but there was no bleeding. Slowly she picked up her baby and looked at him properly for the first time. He was tiny and plump and sturdy with a fluff of dark hair. He nuzzled his head against her, seeking and crying and she felt her breasts ache and prickle almost unbearably. She opened the gown and put him to the breast, wincing at the pain as her milk began to flow.

Hector came home at dusk and found the fire out and the kitchen empty. For a few seconds he stood absolutely still. Suddenly he saw the bedroom door standing open and there they were, both of them, asleep on the bed he had made; Hannah lay on her back, the dark hair usually so neat all astray on the mattress and the baby asleep in the crook of her arm. He looked for a long time and then turned away to fill the great kettle and relight the fire. Coming in with an armful of kindling he paused and looked up at the darkening sky.

"Thanks to You," he muttered, "Whoever You may be, that they're both safe . . ."

Hannah woke and it was night and much cooler; Roderick Dominic washed and dressed lay quietly in a crib beside her and her room was clean and sweet again. She sat up to look at him, and the crib which she hadn't seen before, and Hector appeared at the door. He was so tall and broad he almost filled it, his head a little to one side to clear the lintel.

"Aye, lass," he said, "so you're awake. I've water heated and you can have a wash. There's a clean gown airing before the fire."

Without further ado he lifted her and carried her into the kitchen where her washtub was waiting with the kettle steaming beside it. Towels were draped over a chair.

"And this time," he said grimly, "call if you need me. You can take this independence too far . . . away too far."

Hannah kept her bed until midday the next day; Hector, back to make the dinner, found her stirring the mutton stew he had left ready. By the end of a week she was almost as busy as usual and Roderick Dominic was thriving. When the Minister arrived, as he had promised, the following Monday she was sitting darning outside in the sunshine, the baby asleep in the crib beside her.

"Well, well," marvelled the Minister, "so I'm late at the fair. My word, but he's a bonnie youngster. Are you well enough, yourself?"

"Fine and well," she answered composedly and blew three blasts on a whistle. Hector and she had evolved a code: two blasts meant a meal ready, three a visitor and one long blast, 'come at once'. Moss, the old sheep dog, came loping up in the silent menacing way that sheepdogs have and lay down under the crib, his yellow eyes fixed on the Minister.

"Moss has decided to be nursemaid," Hannah explained. "Heaven help anyone who goes near the bairn without Hector or me there."

"Have you registered the birth?" McVean asked.

"Not yet. I'm taking him north presently, to Auckland. I'll do it then."

She smiled at the thought, looking at her son and wondering what his father would have to say when he saw him. The Minister watched her.

"And what will Hector do when you've gone?" he asked.

"He'll ask you to find some widow-body, glad of a home, to keep house for him," she said.

"And if there aren't any or they won't come?"

"There's plenty widows in this country, more's the pity, and once I'm away they'll come fast enough," Hannah declared. "Men's sins is quickly forgotten. It's women who suffer a lifetime."

McVean looked rueful.

"That's true enough, for all I wish it weren't. What name are you giving the youngster?"

"Roderick Dominic Hector," she said at once.

"He'll never lack for a name."

"He'll lack the one he should have."

"Aye," agreed the Minister, "but there've been good and great men in the same predicament. What will you call him? Roddy?"

"Nick," said Hannah and bent over the crib, "wee Nick . . ."

"Mmm . . . Nick is it? Let's hope he's not a wee nickum then."

"My father was Alexander," Hannah said, "and he was the nearest thing to Old Nick I've ever met or expect to meet. Names don't make any difference to what people are."

"Hannah!"

"It's the truth," she said defiantly. "He'd set about to hurt folk just to suit his book . . . aye, and he enjoyed it. Here's Hector. I'll make a pot of tea while the pair of you have a crack."

"Bring a bowl of water with you when you come back," McVean instructed, "and put a splash from the kettle in it. No need to startle the poor wee fellow with ice-cold spring water."

Hannah chuckled and agreed.

The ceremony was short and informal. Nick let out a sleepy howl of protest at being thus damply admitted to Christendom. When Hannah retired to feed him Hector produced a black bottle.

"Not whisky as I remember it," he admitted, "but we must wet the bairn's head with a dram."

The Minister accepted his share with a guilty gleam in his eye.

"I'll not enquire where that came from. And if they knew about this the good folk back there would have my hide, but here's long life and good health to wee Nick, Hannah's bairn and your godson."

They drank and there was a pause while they savoured the dram.

"So Hannah's for the North?" McVean said at last.

"Aye," Hector agreed expressionlessly. "She'll go down-country with the Gallahers in a month or so."

"You'll miss them."

"Aye. I'll miss them."

The Minister said no more on that subject. He was a man who disliked prying. Instead he began to talk sheep: Hector had had a good clip that year and got a good price for it. English mills were beginning to appreciate the qualities of antipodean wool. It was the clip which had paid for the re-building of the homestead. When he had come back with a load of timber Hannah had protested,

"But man, you're never in the place but to eat. What do you want with a new farmhouse. You'd do better to fence in the creek along the paddock."

"Time enough for that," he'd replied. "We must have a kitchen fit for the fluted cups . . ."

"Away . . ."

"And I'll not have your bairn born in a mud hut," he added.

"He'd not be the first," Hannah protested but Hector had taken no heed.

The Minister commented on the prospects for wool and the difficulty in finding shearers for a big flock but he sensed Hector was not really listening. He reached out and touched the crib. It was beautifully made for all it was so simple, no more than a box on rockers. The tops of the posts at each corner were carved into thistles and the sides fretted into a curving elegant pattern.

"Your work?" he asked.

Hector nodded.

"You couldn't have done more for your own bairn," McVean observed.

Hector thrust the crib aside and refilled the glasses.

"These are Hannah's," he said. "Edinburgh crystal and the Lord knows how they came here safe. She brought a deal of stuff, linen and silver and the like. There wasn't a break or a scratch for all the way they came."

"Not even in Maggie Gallaher's ox-cart? Oh, my word . . . I nearly forgot."

McVean stood up and began to search through his pockets. He drew out a battered packet and gave it to Hector.

"Maggie and Jem were over in Riverhead last week and they left this with the Grimonds and they brought it over when they came to the kirk. Well, I'd best be off. I'd like a word with the Craigies before I go home."

This was not strictly true. McVean had timed his visit for what he had been told was the expected time for wee Nick's birth and had meant to stay as long as was necessary. However, he realised that Macadam could think of little else than Hannah's coming departure and would prefer his room to his company. He shouted farewell to Hannah at the doorway and was gone, cantering down the creek path on his big roan gelding.

Hector stared down at the packet on his lap. He turned it over and saw that it had been sealed with black wax: there was a blob nearly the size of half a crown with the imprint of a seal-stone. It seemed to be a kind of creature, half-lion and half-bird. There was a motto too: Hector strained to make out the tiny letters and found them incomprehensible when he did, 'Semper fidelis'.

When Hannah came out she found him staring gloomily at the home paddock dotted with sheep. Nick was sound asleep in her arms, milky-mouthed.

"He didn't stay long."

"No," Hector agreed, "I wasn't the best of company mebbe. He's away to the Craigies. He left this for you."

He gave her the packet and looked away. Hannah never read Innis's letters in front of him. She put it in her apron pocket and then laid Nick down in his crib, taking a long time to hap the blankets about him.

"Aren't you going to read it then?" he demanded harshly.

Hannah looked at him with a slight frown but didn't answer except by pulling the packet out and looking at it.

"I'm feared to open it," she said slowly.

"Can you see through the envelope?"

"The seal's black," she said.

"The writing's his," he returned. "He'd not announce his own death. Mebbe yon wife of his has drunk herself to death."

Hannah stared at him in dismay.

"Dammit, woman," he shouted, "open the thing. I'm away up the hill."

112

He strode up the path without looking back and Hannah watched him for a full minute before she fetched a knife and opened her letter.

Hector returned just before dusk with an angry sunset behind him. He found a meal ready for him on the table but no sign of Hannah. She didn't answer his call and he was somehow relieved to see Nicky asleep in his crib with Moss in attendance. Hector considered the baby for a few moments and his face was like rock. The fire was low so he cast on a log or two and then went to the door. His eye was caught by a white patch on the hill, up beside Roddy's grave. He narrowed his eyes and could just make out a figure crouching beside the stone slab he had put there. Hannah had her head buried in her arms. He watched for a full minute but she didn't stir. The light began to fail as the sun vanished behind the hill. Hector moved restlessly back to the table where he looked at the meal laid ready, mutton pie, bread, the teapot on the hearth and the kettle singing. He fingered the china plate and the linen cloth laid ready on the scrubbed planks of the table. There was even a posy of flowers in an old mug. He swore, suddenly and blasphemously so that Moss flattened his ears and whimpered. On the back of the fireside chair was his nightshirt, ironed and aired, and a folded pile of shirts and socks ready to be taken to the whare where he slept.

He sat down and began to eat but after a couple of mouth-fuls scraped back the stool and went back to the door. She was still there: darkness was coming fast. He dragged Hannah's shawl from the peg beside the door and set off with it up the hill. She heard him coming, as he meant her to and was standing waiting for him beside the stone, her arms wrapped about her and her face a pale blur in the dusk. Hector said nothing but happed her in the shawl and led her down the path to the house where he lit the lamp and made the tea.

"Now," he said and put a cup before her. "Tell me. What's amiss?"

Hannah stared at the cup as if she had never seen one before and he saw her swallow convulsively.

"It seems, Hector Macadam, that we'll be with you a while

yet," she said harshly and looked at him dry-eyed. "I hope you've no objection."

"None in the world," he returned calmly, "and fine you ken it. This is your place as much as mine. Drink your tea . . . you're shivering."

He reached for the black bottle and poured a tot into her cup.

"But you know I don't taste . . ." she protested.

"Then you'll taste tonight. You've had a blow, a blind man could see that. Drink it."

Hannah picked up her cup in both hands as the warmth was comforting.

"It was his father who was dead," she explained. "They're away back to Scotland. They were to sail the day after he wrote. Five weeks ago."

Hector frowned, watching her face.

"Are you to follow?"

Hannah looked at him blindly.

"No . . . no . . . I'll not be seeing him again," she stumbled and put down her cup because her hands were shaking. Hector stayed stock-still, trying to control the mixture of rage and joy which surged within him.

"He's heard . . . he thinks . . ." she began and fumbled in her apron pocket. "He says . . . 'I gather you have found consolation elsewhere . . .' "

She paused and took a deep breath.

"I need not follow him Home as this would be inappropriate in the circumstances. He doesn't blame me because he knows he could offer me nothing. I was right to forget him and to make what I could of my new life though he can't deny that he expected more of me . . ."

Under the table Hector's great fist clenched hard.

"He will always think of me kindly," she went on like a child reciting a lesson, "but thinks it best if we do not communicate again."

Silence fell between them like the silence which follows the closing of a book.

"And Nick?" asked Hector at last. "When he hears about wee Nick . . . what then?"

"He won't hear," Hannah said wearily. "I won't have him looked at like a doubtful fish on a barrow. I could prove him

114

to be Innis's but I shouldn't need to. He might have trusted me . . . whatever the circumstances."

Hector sighed.

"You ask a lot of the man, Hannah," he told her. "Too much, perhaps."

"Too much!"

She looked at him indignantly.

"In his place wouldn't you at least have given me the benefit of the doubt instead of listening to some third-hand gossip?"

"In his place, after the way he behaved when his wife came, I wouldn't be sure of anything . . ."

Hannah stared.

". . . in my place," he smiled, "I'd believe you if you told me the moon was green cheese."

He refilled her cup.

"Drink that up. But then I daresay I know you better than he does. Don't think too hardly of him. It'll hurt you more than it does him."

"It was the easy thing . . . to believe it," she blurted out angrily. "It solved his problem, removed me from his conscience . . ."

She jumped up and stood beside the crib.

"He can go home now and play the laird and there'll be no awkward questions. He'll watch yon Amy drink herself into an early grave and marry a nice well brought up girl from his own kind with a good tocher and he'll never need give me another thought."

Nick, wakened by his mother's voice, made a querulous little noise and she plucked him out of his nest of blankets putting the little dark head in the curve of her neck.

"Why don't you tell me what a soft fool I've been, Hector Macadam?"

"Don't belittle yourself," he told her.

"There was no need for this," she went on almost inaudibly, "I knew I had no right . . . no claim on him. I told him so. He needn't have made me feel like a hired slut dismissed for a fault."

The tears began to run down her cheeks. Hector sat unmoving in his chair.

"He doesn't see you like that . . ."

"Then he sees me as an abandoned creature with an eye to the main chance," she cried.

Hector rose and put his arms round her as if she had been little Nicky.

"No one could see you like that . . . not if they knew you," he comforted.

"I thought he did know me," she muttered. "I was sure he did."

Hector took Nick away from her and laid him down while she regained her usual calm.

"You're a kind soul, Hector Macadam," she told him with a rather uncertain smile. "And you've an unfailing habit of acquiring lame dogs called Lindsay."

"Away," he said. "I'm a man like other men and as selfish as the lave. I'd not have you think otherwise. I'm sorry to see you take a blow like this but if his foolishness means you'll be staying here a while I can't be sorry for it and now I can tell you so . . ."

He straightened his back and looked at her very directly and Hannah's smile faded as she realised what he was saying.

"I'm no better than him," he declared wrily, "for I've no more to offer. But it might make you feel a thought better to know."

10

During the weeks which followed, Innis was not mentioned again. Hannah worked all the hours of daylight, harvesting the garden she had planted, preserving, sewing, darning, cooking, baking and cleaning. She worked through many of the hours of darkness, too, because it was easier to work than to lie and try to sleep. And all those hours were fretted by Nick's crying. It seemed to Hector that he never approached the house but the child was crying; not the angry hungry bawling he remembered from his younger brothers and sisters but a thin plaintive wailing as if the baby was giving voice to what his mother was feeling. Nor did he thrive as Hector thought he should. Worried by this, Hector made up his mind to buy a cow. He led her home, nearly twelve miles over rough hill tracks and brought a kitten in his pocket at the same time, a skinny little black and white creature. Hannah walked around the cow, a bony indeterminate animal with a rough dun coat and a wild look in her eye and sighed.

"Do you mind I told you how I was to wed the Minister?" she observed to Hector who was watching her with some amusement.

"Aye, I do."

"Do you mind my father was that set on being rid of me that he was to let me have the cow Maggie?"

"Aye."

"It's a real pity I couldn't have packed her up with the crocks in the hope chest," she said, "for I've never seen a beast that thin and not soup. Man, Hector, did the Craigies starve the poor creature?"

"They haven't the grazing," Hector explained. "Their creek's dry and their high pastures burnt with the drought and they're being gey careful with their hay. The Maori woman there says it's to be a bad winter."

"Careful! Mean, I'd say . . ." sniffed Hannah and put a

117

fragrant armful of cut grass in front of the beast. "She's nothing but a bag of bones."

"Then there's a pair of you," Hector said bluntly, "for you don't eat enough to keep a sparrow alive, and you're never still long enough to eat. You're up before it's daylight and the dear alone knows when you go to your bed. I've never seen your candle go out this last eight weeks. If you've no heed for yourself you might think of wee Nick."

Taken aback, Hannah opened her mouth to protest but Hector took her hand and held it in front of her face.

"Look!" he said, "you can see through it, near enough. Do you want to go the same way as your brother? Nick needs his mother more than most bairns as you well know and he doesn't thrive as he should . . . or hadn't you noticed?"

Hannah hung her head and pulled her hand away from him.

"I didn't think," she muttered.

"Well, it's time you did," warned Hector grimly and then added, "and if you've to milk twice a day you'll need to sit down to it. I never met anyone yet who could milk standing up."

Hannah giggled.

"That's more like the thing," said Hector, "and while you're at it here's a customer for the milk."

He presented her with the kitten. Almost at once a flea leaped on to her white apron and she made an exclamation of disgust.

"What'll you call her?"

"Minnie," she said and went away to bathe the wretched little scrap.

Autumn came in a blaze of frosty sunrises and then winter. It was a bitter, bitter winter. Snow blanketed even the low paddocks and the creek froze over so that Hannah had to break it every morning to fill her buckets. Hector spent hours carrying hay to the in-lamb ewes and Hannah's mare learned how to pick her way through the drifts with sacks of fodder slung over her saddle. The wind pounced out of the mountains like a demon and howled and whistled through the tiny chinks between the logs and planks of the new homestead. Hannah picked over the books she had brought with her and decided to sacrifice the *Young Lady's Companion* so that she could stuff the gaps with wet paper. It was not wholly necessary on Bennachie to know how to address a bishop or drape Nottingham lace over a casement: the sections on home nursing she kept and sewed into a little booklet, praying she might never have need of it. Snowy July shivered into a wet and windy August and supplies began to run low as the creeks and rivers ran high with melted snow. The flour was low in the barrel and full of weevils which Hannah sifted out with a sifter made from a piece of lace from the chemise which Minnie had coveted. The hens appreciated the weevils for there were few pickings around their shed, but they laid no more eggs. The beans and peas were long since finished and tea was a treat reserved for Sunday. They lived on mutton and the potatoes Hannah had grown in the summer. It was a monotonous diet. Even with the carried hay some of the ewes died and scarcely a week passed without Hector's bringing down a limp sheepfell.

However, the sheepskins were a godsend: they provided warmth in half a dozen different ways. They could be used on the beds, on the floors and on the chairs: Hannah sewed a massive garment for Hector, using a nail to pierce holes in the skin and strips of leather for thread. It made him look like a biblical patriarch for he had let his hair and beard grow long for the sake of warmth. When the lamp-oil ran out Hannah made mutton tallow candles using a bottle-top for a mould: they spluttered and stank and needed constant attention so that little could be done after sundown.

Just towards the end of September when they had begun to hope that spring might not be far away there was a black frost; it became so cold that Hector abandoned the whare and came down to the homestead to sleep before the fire on the sheepskin rug until the weather improved. The late spring brought the worst floods they had known and Hector was out day and night raking the sheep uphill to keep them away from the treacherous creek. By the time there was a little heat in the sun and the creek was beginning to go down Nick was sitting up by himself and disputing the possession of the hearth rug with Minnie the cat. She had grown into a handsome beast and when the homestead was invaded by mice during the floods she had reconciled herself to Hannah. The lambs began to arrive and Hannah added a number of leggy orphans to her household and Cinderella the cow dropped her calf, a charming little heifer. By the time the handfed lambs had reluctantly joined their fellows on the hill pastures Nick was staggering about the house and garden and into mischief twenty times a day. At the end of the summer he was as brown and sturdy and healthy as anyone could have wished.

The trees had turned and the days were drawing in again to winter when McVean rode up. He arrived towards evening and found Hannah salting late beans into crocks. Nick took one look at the stranger and took refuge in his mother's skirt.

"He's shy," the Minister commented.

"Small wonder," said Hannah, busy topping and tailing the beans, "you're only the fifth human being he's ever seen."

McVean grimaced: he was all too well aware of the attitude of his parishioners. The household of Bennachie was simply not respectable or acceptable and the friendliness and neighbourliness which softened the lot of wives on other isolated farms was never extended to Bennachie. Hector was not ostracised: he was the only professional builder for a hundred miles around and his help and advice was essential when his neighbours began, as he had done, to replace the sod cabins with frame houses. Hector never refused these requests but neither did he accept proffered hospitality, refusing to enter any house except the Manse and grimly ignoring the women. No one, apart from the Minister and the Gallahers, ever came to Bennachie and Hannah had not set foot beyond its bounds since the day she arrived. Nothing McVean had said or done had served to change this attitude.

"He's a fine laddie," McVean said and Hannah smiled down at the little figure peeking at the Minister under the table.

"He's no bad," she admitted.

Just as she said it Hector came in, his big blue bonnet in his hand: Nick gave a squeal of joy and scuttled towards him.

"Eck'or!"

The big man grinned, dropped the bonnet over Nick's head and then picked him up, whirling him round and round still blinded by the bonnet.

"If I haven't caught a mouse, a wee, wee mouse!" he cried out.

This was evidently a nightly ritual.

"Not a mouse . . . I'm a wee, wee laddie!" came from under the bonnet.

Hector set him on the floor, plucked off the bonnet, looked astonished and bent down to examine his catch.

"Mercy on us but it *is* a wee laddie! What's your name, wee laddie?"

"Nickie, Nickie, Nickie . . ."

Nick was rolling about in glee on the floor until Hector lifted him up and set him on his shoulder where he clutched happily at Hector's thick hair and drummed on his chest with his little bare heels. Undeterred by this Hector shook hands with the Minister.

"Good day, McVean, what brings you this far?"

"Couldn't it be a liking for your company?" suggested the Minister wrily.

"Unlikely," observed Hannah from the fire where she was stirring a pot hanging from the swee. "It's a liking the good folk aren't going to let grow on you."

"Hannah!" Hector reproved her.

"Let be, let be," said the Minister. "She's in the right of it, alas. Some busybody's been ferreting in the Register in Dunedin and they tell me that the wee lad's not registered there. Is that right?"

"Aye," Hannah agreed, "I never registered him. I meant to do it when I went to Auckland but I never did go."

"It must be done," McVean told them. "It's the law."

"I'm to go down-country for the winter stores," Hector told him. "I'll do it then. But we'll be hard put to it to find a witness for there was no one but Hannah there."

"I'll stand witness," said McVean. "I've a notion to ride down-country myself. There's an old friend of mine just arrived from Melbourne."

He smiled up at Hector.

"Maybe you'll do the same for me," he said. "I'm to be married."

About a week later Hector saddled his own horse and strapped the pack-saddle on to Hannah's mare. While he was buckling on the saddlebags Hannah came out with a parcel of food.

"There's enough there for four days," she said. "That should do. There's plenty for two for I daresay McVean's housekeeper won't give him enough. Not if the way he eats when he comes here is anything to go by."

"He appreciates a good cook," said Hector hauling a strap tight. "Now, are you sure you'll be all right?"

"I'll be fine," she said.

"I'll be ten days or so, depending on the creek."

"I'll be fine," she repeated.

"What'll I bring you?" he asked and Hannah looked a little startled.

"You've my list surely?"

"Aye, I've got it safe. I meant what would I bring for you? A wee present like."

She stared at him, taken aback.

"A present for me?"

Hector looked at his feet.

"Aye."

"Haven't you done enough for me and mine," she asked harshly, "without presents?"

She thrust the food into his hands and ran back to the house. Hector, frowning, put the parcel into one of his saddlebags and followed her. He found her in the kitchen looking at the latest improvement, a fine high dresser where the fluted china was lovingly displayed. The tears were running down her cheeks and he was shocked for he had never seen her cry but once.

"Hannah," he began, "listen . . ."

"I take and I take and I take," she wrenched out. "I've even taken your good name . . . and you want to give me presents."

"I didn't intend," said Hector unhappily, ". . . I wanted to . . ."

"I know, I know," she muttered, "but I've nothing to give you, Hector, nothing that's worth having."

"Have I asked for anything?" he demanded.

"No, never . . . but just look about you. You've built me a palace and you're out there in that leaky whare. I came out and you lose half your own property. Oh, Hector, I've done you such an ill turn coming here that sometimes if it wasn't for wee Nick I'd . . ."

"Haivers!" he said sharply.

"It's true, it's true," she insisted.

"You're my partner, Hannah. Without you I couldn't work the place."

"You'd find someone soon enough if I left," she flung at him. "They'd stand in line."

"Mebbe. But they'd not be you and they'd not do what you do."

"A wife would."

"You've forgotten. My wife's not that sort," he reminded her.

"I don't forget," she said miserably, "but perhaps you could have done if it hadn't been for me."

Nick, alarmed by the exchange, began to cry and she ran into the bedroom to comfort him. Hector followed and found Nick struggling in her arms, redfaced and yelling.

"Eck'or! Eck'or!"

He held out his arms towards Hector and the big man took him gently out of Hannah's arms.

"Good laddie," he soothed, "there's a good laddie . . ."

Hannah looked on forlornly.

"Forget this," he said gently, "forget it ever happened. Don't fret yourself over what can't be helped."

She sat down on the edge of the bed her hands clenched on her apron and Hector stood with the child in his arms looking down at her.

"You could make things much worse for me, you ken that?" he said, his accent softening and broadening as it did when he was very much in earnest.

"How's that?" she asked.

"If you went away I'd break my heart, lass, and sell up and away to the diggings to make a fortune."

"Mebbe that's what you want, after all," Hannah suggested.

"Haivers. Bennachie's my home . . . but only as long as you and wee Nick are here. Just you mind on that while I'm gone."

"I'll mind," she promised.

"Now, take the wee one," he said and put Nick on the bed beside her, "and tell me what name I should write down for his father."

She looked up at that.

"He'll have Bennachie some day," Hector went on. "It might be easier for all concerned if it was my name on the certificate."

"Are you serious?"

"Never more so," he returned, smiling. "A man must look to the future or there's small pleasure in working. And wee Nick . . ."

He put his hand on the little dark head.

". . . he's as much a part of Bennachie as yourself, Hannah."

Hannah bowed her head over her hands.

"Hector!" she exclaimed, "oh, you are such a . . ."

"I'm a man like other men . . . I told you before."

"If that were true," she cried, "the world would be a fine place."

"The world *is* a fine place, lass," he assured her, "and some day you'll find it so . . ."

Hannah looked up at him and her face was white.

"I'm a fool, Hector, fine I ken it . . . but I can't help it."

He touched her cheek gently.

"And what about the name," he prompted.

"No," she shook her head. "Best stick to the truth. Put down Dominic Innis of Inchbeg, Perthshire."

"Just as you wish," he agreed. "But I'd have been proud and happy to lie."

Hector had been gone three days and Hannah 'assisted' by wee Nick had been trying to renovate the whare. She had white-washed the outside as well as the inside and hung newly washed curtains at the window. Looking up as she removed spiders' webs from the rafters she had seen that there were some shingles missing so she fetched up hammer and nails to put them back. It was a still warm day, the very last of the summer, but there was an arch of cloud over the mountains which heralded wind, the wet and blustery south-wester. From her vantage point on the whare roof Hannah looked out towards the home paddock to watch the sheep grazing peacefully. Hector had brought down most of the mob so that she could keep an eye on them more easily. As she watched she realised incredulously that she was going to get visitors. Two horses were being ridden up the trail which led to the house: it was a shock to see that the riders were women. One was riding astride as Hannah did, with her skirt spread out over the horse's rump and the other was riding side-saddle. Hannah hammered in the last nail and then reluctantly gathered up the white-spattered Nick and went towards the homestead. She washed at the tub, cleaned Nicky as best as she could and then waited on the verandah with her heart beating very fast.

The visitors pulled up their horses and looked towards her but Hannah could not find her tongue to greet them. She watched as they walked their mounts to the hitching rail below the verandah steps. One of them was a Maori woman, grey and wrinkled and rather fat; the other was young, barely twenty, not beautiful in any way but with strong striking features. The Maori woman slid to the ground and then helped the younger from her awkward side-saddle.

They came together to the foot of the verandah steps.

"You're Hannah Lindsay, aren't you?" asked the younger woman. "I'm Elspeth Craigie."

"I'm Hannah Lindsay," Hannah agreed stiffly.

"This is Maraea," Elspeth explained and the Maori woman smiled broadly. "May we come in?"

Nick had run for the shelter of her skirt as soon as he saw the newcomers and he was peeping at them.

"Is this wee Nick?" asked Elspeth and at the mention of his name he dived back into the shelter of his mother's skirt. Maraea chuckled.

"He a shy one," she said. "You come to Maraea, Nick . . ."

"Come up if you wish," Hannah said unsmilingly.

Elspeth came up holding her habit high, too high perhaps for grace for her thick flannel petticoat was plain to see and the high buttoned boots.

"I've come to say I'm ashamed of my parents," she announced bluntly as she reached the verandah and held out the hand which had been clutching the habit. "Black ashamed of them. I didn't even know you existed till three days ago. If I had I'd have been over ages ago."

Hannah took the hand feeling slightly overwhelmed at this declaration.

"I saw Hector Macadam come over and I always knew there

was something about him that my parents didn't want me to know so I went into Pa's room that he calls his office and listened at the door. It wasn't very interesting at first because all he wanted was for Pa to keep an eye on things till he got back from the coast. May I sit down?"

"Please do."

"After that my Mama came in and I could hear the cups chinking and she said would he like a cup of tea and Mr. Macadam said no. Just like that . . . no thank you or anything . . . just no. And his voice sounded like the south wind. Then Pa said he'd be happy to do as he asked of course. Then, before Mr. Macadam could say anything Mama said 'Of course you cannot expect us to visit the Lindsay woman. We have Elspeth to consider.' And Mr. Macadam said he wished he had not troubled Pa and I heard him leave."

Hannah had gone very pale.

"Pa ran after him saying he wasn't to worry, he'd keep an eye on things and then I heard him scold Mama, saying that people had to be neighbourly. So . . ."

She looked mischievously at Hannah.

"I went straight down to the kitchen and I winkled the story out of poor Maraea."

The Maori rolled her eyes comically and Nick gave a little chuckle so she did it again.

"Then," Elspeth went on, "I thought about things a lot and this morning I told Pa I was going to ride over and see were you going along all right."

Hannah raised her eyebrows.

"They both had a conniption fit," announced Elspeth, not without satisfaction, "but I said I was coming anyway. And told them they were proper Pharisees. Mr. McVean comes here, doesn't he? Why not me? When they saw I meant it, Pa made me promise to take Maraea and here we are."

She laughed at Hannah's bemused expression.

"You don't really mind, do you, Miss Lindsay?"

"Of course not," said Hannah rather uncertainly. "But wouldn't like you to be punished for it . . ."

"Oh, pooh," said Elspeth. "They won't punish me. They never do. You see I didn't come along until Mama was nearly forty years old and thought she'd never ever have a family a

126

all. They were both so surprised they never quite got over it. Pa'll be over to bring me home I expect."

Hannah stiffened.

"I'd rather that . . ."

"Oh, pooh," said Elspeth again. "*He's* all right. He'd have been over anyway, I bet you. Even if he didn't knock on your door and ask if you were all right. It's Mama thinks about sin and hellfire and God all the time. I told her when she was going on about the scarlet woman that it was a pity she didn't think more about Jesus and Mary Magdalene. Not that you're like Mary Magdalene really, are you? I mean she was like those women in the dance-halls in Sydney wasn't she? And of course there was the woman taken in adultery . . . look at her. Jesus wasn't all whispery about her, was he? He didn't approve but he didn't like people trying to punish her when they were just as bad themselves. Mama's trouble is that she's daft about the Bible and all that but to my mind she doesn't read the right bits or if she does or someone like Mr. McVean reads them to her, her mind sort of skids over them . . . if you see what I mean."

"Miss Elspet talk you deaf," said Maraea who was coaxing Nick out of his ambush with her long string of amber beads. "On she go like running water, never stop."

"I don't," protested Elspeth. "Well, I suppose I do. But I think that's better than sitting about inspecting my soul every five minutes to see if it's acquired any spots and waiting for the great Day of Judgement so that I can see all the rest of my friends and neighbours bundled off into the Bad Place like so much kindling. What do you think, Miss Lindsay?"

"I think you'd better call me Hannah and I think you ought to come inside and have something to eat," said Hannah whose initial suspicion had long given way to amusement.

127

11

Hannah made a meal while Maraea played with Nick and Elspeth perched on the table and chattered, admiring the house and the furniture and Hannah's rag rugs and the fluted china on the dresser. Nick had outgrown his crib but Hannah couldn't bear to put it away and it stood in its old place by the fire holding Hannah's precious collection of books. Elspeth pounced on them. When she had bespoken two which she had not read she admired the crib.

"Is it true you had your baby all by yourself?" she asked. "With no one at all to help you?"

"Yes," Hannah agreed, "the wee limb didn't give me time to call anyone."

"I thought the first one always took a very long time?"

"Miss Elspet . . . your Mama not like you talk about babies and all that."

"Pooh," Elspeth returned. "If my Mama thinks I can live on a farm and not know all there is to be known about babies and all that she's shutting her eyes. That's really what made me ashamed of her."

"I don't understand," protested Hannah.

"She could have let Maraea come. Maraea told me. Mr. McVean came and told her all about the baby coming and nobody up here to help except Mr. Macadam and Mama said she wouldn't set foot in a house of sin and Mr. McVean said couldn't Maraea go and Maraea wanted to go but Mama wouldn't let her. I was ashamed to my very bones when Maraea told me that and I told Mama so. It's awful to be ashamed of your nearest and dearest but I don't think that you should think everything people do is right just because they're your parents. Especially when it's not," she added emphatically.

Hannah saw to her amazement that there were tears in the girl's eyes.

128

"If you had died she would have been a murderess. I told her so."

"Oh, but you shouldn't have done that," Hannah exclaimed.

"She makes me examine my soul," retorted Elspeth, "and I thought it was time she gave hers a proper spring-clean instead of just a dust-off."

Hannah looked helplessly at Maraea who shrugged and rolled her eyes at the ceiling.

In two and a half hours Hannah learned more about the township of Inchture than she had learned in the past two years and for the first time in all her twenty-six years she had found someone who shared her own trenchant views on people and life and living. She laughed more in those two and a half hours than she had done in twenty years. Afterwards, when Elspeth had gone, Hannah found herself smiling at the memory of some of the things they had said, even chuckling aloud to wee Nick's great delight. Mr. Craigie had appeared mid-afternoon while they were out in the thin sunshine playing with Nick. He had watched them from a distance for quite a while, making Hannah uncomfortable.

"Should I go inside?" she asked Elspeth. "I daresay he'll not wish to meet me."

"Tosh!" Elspeth had said. "It's your place. Shout for him to come over."

But this suggestion was too unceremonious for Hannah. She had gone across to the slight figure on the clumsy piebald horse and made her curtsey.

"Mr. Craigie, I believe," she had said. "My name is Hannah Lindsay. Will you come in?"

He had come in, he had accepted a cup of tea and one of Hannah's scones and if he had said very little it was because no one had a chance to say very much when Elspeth was about. When he protested at her chatter Elspeth had turned on him.

"Your fault, Papa, all your fault. You sent me to school and we were *never* allowed to talk: no talking in Assembly, Miss Craigie, no talking in class, no talking in the corridor, no talking in crocodile, no talking during preparation, no talking after lights out . . . I'm just making up for lost time."

School it appeared had been in Melbourne.

"And now I'm home I'm going to lead you all a life of it and get my own back. Mama thinks I'm going to marry and have a whole brood of chicks instead of one lone, lorn, ugly duckling like her . . . well, faces like mine don't *get* married so I'm going to teach school and wee Nick'll be one of my pupils . . . won't he, my wee lambie?"

She swept him up crowing with glee and held him high above her head.

"If we have a proper school in Inchture," she had continued, "folk won't need to send their ewe-lambs away to horrid Melbourne."

More than three weeks had passed since Hector's departure when Hannah had her second visitors. This time, she and Nick had been out round the paddocks to make sure all was well and came home towards dusk to find two horses tied to the verandah rail and two men sitting on the steps. As she came nearer she saw they were in uniform and realised slowly that they must be policemen. As she approached they stood up and touched their caps.

"Miss Lindsay?" the elder enquired.

"That is my name," she agreed.

"And this is the homestead of Bennachie?"

"It is."

"And the owner's name is Macadam?" said the other.

"We are joint owners," Hannah said and saw them exchange a glance. "Mr. Macadam is not here. He's on a visit to Dunedin. Can I help you?"

"We are trying to locate a man called Angus Ramsay," said the older man.

Hannah looked blankly at them, thinking very fast indeed.

"I've not heard that name," she said and bent to pick up wee Nick. "Come inbye and I'll have something for you to eat in a wee while."

"We've made camp down near the creek," the younger man said and pointed to a neat canvas triangle in the lee of the manuka, "but a cup of tea wouldn't come amiss."

By the time the lamps were lit and the tea made Hannah was ready for them.

"Now," she said, "what was the name? Ramsay?"

The policemen nodded.

"Angus Ramsay."

"I can't think of anyone of that name . . . what does he look like?"

The older policeman pulled a paper out of his breast pocket.

"A big man . . . very broad in the shoulder . . ."

Hannah bent over his shoulder and read for herself. It was a description which fitted Hector like a glove, barring the beard: there was a trickle of ice under her heart.

"There's plenty big folk like that hereabout, so they tell me," she said calmly enough, "why are you after him?"

"He's wanted back Home," said the elder, "wanted for murder."

Hannah's heart beat right up into her throat.

"Seemingly they'd news back in the old country that he'd written from hereabouts. His wife wasn't pleased. She thought he was dead and she'd another husband and children by him."

The younger man laughed and Hannah saw the elder give him a reproachful look. She heard, very faintly, a sound from outside, a step on the verandah.

"Murder!" she exclaimed. "You don't mean it."

"Aye," said the elder, "he threw a man down the stair and broke his neck. Hasn't been seen in Edinburgh since."

Hannah moved to the window and adjusted the curtain.

"I wonder," she said and wondered if the policemen would think she always spoke so loudly, "would it be Jimmie Leslie you were after?"

"There's been no mention of that name," said the elder.

Hannah moved back to the table and poured the tea.

"When was it they'd news of him?" she asked.

"Eighteen months ago, near enough. He asked the man he wrote to to send him news at Bennachie."

"Then it could be Jimmie Leslie. At least that was the name he gave us. He was here about that time. It wasn't long after my brother died. He was here a few weeks during the worst of the winter and we hoped he'd stay a while and lend a hand with the lambing for wee Nick there was on the way and Macadam shorthanded. But he didn't stay. He went off as soon as the trail was open. Macadam thought he might have gone to the diggings."

The elder policeman pulled out a notebook.

"What was he like, this Leslie?"

"Quite like yon man in the paper," Hannah said, "but his hair was thinning and he'd a big moustache. He was near as big as Macadam. I mind for we'd to give him clothes and Macadam's fitted him fine."

"No one else about here has mentioned any Jimmie Leslie," said the younger.

"I doubt no one knew he was here," Hannah observed drily. "If you've been asking about you'll have heard folk don't visit much at Bennachie."

The policemen looked at one another.

"Hector brought him in one day out of a snowstorm, half starved and more than half frozen. He said he was trying to get to Dunedin. From what he let drop we gathered he'd been working Canterbury way. He didn't talk much. Hector always thought he must have jumped ship somewhere."

The younger policeman was writing busily. She looked up, her heart hammering, as the door creaked open and they all saw Hector standing there, looking gigantic in his sheepskin coat. Hannah rose and went to help him out of it.

"So you're back," she said briskly. "And not before time, Hector Macadam. These two gentlemen are policemen."

Hector nodded acknowledgement and bent down to unlace his boots.

"They're looking for a man Ramsay."

"Aye?" said Hector enquiringly.

"Do you think that could be Jimmie Leslie?" Hannah asked. "Mind on him? the one . . ."

"Him that went off to the diggings with my good shovel? Aye, I mind on him."

Hannah's heart began to beat at a more normal rate. She went off to fetch another cup and saucer while the policemen showed Hector the paper. He described the mythical Jim Leslie much as she had done and indicated that he had been on his way to Melbourne.

". . . and if you catch up with the critter," Hector added, "you might remind him he owes me a shovel. Why do you want him anyway?"

The policemen looked at one another.

132

"Well, Mr. Macadam . . ." said the elder hesitantly, ". . . we're none so sure we do. The man we're after's called Angus Ramsay."

"Ramsay . . ." Hector took a gulp of tea and stared thoughtfully at the table. "Ramsay. I don't think I've ever heard the name around this district."

"I don't think he'd be using the name," said the elder man. "He'd not dare. He's wanted for a killing in Edinburgh, eleven years ago."

"That's a while back," said Hector, looking mildly interested. "You've taken your time, surely?"

The policeman cleared his throat.

"He wrote to Edinburgh some eighteen months since enquiring about his wife. She laid information with the Edinburgh police."

"Did she now?" observed Hector and gave his cup to Hannah to be refilled.

"You'll understand, Mr. Macadam that once it's passed to us we have to follow it up."

"Aye, I understand."

The policeman consulted a notebook.

"According to our information you arrived in this district about ten years ago. Is that right?"

"More like eleven," objected Hector. "I was the first up this creek. It would be September 1848 . . . I'd been here a wee whilie before Craigie came."

"Your title's dated 1849," the younger man put in.

"Folk weren't that fussy in those days," Hector told him calmly. "And it's a long step to Dunedin. I'd been here more than a year before I registered my title."

"Where did you come from?"

"Australia. I shipped out in a whaler from Sydney. But I was born in Dumbarton. My folk died there in the bad years when I was a laddie and left me on my own. I starved for a month and then shipped on a collier bound for Capetown. After that . . ." he shrugged his great shoulders, "I never went back. Nothing to go back to."

"So . . . in September 1847 you were in Australia?"

"I'd be hard put to it to say where I was . . . at sea likely," Hector said.

The policemen exchanged glances again and both of them closed their notebooks.

"Well . . . what can you tell us about this Jim Leslie?"

Later when Nick was being put to bed Hannah left the bedroom door open a crack.

". . . you'll not take it amiss, Mr. Macadam, but we've got to ask these things, you understand, or they'll be on our top for not doing it . . ."

"Ask away."

Hannah listened with her breath held.

"We were wondering, after everything we've been told round this district, why you and Miss Lindsay haven't married?"

Hannah could hear her heart beating.

"Could it be because you have a wife already, Mr. Macadam?"

Before he could answer Hannah went in briskly.

"You'd be better asking me that question," she reproved. "Macadam's not one to tell my secrets."

The policemen stared at her uncomfortably.

"The boot's on the other foot. I have a husband. And what's more," she added, "I've no wish for him to get word of where I am. I've run half the world away from him and that's none too far. It's maybe a sin what I've done but it's no crime and I'll thank you to leave well alone."

When the policemen, willing enough to be convinced, had gone back to Dunedin to try, so they said, to pick up the trail of a possible Jimmie Leslie, they admitted that they had no real enthusiasm for their task.

"A vindictive piece, yon wife," said the younger when they mounted up.

"Aye, so it would seem," Hector agreed mildly.

"Half the folk in New Zealand's got a reason for being here they'd not want broadcast to their neighbours," added the other. "I expect you'll hear no more about this Jimmie Leslie, Mr. Macadam."

Hector closed the door on them and turned to Hannah who was standing very still by the door to her room. He looked grim and anxious.

"Lies," he muttered, "all those damned lies. You'll be in trouble if all this ever comes out. You could go to jail . . ."

"Rather that than see you hang," she returned fiercely, "and for a wretched little trollop. To set the police on you! If I could get my hands on her! Never you mind, like someone else under this roof, I'm proud and happy to lie."

After that they slipped back into their old routine and the farming year went on its inexorable way; but their relationship had changed subtly. Now Hector owed something to Hannah she felt less resentful of him, less dependent, and Elspeth's friendship made her feel less of an outcast. Mr. McVean's new wife Judith quickly followed Elspeth's example and visited Bennachie despite all the pointed comments of her husband's parishioners. While no one else followed their example their friendship was enough to restore Hannah's confidence and her self-respect: be anyone never so independent to be rejected by one's fellows is a lowering experience. Hector heard her singing about the house and laughing with wee Nick. She looked younger and prettier and she smiled much more often and he was happy for her. The longing which had overcome him so often during the first two years, to have Nick's father where he could teach him a lesson he would never forget, began to diminish. Wee Nick at the end of his third winter was a sturdy little imp of a laddie with Innis's startlingly blue eyes and dark hair and his mother's fine features. He trotted at Hector's heels like a terrier pup.

In the spring of that year when the mountain lilies were just coming into bloom and the floods were subsiding Maggie and Jem Gallaher came by with a wooden Noah's Ark for Nick, some much-needed stores and a packet of letters. Hector had a few from his buyers in Dunedin enquiring about his prospects for that summer. Bennachie had had a fairly good winter and the prospects were encouraging. Hannah's were, all but one, from Kirkton of Langmuir. It had taken some time for news of her whereabouts to reach the Kirkton but now her brothers and her friends wrote by most sailings. The other one was postmarked Perth and the handwriting had once been painfully familiar. She frowned at it and then thrust it away to open in private, unaware that Hector had seen her do so. Maggie and

Jem enjoying roast lamb and spring cabbage in the kitchen were entertained by news of Alec Lindsay's marriage to a girl from Falkirk:

". . . very refined and high-and-mighty is our new Mistress Lindsay," wrote Chrissie Lapraik once she had given the news of her family, now six in number, "and she has Overlangmuir new-papered and painted till you would not know it for the same place. She had what she cried a swarry the week afore last, a cup in your hand and a wee thin sandwich and a tune on the new piannyforty. He's a grand hand at the singing, your Alec and Davie was rumbling away down there in the bass and Sarah his wife piping high as a bird. We had Tom Bowling and Sweet Afton and a dozen others but my Dougal came away home and ate half a pound of cold beef out of the larder . . ."

". . . Mr. McLagan's got a call," wrote Davie from the Smiddy, "and he is to go to a parish in Glasgow in a very nice district, so I was hearing. He came to take his leave yesterday and my Sarah says he is fell blythe to quit the Kirkton for folk still chip him about you leaving him standing the way you did. It was a great speak yon. Father's no better, but he is no worse either and a bad man to have bedrid for he is aye thumping down to ken what is going on. Minnie is as much use as the fifth wheel on a cart, my Sarah says, but her Effie's going to be a spry wee miss . . ."

". . . we're to have a bairn in the New Year," wrote brother Alec from Overlangmuir, "and if she is a lass she is to be named Helen Hannah. My Helen sends kind regards and best love to her new sister. When will you be coming home? Now poor Roddie is dead and the minister away to Glasgow there's nothing to stop you. We have plenty room at Overlangmuir for you . . ."

Later, when Maggie and Jem had gone back to the bullock team and their new ex-army tent, Hannah watched Hector go up to the whare, lantern in hand. She went into her own room to open the other letter. It was addressed in Innis's writing to 'Mrs. Macadam' and was more like a small parcel than a letter. She looked at the writing for a long time before she opened it wondering why he should have written and half-dreading what she might find inside. When at long last she broke the seal and undid the covers it was to find a tiny leather box, very old and worn. Inside, in a velvet nest, lay a ruby ring. The accompanying letter was not very long:

My dearest girl, [Innis began]
In spite of all I could do to forget I still think of you every day. I miss you more, not less. I look at Amy at the other end of the table sometimes and pretend I see you sitting there. I wish I had not written as I did. I was in a passion of jealousy and wretchedness. You had a perfect right to marry where you could for I had nothing to offer and I still have nothing. Amy and I live in the same house but we have little to say to one another. She would leave me tomorrow but there is nowhere she can go. I have Inchbeg at least and the care of that to occupy me but it is an empty way to live.

Don't think I am reproaching you with this emptiness, I know better now. I had no right to expect more of you than you gave . . . no right to expect so much.

This ring was my mother's. It has always belonged to the Laird's wife. I want you to have it. Wear it with my dear love and leave it to your children. I will not have any children now and Inchbeg will be sold when I die for there are no heirs.

I've come to see that I shouldn't be resentful for having lost you but grateful that I ever knew you.

Yours, now and always,
Dominic.

Hannah was slightly ashamed to realise when she had read this that her immediate reaction was not grief and longing and pity but an upsurge of affectionate impatience with such resigned gloom. She smiled at herself and shook her head over the single sheet: it was somehow not surprising that the ring proved too small for any but her little finger. She put the ring and the letter together at the bottom of the kist which stood as it had done in the Kirkton at the foot of her bed. Wee Nick was sound asleep in his little bed and she bent over him, the candle shaded by her hand, and tried to trace a likeness.

"But I can hardly remember what he looked like," she said under her breath and sighed a little. Like others before her she had been too busy to nourish a grand passion and it had dwindled and died and left behind only the place it had occupied in her thoughts, a habit of thinking herself to be in love, of dramatising her short encounter into something of importance. Only Nicky was really important. She thought of Innis with a brandy-glass in his hand superimposing her own skinny image upon his plump Amy towards the end of a long elaborate dinner and chuckled.

'I expect you need leisure to be in love properly,' she thought and began to get undressed. When she was ready for bed with her hair plaited and hanging down her back and her white-embroidered gown buttoned at throat and wrist she looked at herself in the mirror, her eyes shadowed and her high cheek-bones softened by the candlelight.

'I wonder if he really remembers me?' she pondered, 'or whether he just wants to think he does because it dignifies all that emptiness.'

She grinned at her reflection.

'Vain besom,' she chided, blew out the candle and went to draw the curtain, remembering as she always did that the rose-patterned print had been bought to hang in the Manse parlour.

"Habits," she said aloud, "habits; brushing your hair, re-membering the day you bought the curtains . . . thinking about Nick. Habits are like corsets . . . grand to be shot of."

She looked up at the whare, which was another habit, and saw that Hector's lantern was still alight.

Next morning Hector was morose and silent, even with Nick, and when the Gallahers had departed he set off up the hill without a word to Hannah and did not come home till dark. When he returned he brought with him a moribund lamb and before he sat down to his supper saw it laid in a nest of old blankets among the hot bricks which were always ready at the side of the fire during lambing. Hannah set out his supper and then found the bottle and the glove finger which had already saved half a dozen lambs that year. He toyed with the food on his plate and watched her while she warmed the milk. The feeble little creature was finally persuaded to suck and Hannah smiled triumphantly at Hector. He smiled briefly and then whenever Hannah looked up from her task she found him watching, his expession unreadable. The lamb fell asleep and was settled in its box.

"Nick'll be fine pleased," Hannah remarked. "He likes to help feed them."

Hector nodded but said nothing.

"What's amiss?" Hannah enquired.

"What should be?" he returned. "Everything's going just fine. The weather's no bad and there's plenty feed."

"Do you think I'm wee Nick?" she asked reproachfully, "I ken fine there's something wrong."

He pushed his plate irritably.

"There's nothing," he said.

"Did you see I'd a letter from Nick's father?"

Hector sat very still.

"So?" he asked after a moment.

"So he's sorry he miscalled me," said Hannah calmly, "nothing more. What should there be after all this while?"

Hector stood up suddenly, scraping his chair across the planks of the floor.

"Are you to be going Home?"

"No. He didn't ask it and if he had . . ." she was speaking very deliberately, "I'd not go. Not now."

Hector kicked at the fire with his hill boots and a shower of sparks flew up into the chimney. He made no comment on what she had just said but it was clear that his black mood had lifted.

"Forgetting's not something you can do . . . it just happens," Hannah said, almost to herself. "You realise one day that you can't even remember what a person looks like. Thinking about them has become a habit, like brushing your hair or pulling the curtains, and no more important than either."

She looked up and found Hector frowning down at her so she smiled and got out of the fireside seat.

"If I'm to be up in four hours and feed this wee lad I'd best get to my bed now," she said. "Good night, Hector."

12

Hannah went to bed but not to sleep. She lay wondering how she could show Hector, or find the words to tell him that she was willing to be more than a partner and housekeeper. It was a delicate matter for she knew very well that Hector would never approach her. He could not offer marriage while his wife lived nor could he enquire without danger whether she was alive or dead. For herself, she knew now exactly what she wanted: Innis's letter had brought home to her all at once something she had been reluctant to admit, that her attachment to him had withered. It had been a forced growth and its roots had not gone deep enough for it to survive a long separation. Hannah was too honest not to admit either that while she had loved Innis she had found it hard to admire him. Her years with Hector had bred slowly, almost imperceptibly, a love and respect for him which would make a return to Scotland not a happy reunion but a parting which would be more painful than her parting with Innis. Bennachie was her home and Hector Macadam was her man . . . the question was how to let him know this and whether he would listen to what she told him.

Next morning, Hector went whistling down to the lambing pens and Hannah busied herself about the house, still no nearer to a solution than she had been during the night. For all that she felt light-hearted. She began to sing the *Wee Couper o' Fife*, her mind less on her work than on Hector. She scrubbed the kitchen table keeping time to the jaunty tune and relating the trials of the little tradesman who married above him and found he had gotten an idle creature who would neither bake nor brew nor spin: little Nick knelt up on his chair making finger patterns in the wet sand from the creek that she used to scour the table-top. She had reached the point where the cooper was belabouring a sheepskin draped over his wife's back when she realised that Nicky was singing with her . . . and he was singing in tune. She stopped abruptly and stared at him and he grinned back gleefully.

"Nickety, nackety, noo, noo, noo," he piped.

"But I may beat my ain sheepskin," she sang softly and listened incredulously as he came in with the nonsense of the burden.

"Hey Willie Wallachie," Nick sang, "Ho John Dougal . . ."

"Alive quo Rashetie," Hannah joined in, "Roo, roo, roo . . ."

Her son climbed down from the table and went to the hearth to torment Minnie while Hannah thoughtfully wiped the table clean of sand. In a minute she began on *Lizzie Lindsay*. After a verse or two she found Nick at her side and listening intently.

"Nice," he told her, "more . . ."

When Hector came in he found them still at it, performing a duet of *Bee Baw Babbitie*.

"Hey," he said smiling, "where's my dinner?"

Hannah turned to him, her eyes alight.

"Nick can sing!" she said. "Just you listen to him. Sing for Hector, my lambie, sing about the wee cooper who lived in Fife. Sing for Hector."

She bustled about laying the table and bringing out the mutton pie while Nick stood at Hector's knee and sang his song, sweet and true. Hector praised him and hugged him and demanded more until it was time to eat.

Much later that day when Nick had gone to bed still singing to himself Hector helped Hannah set the supper dishes away.

"He's a right clever laddie," he marvelled. "It's fell early isn't it, for him to carry a tune like that?"

"Aye," Hannah agreed. "But there's music on both sides of my family. My father was a grand singer . . . it was the one good thing I knew of him and both Alec and Davie take after him . . ."

"Their sister's no bad either," Hector interrupted smiling, "whiles I hear her about the place singing like a lintie . . ."

"Away with you," Hannah reproved. "And Granpa Dewar, my mother's father, he played the fiddle at every wedding for miles around. He was a fine fiddler, just had to hear a tune once and he could play it."

Hector put a plate on the dresser, placing it exactly.

"What about Nick's own father?" he asked quietly.

With a slight start Hannah realised she had forgotten the evenings round the tinkling piano in the saloon aboard *Polyxena*.

"He could sing, aye and play the flute and the piano . . . it's no wonder, Hector, right enough . . ."

"He'll maybe turn out a musician, not a farmer," Hector suggested.

"Early days," Hannah said. "Anyway, what's to hinder him being both?"

"We'll see, he'll have his chance to learn if we can afford it. Maybe Elspeth will teach him the piano?"

"More like he'll teach her," Hannah returned and giggled. "Poor Elspeth, she's no hand at the music. She hates her piano practice. 'If I've to catch a husband with my music making, I'll stay an old maid,' she said to me."

Hector chuckled.

"That one doesn't need music to find a husband, she'll be beating off young men with a broom. And a rare life of it she'll lead the one she chooses."

Hannah closed the door of the press and took a deep breath; she knew the time had come to tell Hector. It could not be left for another day.

"Hector . . ." she began and then faltered into silence. Alerted by something in her voice he turned about and looked at her.

"Aye, lass?" he said, very quietly.

"Music's all very grand," she managed to say, "but it's not what you'd call practical in a farming family. We need another builder . . . or a carpenter . . . or a shepherd . . ."

Hector said nothing.

". . . and mebbe a wee lass to keep me company."

She looked at him across the kitchen with her face so hot that she had to put her hands on her cheeks. The silence stretched, thin as a hair between them.

"You ken fine what I'm saying to you," she cried out suddenly and turned away, hiding her face, "surely you'd like bairns of your own?"

Hector crossed the room in a stride and pulled her round to

face him. He looked into her face so intently she turned away her head.

"And what do *you* want?" he demanded harshly. "I'd like bairns, aye . . . but they'd need to be yours. I've wanted you for mine since the day you came. I've never pretended otherwise. But I'll sleep alone for the rest of my days rather than have you lie by me and think of him. Or worse, lie by me for a duty you might think you owe . . ."

"Just for thinking that I'd have come upbye long and long ago," Hannah said, "but I felt you deserved better nor that . . ."

She felt his hands tighten on her arms and a surge of well-being swept over her whole body.

"And now?" he asked softly.

"I know you can't put a ring on my finger," she went on, looking up at him, "but you canna be a better man to me than you've been these past years. And I canna come to you as I'd have liked but I'll be as good a wife to you as any miss in a white gown . . ."

Hector suddenly lifted her high in the air as easily as if she had been wee Nick and laughed up at her startled face.

"If you kenned how I'd hoped for this day," he exulted. "Whiles I thought it might never come."

He set her on her feet again and looked at her with a kind of amazement.

"I can't believe it . . . I just can't believe it," he said almost inaudibly.

Hannah put her arms around his neck.

"You'd better, my lad, I'm wanting yon whare of yours for a calfshed."

He chuckled and hugged her till she squeaked a protest and her knees buckled wanting him.

"I'll build us a room over here . . ."

He jerked his chin at the ceiling.

"I've had it in mind a weary long while. Will you keep me waiting till I build it?"

Hannah shook her head, her heart beating hard. Slowly she began to unbutton her bodice.

"I can't leave the wee one alone in the house but I'll lie with you here by your own hearth where you slept last winter for I'll not wait . . ."

She let her dress slide to the floor and stood there in her petticoats trembling a little.

"Put out the lamp," she asked.

"Let me see you, lass," Hector pleaded, "or I'll think it another dream. Let me see you . . ."

She untied her petticoats and let them rustle into a heap round her feet. Hector watched her step out of them and come towards him wearing nothing but her fine linen shift. He reached out his hand and pulled the pins from her hair so that it tumbled down over her shoulders cool and silky: she felt his hand trembling too and reached in her turn to undo the buttons of his shirt. He raised his hand and touched her breast and she gave a little gasp.

"Hector . . ."

He unbuckled his belt and dropped it and then tore off his clothes as if they had been made of stinging nettles. Hannah, shivering a little, pulled off the shift and lay down on the sheepskin, conscious of nothing but the warmth of the fire, the soft sheep fell against her skin and her desire for the man who came to join her, kissing and caressing with an intense gentleness.

Hannah woke in the morning in her own bed, blankets happed round her bare shoulders. She lay quietly for a few minutes bathed in the memory of the night which had passed. For the first time she understood she might enjoy making love as much as her partner, that her own pleasure need not lie wholly in giving pleasure: with Hector and her there had been a passion of giving which had flowered into a delight she had never expected. She stretched like a cat under the bedclothes aware of every inch of herself. She could hear Hector whistling in the kitchen and Nick chattering to him. At that precise moment she was conscious of being utterly happy: it was as if the sun had blazed out from behind clouds.

"When I am dying," she told herself, "I'll remember this morning and I'll smile."

ENTR'ACTE

13

Grand Circle Row D.

'. . . the composer comes of a family with strong musical traditions . . .'

They were young and well-heeled, they were earnest and they were arguing with all the fire and fervour of those in complete fundamental agreement.

"It's breathtaking," one of them declared, "simply breathtaking . . ."

"But it's so bloody simple really . . . just a handful of tunes from 'Shuttle and Cage' and a few newspaper clippings. How can he make so much of so little?"

"Look what Shakespeare could do with that old bore Holinshed," the first speaker pointed out.

"You're not trying to say this man's a genius!"

"There ain't no such animal."

"People don't always recognise them when they meet them."

"Or they get hyped into thinking any little third-rater is," put in the man in the middle.

"They don't get recognised till they're dead. Look at Mozart and the imperial schweinerei."

"Look, you're not trying to compare this chap with Mozart," protested the first speaker, "that's . . . that's . . ."

"You can't compare geniuses with other people. They sort of put them out, like candles in the sun. Anyway, we'll all be dead before anyone knows for sure."

"Look, he doesn't have to be a Mozart," said the man in the middle, "but he is a musician. You'll all be telling the world for the rest of your lives that you were here tonight."

"It's the way he just came out of the blue," the girl said. "I mean, no one ever heard of him before, not really, did they?"

"I knew about him," objected the first speaker, "and he didn't come out of the blue, exactly. His great grandfather was Lindsay-Innes."

"Who?" someone asked after a brief bewildered silence.

"Composer . . . late Victorian. He wrote that thing they played yesterday at the Usher Hall. *Four-leaved Clover Variations*."

"I liked that," reflected the man in the middle, "it didn't sound a bit Victorian. It was sort of . . . well . . . elegant."

"Bet they only dug it up because of tonight."

"Rubbish," said the first speaker. "If either of you ever listened to chamber music you'd know it had been in the repertoire for years."

"Having a minor composer for a great grandpa doesn't make him a genius."

"Every little helps," put in the girl.

The houselights began to dim and the hum of conversation died down.

Earlier, in the box, John had been looking at the same bland sentence. '. . . his great grandfather was Dominic Lindsay-Innis, remembered today chiefly for his *Four-leaved Clover Variations*, a work of great charm and delicacy . . .'

"Do you know," John said to Lucy who was watching the musicians slip back to their places in the pit, "I was nearly fourteen before I knew Grand was a composer?"

Lucy looked at him in surprise. John rarely talked about his early childhood; it was as if he had been born aged fourteen at Bennachie.

"Grand didn't talk much and never about himself. We were good friends but we didn't talk a lot. I hated asking him questions."

"Why?"

"He sort of shrank away from them, like a sea anemone. After a bit you didn't want to ask any."

"How did you find out?"

"Dan told me. He couldn't believe I didn't know. He just sat and gaped. I remember that."

"But surely," Lucy protested, "surely your Grandmother would . . ."

"I don't suppose she'd think it was important. Or perhaps she was upset because he'd stopped writing. He never composed anything while I knew him. He played a lot but I don't think any of it was his own stuff. Mozart and Haydn, mostly. As far as I know I don't think he composed a line after the war. It was as if the war extinguished him, snuffed him out."

John stared out at the curving rows of stalls, cobbled with heads and thought about Grand. The quality he best remembered about him was his humility . . . no, it was a more positive quality than humility. Humility was negative, an absence or a suppression of self-esteem; what Grand felt was self-contempt. He shrank from questions because he believed his answers were without value; his affairs were of no importance. Perhaps it had been the same with his music; the war had made it seem trivial so that afterwards it could not be important to him any more and so he thought it was unimportant to everyone. It seemed to John, looking back over fifty years, that after the war nothing had been very important to Grand, except, perhaps, John himself. Not all the casualties of war lay under the silent geometry of the war cemeteries. And yet, within that self-doubt, that despairing silence, there had been no weakness. He had done what Grandmother ordained because he wanted nothing, not because she was the stronger. In the end he had proved that.

The lights dimmed and the 'cellos throbbed like a heart-beat heard through a stethoscope, strong and insistent . . . but still a reminder of mortality. The beat could stop, so quickly and so easily.

NICK'S STORY

14

Nick woke early on his wedding morning and lay watching the sun struggle between the heavy velvet curtains. It was the last time he would waken in this room. When he returned to Inverbeg Caroline would be with him and they would share the stately guest room which overlooked the gardens to the west. He sat up restlessly and swung his legs out of bed. He was a slender, rather gangling young man, dark-haired and pale. He pulled on his dressing gown which was an elaborate brocade affair, braided and frogged and quilted, suitable for a bridegroom about to escort his bride to Germany and dwell for a time in public hotels. He found himself wishing resentfully that he need not go. When he pulled back the curtains he saw old Donald below in the stableyard polishing the carriage, preparing it for the wedding. In it, Nick would ride to the little church at Netherknowes and there he would be married to Caroline Ruthven. He found it impossible to believe that from midday onwards he would be a married man. Tomorrow morning he would waken with Caroline at his side and every morning after that he would waken to find her there.

He stared down unseeing at the stableyard and wondered how he had arrived at such a prospect. He could not remember any moment when he had said to himself, 'I would like to marry Caroline'. He remembered very clearly the moment when he had realised he could do nothing else; his proposal had been a formal acknowledgement of a situation he had done nothing wittingly to bring about. He had a sudden vivid memory of a scene half a world away, grey-gold tussock, the snow-tipped hills stretching away to the north and Hector's two dogs shedding a ewe from the flock, running and dropping and pressing until the ewe trotted reluctantly the way she was meant to go. As he had done. As his father had meant him to do. Some people might say, did say, that he had done very well. Caroline was a handsome girl, plump, rosy, seemingly goodnatured . . . and rich. His father-in-law to be had made gas-fittings: Ruthven's patent safety gas taps were found everywhere gas was used. Now Ruthven had retired he had set up in Netherknowes House and Caroline was his only child. Her Mama had not come to Netherknowes but had died in the little shabby house in the City Road before her husband had been translated from business man to laird, from Glasgow street to Perthshire countryside. Ruthven was a nice, commonplace, shrewd little man, perfectly content to have Sir Dominic's son for his Caroline and never mind if he was born on the wrong side of the blanket. All the countryside knew the story of remote cousinship to be a polite fiction. Nick's likeness to his father was marked and Lady Innis's patent hatred of him told its own scandalous tale. Mr. Ruthven anticipated with satisfaction the day when his Caroline would be chatelaine of Inverbeg. Lady Innis she could never be: Nick could not inherit the title, only the property and there was not much of that as he knew. Still, Mr. Ruthven reflected, there was always the lad himself, quiet and dreamy maybe, but no fool. Nick would have been surprised at this verdict for he had little opinion of his own qualities.

The bedroom door opened and Swann padded in with an armful of towels and a steaming copper can. Swann was his father's servant. Nick had not been at home for long enough at a time to need a servant of his own. He read into Swann's customary silence suspicion and contempt for a chance-come new arrival from the colonies. Swann raised his eyebrows to find his charge already up and the curtains drawn, but wished him a 'good morning' and began to prepare the washstand. Nick reflected that once he was married he would be able to do without a man-servant: Swann made him self-conscious, aware of his speech, aware of his colonial upbringing, aware of his short-comings. He sat down and was prepared for shaving. When he was married, he decided, he would grow a beard. Swann enveloped him in a towel and began his meticulous ritual. The bridegroom would lack nothing which Swann was able to bestow. Swann's silence and formality hid an affection for the master's heir which would have surprised Nick. It was plain enough to him that the groom lacked the good spirits to be expected on such an occasion. Swann cleared his throat.

"The rest of the staff," he began, "have asked me to say that they wish you every happiness and trust all will go well today. Mrs. Robertson requested that I give you this . . ."

Mrs. Robertson was the elderly widow who had been housekeeper at the Castle since Innis was a boy. Swann laid a tiny fold of paper on Nick's lap; inside was a four-leaved clover, old and frail and mounted on a scrap of yellowing card. Nick looked at it in amazement.

"Why, thanks," he said, "I didn't think . . . I mean . . . how very kind . . ."

Swann said nothing, rinsing the razor.

"*Really* kind . . ." said Nick, almost to himself. "She must have had it a long time . . ."

"Robertson gave it to her on her wedding day, Master Dominic," Swann told him. "I am to put it on your waistcoat pocket. And, in order to protect it I have, myself, contrived this . . ."

With pardonable pride he laid a tiny leather object on Nick's knee. It was a minute frame with a tooled pattern and an oval of glass set in it. There was a flap at the back which fastened with a brass catch. Swann dried his hands and demonstrated how the four-leaved clover would slip into the space behind the glass.

"There," he said. "That'll keep you safe, Master Dominic."

He placed it in Nick's hand.

"I don't know what to say . . ." stammered Nick, "I am so very . . . so . . . I didn't expect . . ."

"Tut, tut, Master Nick," Swann cut him short, "it's just a trifle."

"No," said Nick decidedly, "it's not a trifle. I'll treasure it, I promise you."

And indeed he felt comforted.

At breakfast he sat opposite his father and looked over at that rather remote figure. Innis was still neat and spare and soldierly but was slightly stooped and his hair was thinning.

"It's a fine morning for you," he observed. "Too fine perhaps."

Nick agreed quietly that they might have rain later and helped himself from the dishes on the sideboard. Innis ate nothing and fidgeted with his knife as he drank his tea. The silence settled between them like a stifling blanket. At last Innis pushed away his cup and looked at his watch.

"Want to talk to you, m'boy."

He led the way across the stone-floored hall to the library. There was the thick musty smell of neglected and decaying leather and dustmotes swirled in the sunbeams. Innis went to perch on a windowsill and Nick sat facing him, a bar of sunlight striking between them.

"Got something to tell you . . . been trying to for days. Not easy."

Nick waited, slightly apprehensive. Innis frowned across at the garden.

"Daresay, you're none too enthusiastic about this wedding, Nick," he said unexpectedly. "I mean . . . it wasn't your notion. I'm not proud of the way you've been forced into it."

Nick was startled at such plain speaking.

"It's in the family tradition," Innis went on. "My own marriage pleased me no better."

His voice was flatly expressionless.

"Then, why . . ." stammered Nick, "why . . ."

"Because I can't provide for you any other way," Innis jerked out. "I can leave you this place when I die . . . and I have . . . but there's hardly a penny-piece to go with it. The land's mortgaged mostly. I'd have had to sell it all years ago if it hadn't been for . . . for my wife's money."

He glanced upwards. Amy Innis's room was above the library: she rarely left it. When Nick was in the house she never left it at all.

"And the way that's tied up, it can't come to you . . ."

Nick was speechless: he had never really considered the source of the money which had fed, clothed and educated him since he was fifteen. To understand that it had belonged to a woman who detested him so much that she could not bear to be in the same room was like being plunged suddenly into cold water; it left him breathless with shock.

"If I died now," Innis went on calmly, "you wouldn't have so much as your fare back to New Zealand for Inchbeg wouldn't fetch enough to pay my debts. After today, there'll be money enough for you . . . and for Inchbeg."

"I wish you'd told me," Nick said unhappily," I wish I'd known . . ."

"Better you didn't know," interrupted his father, "what would you have done? What could you have done?"

It was a home question. Nick knew he could make only a bare living as a musician: he was talented, there was no doubt of that, but he lacked the drive and the ruthlessness which might have made his name. His studies in Germany had shown him this. As a scholar he excelled, as a performer or a teacher he was mediocre. As for being a composer, he had had one work performed and published; he had composed nothing since, he might never conceive another line of music. Sometimes he felt that he could produce great surging symphonies but when they emerged mangled by their birth he knew them for poor mewling things.

"This way you're secure," Innis said, "and so is Inchbeg . . ."

Again, Nick saw the sheep driven into the pen and the gate clapped to.

"I owed that to your mother . . . to see you well-provided for . . . you gave up your claim to the farm when you came . . ."

Nick's father never spoke of Hannah. When Nick had first come from New Zealand he had been asked questions about Bennachie, about Hector, about the countryside, his half-sisters and his little half-brother but not about Hannah. He never sent her messages when Nick wrote and never asked what was in her letters.

"You see, I never explained to her," said Innis. "If she had known that the money was Amy's she wouldn't have let you come to me."

Nick swallowed hard, horrified.

"I wanted an heir," Innis said, "I wanted one so much that when I heard of you I couldn't risk . . . we've been here since the time of James IV and that must count for something. Your mother's letter was like a miracle . . ."

Nick found himself unable to say anything.

"It was your due," insisted Innis, "however I managed to bring it about. It's your heritage . . . your *due* . . ."

He was overwhelmed by confusion of mind; part of him responded to the idea of continuity while another part cried out in horror at the price. He thought of the bitter sterility of the relationship between his father and the woman upstairs, gross, unclean, sodden with drink. Something of what he was feeling must have shown on his face for Innis cried out,

"Caroline isn't another Amy!"

The thought which rose to the surface of Nick's mind was that his stepmother had become what she was because she was chained to her husband when there was neither liking nor respect between them.

"Caroline's a good, sensible creature," Innis was saying, "she knows what she's doing and she'll make a good wife. She . . ." he jerked his head upwards, "was a very different creature . . ."

Not persons, Nick thought and felt sick, just creatures.

". . . and you'll be a better husband than ever I was. A soldier's a poor bargain if he's a good soldier and that was all I ever wanted to be."

"How can you know?" Nick demanded jerkily.

"About you? Or about Caroline?"

"How does anybody ever know about anyone?" asked Nick bitterly. "I didn't know about you . . . I don't even know about myself!"

"That's a very different matter," his father said and smiled faintly. "It's what people expect that shows you what they are. Caroline expects to bear your children, run your home, look after you and your indigent relatives . . ."

Nick shot a horrified look at him.

". . . oh, yes," said Innis, "you'll find that Caroline knows more about your circumstances than you do. Her father's no fool."

"And what do I expect?"

Innis looked at him with a kind of cool amusement.

"You're like your mother," he said. "You expect nothing. You never look ahead. You live in the present because the future frightens you. And half the time you're not even in the present but in a kind of limbo with music sounding in your ears."

"And what did your wife expect?"

"She thought it would be romantic to follow the drum. She expected travel, excitement, change and the unreserved

158

adulation of a whole regiment. Instead, she found that it meant poor lodgings, heat and cold and boredom and the company of other wives. At length she decided she would stay at home. There she was easy prey, poor silly creature, and threw her cap over the windmill . . . and paid for it."

"And you?"

"Oh, like you, or I was. I dreamed vague dreams of military glory, and never thought of the future. But to have children is to have to think of the future. I had to do what I could to look after you."

"At Caroline's expense?"

Innis shrugged.

"She may not count it such a cost as you think. Her eyes are wide open."

"I don't know that I like what she's looking at," Nick said despairingly.

But, if Caroline misliked the prospect she gave no sign of it. She sailed through the elaborate wedding celebrations, serene and smiling, with Nick at her side, quiet and colourless, responding with an effort to the jollity and jocularity surging about them. The guests were a curiously mixed party: there were Glasgow businessmen and their plump, overdressed wives who clustered in corners to compare the iniquities of their servants, a sprinkling of local gentry there to enjoy the good food and drink and show the flag for Innis. Ruthven beamed and bounced among them all like a benevolent M. Jourdan urging them all to eat and drink and dance; he was a good host and by the time that Nick and Caroline were ready to leave for the night train to London many of the guests had almost forgotten why they were there. The reappearance of the bride bereft of her white satin and guipure lace and clad in a sensible travelling outfit of brown linen with a neat straw hat recalled the company to their duty. Nick and Caroline ran the gauntlet of rice and rose leaves to the shiny new barouche which was to take them to Perth and the train. The baggage had gone ahead in the waggonette. On the box was old Donald, back straight and face flushed with toasts; he had fastened wedding favours on his hat and his whip. Mr. Ruthven's talent for detail was revealed when the bridal pair were being handed in by willing arms. A piper appeared on the top of the portico over the front door and began to play a spring. Unfortunately it was a surprise for the horses as well as the guests and old Donald's moving lips as he fought to prevent their bolting down the immaculately raked gravel drive shaped words which were unsuitable for any public occasion.

"Well," said Caroline, once they were under control again. "That went off very well, don't you think?"

"Yes," Nick agreed.

"Father does so enjoy a party," Caroline remarked. "Such a pity he has just the one daughter to marry off."

In Nick's ears a phrase from the piper's spring was singing and echoing, building itself into a set of variations. It would sound well on clarinets with a string accompaniment, a continuo . . . then it could be caught up by the flutes and inverted perhaps . . . then the cellos only in a different rhythm, a much more marked beat. He became conscious of Caroline's voice, a note of deliberate patience in it that he recognised.

"I said, are you feeling out of sorts?" she asked. "You haven't said a word to me for ten minutes and more."

"I'm sorry . . ." he said absently, "I wonder, have you got paper and pencil?"

She stared at him and for the first time since she had lifted her veil in the church he saw her clearly. It was as if he had turned a light on her or donned spectacles which brought her face into proper focus. It was a plump face, rounded and smooth and clear-skinned with round blue eyes. Her cheeks were slightly flushed either with irritation or champagne and her mouth a little open: it was a biggish mouth, he noticed, with the lower lip turned very much over. Nick found himself thinking that soon he would have to kiss that mouth and knew a surge of panic.

"Paper?" she repeated.

"Paper and pencil. The piper gave me an idea. If I can just jot down a note or two . . . I can work at it while we're travelling."

Her chin bulged unbecomingly over the high tight collar of her dress and there was a gleam of perspiration on her upper lip. The cameo brooch which had been his engagement present was pinned on the pleated bosom of the dress and he thought suddenly of the breasts underneath.

160

"Would these do?"

She was holding out a little leather-covered notebook and a gold-mounted pencil of the kind given as small gifts and rarely if ever used. He took them with a vaguely grateful smile and began at once to jot down the ideas crowding into his mind. On the first page he wrote down *The Four-leaved Clover, Variations on a Theme*. Caroline watched him in silence for a little while and then rather sulkily turned her attention to the countryside, which was beautiful enough under the June sunshine to deserve more than the slightly disapproving glances she gave it. Busily Nick outlined the theme and the three main variations in his own form of musical shorthand, hearing them form with that kind of inevitability which heralded something he knew could be good. Just once before he had had this sureness. He jotted frantically, longing for a piano, unaware of Caroline or the summergilded country.

By the time old Donald turned into the station square with a flourish Nick had filled every page of the little notebook and was intent on finding more paper. He was aware of Caroline beyond the music as one is aware of an impending event. While the porters fussed with the baggage and Caroline gave crisp orders for its disposal the finale swam into his mind as surely as a swan: he spied a stall selling magazines and books and went over to it. They had cheap notebooks with coloured covers and he bought half a dozen and a bundle of pencils. As an afterthought he added a copy of the *Illustrated London News*, a copy of *Blackwood's* and a newspaper. Caroline was likely to find him a dull companion for a long journey.

While the light lasted he worked. Twice Caroline recalled him to the commonplace, first to share a basket of sandwiches and fruit; he ate next to nothing and returned to his notebooks as soon as he could. Caroline laid the newspaper aside and resignedly began to acknowledge the pile of letters and gifts. He was dealing with an awkward string passage when he heard her repeat,

"Nick . . . *Nick*!"

To his relief she had not decided to call him Mr. Innis. Her mother had called her husband Mr. Ruthven in public till the day she died.

"Surely you can spare me a moment . . . who on earth are these?"

She handed him a letter. It was written in a florid elaborate hand; the beginning had the stamp of a set letter from a book of etiquette as had the end but the middle lapsed into humanity.

. . . and maybe, [wrote Helen Lindsay] you'll be a thought surprised to hear from us but when I see in the paper you were to be wed Alec and me thought we must wish you well on behalf of your mother's kin here at the Kirkton and we would be fine pleased to have you come and visit us one of these days after you come back from foreign parts. The other day we had a letter from your mother and were awful vexed to hear of the accident but I hope they are fine the now . . .

Nick let the sheet drop to his lap and stared out of the window, conscious of a vast disquiet.

"Who are they?" insisted Caroline.

"My uncle and his wife," Nick said, and put out his hand towards the bundle she had spread on the table between them. "Is there a letter from my mother there?"

Wordlessly, Caroline handed it over and Nick read it with care. He could find no hint of an accident in the quietly formal good wishes.

"I didn't know you'd an uncle, a farmer," observed Caroline eyeing the address on the first letter.

"I've two in the Kirkton," Nick told her. "The other's a blacksmith."

Caroline pursed up her lips.

"Have you been to visit?"

He shook his head.

"I meant to go. My mother asked me to. But I've been in Germany most summers and winter's no time to visit in the Carse of Stirling."

Caroline considered the letter a little doubtfully before beginning an acknowledgement which, she hoped, would discourage the idea that Overlangmuir Farm might consider itself on calling terms either in Rose Terrace or Inverbeg. She had better begin, Caroline thought, as she meant to go on. She had

162

married Sir Dominic's heir, not Hannah Lindsay's chance-come son.

Hannah's son did not see her expression for he was still wondering uneasily what sort of an accident had befallen whom. Was it his mother, the brisk, the imperturbable? she would take ill to any handicap. Gentle, cautious, little Elspeth would bear it better but she rarely left her mother's side. His own Judy, on the other hand, was an imp, dark-eyed, dark-haired and never silent and tumbling in and out of mischief like a collie pup. All too easily it could be tomboy Judy. He swallowed with fear. Then there was Ian Angus. He had been a baby still when Nick left but by now he must be a child of ten. And if it were Hector . . . what would his mother do? Surely it could not be Hector? Hector was not so much a person as a presence like the great mountains which dominated the farm. Suddenly he longed to be a boy again, to be like Ian Angus, trailing at Hector's heels all the summer long to the high pastures. He drove this nostalgia from him and once more immersed himself in the music.

He finished the outline an hour before midnight. He sighed and closed the last of the notebooks, shuffling them together. It had been full dark for some time but Caroline, her letters disposed of, was sitting opposite staring out of the window though there was nothing to be seen but the flickering lamp and their own reflections riding outside in the dark. Nick felt suddenly tired and empty and light; he was afraid momentarily that he was the reflection and would vanish as easily with the dowsing of the lamp.

Caroline turned her head and looked at him.

"You've done?" she enquired and her voice was dry.

"As much as I can do for the moment," he said and realised with a qualm just how long he had spent. Plainly Caroline was feeling herself neglected. He set himself to appease her.

"It just happens like that," he tried to explain, "an idea comes and if I don't set it down as often as not I lose it."

"Well," she observed, more approachably, "I'd no idea what a business music was, to be sure. Hardly a word spoken since we left Perth and on our wedding day too. And I've been ready for my bed this hour and more."

Nick got up hastily and began to prepare the beds.

163

15

The sleeping compartment had an upper and a lower berth. Nick waited until Caroline called to him before he ventured inside. He found that she had lain down on the lower berth and covered herself with the blankets.

"I thought I wouldn't undress," she told him. "Suppose there were to be an accident. I should hate so much to have to appear in my night clothes."

Nick agreed quietly, removed his coat and his cravat and climbed into the upper berth where, with a good deal of contortion he succeeded in taking off his trousers. He turned out the lamp and lay for a time thinking that his forecast of events in the morning had not been strictly accurate. He would wake, not with Caroline at his side, but with her below him. He wondered vaguely whether she had succeeded in removing her corsets without the help of a maid. They had, or rather she had, decided not to take any servants but to find one when they reached Salzburg. He wondered whether he should enquire. From what he knew of corsets they would not make it easy to sleep.

"Caroline?" he called softly.

"Yes?"

"I was wondering . . . do you need help with anything . . ." his voice tailed off.

"No," she said decisively. "I was able to do what was needed. Aren't you sleepy yet?"

"No . . . not really."

There was quite a long pause.

"Would you like me to dedicate *Four-leaved Clover* to you?" he asked. " 'To Caroline on our wedding day'. . . ."

"I think it's the least you can do." There was a note of amusement in her voice. "But I was wondering what it was you were composing?"

There was a note in her voice as she said the last word, as of someone attempting to make use of a vocabulary to which she was unused. She sounded like someone trying for the first time to make herself understood in a foreign language.

"It's a set of variations," he told her. "I've used that theme from the spring your father's piper played."

He whistled the engaging pattern of notes.

"Oh," she said. "Is that a song?"

"No, it's for a small orchestra."

"I see."

It was plain from her voice that she had lost interest. She began to talk about their wedding, who had come, what they had worn, what they had said . . . Nick responded automatically, wondering as he made appropriate comments why a song would have been of interest whereas an orchestral piece was not. Suddenly a picture came into his mind, as sharp as an ink drawing of a sheet of music open on the pianoforte and the dedication plain for all the singers to read. The fact of dedication was not enough for Caroline, she wanted the world to know. He smiled at the roof of the carriage and resolved to write a song for her one day . . . some day. He remembered his very first song. It had been a very long time ago: he could not have been more than seven or eight. He had picked it out on the ancient piano in Inchture schoolhouse. He could see that piano, smell the musty smell of it and hear the tinny sound. The violent changes of temperature around the head waters of the Clutha were not good for pianos and the school piano had had a long hard career before it was retired to the little wooden schoolhouse beside the church. It was after that when Mrs. McVean had come all the way out to Bennachie with him, one hot summer afternoon, to tell his mother that he should be given a chance to study music seriously. She had written down what he had heard in his head and he had been marvelling at the pattern of dots and lines which could contain what he had heard in his head. It was like a miracle to him then, better even than books which could tell you stories. His mother had sent him out to feed the hens while Mrs. McVean had argued, but he had given the hens short rations and hurried back to over-hear what they were saying. It hadn't really meant very much at that time except that he was delighted in being again the centre of his mother's attention. Somehow it was not a pleasant memory and he flinched from it without quite knowing why. In the half consciousness between sleeping and waking he recalled the voices.

"His father will be so pleased," Mrs. McVean had said.

"Hector is not Nick's father," Hannah had replied.

It had been a blinding, bewildering idea: something incomprehensible and terrifying like the thunderstorms which racked the hills about the homestead. He remembered running to the stable and hiding there until Hector came, huge and puzzled and comforting.

"Elspeth calls Hector, Papa."

His mother's face had stilled when he had said that. When had it been? Days later? Hours later? He couldn't remember now what she had replied but it was after that he knew for certain that he was not the same as his sisters and longed miserably for it to be 'then', not 'now'. . . to be able to go back to a time when he didn't know.

Strangely, he had sought comfort from Hector himself and found it: the knowledge had gone to the back of his mind and become overlaid just as the landslip had been overgrown within a year of the day when it had engulfed a mob of ewes and their lambs and almost killed Hector.

"I wonder what sort of an accident it was my aunt was talking about?"

There was a short irritated silence from below.

"What accident?"

Caroline's voice had a note of restraint which he recognised.

"The one my Aunt Lindsay mentioned in her letter. So many things can happen on a place like Bennachie. I remember a landslide . . . there's a place just above the creek where there have been lots of them. This one cut us off from the township for more than a fortnight and killed fifty sheep. It must have been just about the end of the winter, when the snows were thawing . . ."

"Good gracious," Caroline exclaimed.

"Hector was caught in the edge of it," Nick went on, very quietly, as if he was talking to himself. "We could see it from the homestead and my mother ran out with her hands all floury. She'd been baking scones."

"You could see it?"

166

"It was just above the creek where the path ran beside the water. But we didn't need to see, we could feel it. The pots flew off the shelf and the china clattered on the dresser. It was as if the whole hill was falling on us. It was over the track by the time we got to the window . . . the whole house was rocking and groaning. Wooden houses cry out like humans."

"What did you do?" asked Caroline.

"Mother caught up the fire shovel and ran like a girl, her skirts above her knees. I ran to the shed and found the garden spade. When I got there the earth was still shifting and I could see the dog drowned in the creek under a boulder. It was that caught my eye. I didn't realise about Hector. My mother had seen him and she had cleared his face and part of his chest by the time I reached them."

He could see his mother crouched beside Hector, her head bent over him and the tears pouring down her cheeks.

"He was just coming round."

Nick relived that moment often, he heard Hector's voice, faint but urgent, 'Leave me alone for God's sake . . . there's more to come . . . run . . .' Hannah had shifted herself till she was half-lying half-sitting above Hector with his head in her lap. 'Dig, Nick!' she had cried, 'dig for all you're worth . . . but if I say to run, don't wait to argue . . . run!'

Hector's voice had been feeble and Nick hadn't heard what he had said then above the noise of the fire shovel against the stones and gravel but he had heard Hannah reply, her voice calm and determined.

"I'll never leave you," she had said. "I'll not live without you."

He could taste and smell the dust even now. He dug frantically and felt the earth shift and sink under him. He heard the creak and rattle as the slide settled; the rain had begun then, not pouring down but hurtling, hard as pebbles. He had dug blindly after that, the rain running all over his face and eyes and washing the dust into his mouth. Suddenly there had been a movement and he had flinched until he realised that it was Hector shifting for himself with a groan. Hannah and he between them had drawn him out of that wet grave and dragged him clear, desperately dragging him to the shelter of the trees.

"We found he had a broken hip," Nick said aloud. "My mother set it . . . there was no one else and we couldn't reach help."

"Good gracious me!" Caroline exclaimed. "How could she?"

"Hector told her how. He knew a good deal about these things, looking after the sheep."

Hannah had had a tiny booklet, just pages torn from a bigger book, sewn together. These contained instructions for nursing simple illnesses but there was nothing there about injuries. The 'Girl's Companion' had not visualised their situation for their readers. Hector, his face sheet-white under the grime and the mud, had given the terse instructions and hauled himself to a place where he could hook his arms over the lower rail of the verandah. Nick had fetched and carried the things they needed until his mother had said briskly, 'Away and mind wee Judy.' Judy had been safely asleep in her crib and Elspeth beside her. He had crouched down in the corner his hands over his ears and his heart bursting with shame that he had not disobeyed his mother and stayed. He could still hear the groan which had been wrenched out of Hector . . . he would never forget it. A minute later his mother had called to him again to help her splint the break. Hector had been unconscious, lolling against the verandah rail, his head on one side and his eyes white under their half-closed lids. Nick had held the wooden fence slats for his mother while she hauled the bindings taut. When it was done she had sunk back on her heels with her face in her hands, shivering. Nick had run in for her black crochet shawl which hung in its place by the door and laid it over her but she had pulled it off again and laid it over Hector. Between them they had brought him inside, inch by inch, but he was too heavy for them to bring upstairs to his bed and they had made up a bed on the floor by the fire in the kitchen. 'It'll not be the first time he's slept there,' Hannah had said and smiled for the first time since they had heard the slide.

"Did he recover?"

With a start Nick realised he had been telling Caroline about it.

"Yes. My mother made a real good job of it. He recovered but he was lame a long time. After that, he used the horses more on the hill."

Hector had been least affected of the three of them, Nick thought. The slide was a turning point for him. His mother had made her choice and after that Nick knew, or thought he knew, that he existed on the edge of his mother's life. In a curious way he was more important to Hector than he was to his mother. It was after the landslide that he had begun to wonder about his own father. After the slide he knew he would leave Bennachie.

The first thing that Nick did at their Salzburg hotel was to ask for letters; when he was given the bundle awaiting their arrival he leafed through them urgently, forgetful of Caroline's presence. He found what he wanted and thrust the rest into his pocket.

Dear Nick, [Hannah wrote]
By the time you get this you will be married and all here at Bennachie wish you very happy. Please give my kindest regards to Caroline. I enclose a little note for her . . .

It had fallen unheeded to his feet to be retrieved by the porter.

I did not wish to cast a gloom upon your wedding day, but we have had trouble with the hillside again. We had another slide, worse than the last. We were lucky no one was caught in it and we lost no stock but it has dammed up the creek and the home paddocks are flooded and so is the homestead. We had time to save everything that was in it and we have moved for the time being into the old calf shed. The water has gone down a little but folk say that it may never go down completely so we have a little lochan now, where the lambing pens were. Hector has already begun to build another homestead further up the hill. It has been a difficult time but we are all well and it could have been much worse. But it means that we cannot think about coming Home for a while to come. We are breaking a new trail over the shoulder of the hill which will let us take the stock out, but as Hector says, it is uphill work.

Nick folded that letter without finishing it, conscious of an enormous relief. If Hector had been dead or crippled he must have gone back. He would have been needed. He did not want to go back. He could no longer have endured the life on Bennachie: he wanted never to see Bennachie again. The knowledge struck him like a blow on the face.

"Nick . . ." not for the first time on the long journey, Caroline's voice indicated suppressed irritation, and none too well suppressed. "Nick . . . *please*! You know very well I don't know a word of this language. What is this person saying to me? And I would be grateful to have my own letters, thank you very much."

Nick found himself the object of the gaze of at least five pairs of eyes, the proprietor and his wife, the porter and a plump woman with a bunch of keys at her waist and, of course, Caroline, who looked weary and discontent and plain. He smiled tentatively at them all and began to attend to the present.

They had a pleasant suite of rooms overlooking the square. There was a wooden balcony on to which all their windows opened, positively overwhelmed with red geraniums. Inside the light gauzy curtains the furniture was simple and heavy, carved in the peasant style which Nick remembered. The bedroom was small and contained little other than a vast tester bed draped with white and piled high with feather beds and square pillows. Between that and the sitting room there was another room of the same size fitted up as a dressing room with chests and clothes cupboards and a marble-topped wash stand. The sitting room had a table and some high-backed carved wooden chairs and, incongruous in such surroundings, a velvet covered sofa of modern design. In one corner, as Nick saw immediately, was the piano for which he had telegraphed from London.

Caroline considered the suite with a critical eye while the porter went to and fro with their luggage.

"I would like a bigger looking-glass," she observed, "preferably one which doesn't make me look like a clown from a circus. Tell them to take away those feather beds and make up the bed with the sheets and blankets in the trunk. Feather beds make my eyes run."

A young Austrian girl came into the room and made

her curtsey. She addressed them both in a flood of voluble German.

"This is Lisl," Nick translated. "She comes from Fuschl-am-See and she is to look after you while you are here. Is there anything you would like her to do for you before they send up the luncheon?"

"Could you ask her to unpack?" asked Caroline when she had nodded to the girl and exchanged a smile. "And then we'll have to see if she can dress my hair. It's not fit to be seen after that long journey."

While Nick translated that to Lisl, Caroline wandered about pulling open drawers and opening cupboards.

"This is only just adequate," she observed discontentedly, "but I suppose . . ."

"This is the very best suite they have," Nick assured her. "And I know this to be the best hotel."

Caroline sniffed.

"Then I wouldn't care to spend a day at the worst . . ."

"Would you have liked it better if we had gone straight to Vienna?" Nick asked anxiously. "It's just that I thought you might like to see Salzburg."

"I expect the food will be all goosefat and dumplings," she commented and wandered over to the window. "How very picturesque the clothes are. Does no one in the town dress in a more, well, ordinary fashion?"

Nick was wise enough not to reply: it had been a long and troublesome journey with unexpected delays and other mishaps and Caroline was unaccustomed to travel of any kind. He turned about and stared at the bewhiskered Emperor Franz Josef hanging patriotically above the chimney piece; he wished that he had chosen to go to Paris or Vienna or Venice. Plainly Caroline was unlikely to enjoy the quiet of the mountains or the staid delights offered by Salzburg. He saw it through her eyes as a shabby little provincial town where such friends as he had were neither wealthy nor fashionable.

"We'll stay a week or so, no more," he promised. "Then we'll move on to Vienna. You'll like Vienna and it isn't so far away. I would just like to greet my old tutor and see some acquaintances." He smiled at her in a rather strained fashion. "I must show them my pretty new bride."

"Once you get on to your music, you'll forget my very existence," Caroline observed tartly. "Don't tell me you're not longing to sit down at that . . ."

She jerked her head at the piano.

"I thought that Salzburg would be a good place for us to become acquainted," Nick went on haltingly. "We need a little quiet. We've hardly seen one another except in company."

Caroline came over to him.

"Do you mean that? It wasn't just for the music?"

Nick shyly put his arms round her and felt her nestle against him.

"Of course it wasn't."

She turned her face up to his, and Nick realised that he must kiss that wide red mouth; he saw her face as if his eyes had become a camera registering every detail of skin and eyebrow and eye and eyelash and nose and mouth. He bent his head and as he did he thought, 'I don't want to do this, I don't want her. I can't do what she wants . . . I can't . . .' He felt her breasts pressing against his chest, her arms tight about his waist and that wide mouth moving against his own and he wanted to do nothing but push her from him. The thought of the night to come made him sweat with panic and a consciousness of his own inadequacy. 'Why can't I just do what any man does?' he demanded of himself, 'surely they would never feel like this . . .' With an immense relief he heard approaching footsteps and the chink of crockery at the door. He was careful to let her pull away from the embrace and again wondered why he should do that. Was it vanity? Was it reluctance to hurt her feelings . . . and if so why, when he was likely to hurt them much more? Was he merely postponing the point when he must admit how he felt?

The porter set their table for a meal, chattering to Nick, complimenting him on his German, remarking on the fine weather.

". . . there is to be a grand concert," he said, "in the square they will play. It is a fine band. The Concertmaster, he has these left . . ."

He produced a crumpled advertisement and laid it upon the table, bowed to Caroline and scuttled out. She picked it up, saw it was in German and gave a little exclamation of annoyance.

172

"It's a small group of string and wind players," Nick explained. "They are playing Mozart."

He took it from her and a name leaped out at him like a fist.

"I suppose you'll want to go?" she said.

"No!" he heard the panic in his voice; "no," he repeated more calmly. "There'll be plenty of time for concerts. We've had a long journey. We'll ask if we can dine early and then . . ."

He saw Caroline blush fiery red and felt himself in hazardous territory.

After luncheon, Caroline retired to the dressing room saying that she felt as if she had been born in the gown she had been wearing and must change. He heard her moving briskly about, speaking to Lisl in the slow loud tones which the travelling English think will be comprehensible to foreigners and he smiled. He took the bill to the window and read it again. Adam Heilbron, first violin: it could be no one else. The sunny square in front of him seemed to darken. Four years ago he had run along the far side behind those trees, his violin case under his cloak. A storm had been on the point of breaking over the old city; the sky was yellowish-black, shot with flickering lightning and thunder was rumbling continuously round the surrounding hills. He was running because he hated the thunder and because in his lodging by the river he had no fire by which to dry clothes. He remembered the noise, the swirl of hot wind which raised the dust and the dried horse-dung into an eddy, and the splatter of huge warm raindrops spotting the dry cobbles. A hand had grabbed his elbow and he had been steered into a café; there, across a table littered with glasses and cups he had seen Adam. It was not for the first time. Adam was a much-admired figure among the students of music and Nick had watched him often. It was just that even after two years he had made few friends and he would not have approached Adam of himself. A warrior in the army of Saul, that was what he had looked like; not in the least like the ringleted, behatted Jews who walked the streets of Vienna in earnest pairs. He had seemed heroic to Nick, heroic in his certainty, his enormous talent and his unquenchable energy. Nick had been unable to believe that such a figure was ready to befriend him. He had been lonely, unsure of his abilities and still guilt-ridden over his leaving Bennachie. Adam had convinced him of his right to lead his own life.

"You have a talent, maybe more than a mere talent," he had said. "Surely they wouldn't wish you to let it wither for the sake of a flock of sheep?"

But, not even to Adam would he admit the real betrayal.

Adam had made him speak German, forced him to mix with his fellow-musicians.

"You cannot make music alone," he had cried, "you need us, we need you!"

Adam had watched over his first attempts at composition, criticised them mercilessly and then bullied their friends into copying them and playing them. Adam had bullied him out of the morass of guilt, forced him to live and to respond. The price of this friendship had been to become Adam's lover . . . and this he had done. He had been conscious of reluctance, not distaste, that was too strong a word, but he had been unwilling to lose Adam and to rebuff him might have been to lose him. Without Adam the unhappiness would have come back like the thunder; only in Adam's company did he feel whole and himself. Nevertheless, after two years he had lost him.

"My family," Adam had announced one morning, "have been busy. They have arranged my marriage. On Monday I must go home to Vienna and prepare for the wedding. And after it I must be a good husband and work for a living. They have found me a place with the Opera."

Nick had felt as if the earth shifted under him.

"My bride is called Sarah," Adam had gone on. "I am lucky, for I have seen her twice . . . spoken to her even. She is like a little brown robin."

"I feel she should be called Eve," Nick heard himself say.

Adam hadn't laughed.

"You have been my Eve," he said roughly. "You should hate me, Nick. Do you?"

"Never," he had said and he had meant it.

"Forget me," Adam had replied sombrely. "You must forget what we have been. It isn't for you. I knew it, but . . ."

He had made one of those huge gestures which replaced words for him and which were so much a part of him.

He did not come back from Vienna and he wrote only once,

saying again, 'Forget me'. Nick had learned to do without him: his confidence remained, as long as he was with musicians, but he lost the zest and the enjoyment which Adam had lent him; gradually the guilt had engulfed him again. There were times when he felt as if he were enveloped in a hampering blanket. As he stared out of the window he began to wonder whether his chance to be a composer had been bought too dear, like Adam's friendship. He shifted restlessly and looked up at the Palace on its rock. Perhaps to pay too much for anything devalued it? He had gained his music by betraying Hannah, he had gained Adam by betraying himself. And now there was Caroline. His father had brought him security but at a price he might not be able to pay . . . a price which Caroline must pay as well. His life had been expensive, he reflected, and turned his head to look at the river surging under the old bridge. Had it been too expensive to have any value? If he died, who would care? Caroline might be hurt in her pride, that was all. She would soon find another, better man. His father might grieve, but Nick found that he did not much care for what his father might feel. They had never become close. It was difficult to overcome the feeling of being a lanky chicken come home to roost and, after their conversation in the library on his wedding morning, Nick could understand why. What the circumstances of his birth had been, no one had ever told him but it would seem that Innis had clung to his wife's money and deserted Hannah: Nick was not so much his son as his heir . . . and to what? His heritage was worthless without Caroline's money and that made it too dear to be valuable. There were the people at Bennachie, but was he more to them now than a name on an envelope? If the envelopes ceased to go to and fro, would it really matter to them? Did he deserve that it should? The river was deep and fast and cold; he could conceive of a limp body turning and tumbling in the icy snow-melt . . .

Even as the picture came into his mind it turned imperceptibly into music, tumbling, impetuous music, ringing for him, building rapidly in his mind, born almost full-grown . . .

When Caroline emerged from the dressing room she found him at the pianoforte, writing frantically. Ruler and five-nibbed pen lay on the table with an untidy pile of paper beside them and an uncorked bottle of ink.

16

Caroline watched Nick at the pianoforte for a full minute;
then, slowly, she removed her elegant straw hat and her
gloves. She had put on a new walking dress and had been
about to suggest a stroll round the town. Instead, she sat down
at the table and began to rule lines meticulously across the
paper. Unheedful, Nick scribbled and noted and scrawled,
occasionally trying out a phrase or a rhythm on the tinkling
pianoforte, or singing a line above his own accompaniment.
The journey from Scotland had shown Caroline that Nick
could not be distracted when this mood was on him. She could
make him walk, or eat, or lie down to sleep but she knew now
that the music went on.

Ruling lines was an undemanding occupation and Caroline
found herself thinking, not a procedure to which she was
much addicted. Such thoughts as she had permitted into her
consciousness had been, up till then, neat, orderly and acceptable. Because she was an only child and encouraged to see
herself as the centre of her parents' life her thoughts had always
turned around herself. For the first time in her life she was
being forced to consider the ideas and feelings of another
person. Before her wedding Caroline's view of Nick had been
without detail; he had fitted adequately into a frame prepared
for the 'eligible match', the husband needed to complete the
idea she entertained of herself. Nick, as himself, she had not
considered at all; if she had thought about his music it had been
as an unusual and mildly prestigious hobby about which she
might boast to her friends whose husbands owned to no
pastimes beyond a taste for tobacco or fishing. In the four days
of their journey together she had discovered with dismay and
amazement that music was far more important to Nick than
she was; it was borne in upon her with great distinctness that if
she had merely thought of Nick as a lay-figure to furnish forth
her own portrait, Nick had scarcely thought of her at all. He

had had no frame into which she might fit; no vision, however undefined, of himself in relationship with her. Plainly he was discomfited by the marriage. He was too courteous to let her know but it was not something he could conceal. Caroline was no fool.

Ruling the lines, neatly and competently as she did most practical things, she tried to identify the misgivings creeping to the forefront of her mind. She felt in this new situation as uncomfortable as she might feel if she were visiting an acquaintance who neither expected nor desired a visit. The word 'intruder' stared at her, and none of her arguments could blot it out. Her first impulse had been to sulk, to protest, to break in on his abstraction and shout, 'Look at me! I'm your wife! It's your duty to see me!' On the journey she had done this, complaining politely of his neglect of her, making a slightly edged jest of it. He had given her a semblance of attention, turning his face towards her but not his mind. He had smiled and talked but his eyes were turned inwards and his ears tuned to sounds her voice could not penetrate. He heard what she said but not what she was telling him. And he told her nothing at all.

When the paper was all ruled she piled it neatly on the table where it might easily be reached. Discontentedly, she contemplated Nick's back; he was like to make a poor bargain, she thought. The word brought her father to mind and she remembered him with his back to the high grate in the City Road parlour, bouncing a little on his heels, while her mother laid the table for tea.

"Let the buyer beware," he was saying gleefully. "A bargain's only a bargain where both sides are pleased."

Caroline frowned wondering why she should think of that after all those years. She had wanted this match, but had Nick? If he had not, then it was no bargain. And, in a very real sense, under the froth of lace veils and wedding cakes and good wishes she, or her father, had bought him. 'Let the buyer beware.' She could not protest that Nick had shown enthusiasm for the match. The chase had been long and subtle and the quarry ensnared because he was, for the most part, unaware of the pursuit. One of his more endearing qualities was that he had no conceit of himself. He never saw the caps set for him, and there had been a fair few cocked in his direction. Alison Mitchell had taken extra music lessons and sung at him. Caroline smiled at the memory. Mrs. Mitchell had arranged 'little concerts' and invited Nick to play. But, he had never looked Alison's way: nor, if she were honest, had he looked Caroline's. Sir Dominic and her father had made the match between them and she had been content to have it so.

Nick played a series of arpeggios which disquieted her somehow: he played them again and again and then a succession of long, muted, rolled chords. In her unusually receptive mood they seemed to her searchingly melancholy. When the sound died the room fell quiet. Caroline waited for Nick to turn round and marvelled at herself; a few days ago she could not imagine adapting her actions to anyone, no one else had been of that much importance to her. She felt resentful and humble at the same time. When Nick did turn round he looked, she could not quite find the word to describe how he looked: it was a new thing for her to need real words not the little, handsmooth collection she had used all her life. He looked quiet, she thought, the way the room felt in the late afternoon light, quiet and apart.

He saw the ruled paper and looked sharply up at his wife. It was as if he had seen the person she was for the first time.

"Why, thank you . . ." he said.

"What is it this time?" she asked uncertainly.

"I'm not sure, it was an idea which came to me looking at the river."

"It sounded terribly sad."

"I suppose it might," he admitted.

Caroline took a deep breath, like a sigh.

"Are you unhappy?" she asked gruffly and stared hard at her square plump hands as if she might find the answer there.

Nick was taken aback. He knew his answer was important, that it must be truthful, that he must not parry the question.

"I suppose I am. I haven't been happy since I came to Inchbeg," he told her. "Sometimes I wish I had never come."

Caroline was astounded. She had expected him either to deny that he was unhappy or to admit to her face what she had come to suspect that he had had no real wish to be married and in that case she had had a vague notion that she could reassure

178

him, offer some comfort. To hear his melancholy had nothing
to do with their own situation took her breath away.

"Then why did you come?"

"Because I had to be a musician . . ."

He flicked at the paper on the table and frowned.

"Because I wanted to know my real father . . ."

'Because I felt unwanted,' he added silently, 'because I knew
my mother loved Hector more than me, more than any of her
children. The others had Hector but I persuaded myself I had
nobody . . .' But he could not, would not tell anyone that. 'I
was wrong,' he cried to himself, 'I was stiffnecked and obstinately wrong. I set myself apart, looked for slights where there
were none, destroyed my own place in the home, tore up my
own roots, hurt them both beyond bearing . . .'

"Most fifteen-year-olds are fools," he said aloud and smiled
faintly, "and I was more foolish than most. I had the finest
notions of what I would find at Inchbeg. I didn't expect a
crumbling old house, a handful of sour farms and all mortgaged
to the hilt. And my father was no more than half glad to know
that I existed . . . he was embarrassed by me. . . relieved to see
me disappear to Germany six months at a time."

Caroline having torn down the screen between them found
herself dumbfounded by what lay behind it.

"Lindsay-Innis . . ." Nick mused, ". . . he calls me adopted,
but you know what I am. The whole countryside knows what
I am, and they smile . . . oh, quite kindly and secretly, but they
smile . . ."

"No they don't," Caroline protested. "Folk were pleased
for Sir Dominic and he was that proud of you. My father told
me and I heard the same from other folk. You aye make too
little of yourself, Nick."

"Easy to make little of little . . ."

Suddenly his humility irritated her.

"For heaven's sake, Nick, have a proper conceit of yourself!
Aren't you a man like other men?"

A silence stretched out like a muted string.

"That I don't know," he said harshly.

Caroline put her hand to her mouth. Nick turned away and
shut down the lid of the piano as if his life depended on making
no noise. Caroline could find nothing to say. She did not

pretend to misunderstand him; and she found she was not surprised. Nick had been like Fair Ellen's abandoned groom, a laggard in love. Before their wedding Caroline had rather approved of this. She had had no wish, as she had put it to herself, to be kissed behind doors like a kitchen maid. And instinctively she had not wanted to frighten him off by too much affection. Even now she did not know whether to be disappointed or relieved for she had no very clear idea what to expect. Her mother was dead and none of her female relatives or friends had thought it necessary to explain precisely what would be required of her. Caroline was not the sort of person to whom one might volunteer information. Staring at Nick's back she understood that she had never really envisaged this moment; the wedding she had planned to the last detail, likewise her house in Rose Terrace and her life in Perth society. She had even decided what was to be done with Inchbeg when she fell heir to it. But she had not considered how she must set about adjusting her life to another's. Her plans had included children, three, she had hoped, she had a suitable nursemaid in mind and distinct ideas about their upbringing; their actual begetting she had disregarded. It was, she had considered, his business, not hers. For the first time in her life it came to her that ignorance might be a handicap.

"Och, well," she said calmly, "time will tell and we've the rest of our lives to listen . . ."

Mr. Ruthven had a store of little phrases like that and his daughter used them as he did: to cover a gap in the conversation, overcome an awkwardness or give time to think. Nick accepted this one at its face value and turned about gratefully.

"You're right," he agreed, "we need time."

Caroline felt a little disconcerted at this; the phrase had come to her mind without conscious thought. She had not proffered a remedy, merely a kind of verbal bandage. She looked at Nick and saw him clearly, perhaps for the first time. A bonnie lad was how her father had described him and up till that moment she had seen him in those terms; tall, handsome, slender with a face as bonnie as anyone might wish. Her cousins had exclaimed in envy after they had met him and teased her about her 'Adonis'. Nick was quite remarkably good to look at but what she had never seen before was his expression. The blue eyes were shadowed and the shapely mouth set in a way which suggested that it seldom laughed or smiled. It seemed a marvel to Caroline that she should never have seen this before. The man she had married was no lay-figure, not the 'my handsome husband' of her imagining but someone who was uncertain and unhappy. Caroline had never been unhappy in her life and could not imagine why Nick should be so. Her first reaction was one of resentment; why should Nick be unhappy when he was married to her? The advantages, as she saw them, were mainly on his side. The resentment was short-lived. Behind Caroline's conventional, rather narrow outlook there was a brisk sense of justice and she knew very well that neither her father nor Sir Dominic had considered Nick's wishes any more than she had herself. Nick was not a dominant character. Her father had put it plainly, 'You'll wear the breeks lass, and mebbe no bad thing. He's a good lad but half the time he's in a dwam and wouldn't know whether it was dinnertime or next fair day. But he'll never misuse you . . . or what's yours . . .'

Caroline had taken for granted that Nick's passivity had been weakness; it came as a surprise to find that it had quite another source. It was one thing to think that Nick had married her because he was too weak to resist the pressure put on him; it was quite another to understand that he might have accepted the situation because he really did not much care what happened to him. Resentment died and was replaced with a great if uncomprehending compassion, an emotion so overwhelming it shocked her into moving towards Nick and putting her hands on either side of his face.

"You shall have all the time you want," she declared and then, startled by her action, drew back, letting her hands fall Nick caught and held them. He, too, was startled by the spontaneity of her action; he heard the emotion in her voice and knew it to be genuine even if he was uncertain how it arose or even what it was. Whatever it might be it was reassuring and he felt his desperation subside. Her hands were cool and smooth and plump and he thought of the joy he had had in Judy when she was tiny and her little starfish hands tugged at him, and the memory made him smile.

"That's more like the thing," Caroline said briskly, her

words down to earth but her pleasure in seeing him smile written clearly on her face.

"We'll go for a walk," Nick declared. "There's so much I want to show you and there's plenty of time before dinner. You aren't too tired?"

Caroline, alerted by her own feelings, heard him telling her that this was a place he loved and offering to share with her his pleasure in it. If she had been worn to a thread she must have accepted.

"Och, I'm never tired," she announced happily and picked up her hat.

"And that's a very fetching hat," Nick observed and the commonplace little compliment admitted her presence there with him once and for all . . . for better or for worse.

17

They came back to the hotel some two hours later. Nick had leaned over the bridge and recalled as he watched the waters surge below that in some corner of his mind he had contemplated suicide; it would have seemed unbelievable at that point except that he had that disquieting first movement of a quartet to prove it. As they turned back dusk had begun to fall and lamps were being lit so that the river glinted here and there with yellow: he had known then how he would shape the next movement and the quality of his silence had changed. Caroline had glanced at him and smiled resignedly, even after a mere five days she knew that expression.

"Back to the piano," she said with a chuckle and took his arm.

"How on earth did you know?" Nick asked.

"Och, a blind man in a hurry might miss it," she told him drily and felt rather than heard him laugh.

"It must be that you inspire me," he offered in an unpractised fashion.

"I doubt I'm not the sort," Caroline said. "It's a more die-away female you're needing for that role. If I landed by your side you'd jump out of your skin for the noise. And all those draperies . . ." she wrinkled her nose, "not my style."

They strolled back along the narrow, quiet streets and Nick settled the new motif in his mind. Suddenly it came to his attention that he had not had such a flow of ideas since he had been in Salzburg four years before. Was it the place which brought them to birth? Or had it been Adam? Perhaps, in all seriousness, it was Caroline who gave him the peace of mind he needed. Startled by this unexpected notion, he hesitated outside the hotel door and turned his wife to face him looking at her intently in the light which streamed from its windows. She was surprised in her turn by this scrutiny but underwent it good-naturedly.

"What is it?" she asked after a few seconds. "Have you decided you don't like my hat after all?"

"No," said Nick, "I think I must like it even better than I thought I did."

Caroline could make nothing of that. She turned away smiling and went to the door.

"Music may suffice for you, Nick, but I am hungry."

It was a good well-served meal and Caroline did it hearty justice. She was careful to see that Nick did as well.

"Just keep your eyes off that piano for another few minutes and try some of these delicious apricot affairs . . ."

"Marillenknoedeln . . . apricot dumplings," he supplied.

"Dumplings! Never! They're light as feathers. If I were to ask them for the recipe, would you interpret for me?"

"I could try. I don't know that my German runs to cookery terms."

"I doubt if even your English does."

"Oh, you'd be surprised," Nick retorted. "I was taught to be a fair cook, I can make bread and scones, roast meat and concoct a stew."

Caroline stared.

"Surprised is the word."

"Mother insisted that I could make a meal in case she was ever sick or I was left on my own with the girls."

He remembered again the time when that had so nearly happened; his face stiffened with remembered fear.

"We were very isolated, you know. Our nearest neighbour is more than a day's walk away . . . half a day on horse back if the weather's fair and the creeks are fordable. If not, it might take a week."

Caroline sensed rather than saw his retreat into the fastness from which he had emerged that afternoon. He stared at the little cinnamon-coloured morsels on his plate but he was seeing his mother making her own body a barrier to the threatening slide and reliving those frantic moments when he had understood that any moment he could find himself alone with his two half-sisters . . . Distantly he heard Caroline's voice, but not what she was saying.

"What *is* it, Nick?"

"Oh, nothing . . . nothing much . . . I was just recalling
something which . . . Perhaps I should ask them in the kitchen
to write the receipt down. Then I can ask them what are the
words I don't know."

"If you like. It would be interesting to have the receipt in
German for my kitchen book."

The new slide must have cut the trail to the Craigie homestead completely. Now, they would need to climb the hill. He
forced his mind away from the memory of the grinding,
thundering bellow of the slide, more a sensation than a sound,
and the shaking of the ground when even the earth turned
traitor and the world would never be the same secure place
again.

There was a knock on the door, a brisk rat-tat, unlike the
polite warning tap given by the waiter or by Lisl. Caroline
looked up in surprise and Nick caught her eye and nodded.

"Come in!" she cried.

The door was flung open and a very tall, swarthy man came
in and devoured Nick with a hungry affectionate regard. He
had a beak of a nose and a mane of dark curls, receding slightly
at the temples and his eyes were almost black. He was dressed
in a plum-coloured velvet jacket and narrow dark trousers and
his shirt was so white against his dark skin that it was almost
the first thing after his eyes that one saw.

"I take it very ill, Klauschen, that you should give my little
concert the go-by," the newcomer said, reproachfully. "How
are you, my dear fellow?"

"Adam!"

Caroline noticed that Nick had gone very white. Adam
turned and looked at her until she felt that he was examining
her very soul.

"And so, Klauschen, you are married . . . I congratulate you
. . . I wish you both all imaginable happiness."

He hugged Nick obliteratingly, then took him by the
shoulders and looked at him keenly.

"Ach, was it such a shock to see me?"

"It . . . it has been a long time," Nick said quietly and
collected himself with a palpable effort. "But, I'm damnably
glad to see you, never doubt it."

"Well, I did," Adam said. "I expected to see you out

there. . . ." he jerked his head at the square outside the window. "Herman told me you were staying here. I changed the programme specially to include your favourite. Remember the Mozart piece?"

He sang a phrase from it, swaying to the rhythm.

"When you didn't come I had to find out why."

"We arrived only this morning," Nick explained, "and it has been a gruelling journey. Caroline, let me introduce to you my good friend, Adam Heilbron. Adam, my wife, Caroline."

Adam took her hand in his long bony one and kissed it with a flourish.

"Gnädige Frau, we shall be friends, shall we not? I am not as outré as you think and I may commend myself to you by a very deep regard for your husband."

Caroline, slightly breathless, murmured polite agreement and begged him to sit down. He did so, pulling up a chair to the table with the suppressed energy which characterised his every movement.

"Is this not a most notable occasion?" he demanded. "I have told them to send up a special bottle . . . not champagne, a much over-acclaimed drink in my opinion, but a Moselle which, I think, must please you . . . ah!"

The waiter entered on a wave of smiles with bottle and glasses.

"This is a Himmelreich of Graach and as fine a wine as any I have tasted."

He watched with keen interest the cork drawn and the glasses filled.

"Now, let me drink to your health and happiness . . . and now, you and I, gnädige Frau, will drink to your husband's music . . . so . . . and, Klauschen, you and I will drink to your wife . . . so! And now, we will refill all the glasses and talk. We have three years of talk."

Nick looked at the golden wine in his glass.

"Is your wife with you?" he asked.

"She is dead," Adam said. "She gave me a little dark daughter and died a week afterwards. My poor little robin, I miss her still. But life goes on and time passes and my parents have arranged another marriage for me and little Sari will have a step-mama. In two weeks time I am to be married. It is in

Vienna. Are you to visit Vienna? Will you come, my friends, and wish us well, as I wish you well? It is possible? It would give us both such pleasure and then you shall see my little Sari, gnädige Frau, such a little black one, as like her father as she can stare . . . it is quite laughable."

Caroline looked across at Nick who was smiling faintly into his glass.

"We do intend to visit Vienna, Mr. Heilbron, and I see no reason why we should not come to your wedding. How kind of you to ask us."

"Then it is settled. I shall write at once to Rachael's parents."

Nick held up his glass.

"Our turn, Caroline, let us drink to your happiness, Adam."

They drank and Adam came to his feet, overpoweringly tall, and bowed his acknowledgement. Suddenly he turned to Nick and blurted out in German, "Your wife cannot speak German, nicht wahr? I meant to wait, but I find I can't. Is it that I am forgiven? I blamed myself very greatly for what I did."

"There was nothing to forgive," Nick replied gently in the same language, "I have so much to thank you for . . ."

"If I am happy, I sing," Adam continued as if Nick had not spoken, "if I am sad, I weep . . . and when I love, and I love you very dearly, Klauschen, words are not enough for me, do you understand?"

"Very well," Nick said, "I did then . . . I do now."

Adam turned back to Caroline and shifted his speech to English.

"I envy Klauschen, gnädige Frau. What he feels, and he feels deeply, he can transform into music. I must use the music of other men. I perform . . . he creates, fortunate man. What has he been writing lately? Have you inspired him?"

"He has been very busy," Caroline replied placidly. "He was writing all the way here, all the while . . ."

"Ah, ha!" Adam turned to Nick. "What? What? Tell me!"

"A theme and variations. I've called it *The Four-leaved Clover* . . ."

Nick whistled the theme and got up to rummage for the notebooks he had filled.

"Ah, one of your Scotch tunes . . . what ensemble?"

"Chamber orchestra, woodwind and strings . . ."

"Ach, splendid!" Adam cried. "Let me see! Let me hear!"

Caroline hastily removed the remaining dishes and set them on the chest beside the door while the music was set out among the glasses and the bottle of Himmelreich. Quietly, she fetched her crochet-work: she was planning a white lace table-cover and had, perforce, made a good start on it during the journey. As she chained, doubled and trebled she marvelled at her readiness to accept being ignored for a parcel of notebooks: her father would never have believed it. She watched Nick's face and felt content to see him so absorbed.

Adam hummed, read, re-read, whistled, tapped his fingers, sang aloud and generally did his best to turn himself into an ensemble. Occasionally he would pounce and criticise and Nick would argue with a certainty that Caroline had never seen in him before. Sometimes he would give way and make a change with his pencil; more often Adam conceded the point with a shrug.

Soon, after all the clocks in the town had struck eleven, an event which took a good five minutes, Caroline said good-night. It had been an exhausting and eventful day in every way. She got a flashing smile and a kiss on the hand from Adam and a shy kiss on the cheek from Nick before she went into her dressing room. Lisl was not there and she had to undress herself which was not easy. She gave her long, thick, shining, toffee-coloured hair its customary hundred strokes of the brush and braided it into two long plaits which, under a lacy cap, made her look like an illustration from the Idylls of the King. Scrubbed and shining, she clambered on to the high bed, slid under her own Irish linen sheets and promptly fell asleep. The lighted candle left for Nick burned lower and lower till it guttered at last into a smelly demise.

In the sitting room, they came to the finale soon after one in the morning. Adam shuffled the notebooks and the loose papers together energetically.

"So!" he said with satisfaction, "you have become a composer. This is music . . . your music . . . not a rechauffée of other people's ideas. We will have it copied. I know where. It will be well done but it is not cheap. Can you afford the fee?"

Nick was about to deny this regretfully when he realised for the first time that he had married a wealthy woman.

"Yes," he said, torn between resentment and relief, "yes, I can."

"Two days to rehearse, under your eye, Klauschen, but *not* under your baton, I think . . ."

He grinned wickedly at Nick whose ventures into conducting had been reluctant and unsuccessful.

". . . after that we will play it for you on Friday night. It will go well. My players, they will like it."

Nick stammered his thanks. Adam made a staccato sound, compounded of deprecation and derision. He gathered up the notebooks and the ruled sheets and thrust them into the recesses of his tall hat.

"Your wife will hate me," he declared. "It is nearly two. Off with you, to bed. I'll be at Liebermann's till midday and if there are any difficulties I'll send to you here."

He strode to the door and turned back to smile his good-night. Something about Nick's attitude struck him and he came back to the table.

"What is it?" he asked. "What is the trouble? Tell me, Klauschen."

Nick shook his head.

"No trouble, Adam. I'm tired. We came from Munich today and left before dawn. We've been travelling for four days . . . five really."

Adam scrutinised Nick's face intently and then swung round the chair he had been sitting on and sat down astride it, his hands along the back and his chin on his hands.

"All the same," he declared, "it is not well with you. I know you. Who better, indeed? I know that look. Tell me."

"I tell you, there is nothing the matter. Goodnight, Adam."

"Then, if you will not tell me I shall guess," Adam went on inexorably, "for you have a saying which I cannot remember about fools and angels and I am no angel and have no wish to be one. You are unacquainted with women. Nicht wahr?"

Nick went scarlet and stared ruefully: he had forgotten Adam's uncanny knack of putting his finger firmly on the very nub of a problem.

"Why, I wonder? Is it my fault? If so, I am very much to blame. It is hell-fire I deserve . . ."

"No, no," Nick protested. "It has nothing to do with you. There has been no opportunity . . . I have not met any . . . I'm not . . ."

"I will tell my tale," Adam interrupted. "When I married my Sarah I was not happy. The marriage was forced on me. I am an only son and with us the family is all. It was necessary that I should marry. I was angry. Ach, not with Sarah, no one could be angry with my Sarah, any more than they could be angry with a bird. But I was angry with myself, with circumstances . . . with you . . ."

"With me?" Nick was startled.

"Because you were not angry. If you had been angry it would have been easier to part. But you were not. You were just desolate. I could see your face all through the wedding. Jewish weddings go on for hours, I warn you. Afterwards, for weeks I could feel nothing for poor Sarah, nothing but a kind of exasperated affection. Yet there she was."

Nick looked involuntarily at the door to the bedroom.

"Yes, there she was . . . and it was no fault of hers. I have never felt more inadequate."

He laughed.

"What did you do?"

Adam gave him a sardonic look.

"But nothing . . . that was my point. But listen, we lay together and I cuddled her and we talked. We learned about each other. That is all."

Nick stared in bewilderment.

"That is what you say . . . verhätscheln . . . cuddle, nicht-wahr?"

"I don't quite follow."

Adam grinned at him.

"Women are good to hold. They are warm, soft . . . they like to be cuddled. They feel safe, wanted. It is pleasant for both. And in a little time, a very little time, the rest will follow . . . you will discover."

"And if not?"

Adam rose to his feet and the mockery fell from him like a cloak.

"Then, Klauschen, she may live longer. I do not forget my little Sarah. She was very young to die. Better for her if the rest had never followed . . ."

He raised his hand in salute and left the room. Nick stared after him smiling faintly.

In his bedroom, light filtered in from the square outside: Nick stood there in his nightshirt and found the hump on the far side of the bed endearing rather than frightening. One long plait lay outside the sheet, as if it had escaped, and the frilled night cap was comically askew. He climbed in very gently at the other side and slid down between the cool sheets. Caroline muttered in her sleep and shifted a little. Nick lay with his arms behind his head and watched the shadows on the ceiling. The room smelled of candlewax and lavender and scented soap; it was peaceful. Outside some late revellers went by singing pleasantly in harmony and laughing: a horse trotted urgently under the window and dwindled into the distance. Nick's eyelids drooped and he slid into a half-sleeping half-wakeful state.

"His heart's set on it," Hector was saying, "we'll need to let him go."

"Why?" Hannah's voice had been strained and harsh. "Why? What have we done?"

"We've done nothing, lass. It's what he is."

"Or what I've made him. You forgot he was none of yours, Hector, but I never could. Every time I see him, I see his father. While's I think I've driven him away seeing that."

Nick started full awake with the voices sounding in his ears; his movement disturbed Caroline who made a comic little sound of protest. Nick smiled at it and then lay back wondering why he should have recalled that exchange so long buried by other more painful scenes. It had taken place not long before he had left with the McVeans. His mother and Hector had been outside on the verandah and he had been in his own room, lying awake, as he was at that moment. He examined the implications gingerly rather as a sufferer from toothache might probe at the place where the pain had been. Could it have been a relief to his mother to see him go? Could that have been why she argued so vehemently against it? Why she had been so angry that he had written to his father at Inchbeg? Guilt need not be a monopoly of his, after all. He frowned into the darkness. Suppose Caroline had come to him with another man's child? He remembered Hector's patience, his readiness to listen, his enormous safe presence. He had not cared whose child Nick was. Perhaps in the same circumstances Caroline might feel worse than himself. Perhaps the stifling blanket of guilt he bore was not all his own.

Nick turned towards his wife who lay curled up like a puppy with her back to him. Gently he put an arm across her waist and lay pleasantly conscious of the soft warmth under the folds of cotton and the faint hint of scented soap which stirred when she moved to lie against him. For the first time since he was a child he felt that life might someday be a pleasant affair; it was not a revelation, just a quiet intimation, no more dramatic than the slow lightening over the mountains to the east which foretold the ending of the short summer night.

18

From the summit of Kinnoul it was possible to see the whole of Perth, laid out like a picture map, and to trace the River Tay curving through the Carse of Gowrie into the autumn haze with reaped fields lying on either bank like a faded patchwork: Nick, slightly breathless, found his favourite vantage point and settled down with his back to a rock in the thin September sunshine. He was careful to stay out of the wind which was light but bore on it a hint of cold to come as searching as an intimation of mortality. The leaves in the woods which clung to the steep slopes beneath him were autumn-coloured: the whole hillside was quietly melancholy, relinquishing summer with regret. Nick gazed across to the misted Ochils and tried to put his thoughts in order. It had been an eventful summer, too eventful to enjoy, and he felt the need to come to terms with what had happened. His hand went to his breast-pocket but fell away again without the letter it contained. He would read it again but not until he was ready. He looked out across the landscape but could find little reassurance there; spring was a long way off. Once, he had enjoyed autumn, revelling in its fruitfulness, its colour and even in its melancholy; for anyone born in the antipodes there was the double vision thinking of the spring which was creeping across the northern slopes of the hills on the other side of the world. However, these days things were different, because autumn was now the time when his son had been born and had died: when Caroline had almost died. From where he sat it was just possible to see the graveyard where his son lay. Nick looked at it and wondered how he would have felt if Caroline had followed their child there. It seemed unbelievable that there had been a time when Caroline had not been part of his life, that a time might come when he would have to do without her, live without her. The doctors could be as reassuring as they pleased, but what did they know about it when all was said. They weren't women.

193

He remembered Caroline two years ago when it was all over, that hideous three days, and her face was old and sunken and grey and those busy, plump, little hands had lain flaccid and still in his own. He dropped his head in his hands and cursed, ugly, dirty obscenities which welled up like pus from the depths of his memory, hating himself for putting her into the same danger, hating the comforters, the reassurers. Even the undoubted fact that Caroline had wanted another child couldn't obscure the danger to come: the baby would be born in the spring, sometime in April. He found himself wondering if Caroline ever compared herself to a condemned criminal awaiting execution, knowing that nothing could prevent the day dawning when a knock on the cell door would summon him to that walk across the yard to the hanging shed. Nick's eyes turned to the grey walls of the great jail on the South Inch and he wondered whether any of the inmates was lying there with this dread upon him.

However, if Caroline felt like a condemned felon she gave no sign of it: she was her usual brisk and cheerful self and ridiculed his own ill-concealed fears. In fact, Kinnoul was the only place in which he could indulge them for it seemed that no one shared them, neither Caroline, nor her father who had lost Caroline's mother in child-bed, nor his own father who instructed him matter-of-factly to be done with his long faces and think of an heir. He had fled to the summit of Kinnoul from a luncheon in the club with the pair of them. Obviously, they had been instructed by someone to 'cheer him up'; someone was probably Doctor Forsythe whose brusque impatience with Nick's vague terrors was imperfectly hidden.

"It's a perfectly natural process, m'boy, babies are born every day. She'll wear through it much better this time, I promise you."

"Natural to be a little sickly at this stage . . . wouldn't regard it if I were you. . ."

Nick knew a desire to empty the little black bag over that pink, self-important face. And there were the others.

"Don't you go frightening that lass of mine into fancying herself ill," Mr. Ruthven had said. "Just leave her to manage the business on her own . . . your part's played eh, Innis?"

They had both laughed at that time-worn jest and Forsythe

194

had come across to them with the whisky on his breath and joked about never losing a father yet, and his crony, Mollison the stationer, had chipped in with, "You've fish of your own to fry, Mr. Lindsay-Innis; I'm looking to you for a piece for the Choral Society's December concert. Have you anything in mind?"

Mollison meant well; he was a good amateur musician and fancied himself as a conductor.

"I'm afraid I've nothing ready, just at the moment," Nick had said.

"Even if you had," said Morrison and clapped him on the shoulder, "it's no likely to sell like *The Empty Cradle*. Man, there was a song. Every wifie's got to have a copy in her pianny stool and Gilchrist the draper's made a fortune selling handkerchiefs for folk to greet in, hearing them sing it."

"And our Nick's made a bonny penny," Ruthven had pointed out proudly, "and now his name's kenned no saying but he'll not make more. If he'd leave his quartets and his quintets and the like and put his mind to writing songs he'll make his fortune yet."

It had been at that point that Nick had muttered his excuses and left the club. He had crossed the old bridge and set himself at the hill as if he wanted to create a record. The song was a sore point with him, and Mollison and Ruthven between them had rubbed it raw again.

He told himself fiercely as he strode up the leaf-deep paths that it was not that he did not want to be recognised; he knew he had some qualities as a composer and on the continent the quartets and quintets of which Ruthven spoke so disparagingly had found a small but growing audience and the *Four-Leaved Clover Variations* was in the concert repertoire even in England. What stuck chokingly in his throat was not even that *The Empty Cradle* was far from being his best work, though it was the most profitable; it was that he felt as if he had exploited Caroline's grief and his own over the dead baby. In his eyes it seemed almost obscene to make money from such a thing and he had seen his bank balance swell with feelings so mixed as to be explosive. It was a relief not to be totally dependent on Caroline's fortune, the more of a relief because he had become so dependent on her in more important ways: moreover, it was satisfactory to assure Bennachie that he had justified their faith in his abilities, but, in a very real sense, he felt ashamed beyond bearing of having revealed what should have been kept decently hidden.

The truth was that Caroline had found it inexpressibly difficult to come to terms with the loss of her baby. To outward appearance she had remained her usual brisk, practical self, running her household competently from the sofa in their sitting room. When visiting friends tried to mourn with her they had been rebuffed. Caroline found sympathy hard to accept because under her cheerful and stoic manner she despised and condemned herself for failing to do what any beggar's slut could do alone beneath a hedge, bear a healthy living child. She hated her failure and her inadequacy and grieved for the dead baby with an intensity which only Nick was permitted to glimpse. She had not turned at once to him for comfort because she felt she had betrayed him as well as his child and so could not demand comfort as a right. Nick, uncertain, as always, of his ability to affect others, had been slow to let her see that he guessed at this depth of misery, but when he was not rebuffed as the others had been he had offered as much of comfort as she would allow and this had let them grow together in a way Nick could never have imagined when they had first been married.

Caroline, forced to spend hours resting on her sofa and not being, as she said, a dormouse or a hedgehog to sleep her way through the winter, found it painful to sew or knit because of the pleasure she had taken in preparing for her lost child. Reading had never been a preferred pastime with her; like her father, she had thought time spent reading was time wasted. However, even reading seemed better to her than lying idle and thinking about what might have been and she had begun to raid Nick's collection of books. Nick's one extravagance, as she saw it . . . and she did not grudge it, merely observed it . . . was the amount he spent on books. He bought for himself and for Bennachie: twice a year a chestful of volumes was despatched on its long journey, as eagerly received as it was carefully chosen. Nick found his wife's tastes surprising: fiction she rather despised.

"Such a fuss as they make over the way they feel," she said

about the characters of the Misses Brontë. "Half the time they'd have no problems worth the mentioning if they'd just say right out what was on their mind. And I don't hold with hiding madfolk in attics," she added disapprovingly. "You'd not keep yon wife of your father's a secret long if you put her up-bye."

About the characters of Mr. Trollope she maintained that most of them would be better off if they had more to do with themselves. Even the novels of Jane Austen seemed to Caroline to twitter on about trivia:

"Getting married isn't the be-all and end-all," she observed to Nick after she had finished *Emma*, "Yon Knightley would have a time of it with that one. She ought to have started with their wedding and told us how they went on. It's plain as porridge he hadn't a morsel of respect for her . . . and he was a cold stick, forbye."

She read history with more attention, for it was something real and it meant something and so did biographies though some of those were dreich enough. She found it harder to sort out her reactions to poetry.

"I like the sound it makes," she decided, "but half the time I can't make out what the mannie's getting at and some of them, when I do, it's not worth the bother. But there's a few I'd not have missed for the world and all."

Amongst these were the border ballads: she read and re-read them until she could recite many of them by heart. Soon after the New Year when Nick was choosing books for the shipment she asked him to look out for any ballads she had not read. Nick, fossicking round the bookshelves in Mollison's shop had found a small blue book called *Ballads For a Later Day*. The first had been a tale of the war in the Crimea done clumsily into ballad form and though he had never heard of any of the writers whose names appeared on the list of authors (except, of course, Anonymous) he could find nothing else with ballads and he bought it. He thought with a smile that Caroline would like pulling the verses apart; she was nothing if not a critical reader.

He had been stunned and horrified to find her the next day lying with the new book open on her lap and the tears pouring down her cheeks: Caroline never cried. She had not even wept when he had had to tell her the baby was dead. Even in the difficult early days of their marriage he had never seen her cry. He came quickly to the sofa, kneeled down and put his arms round her searching for words and finding none fit. After a little while she hiccoughed, sniffed and pulled his handkerchief from his pocket to blow her nose.

"Why you must use good linen handkerchiefs as penwipers . . ." she reproached him and blew her nose again.

"What's wrong?" he asked. "Are you ill? Have you got a pain?"

"No, no, I'm fine . . . right as a trivit. Really. I feel the better for a good cry, Nick, truly. I doubt it's what I've been needing. My nurse used to say, no one was ever the worse of a good greet . . ."

She smiled at him waterily and dabbed at her eyes.

"Lord, I must look a sight."

"But why?" he persisted.

"Och, you know me, I never know the whys and the wherefores. I was needing a cry maybe and this started me off . . ."

She lifted the book and showed him the verses on the page where it lay open.

"It said what I felt . . . I didn't know, you see, until I'd read it. I didn't understand why I was feeling the way I was. Perhaps, now I do, it'll not be so bad . . . och, I can never explain things. Nick . . . don't look like that. It's no fault of yours. And you can't be careful of my feelings if I don't know what they are, can you? Go on, read it. It's not much of a poem, I daresay, but I'll not forget it."

She pushed the book into his hands and he saw to his dismay that the title of the verses was *The Empty Cradle*.

"I should have read it through before I gave it to you," he reproached himself. "The last thing I would want to do is distress you. My dear . . . I'm so sorry."

"Well," she said, with a touch of her usual briskness, "there's no call to be. It's done more for me than all Forsythe's potions. Go on, read it."

As she indicated, it was not much of a poem, a crude pastiche of a ballad. Nick read it with more attention than it deserved.

I canna bide the crying whaup,
That calls abune the grassy ride.
My bairn is cauld beneath the ground,
His cradle gaping at my side.

I canna bide the mewing gull,
That cries across the glass-green sea.
My bairn was deid afore he breathed,
Yet, sure am I he greets for me.

Leave me, leave me, bonnie birds,
I canna thole sic waesome cries.
My wee, wee lad is ta'en frae me,
O, stark and still and quiet he lies.

That I micht dee and comfort him,
Alane and cauld and laid in clay.
I canna bide to live and breathe,
And mind on him awa' frae day.

Nick read it through again and in his ears a melody stirred and entwined itself around the words; simple, plaintive and inevitable, it was as if it had been lying there in his head waiting for them. Caroline, watching him, suddenly chuckled and Nick smiled with pleasure for she had not done that in months.

"My, but I know that look on your face. Genius stirs. What is it this time?"

"A setting for your ballad . . ."

He took the book to the piano and set it on the rack.

"Listen."

He sang it to her and improvised an accompaniment almost without hesitation. When he had finished he turned round and saw she was crying again.

"Caro . . . I'm sorry. I should have realised that . . ."

"Away! Don't you know a compliment when you see it?" she demanded. "It's just what it ought to be. It's perfect."

"Do you really think so?"

He had written out words and music very carefully and had the sheets bound in calf at the book-binding shop in the jail. A week later he had presented it to Caroline.

"There," he said. "That's yours. All your own."

She had looked at it and admired it and hummed the tune.

"Can I really do just as I like with it?"

"Of course, it's yours."

She got up from her chair at that point and gave him a hug, much to the scandalisation of Bachelor, the parlour-maid, who was bringing in the tea-tray.

"It's the best present I ever had," she declared. "And it's too good not to share. We'll have some people in, Nick, and I'll ask Alison Mitchell. She'll sing it for you."

He must have looked taken aback at this decision because she hugged him again and ruffled his hair.

"We know fine why it's important to us," she assured him earnestly, "but it'll just be a bonnie song to other folk. And it is a bonnie song, Nick. I can't just put it past in a drawer with the baby clothes and let it lie."

And so, *The Empty Cradle* had seen the light. It had quickly caught the public fancy, being easy to sing, agreeable to listen to and of a delightfully pathetic nature: moreover the words were scotch and the dear Queen was well-known to have an eccentric devotion to things scotch. As it gained popularity, Caroline regained her strength and her spirits. She poked gentle fun at Nick's scruples about making money from the song until he accepted his good fortune with a better grace. With the money there came other marks of public favour; requests for locks of his hair, his discarded pens and other mementoes, and drifts of verses for his consideration, ranging from the merely vapid to the actively ludicrous. Caroline dealt with these and with the visitors who converged on the house in Rose Terrace. Many of these claimed to have written the words of *The Empty Cradle*, for the author had been anonymous. However, the publishers of *Ballads for a Later Day* knew that the author was a purse-pinched minister's wife who was allowed to keep her anonymity. Her ingenuity was stretched to some degree to account to her husband for unexpected affluence for he did not approve of verse, or of women who so far forgot their place in the scheme of things as to write it.

Commissions began to come Nick's way: the most ambitious being a suggestion from a famous choir in the north of England that he should supply them with an oratorio on the subject of the prophet Ezekiel. This, after refreshing his memory of that bizarre figure, Nick politely declined. He could not, he wrote, really consider Ezekiel as a suitable subject, incoherent anger and incomprehensible allegory being difficult to convey in words, let alone in music. Others, he accepted. After eighteen months he had a body of work on hand and was, despite Innis's gloomy prognostications, more than earning his living.

It had been just over a month ago, in August, when a request had come in from a choral society in London that he should set an ode to music in order to celebrate the christening of a royal infant. He passed the letter across to Caroline who read it and then the ode.

"Pooh, mawkish stuff," she observed. "I could write better."

"It's by the president of the society, I expect," said Nick.

"Or his wife. Which is the royal babe so nobly named?"

"I couldn't say. There's one every year and two on leap years it seems. I've lost track of them."

She handed back the letter.

"With different words it'll do very well for our own."

Nick stared at her in dismay.

"In April," she told him.

"But . . ." he began.

"You must have known it was possible?"

"But you said . . ."

"Never mind what I said. I want a child."

He knew then that she had meant it to happen and said nothing.

"It won't be so difficult this time."

And that had been that. The child was a fact; it would be born, it must be born and he must wait for the coming of spring and conceal his fears for Caroline's sake. He remembered Adam's face when he had told them about Sarah.

"I miss her still," he had said.

Nick ducked his head as if someone had aimed a blow at him: why, he demanded of the fading landscape, could Caroline not be like his mother who had born him alone and whose other children had come with hardly a pause in her working life? Reluctantly he remembered the letter in his

201

breast pocket and drew it out. It was from Hector, not Hannah, and it held bad news.

My Dear Boy,
   It is a great grief to me to write this. Your mother is far from well. We had her to the doctor in Dunedin who is a clever man but he says there is nothing to be done and that it is just a matter of time. If you want to see her alive you will need to come soon. She knows she has not long to go but she is cheerful and like herself.
   I have a favour to ask of you. Will you enquire in Edinburgh about a Mrs. Ramsay. Her husband killed a man and vanished in 1847. I just want to know whether she is dead or alive. You will have to mind how you set about it because I'll not hide it from you that I was the man who vanished. I was her husband and may be yet, for all I know. If she is dead I would like fine to make your mother my wife at last, in fact as well as in truth. Here are the things you need to know . . .

When Nick had first read the words they had not meant much to him. He had been told that often after a serious hurt no pain was felt, that shock numbed. Now, he knew this to be true. His mind had rejected the news and its implication. If he was to see Hannah again he could not be here in April. It was a dilemma he could not bear to face. Slowly he rose from his seat under the rock and folded Hector's letter. It was time to go home. He would not tell Caroline what was in the letter until after he had been to Edinburgh.

In Edinburgh, in the Records Office, Nick discovered that Mrs. Ina Ramsay, know as Craig, was to be found in Liberton, in the cemetery. She had been dead for three years. Nick took a cab to see the grave and then rode back to Princes Street thinking about Hector's confession: it seemed incredible that the huge gentle man who had been his real father could ever have killed a man. From the General Post Office above the station he sent a tactfully phrased telegram to the Cable Office.
   "Subject of enquiry dead stop letter follows stop Nick."
   In the train going home to Perth he decided he would say

nothing at all to Caroline. To tell her would simply shift the
decision to her shoulders and he knew what she would decide.
He would explain in a letter how it was . . . then in his mind's
eye he saw them opening his letter at Bennachie. He winced at
what they would think, how his mother would feel. During
that journey Nick made and unmade and remade his decision
time and again and when he got out at Perth he was no nearer
knowing what he should do. He walked home across the
town, putting off the time when he would be face to face with
Caroline.

When he let himself into the house he found the place in a
state of turmoil. There was a massive trunk open in the hall
and a waft of lavender from the sheets and blankets and towels
which were being packed in it. Nearby there was a tea-chest
half-filled with jars and packets and bundles and the smell
from that was like a grocer's shop. Bachelor came downstairs,
picking her way and peering round an armful of towels.

"Bachelor, what is going on here?"

The parlour-maid dropped her load on to the hall chest.

"You may well ask, Mr. Innis," she said disapprovingly.
"It's not what I hold with at all. To go traipsing off at a
moment's notice in this way, putting people about . . ."

"Traipsing off where?"

Bachelor sniffed and kneeled down to start packing the
towels into the trunk.

"Best ask the mistress, sir. All I know is that there was a
letter for her this morning and she came into the kitchen before
cook and me had swallowed our breakfasts and we've been on
the go ever since. There's been folk coming and going all day,
and messages hither and yon and packing this and that. John
Coachman's away to Netherknowes with the horses and there's
two cabs ordered for six in the morning to catch the Glasgow
train. And we're to be on board wages, Mrs. Lumsden and
cook and me and Miss Marshall's in a fine state because she's
going with the mistress and doesn't care to leave all in a bang
and not see her mother. I tell you, sir, it's not what I'm used to
and I don't care who knows it . . ."

Nick bewildered by the long string of complaints heard
Caroline's voice upstairs and left Bachelor grumbling into the
recesses of the trunk. He went upstairs two at a time and found

the landing jammed with cases and boxes and trunks. Most of them were shut, locked and labelled. For an awful moment he wondered if Caroline had decided to leave him. He bent and read one of the labels.

> Mr. and Mrs. Lindsay-Innis,
> Passengers to Dunedin
> by the SS *Te Anau*.

He could not believe his eyes.

"Caroline!" he called out. "What in the name of all that's wonderful, is going on?"

She appeared in the doorway of their bedroom, slightly flushed with her hair, usually so neat, escaping from its pins.

"Ah, you're back," she observed. "I was worried you might decide to stay another night. If you weren't off that train I was going to send a telegram to the hotel."

She had a long list in her hand and crossed off an item as she spoke.

"Caroline . . . please, will you explain."

"You've heard from Bennachie?" she enquired.

"Yes. I had a letter from Hector two days ago."

"Then you must know what's going on. We're going to New Zealand. Why did you not tell me your mother was sick? I'm not *ill*, Nick."

"Because . . . because . . . are you sure you are able to travel? Have you asked the doctor?"

"I have." She turned back into the bedroom so that he had to follow her. "Forsythe says that a sea-voyage is just what I need. We'll miss the winter, have lots of sunshine and fresh air and a long restful voyage."

"When did you see him?"

"This morning at nine o'clock. You see, I had a letter too. It was from someone called Elspeth Duncan . . ."

Nick immediately pictured the plain eager face in front of a battered blackboard.

"That would be Miss Elspeth, the school teacher," he said. "She married Geordie Duncan over at White Waters. Elspeth was named for her."

"Well, I've plenty to thank her for. I take it you'd have left

204

me in ignorance for some scruple about the baby. She said
straight out your mother was very ill and pining to see you and
that I ought to know about it. What do you think I am, Nick?
How do you think I would have felt afterwards if you hadn't
gone?"

"I didn't know what to do," he muttered. "I've been on pins
over it."

She looked at him and shook her head.

"I might have known. Anyway, everything's arranged now.
I went right out and saw Forsythe and told him what I wanted
to do and then I went to see Mr. Parker and he booked two
passages on the *Te Anau* by the telegraph. We're going aboard
tomorrow afternoon at Greenock."

Nick gasped.

"I've written to my father, and to yours, and sent off the
letters with John Coachman. All you need to do now is eat
your dinner, pack up your paper and pens and ink and pray
that there's a decent piano in the saloon."

"But we can't possibly get back before . . . heaven knows
when we'll be back."

"Then our child will be born in New Zealand," said
Caroline. "Like you. Why not? I think it would be a fine thing
if your mother could see her grandchild, don't you?"

"But, what about doctors?" Nick protested. "You've no
notion how remote Bennachie is. I couldn't be easy . . . I
couldn't . . ."

"It's me that's having this baby," Caroline told him, "not
you. This Miss Elspeth tells me that there's a fine new doctor
in the township and a midwife as well. I'll be fine unless you
fuss me into a frenzy. We're going and that's the end of it."

Nick took a deep breath and sat down on one of the trunks
which was marked clearly NOT WANTED ON VOYAGE and began
to laugh.

"To think I never even considered that you might be able to
come with me. Dear God above, when I think of the two days
I've spent trying to decide what to do for the best . . ."

Caroline put her arms round him and pressed his head to her
breast so that Miss Marshall entering with a pile of his shirts
was quite put about.

"For it's not what you expect in a respectable house," she

said later in the kitchen over a belated supper. "Hugging and that in front of folk. It's no decent, so its no."

"When you've a man, you'll think different," said cook placidly. "And maybe you'll find one, out there. Lassies is scarce, so they tell me."

Miss Marshall exchanged a look with Bachelor expressive of distaste for such vulgarity but secretly she wondered whether cook might be right: she might stand a better chance of bettering herself in the colonies where Jack was as good as his master.

And so Anna Lindsay-Innis came to be born in New Zealand.

ENTR'ACTE

19

In the Stalls. Row G. 14 and 15.

In the dark between one scene and another.

"What are you fumbling for, woman?"

"Hankie . . ."

"Here, have mine."

A nose blown very thoroughly.

"How could he *know* like that?"

"Know what?"

"How she had to be feeling. Oh, blast it . . . I didn't mean to cry . . ."

"How does anyone know what anyone feels? Unhappiness is the same in any language. Everyone's been unhappy, one time or another."

"I didn't expect . . . usually tragedy in opera makes me want to giggle. All that noise and the orchestra all hammering and sawing away. But this was *real*. How could he know like that. He's a man."

"Men aren't immune to grief."

"I'm sorry . . . really . . ."

"You know about grief and he makes you remember you know. It's you who puts the grief into the music."

"But it doesn't always happen, does it?"

"No."

"I mean, think of all the plays you can just sit through and never shed a tear. Tragedies I mean."

"Tragedy doesn't make you cry."

"I thought that's what it was supposed to do."

"Tragedy's too big for tears. It makes human beings too small and unimportant. Like a thunderstorm. This isn't tragedy. The scale's wrong."

"What then?"

"Desolation . . . grief unending . . ."

"Oh, God, I wish I hadn't come . . ."

"It'll help . . . just a little perhaps . . . but it will help."

"Nothing helps much, does it?"

"My poor lamb. That's what it's about."

ANNA'S STORY

20

There was something nudging at the edge of her consciousness, a sound, a thin plaintive sound and she felt she should know what it was. She knew it ought to matter but she was too light to speak . . . to make a sound would send her spinning into space and she might not be able to return. But the sound mattered, she knew it mattered. There was a smell. A thick, sweet smell which frightened her. Under it was another she knew. She knew it well but did not want to remember what it was . . . it meant . . . but she must not remember what it meant . . .

"She's coming round," murmured a voice.

Anna fought against consciousness: she did not want it, she wanted the dark, the lightness, the not-being, but it slipped from her slowly like the tide going out, leaving rocks uncovered, black and hard and unchanging. There was a moment when she knew there was a pillow under her head, she felt the smooth sheet and a hollow aching body lying on it and slowly came to understand that she, Anna, lay there. Anna.

"Anna! Anna . . ."

Another voice, another rock uncovering, her mother: she knew she should answer but the light was lying in wait for her outside her eyelids, like sunshine outside a tent, waiting to pounce and dazzle. She lay still and knew she lay, but her eyes would not open nor her hand stir; she was hollow, empty, heavy as iron. Unmoving, immoveable. A hand touched her face.

"Anna?"

Her nurse had woken her when she was small, calling like that, softly in her ear, as if she half-hoped not to waken her at all. A little dumpling of a girl she had been and her straight hair Morag's despair. Brushing and brushing, brushing and brushing, curl-papers and rags; she would have to bunch her pillow under her neck not to lie on the knobs and by midday the curl had gone and Mama would send her back up to Morag to have it braided after all. The plaits were like rope, heavy and thick and shining. When she went to Glasgow she had had it cut. With the sort of patients who came into the Infirmary short hair was an advantage. It could be washed and dried quickly. She had sat on the sill of her window high above the bustle of Rotten Row and dried it in the sun, reading and drinking tea.

Oh, the illicit tea they had drunk in those days, made over the little spirit burner she had brought back from Inchbeg after that first leave of absence. It had been in the big room over the library and old Lady Innis had used it to make her toddies. Anna had only seen her once. They had gone to Inchbeg when Grandpa Innis was dying. Morag had gone down to the kitchens to lend a hand and hear all the gossip and left her alone in the nurseries on the top floor. The nurseries were dull and brown, the only toy left in them a rocking horse with no tail and only one eye which glared menacingly at her. The stairs were shiny and dark without the drugget which quieted the nursery stairs in Rose Terrace; they complained when she stepped on them. On the landing below was the door which was never open. That afternoon everyone had been busy, rushing in and out of Grandpa Innis's room. They had brought a nurse from Perth, very tall and starchy in her uniform and white veil; the first nurse she had ever seen. Anna sat on the bottom step of the nursery stairs and watched her moving to and fro in Grandpa's room. She had sat there for a long time, chewing the end of her long pigtail; there had been no time for curl-papers.

The nurse had seemed so sure, so calm and self-contained, the still centre of that turmoil which surged in and out of that room at the end of the passage. Anna heard Morag call her the Traynurse in respectful tones, tinged with resentment, and she had thought it was because of the trays which she saw carried to and fro. The child who was Anna-on-the-bed and Anna-on-the-stairs remembered her certainty, her confidence. After a while the doctor had come, looking grave and worried and the door of the bedroom was shut. Mama and Papa went

downstairs without seeing her and everything went very still
and quiet. Anna waited and waited but the door stayed shut
and she could hear no sound. She got stiff and bored and a little
afraid. Then, all of a sudden, she had seen that the door which
was never open was standing just a tiny bit ajar. She tiptoed
over and stood trying to peep inside: there was nothing to be
seen but the blank side of a wardrobe. She pushed the door a
tiny bit more and it swung swiftly and silently wide open. The
snow outside lit the ceiling with a cold pale intense light; there
was a fire burning low and a great luggie chair drawn close up
to the hearth. Anna crept just over the threshold and stared. It
was the smell which struck her first and last; it was so unlike
the clean snow-light. The air of the room was stagnant, hot
and stale, impregnated with the stench of unwashed flesh, the
fumes of whisky and urine from the chamber-pot behind the
chair. The stench was so strong she had put her hand over her
mouth and nose. The luggie chair creaked and a face peered
round at her.

"There'sh draught . . ." complained a husky, slurred voice.
"Shutter door!"

It was a face from a nightmare, bloated yet flabby, purple
with ruptured veins and the eyes prominent, glazed and
bloodshot. Thin, uncombed hair straggled around it. Anna
was transfixed, stunned with disgust.

"Know you," said the voice, "bashtardsh' brat. Pshaw . . .
ugly creature . . . g'way brat! G'way! G'way!"

Anna had slammed the door on the nightmare and scam-
pered upstairs to hide in the nursery cupboard.

Lady Innis outlived Grandpa Innis by more than five years
but Anna never saw her again, even after they all went to live at
Inchbeg. She would tiptoe past the door, holding her breath in
case the monster would pounce out and drag her in among the
smells. Mother had gone in. Sometimes that awful voice was
to be heard all over the house, yelling incoherent abuse and
screaming and there would be the crash and tinkle of crockery
hurled against the walls. Sometimes when Anna tiptoed past
she heard the sound of hoarse sobs and that was worse than the
screaming. On those days she would run to the music room
and sit as quiet as a mouse on the deerskin hearthrug while her

father worked at his desk or played on the piano. Sometimes he would talk to her about what he was doing in that hesitant way which was so much a part of him, as if he was never quite sure you wanted to listen. On winter days the wind howled in the chimney of that room like an imprisoned demon and Papa could be tempted by a tray of tea and toast to leave what he was doing and tell her about a place on the other side of the world where the winds howled in the same way but the seasons were upside down, where spring came in September and it was high hot summer at Christmas-tide. There were times when this place was real to her, when she knew it was waiting over on the other side of the world. The people who lived there wrote letters which she could read, sent photographs of themselves and presents for her birthday: it was the place where she had been born, though she could never quite accept that. It seemed unfair that she could not remember. At other times it was their own private world where Papa was a boy again and it had no real place except on that hearthrug. It was a world which was a refuge from her straight hair, her ungainliness and the spectacles she had to wear. In that world she could be a boy, not a disappointing, plain, untalented girl; she could be a boy who ran barefoot over the hill, or rode a half-broken pony through the creeks to reach his school. In bed she would daydream wild adventures for this boy, living in him a life quite different from her own daily round of lessons, walks and meals; meals, walks and lessons. Bennachie became her escape. From Papa's stories she spun herself a detailed other life, a family, brothers and sisters, a life where she was important . . .

Papa had never quite understood her hunger to hear about Bennachie though he was willing enough to feed it. It amused him that she never forgot the least detail that he told her. She wondered if he had ever guessed about her secret life there; she had only ever told one person about it and he . . .

"Anna . . . Anna . . ." The voice was gentle, tentative, but for all that there was a hint of impatience. Anna lay still, hiding behind her weakness as she had sheltered from the searching wind of her mother's criticism in the nursery, in Papa's study, in her daydreams. For Papa she might have opened her eyes, tried to speak . . . not for her mother, for it was little use trying to please her. Anna lay there, deaf to the voice, drifting to and

216

fro on an inconsequent wash of thought, half dreams, half memories . . .

For the first time in years she remembered a broad, rather red face, the fair crinkled hair and the great silky moustache; it was a benign face, even a little stupid, not the kind of face one would think would wound unmercifully, but she had learned since how cruel the stupid and unimaginative could be. Lamond, his name, James Lamond and her mother had wanted her to marry him. How old had she been? How old? Seventeen, perhaps, nearly eighteen . . . but still plain as a plate of porridge. The old queen had died that year and black mourning had made her look plainer than ever. She had *known*, known with the cringing certainty of the loving and the unloved, that he found her utterly unattractive. He had never found excuses to touch her, never smiled secretly at her, never even looked at her except as politeness dictated. She had worshipped him, waited for these things in vain and hoped and hoped . . . and hope deferred made the heart sick. Why had he even considered her? She could only suppose he had seen her with a farmer's eye. His land was his real love. She was of strong, healthy stock with enough breeding to throw good progeny; docile too. But even these virtues and the dowry had not been enough to bring him to the point; not all her mother's tactless-tactful moves, the new clothes, the new hair-styles, her own pathetic and obvious devotion. He had been to an agricultural show in the Borders, met and married a girl from Biggar, all in a month, and all of Perthshire had smiled behind their hands. Mother had been quiet-angry for weeks, blaming Anna and trying not to show that she blamed Anna. Anna would have been more miserable except that she had never in her heart of hearts expected anything else.

Agnes Lamond was a good soul. They had become friends, to her mother's dismay. And now she was a widow, a widow with four children trying to run that fine estate where mother had hoped to visit her own grandchildren. James Lamond was dead. When . . . where . . . it didn't matter. The brawny body and ruddy face which she had once worshipped were rotting in France somewhere, with all the others . . . those others seen and unseen, heard and unheard . . . the faces swooped and swam around her and she flinched from them. There was a hand against her cheek.

"Anna? Anna . . . can you hear me?"

After Lamond's wedding she had ceased to listen to her mother. After a while, her mother had ceased to criticise, to harangue, to discuss clothes and styles. The evening parties had become fewer, the carefully chosen house-guests had ceased to come. Very deliberately she had abandoned all efforts. Anna had been at once relieved and hurt. Once more she had begun to find refuge on Bennachie, a boy no longer, locked now into the physical inevitability of being a woman, but on Bennachie she could be the sort of woman she longed to be, the kind she could bear to be. On Bennachie she could be steadfast, enduring, courageous and beloved . . . plain or not. Even in dreams, Anna could not make believe to be beautiful. What had ended this dream . . . stolen her refuge?

". . . really very weak . . ." murmured a strange voice.

Anna-on-the-bed knew the voice was talking about that empty, aching, hot and weary thing which anchored her. How could it be weak when it held her down, pinned her on the bed. If the voices would go away and leave her alone she might be able to free herself. Twice before she had freed herself from the unendurable. Why had the dreaming ended? Because it was not enough?

A hand gently pulled her nightgown open at the neck. There was a cold, thin sensation under her arm, fading and then with-drawn and a cool, rough hand rested momentarily on the hot skin of her chest. Her hands must have felt like that. She could often tell a temperature almost as accurately as a thermometer. Her hands had been so clean, so achingly clean, scrubbed, scrubbed, scrubbed . . . never quite dry, never quite warm. The hand at the neck of the gown was quite different, smooth, pampered, plump . . . it smelled of lavender, not carbolic, mother's hand. She had a sudden picture of Papa's hands on the keys of the piano, long, bony, ugly and sure . . . the only sure things about him. He had played for Adam the night she had decided what she must do. Adam had shown her that she must not blame other people because she was unhappy. He had said that she was the mistress of her own fate. Strange to think that his son was fighting on the other side of the Front, if

218

he was still alive. The Front was the Front; after a while it ceased to matter much on which side people stood; they died . . . they all died, sooner or later. Adam would lose his son, his bright-eyed, beloved son . . . had probably lost him already. Anna had never had him to lose. He had not seen her at all while she had fallen headlong and humiliatingly in love. It was unfair that the plain had the same desires as the attractive. Unfair. . . unfair . . . She had hidden it, Lamond had taught her that much; no one had known, except Adam who knew everything about people. He had said in that headlong English of his, 'To work . . . to work, it is the only sure cure. Find your work and the rest will cease to matter. The pain will die.' He had been right.

But, as far as her mother was concerned, she chose the wrong work. There had been anger, reproach, refusal. She had run down the long drive on the morning she ran away, the winter sun barring the gravel with shadow. Her eyes had dazzled at the light and dark, dark and light, but she never saw a path with bars of light and shade across it but she thought of that cold early morning and the sense of fear and exhilaration which had possessed her. Something of that exhilaration lasted even through those quelling early months in Glasgow. Annie Smith, she had been then, probationer-nurse, always hungry, always tired, always footsore but knowing without a shadow of doubt across her path that she had found her adventure.

21

When the tide went out again it was night time. Anna knew that even without opening her eyes: hospitals, houses, ships, they were always different places at night. The sounds were different and the smells. Places took on a completely different aura, as if they came to life and watched over the people inside them: sometimes you could feel safe and protected (Rose Terrace had been like that), at other times the places brooded inimically as if the wakeful intruded. Night duty was never simply doing the same job at night, it was much more. People were vulnerable at night, more frightened, more unhappy, more alone: during the day they put on their masks and behaved in the way expected of them by others. At night the masks came off. During the day, patients had to be cases: Mr. Stewart's carcinoma of the bowel, Dr. MacDonald's abscess on the lung, Dr. Lassiter's chronic chest: there was so much to be done there was no time to see them as individuals. They were always all–important, but they could not be people. At night, Mrs. O'Connell could confide her fears for her four children after she was gone at last.

"For my man's a thowless, idle creatur'. I doubt he'll never manage. Och, Nurse, if I could just ha' the choosin' o' his second . . ."

Mr. Campbell, weak and breathless, would speculate on his chance of finding another job in the shipyards.

"I've served my time, ye ken, but it's gey hard work. I doubt I'll no be able for it . . ."

"It's yon stour," Mr. Graham would gasp after a paroxysm of coughing. "It's the stour'll kill me the way it killed my father . . . he deed o' the black spit . . ."

None of them really heard what the night nurses replied. It was the tone of voice they heard, soft, reassuring, saying, "You're not alone, we're here, we care . . ." It worked for German prisoners, for French poilus when neither could understand what you were saying and you could barely make out what they wanted.

"We're here, we care . . ."

There was someone in the room. Anna heard the soft breathing and the subdued crackle of starched linen: if she were to open her eyes there would be a lamp, well-shaded, in a corner and a quiet figure beside it, reading or sewing. The rhythmic whisper of cloth on cloth suggested sewing. For herself, she had always read on night duty: it was easier to listen for the sounds which heralded trouble and patients in pain were hypersensitive to sounds and movement. She had read medical books for the most part, sponging up information with an ease which surprised her, and others. Somewhere, there was a medal, lying on its velvet bed to witness to all that reading . . . where? . . . in Glasgow. It would be with the rest of Annie Smith's belongings, in her cheap tin trunk.

The trunk would be waiting for her in the store room of the Home. There were books in that trunk, a few discarded clothes, the blue face-cloth costume she had worn the morning she ran away, a blouse she had made herself, high-necked and unbecoming to someone as short-necked as she was; a few other cheap oddments. There was not much to be bought on a nurse's pay after the tea and the biscuits and the stockings were bought and the tram fares paid. Not much in the trunk to show for fifteen years; the austere uniform which saved one from thinking about clothes and what they did not do for one's appearance, a medal which purported to be gold, a sister's strings, a few photographs . . . she wondered whether she would ever claim that trunk. Annie Smith was dead, that plain, rather solemn creature in the photographs, her eyes narrowed against the sun, looking plain and stolid beside her prettier colleagues. She had lost weight on the wards but she would never be tall and elegant and trim. Annie Smith was dead, her place filled, her ward run in a different way. Someone else was making the illicit tea in the Home, answering the anxious questions from relatives, correcting the bandaging and the bed-making. Someone else was checking for dust and fluff, watching the comings and goings of the doctors and surgeons along the long shining room with the huge elegant draughty windows, someone else was worrying about chipped bedpans, torn pillow-cases, stained towels . . . it would not be Annie Smith . . . never again. Unbelievable that such things had once filled her days. If she went back, would there be anyone left who remembered Annie Smith? Unlikely. No one person could make a lasting impression on a hospital: too much happened all the time, too much urgency, too much tragedy; in a few days the tide of events had smoothed away the gap, memories were overlaid with others and inside six months people who had told her the most intimate details of their lives would be hard put to it to remember her name or her face. Only dangerous eccentricity or disastrous inefficiency was ever memorable for long. Even then, the tales grew with the telling while the characters in them were faded and merged with others who had become legend.

The rhythmic sounds ceased and Anna knew that someone was standing beside her bed. Perhaps, if she opened her eyes, she would find it was Annie Smith. Annie Smith, nurse. Sister Smith. Annie Smith was dead. She had had a short life, born when she had arrived at the infirmary and smelled the all-pervading smell of carbolic for the first time. Anna could smell it now. A doctor had once told her that hearing was the last sense to disappear, the first to revive, but it was smell which triggered memory. If people were to recall Annie Smith ever, what would they remember? Not efficiency among so many who were efficient. A voice sounded in her memory, speaking in that light flat undertone they used at night because it was less disturbing for the patients than a whisper:

". . . I tell you, that won't do for Pernickety Penny . . ."

Annie Smith had resented that name, but not the implication. It was essential to fuss over details. Nursing was living in detail; every least thing counted. Tidiness saved time and thought in emergency, cleanliness saved lives, routine saved thought, reserved initiative for emergencies when it was desperately needed. She had proved this and she practised it, but nicknames described, they never explained. Pernickety Penny. Sister Smith was content to accept it as an accolade, but Annie Smith wondered, a little resentfully, who had coined it.

"Don't you ever laugh, Smithy? Life's not so bad, you know! Cheer up!"

Only one person ever called her Smithy. Elena Scott. They had entered together, trained together. They shared a room in the Home. They shared their books. People regarded them as friends, as inseparable, but they had been wrong. Elena and she looked at one another across a great gulf. Elena was light-hearted, confident, sunny in her profound and unshakeable religious belief. What she did she did for Christ's sake. She made no secret of it, joyfully paraded this priceless gift of unquestioning faith and somehow made Annie Smith question her own motives in doing this work and devalue them. Anna had been brought up properly, the Kirk on Sunday, Sabbath School, hymns learned, texts expounded and prayers said but none of this had come to life for her and she envied Elena obsessively. More, she had resented Elena's sunny simple affection, found irksome her utter confidence that Anna returned it: it was as if she had been given a present she did not want and her gratitude was being taken for granted. Elena did not know what sort of person she was, she had taken no trouble to find out; she had crashed through Anna's reserve, trampled uncaringly on her feelings and all this in the name of friendship, even of love. It had been hard to bear and worse to know that she should be grateful for this offer of something which no one else had been ready to offer.

Elena had persuaded her to write home at last and reveal where she was, or that was how she saw it. Anna had determined that after six months she must write if only to reassure them. When her mother had come to Glasgow, cold-angry and reproachful, Elena had charmed her out of the anger. Anna sat stolidly and silently by, conscious that Elena was just the daughter that her mother would have preferred to have. Papa had come with her and had said less but it was plain that he had spent an anxious time looking for her and Anna had felt remorseful. It had been appalling to have Elena explain this to him.

Afterwards, Elena had spent her leaves at Inchbeg because she had no home of her own. Matron had tried to ensure they had their leaves together. It was somehow ironic that she had done this because of Annie Smith's prowess, as a reward, as a mark of Matron's esteem. Elena had succeeded as easily with nearly everyone else at Inchbeg; except Papa. Papa was not so readily charmed and Anna had exulted inwardly at this and then despised herself for being so petty.

"Smithy! Smithy!"

The light, breathy, rather childish voice was the same as ever. Anna could not decide for the moment whether she had heard it or whether she had conjured it out of her mind; she lay inside that inert thing that ached and throbbed and waited to hear whether it would speak again.

"Smithy . . . can you hear me?"

If she opened her eyes it would not be Annie Smith, it would be Elena Scott. Nell, her mother called her. Nell . . . the curfew sounds the knell . . . each matin bell the Baron saith, knells us back to this world of death. She would not hear, she would not see, she did not want to . . . she would wait for that tide. It must change soon. Tides did not go on going out and out . . .

"Open your eyes, Smithy," coaxed the voice, "I'm sure you can hear me. I've brought your son, don't you want to see him?"

Never, Anna thought, never. If I see him he will drag me back, pull me above the water's edge. She shrank from him, shrank from the idea of him, wished him away . . . wished him away . . . away . . . It was just at that point that she knew she was dying. She forgot the threat which hung over her and thought, 'it will soon be finished,' and a great wave of relief and gratitude washed over her. The aching diminished and she felt light as air, ready to spin away at a breath. When the tide crept back again the rocks would lie covered deep and quiet and away away from the cruel wind and the drying sun and the strutting pecking squawking gulls.

"Is she conscious?"

Her mother's voice. There was no spoken answer but Anna knew Elena shook her head and might have smiled to think that she had defied that probing, searching greedy affection to find her out. This time she would escape.

It must have been a little while later that she smelled the corruption, just a breath across her nostrils where the breaths

224

went softly in and out. The smell whirled her back and back to the narrow wooden hut packed with beds and stretchers. She could see it as if it was rebuilt within her head, the red blankets and the white bandages and the glint of paraffin lanterns on the iron bedsteads and the glistening sweating faces, still or mouthing or resigned; drugged, defeated, astonished, bewildered. She had seen hundreds of these faces, all of them different and she could recall each single one of them. They had depended on her, demanded comfort, reassurance, love . . . things not hers to give, rationed like the food, exhausted like the stores.

She had known as well as any staff officer how the war was going, by the casualties in CCS 13. She could tell by their numbers, by their injuries. First head wounds trickling in a few at a time, hideous splinter wounds from troops under artillery bombardment, a flood of abdominals meant an attack, up and over and into the range of the machine guns. If the wind changed she might see a procession of the burned and the blind winding up for treatment, each man holding on to the man before, blind and choking.

In Glasgow there had been horrors, razor attacks, explosions, axe attacks, hideous injuries from the shipyards, ghastly burns when there were fires in the tinder-box slums. She had thought herself able to withstand most of these. She was trained, experienced, annealed under the hammer of poverty, unemployment, gang warfare. But CCS 13 exceeded nightmare, exceeded any mediaeval vision of damnation. The mud, the smells, the cold, the wet, the vermin, her sheer inability to do all that needed to be done combined during that first winter in France to bring her close to breakdown. She had lost all her fear of death, that winter, familiarity had bred respect. Too often she had welcomed death as the only possible outcome, the happiest outcome. She had prayed for it to come quickly; once at least she had hastened it by an overdose. Afterwards, she had dreamed again and again that he came back to reproach her, the face which wasn't a face looking up at her from the floor and babbling sounds which were almost human, pleading for life.

When the German guns at Lens had found their range just after the New Year she had come close to death herself: they had dug her and two others out of the ruins of her ward. The others were dead and she had lain in company with them for more than a day. While they were burying them and the rest of the patients in her ward she had been sent on leave. She had fled home to Inchbeg and found Elena there, sleeping in Anna's old room, helping Anna's mother organise an officers' convalescent home. Anna had shared her room uncomplainingly, endured and baffled the inquisition which followed her nightmares and taken refuge in the music room when she could bear no more of the questions or her mother's constant pressure for her to come home and to help them. Papa had said very little, asked no questions. He played for her or talked of Bennachie but even that old panacea failed to exorcise the nightmares and the crushing burden of guilt; the knowledge that she was alive still and had seen so many die. Bennachie faded like an old photograph, faded into a primitive sheep-station, no longer an escape, just another place. She could have read about it in a book. It had no reality. There was only one place which was real and she thought about it night and day.

When she went back, her picture of Inchbeg was overlaid by the new picture of the library and the dining room cleared and scoured and shining, set with high iron beds and bright blankets. In the midst of these stood her mother and Elena resplendent in starch and white veils. The first occupants for the beds arrived the day before she had to go back to France. In her shabby civilian clothes she had helped the men to settle in: she saw in her mind's eye what they must have looked like a few weeks earlier, grey-green with pain and shock and fear, alive with lice and filthy with mud and blood and vomit. Now they were clean, recovering, burying the thought of return under a relentless cheerfulness and banter. Some would never go back.

"You work here?" asked a young Irishman who had lost a foot, as she helped him into the high bed.

"It's my home," she said.

"But you're a nurse, for certain sure. I can see by the way you go about things."

"Not here. I'm going back to France tomorrow."

He hadn't said anything to that at once but when he was comfortably settled he had picked up her square ugly hand and kissed it, his eyes sombre.

"There," he said, "may God go with you, so."

In the morning when John Coachman came round with the old governess-cart to take her to the station in Perth, the Irishman had been waiting in the hall, leaning on his crutches. He had wished her goodbye and given her a medallion on a silver chain.

"You'll not have the faith, I daresay," he said, "but this fellah's done well by me and I want for you to have him. To keep you safe, so, and bring you home."

The 'fellah' was a Saint Christopher. She had put it round her neck and thanked him gruffly, her face red because of her mother's faintly amused and shocked expression and Elena's raised eyebrows.

"Och," he said, "sure, 'tis but a little thing when I know where you'll be by this time tomorrow. Bless you, girl, and all like you . . ."

He lurched away awkwardly and when the governess-cart drove away the windows of the library and the dining room were lined with dressing-gowned figures who waved and blew kisses.

At the station Papa had kissed her, not in his usual style as if he expected her to repulse him but fiercely, almost painfully.

"It's a strange world, these days," he had said, "when a man has to see his own daughter go to war. I can't think of another time in all history when this has happened. It's not right. They should have taken me."

"It's war that's not right!" she had cried out. "Nothing can make that right. Never mind me going, there's hundreds like me. But if I could tell you what I've seen . . . I did try. I can't now, there's no time and I'm glad. I wanted to tell you, but I couldn't find the words. I couldn't bear to bring it home."

The train huffed and clanked into the platform.

"It's as if I'll never be able to wash it off . . ."

She had meant the smell of corruption but couldn't say so.

He had stood on the platform, unmoving and unsmiling for as long as she could see him.

22

She did not go back to CCS 13. Instead she had found herself in a hastily converted tannery outside Bethune where the stink of half-cured hides whispered through all that carbolic could do. There she had been plunged into the organisation of two wards and a gaggle of half-trained nurses and V.A.D.s. Stalemate at the Front stemmed the stream of casualties to a trickle, victims of the regular 'hates'. It was a period of waiting, or so it seemed. The guns rumbled and muttered in the background and at night the skies throbbed with flashes: it was 'quiet' everyone said, quiet for the time being.

The quiet continued till early summer when ominous signs indicated a 'push'; columns of cheerful men singing gloomy songs tramped through the town heading north-eastwards, interspersed by convoys of lorries; case upon case of medical supplies arrived till the stores were overflowing; the guns trundled past the doors, shaking the ground, their muzzles yawing and jerking over the *pavé*. In the last beautiful days of June there was a lull, as if the world was holding its breath, waiting.

"Wait . . . it's all we can do. Bound to go one way or the other soon. A difficult business altogether . . . so little one can do . . ."

A man's voice this time. It was familiar but it was too much trouble to rummage for a face or a name. The voice retreated and became an indistinguishable murmur but she knew what he was saying. She had heard the words before. She knew them by heart.

"Just a question of time. Keep him as comfortable as possible. There's nothing more we can do. There's nothing to be done."

If there was nothing to be done the tide would come in, all in good time, cooling, cleaning, concealing . . .

It had been the guns which heralded July 1st. The subdued

mutter became a rolling perpetual thunder which kept every dish chattering, every window rattling and the dust she so detested swirling and settling all over the ward. The V.A.D.s mopped at it with damp rags until they rebelled. It was not what they had come to do, they said.

"Dust is dirt," she had snapped, "and dirt in a ward full of open wounds means death. God knows, isn't there death enough?"

She had heard her voice become shrill and clamped down on herself.

"Before very long there won't be time to dust," she had added in her usual flat tones. "And you'll wish you were dusting again."

She had left them exchanging glances and muttering and went across the yard to the store. There was a dray with two bony Flemish horses harnessed to it backed up to the main door. Its load was being discharged, plain deal boxes, six feet long, eighteen inches high . . . coffins.

"That's what I likes," the Quartermaster Sergeant had said, "folks as looks on the bright side."

He took her requisition slip and wandered along the crowded shelves, peering at the labels.

"But our lot have boxes, poor sods, begging your pardon, sister. There's plenty don't."

For the rest of that day she wondered what the future occupants of those boxes were doing: smoking, laughing, eating and complaining about the food, making lewd suggestions about the origins of Maconnochie; they would be writing home cheerfully and uninformatively for the last time, reading and re-reading letters from home, swapping stories of their last leave, sleeping, whistling, louse-hunting . . . and all the time those boxes lay waiting. And what they would go through before they were laid in them made her gut twist in sweating anticipation. What the human creature could endure and still survive inspired in her a horror which lurked in the back of her mind like a shapeless monster . . . the shape, if shape it might be called which shape had none . . . grinned horrible a ghastly smile to hear his famine should be filled. What was to come could be endured, but the terror lay in knowing it must come, worse to know that it could be stopped but would not be.

Somewhere out under those guns the watches would tick away the last moments of life, of physical perfection, of sight, of humanity and then, with no fanfare more than a whistle and a shouted order, it would begin . . . it must begin.

The guns stuttered into silence just after seven-fifteen on the first of July and Anna listened to the silence feeling cold on that summer morning . . . imagining.

But the reality of that summer was past all imagining.

It was night again and quiet and Anna knew that the tide was on the turn at last. The room was full of presences and sounds which beat imperiously against her closed eyes. There were whisperings over her head, but they were unimportant, quite unimportant.

"She's not fighting," her mother's voice stated aloud, "she's not trying . . . she wants to go . . ."

Even in dying she could call forth that note of impatience from her mother. She would be an unsatisfactory daughter to the very last. If she had had the strength she might have smiled. But for once she was doing as her mother wished, behaving like other people. Death was all the rage, these days, all the best people were dead. She had seen them die, heard them die, helped them die. Now it was her turn. She knew what it meant to fight but this time the fight was over. She didn't want to remember any more: better to let the tide swell, cover the rocks, deep and cool and silent. There was a sound, an engine and tyres on the gravel. Another ambulance and no room for a single stretcher. They would have to stay in the passage until there was space. There would be six spaces before night, six at the very least . . . A door slammed far away, there were voices outside the door and movement near her head. A hand on her shoulder, it must be another convoy. She must waken, cram her feet into her shoes and stand up.

"Smithy . . . Smithy . . . someone to see you. Someone very special . . ."

After all, there was something she wanted to remember but it was fading away now, eluding her like a will o' the wisp. She knew who it must be . . . who else could it be? She tried as hard as she could to lift her eyelids to make sure but now she wanted to, she could not.

"She heard, I'm sure she heard me. Smithy, darling, wake up. Someone has come home specially . . ."

In a very little while the tide would be full. This was the part she wanted to remember when he had come. The sound was hardly audible, a croak but she had meant it to sound glad and grateful and welcoming.

"Hec-tor . . ."

The effort of speech tore her away at last from the thing on the bed and she went fluttering outward like a leaf in the wind.

ENTR'ACTE

23

In the Circle Bar.

"Macadam! It *is* Macadam . . . John Macadam. After all these years! The very last person I expected . . ."

The voice still drawled. John, grinning with pleasure, turned his great bulk about, holding his glass high above the heads of the crowd.

"Parker . . . Westy Parker. Well, I'll be damned!"

Parker pounded him upon the back.

"I thought you high-tailed it back to Kiwiland as soon as Hitler bit the dust."

"Oh, before that. I was posted home at the end of 1944. I haven't been off the station in years. This is just a flying visit. Lucy, this is a very old friend of mine from R.A.F. days. Westy Parker. So-called from his predilection for imitating the Western brothers at the slightest provocation, or none at all."

Parker looked momentarily puzzled and then wriggled into the corner beside them and shook Lucy's hand.

"And here of all places!" he marvelled. "I mean to say . . ."

"I wouldn't have said that grand opera was just your pint of bitter either, Westy," observed John.

"It isn't, it isn't," he agreed hastily. "I'm up for the Tattoo. R.A.F. show this year. Do a stint with the R.A.F.A. still. Actually my wife hauled me along here tonight. Likes this sort of thing. And I must say it's much better than I expected. No busty dames expiring noisily of broken hearts and that style of thing. Quite surprising when the lights came up so soon, eh? She's over there doing the pretty with the *aficionados*. They all seem to think that it's the best thing to happen since King David tooted on the flute, but they all say it differently. Gawd. Tell me, what dragged you two away from the sheep?"

"Dominic's my son," John said.

Parker choked over his whisky.

"Your son? Do you mean to tell me that my old friend and

ivory basher actually fathered the current genius. God, am I one up on that crew . . ."

He pointed over to the corner where a plum-coloured evening jacket in silk velvet was arguing with a frilled evening shirt and a gold lamé dress and then guffawed with enjoyment.

"In the name of the Prophet, I'd never have picked you for the part. You must be proud as bloody peacocks!"

"You could say that," John agreed.

Parker raised his glass.

"Here's to you all," he drank. "How does it feel?"

"Bewildering."

"Don't have to set the world on fire to be that, let me tell you. I've two and they bewilder me more and more every year. Boy's wearin' bells and beads and the girl calls me a male chauvinist pig because Laura gave up music when we got married. Here, is this the one we had a party for? Remember? We dressed Denton up as a baby so you could get into the skin of the part. Those WAAFs wheeled him in on the trolley with nothing on but a bath towel. . . Denton I mean."

John chuckled.

"I remember the flight of the WAAFs when the towel came off."

"You brought a guest along . . . great chap. Told some of the best stories I ever heard," he chortled and then glanced contritely at Lucy. "Perfectly clean . . . but funny!"

"That was Dan."

"He made the funniest speech about how to be a father . . . laid us in the aisles, wish I could remember some of it. He here tonight?"

"No," John said. "He's dead. Died a couple of years ago in Vienna."

"He thought the world of you," Westy declared. "Couldn't hear enough about your exploits."

He grinned wickedly at Lucy.

"Hell of a chap, your husband, ma'am. Don't suppose he's told you a tenth of it. Talk about necks for sale. He'd really got it in for Jerry. Oh, boy! I never quite understood it. I mean what did old Adolf do to bring down the price of mutton?"

"The Nazis killed Dan's father," John said. "Quite early on."

Parker nodded and pursed his lips under the grizzled shadow of his once vast moustache.

"So, that was it. It cost them, by God, it cost them . . . Tell me, Mrs. Macadam . . ."

"Lucy," she reminded him with a smile. Parker again looked a little puzzled.

"Tell me, Lucy, is Dominic Macadam like his old man?"

Lucy widened her eyes and smiled a little.

"Not at all to look at," she said. "But, in every way that matters, yes."

Parker laughed.

"Then he'll do . . . he'll do, I reckon. I hear there's some sort of booze-up afterwards. You two going?"

John exchanged glances with Lucy.

"Probably," he agreed resignedly.

"See you then. Got to get back to the ball and chain. Marvellous to run into you like this after all these years . . ."

He gave a salute with his hand, downed his drink and wriggled back through the crowd toward the gold lamé dress. Lucy swallowed the last of her Dubonnet, now much diluted by melted ice, and winked over the rim of the glass at John.

"Wizard prang," she observed.

John made a face. He was thinking rather ruefully that his strand in the web was a tenuous one. 'If I hadn't been a born bloody young idiot,' he thought to himself, 'the current genius would never have been born at all. But I go at things like a bull at a gate. I always did. I suppose that's my contribution, for Nick is just the same. He never stops to think. That's what Lucy meant. But I'm glad now, though it seemed a disaster at the time . . .'

JOHN'S STORY

24

Afternoons at Springwood were devoted to games: there was rugby football on the pitch which dipped and sloped from one side to the other and from one end to the other. The Springwood fifteen was deservedly renowned for its wind. In the summer there was cricket on that same pitch or tennis on the local club courts for those with bicycles and whose parents were prepared to pay the club fees. Once a fortnight the boys of each house were escorted to the huge echoing swimming pool at Portobello. For the very wealthy there was riding once a week on the riding-stable screws. There were no classes in the afternoon although the C.E. class were permitted to study in the library: everyone else was expected to be outside, either watching or playing. The trouble was that so few could play. One pitch and a paved courtyard offered only a limited amount of opportunity to more than a hundred boys. In the Spring Term the onset of interhouse and interschool matches meant that for days on end the Lower Fourth could only watch from the sidelines. There they shivered while their more favoured seniors plodded muddily to and fro, or they would break backwards and outwards as the play heaved over the line. The 'keen' observed with theatrical attention, occasionally screaming out apt exhortations for the ears that might appreciate them, the games-master, the head-prefect or the god-like head of games.

Those who dared, plunked. John Lindsay-Innis plunked as often as he could. He did not dislike games, in fact he was a useful three-quarter and the head of games had his eye upon him. However, he hated watching and preferred to find a quiet place where he could read. In the afternoon of the Tuesday before they were due to break up for the Easter holidays John had settled down in a space behind the old stables which were now used as bicycle sheds. It was a grim, grey Scottish spring day with low black clouds scudding across below the higher grey and an east wind which bit and worried and spat flurries of icy rain. Behind the stables there was shelter from this wind; John, after two years of boarding school, was almost impervious to cold but to return 'Scissors' to its owner wet and rain-spotted would invite trouble. Two years had also taught him to avoid trouble if it were at all possible. He curled up under the half-shelter of some overhanging ivy and became instantly immersed in the story. This faculty he had learned at Inchbeg but it stood him in good stead at school; he did not dislike school but found escape necessary for survival and books supplied one method. Over the wall he could hear the dunt of foot against ball, the squelch and grunt of muddied runners and the occasional gull-like shrieks of his more sycophantic peers.

A snail dropped out of the ivy and landed on the page, together with a scatter of dead leaves and scraps of mortar. He looked up and saw a face looking over the wall: it belonged to McCaw of the well-known gang of McCaw, Greenhalgh, Geogehan and Luckenham. These were all Upper Fourths and all too well known among the Lower School. McCaw grinned menacingly and disappeared. John closed the book, wrapped it swiftly in his mac, and pushed it under the laurel which grew across the entrance to his hideyhole. With luck they might not spot it. Two heads appeared over the wall and the owners followed quickly to sit astride, looking contemptuously down at him. The clatter of boots running through the stable-yard advised him that his retreat had been cut off. Geogehan and Luckenham pushed past the laurel and confronted him, smiling with anticipation. Luckenham, it was said, had been expelled from a school in England for offences which no one seemed willing to name.

"Ah," said Luckenham in the Bertie Wooster drawl he affected, "if it isn't a little shirker. What are you doing here, dear boy?"

John didn't answer. Silent at the best of times, he knew that speech at this point could only prolong the performance to come. He had been 'attended to' before. He set his back against the crumbling brickwork of the stable wall, stiffening his sinews and summoning up the blood. In any event he had found that his voice was not to be trusted these days: he had grown a good deal since Christmas though he was not so big as the hefty Luckenham. Greenhalgh looked down meditatively from the wall and spat accurately in John's face; accurate spitting was a treasured accomplishment of his, and he had few others. McCaw flicked a snail which missed John and splattered messily on the stable wall.

"House-teams," said McCaw loftily, mimicking the Head, "ought to be supported by their houses. It has doubtless slipped your erratic attention, Lindsay-Innis, that it is the Trojans versus the Greeks this afternoon. I conclude from the colours you sport that you are a Greek. You should be out there and in support, should you not?"

McCaw rooted in the ivy for hibernating snails and lined them up ready to be flicked. Luckenham advanced from the laurel, his wet, red mouth grinning and glistening and his buttony eyes wary. John neither moved nor spoke.

"Dear boy," Luckenham drawled. "oblige me by moving so that I may kick your arse as it deserves to be kicked . . ."

Greenhalgh spat again and two snails hit John's face and head. He felt a surge of anger heating his body and his neck but controlled it. When they touched him . . .

"You are a bastard, I believe," drawled Luckenham, "or have we been misinformed?"

It was a familiar opening. John said nothing.

"Well, now," said Greenhalgh in mock surprise, "how very picturesque. What is a bastard, Luckenham?"

"A little turd who doesn't know who his father was, or which he was. That is what a bastard is . . . the son of a whore. Am I not right, Lindsay-Innis?"

John stared at him expressionlessly, beating back the anger and hatred till his collar began to feel too tight.

"Answer me, Lindsay-Innis. Isn't that what a bastard is? Answer me, dear boy, or I'll kick your bum black and blue. *Isn't it?*"

John remained silent, concentrating on what he wanted to do to that complacent face and would do if he got the chance. He would beat it to a pulp, break the ugly arrogant nose, knock out those yellow over-large teeth . . .

"The Greeks had a word for them," said McCaw, searching for more snails, "god-begotten. Their mothers used to say that the gods had slept with them. Is that what your mother said?"

The blood beat in John's ears like waves and he heard very little.

"God-begot . . . Lindsay God-begot," Luckenham drawled insultingly, "stinking little son of a whore. You keep cave, you lot, and I'll teach the little bastard to sneak away into corners while there's a house match going on."

Luckenham advanced towards John and grinned with anticipation. John's head cleared suddenly and completely and he assessed his opponent as if he was a complete stranger. Luckenham was tall and heavy for his age but much of the weight was flab. He ate too much. He forced the Lower school to pander to his greed, making inroads on their tuckboxes. He was nearly a head taller than John but a blow on that soft belly would bring the grinning face into range. John lusted to drive his fists into that face.

"Well, shall I kick the bastard's bottom?" Luckenham demanded of his cronies. "The god-begotten arse?"

John realised suddenly that his opponent was a little uncertain. He was used to whines and pleas for mercy, even to tears. A spurt of delight rose in him. He rubbed the backs of his hands against the damp, gritty, crumbling brickwork, watching and watching for the exact moment when the Luckenham belly would be in range, well within range. A glancing blow would be worse than useless.

"Bastard . . . son of a whore . . ." jeered Luckenham softly, but John, timing his onslaught, did not hear him or so much as notice the wretched snails ricocheting off his face and head. The moment came and his left hand sank deep into that soggy diaphragm. He heard the breath crow out of Luckenham's lungs, the beefy face came forwards and downwards, eyes starting, and he drove his gritty right hand into it so hard that he felt the nose crunch disgustingly. A third blow with his left was less effective, scraping harmlessly up the spotty cheek. Luckenham went sprawling back, thumping his head against the wall, blood spouting from his nose and John flung himself upon him, pounding and pounding . . .

"Christ!" someone said. "Haul him off, Goosegog . . . he'll kill him!"

John felt hands plucking at him and laughed. He landed a contemptuous openhanded slap across the bloodied face under him which left his fingers numb.

"No I won't," he growled in the bass which afflicted him from time to time. "Not worth hanging for that."

"On the whole," observed a sardonic voice behind him, "I quite agree. Get up, Luckenham, you'll survive, though whether this is a fortunate circumstance for the world is questionable. There is nothing more gratifying than to see the biter bit."

John recognised the Chemistry master, Davidson. Davidson enjoyed the respect of his pupils, if not their liking. He was reputed by those who took 'stinks' to be a sarky brute. He was also reputed to have a remarkable war record though no one had yet managed to draw him out on the subject. Other masters were more than ready to enlarge on their war experiences and this was known to be a useful time-waster. Davidson was not. John secretly liked him, respected him where he regarded the other masters with tolerant contempt. He had reason to like him for Davidson had once hauled him out of the swimming pool and John knew that he had saved his life. Even after a year, breathless and half-blind with rage, the pool at Portobello was so clear in his mind that it was more real than the bloodied Luckenham slumped against the wall. He could smell the stench of the chlorine and hear the sea-gull-like shrieks of the children in the water echoing in the high roof. He could even see the irregular shifting light patterns on the blue tiles under the water. He had thought, quite calmly, that he would drown; that there was only one thing he could do, sink down to the very bottom and then push upwards with his legs until his head broke the surface of the water and he could gasp in a lungful of air. He tried this. It hadn't occurred to him that, fully clad in mac and boots, he might not reach the surface. The desperately needed air just wasn't there. He had choked then and thought, 'I am drowning . . .', incredulously, as if it was happening to someone else.

Then someone had caught at him, held him by the arm and the hair and dragged him up and up and out into the blessed air. He could still remember the pain in his lungs as he coughed up water all over the cracked tiles. Curiously, he had not expected rescue. It was Davidson who had pulled him out though he didn't learn that until much later. All he remembered of the rest of that day was the feel of the blankets in which they had wrapped him and thinking about Rupert Brooke in the ambulance because they had been reading *The Great Lover* in English the week before and the class had sniggered at the bit about blankets. Next day he had been none the worse, barring a sore throat, but Davidson had been kept in hospital. Gas victims didn't take kindly to chlorinated cold water. He had returned after half-term, as silent and saturnine as ever and when John had found words to thank him he had rejected thanks and said an odd thing, ". . . one notch off my tally," he had muttered. Luckenham had admitted nothing. The whole house had been gated but he had still admitted nothing. John knew very well who had pushed him in but, according to the code, he said nothing. But, as he looked at Davidson over Luckenham's body, he knew that the thought of Davidson wheezing in hospital and the memory of the pain in his own lungs had lent force to his fist. It had taken a year, but it was worth it, whatever happened.

"Tell me, Lindsay-Innis, why this determined and on the whole understandable attempt to rid the world of our Master Luckenham?" Davidson enquired in his soft hoarse voice.

John said nothing. Davidson looked from one to another and smiled slightly.

"Perhaps you will enlighten me, Luckenham?"

"Lindsay-Innis was plunking the house-match, sir," said McCaw primly from his perch on the wall.

"And the four of you were exhorting him to demonstrate his allegiance?"

"In a sort of a way," Geogehan admitted.

"In just what sort of a way?"

Davidson looked at each member of the quartet with a sardonic contempt which bit to the bone.

"Not that I need to be told," he reflected. "I have observed the . . . er . . . outcome of your exhortations on numerous other occasions."

He observed Luckenham getting to his feet.

"On this occasion," he said with evident pleasure, "they would appear to have met with a degree of counter-argument. Tell me," he went on very quietly, "have any of you heard of a man called Hitler, Adolf Hitler?"

"The German bloke, sir?" asked Greenhalgh. "That one with the Charlie Chaplin moustache?"

"The very one. His National Socialist Party, the Nazis, as they call themselves, did extremely well in the elections this year."

"My father says it's the best thing to happen in Germany since the war," volunteered Geogehan. "He says he'll do for the reds and all that sort of thing."

"Oh, I have no doubt your father is right," Davidson agreed. "He does for anything or anybody he dislikes or fears or despises. Or rather his delightful bully-boys do it for him. Do I understand that you have been making a study of Herr Hitler's methods?"

The four looked at one another and said nothing.

"The politics of intimidation," reflected Davidson. "Of course, Nazis only choose targets which they think . . ." he laid the slightest amused stress on the word, ". . . are weak and vulnerable. Like the Jews. Have you heard how the Nazis deal with Jews?"

"Oh, yes," Greenhalgh admitted cheerfully, "they put badges and stuff on them."

"And they beat them up and burn their businesses," added Geogehan.

"And does your father approve of those activities?" Davidson demanded suddenly of Geogehan who went red. "Do you?"

"I don't" Greenhalgh said unexpectedly. "I think it's bally awful. People can't help being Jews. I mean people don't have to be reds but they're born Jews."

"People can't help being illegitimate either," Davidson reminded him, his voice as chilly and cutting as the east wind. "It is decided, like Jewishness, before birth."

No one said a word and he looked round the group. When he had finished he sighed as if he was suddenly very tired.

"Save your energies . . ." he advised them. "Fighting each

247

other is stupid and pointless. You'll have fighting enough before you're my age, or I miss my guess."

"But we fought a war to end war," McCaw protested.

"*I* fought a war," said Davidson, "but God alone knows what it was fought for."

The boys looked at him, their faces faintly shocked.

"I thig by doze is brogen," mentioned Luckenham, feeling it gingerly.

"Serve you bloody well right," said Davidson unemotionally and walked away.

"Sarky brute," grumbled Geogehan. "Bet he's a Jew. He's dark enough and look at his nose."

"Dever bind his doze," complained Luckenham, "whad aboud bide?"

"Better get you to matron," Geogehan advised. "Come on."

"And don't you think you've heard the end of this, Lindsay-Innis," McCaw threatened, "'cos you haven't."

From his perch astride the wall Greenhalgh laughed.

"If he can break Lucky's nose he'll murder you, Jim Crow. You can't fight worth a damn. You'll do, young God-begot!"

To John's surprise Greenhalgh winked at him before he jumped down from the wall. John found himself in possession of the field. He was conscious, not of triumph but of unease at the sour dregs of the fighting madness which was dying in him. After that day Luckenham and his gang avoided him. But John had learned more than they had.

For John, the holidays did not begin until the train drew into Queen Street Station and the boys dispersed to catch trains to the south, the far north and west, or just to jolt and sway towards their Kelvinside and Bearsden homes in green trams. The wealthy hailed taxis with an air. John stayed by his case, waved to his friends as they disappeared, doffed his cap to the staff as they dispersed also and then, the last one left upon the platform, relished being once more a person and not a small part of a school or a class or a team. People bothered John; they were demanding of the attention he needed for his own thoughts. He felt distorted by them. On his own he could

248

reassume his own shape, his real shape. Ahead of him were three whole hours before he need meet Aunty Nell at Buchanan Street. He had not lied to Grandmother, he thought uncomfortably, merely not told her that he would be on the earlier train. Grandmother fussed about journeys. He could perfectly easily have taken the Perth train from Edinburgh, but this she would not permit. Aunty Nell combined a visit to her dentist with the end of term. But he had managed to gain three whole hours on his own and in Glasgow. He moved out of the wide entrance and into George Square where the thin, spring sunlight lit the ponderous grimy buildings to a travesty of civic elegance. He had five shillings and sevenpence in his pocket, enough for tea at Fuller's, a book or two from the book-barrows and a tramride back to the city centre if he found himself too far away at train time. He began to walk swiftly and purposefully towards the river and ships and Argyle Street.

It struck him before long that there were an awful lot of people around; not bustling people with things to do and places to go, but men, leaning against the walls apathetically watching the working world go by. Despite the sun the north wind blew cold and he saw the mufflers, the caps drawn down and the inadequate shabby collars pulled up to shield neck and ears from that wind. On the corner of Outram Street, two men stood in the gutter. One wore dark glasses and his face was pitted and seamed and distorted with long-healed scars. Hanging round his neck was a tray with matches and bootlaces and cheap sweets. Round the edge of the tray was a strip of paper which had once advertised the headlines of the *Evening Citizen* and daubed on it in uneven capitals was, BLIND EX-SERVICEMAN. WIFE AND TWO CHILDREN TO SUPPORT. The other man shivered in the wind, watching the passers-by without expectation, his hand under the blind man's elbow. When he came near, John found they were singing. He ascertained the tune with difficulty, *Roses of Picardy*. Further along, a queue of women were waiting outside a fried fish shop with children hanging on to their skirts and grimy babies happed in the tartan shawls which were wrapped round them. Underneath, the wind fluttered at the drooping cotton skirts. Some of the children were barefoot. John became intensely conscious of his thick woollen socks and his warm flannel shorts. Even the thick gaudy scarf in the school colours irked him and the regulation leather gloves, stripped off as soon as the train reached Glasgow and stuffed into his pocket. He turned off the wide street so that he need not run the gauntlet of their eyes and found himself in a narrow street, no more than an alley, littered and filthy. There was a girl sitting at a closemouth nursing a baby nearly as big as herself. Her dress was far too large, a clean threadbare cotton, much too thin and wrapped tightly round her knees and legs. Her feet were bare and purplish-blue. As John came near she looked up, her eyes challenging under the straggling dark hair.

"Whit you efter . . . toff?" she demanded.

"Nothing," said John feebly.

"Nothing," she mimicked. "Get him! You wantin' someone?"

"No."

"Whicher daein' here, then? 'Tisnae the Byres Road, ye ken."

"Just walking."

"Walkin'? Doun here? Ye're daft, so y'are!"

John said nothing but looked at the baby which stared solemnly and accusingly back.

"Be'er get goin', toff," said the girl sullenly. "There's naethin' roon' here fer you, so there's no . . ."

"Would you like a pair of socks?" John asked.

He sat down and untied his laces.

"You daft or suthin'?" she demanded shrilly and incredulously.

"There!" he held out the thick red and grey socks towards her.

She stared at them as if they might vanish in a puff of smoke.

"Here," she exclaimed, "ye mean it! Tak' the wean a minute till I pit them on."

She thrust the warm smelly bundle into his arms and began to pull on the socks. He could almost feel her pleasure in the warmth and comfort of the wool. The baby stirred uneasily and John tightened his clasp. The sight of the girl's skinny, blue-tinged legs made him uneasy, unhappy and angry all at the same time. She grabbed the baby back.

"They're great! My, they're great, but," she crooned. "Great!"

John put his boots back on and tied the laces neatly.

"I'm Jinty," she announced wiggling her toes and looking down at them.

"John," he said.

"You're daft, John, d'ye ken that? Oh, my . . ."

He pulled the gloves out of his pocket and the scarf off his neck.

"There!" he muttered. "I hate them."

He dropped them in her lap and turned away, almost running.

"Ta!" Jinty shouted after him. "Ye're great, just great . . . so y'are!"

His feet felt strange, naked in the smooth leather and the boots worked loosely round them. He wandered a little further along and saw another queue outside a cinema, all children, all ragged and all clasping jam-jars, some still sticky with jam. A doorman in a shabby uniform from which the braid hung in loops and half the brass buttons were missing was trying to control the children.

"Stop yer shovin', but!" he bellowed. "There's room inside for a'body and nae need tae shove!"

A few yards beyond the cinema a small boy was squatting disconsolately over the shattered pieces of a jam-jar. John stopped beside him.

"What happened?"

"The big yins dunted me!"

"Better put them aside before someone gets cut," John advised, for the child was barefoot, and he pushed them into the gutter with his boot. The small boy ran ahead for a yard or two.

"Up here!" he urged. "Up here! We'll pit 'em doon the stank!"

John obeyed and his new acquaintance picked up piece after piece and manoeuvred them between the bars of the storm drain, listening gleefully as they tinkled down into the mysterious regions below. John watched. The urchin poked the last piece down and then looked up at John and grinned.

"Go' a penny, mister?"

251

"What for?" John asked.

"For the pickshers. It's a penny or a jeely jar and my jar's broke. Gaun, be a spor', mister. It's an awfÿ guid yin wi' horses and cowboys and shootin' an' tha' . . ."

He looked up and grinned mischievously.

"Gi' me tuppence an' I'll treat ye!"

John chuckled at such an offer.

"Ye'd like it, mister, it's great! It's warm in there, an' a'!"

"I'd like it fine," John told him, "but I haven't the time. Here!"

He put sevenpence into the boy's hand and walked on, not looking back; he heard a suppressed whoop and felt ashamed. He welcomed the cold on his legs and neck, it made him feel more part of what he was seeing. There was a band playing further along towards the Trongate and a crowd began to gather on the pavement to watch. In the distance, banners could be seen swaying and flapping above the heads of the marchers. The band was partly uniformed, wearing ill-fitting tunics over their own ragged trousers and worn boots. They were playing Scottish tunes and the contrast between the jaunty music and the gaunt marchers was cruel. They tramped past defiantly, the Union banners above them declaring that Unity was Strength, that Brotherhood was Unity and Strength lay in Brotherhood. Crudely lettered placards demanded work. John, like those about him, watched in silence.

"For all the good it'll do . . ." said one voice wearily when the bemedalled ranks had tramped into the distance.

"Better than standin' aboot ootside the Burroo," suggested another.

John caught sight of the clock on the Tron and realised that he had twenty minutes to reach Buchanan Street Station. He began to walk quickly back up west as the lights began to blink out into the gloaming. Halfway up Glassford Street he saw the blind pedlar and his guide making their way home. Then he legged it as hard as he could through George Square and the steep slope of upper Buchanan Street. He paused at a crossing to tie his bootlace and a huge Clydesdale whickered not a foot from his ear. It was waiting in the alley for the carts toiling up from Central Station. A trace horse was necessary on that hill for the really heavy loads. The sound and the smell of the great beast were comforting and he waited a few seconds to pat the pinkish nose, so unbelievably soft and velvety. It was at once dear and alien; hemmed in as he felt himself to be.

It was a short-lived comfort. As the train rattled and chattered its way over the maze of lines outside the station and found it's way unerringly into the countryside John could hear Jinty's voice much more clearly than Aunty Nell's scolding and bewailing and reproaching the loss of socks and scarf and gloves.

"They were cold," he protested. "Her legs were blue and all she had on was a thin dress . . ."

"Boots and no socks," said Aunty Nell, unheeding, "you look just like a keelie. And have you the slightest idea of the price of wool these days and how I'll need to knit another pair and another scarf. Money doesn't grow on trees."

"But she was cold," he said again, this time in the deep bass which came and went. This deflected her well enough, into marvelling how time flew and how he was already taller than she was herself. John heard not a word for he was wondering whether it was true what Aunty Nell had said and that Jinty's father would pawn the socks, scarf and gloves for drink.

Why had he given them to her? If the men at school heard what he had done he would never hear the end of it. He felt hot and ashamed and embarrassed. And yet, at the time it had seemed the only thing he could do, so obvious he hadn't even hesitated. Jinty was cold and he had clothes to spare. You couldn't just watch people being cold as if you were behind glass even if there wasn't a lot you could do to help. School and home was like being in a glass box looking out: you could see, but you couldn't touch or feel, you weren't in what was going on, bad or good.

When over a late supper Grandmother asked sarcastically who did he think he was, little St. Martin? his face burned with his resentment and inside he knew that she thought he was a stupid, soft prig. 'I don't care,' he said to himself, 'I don't care. She liked them and she'd have them and be warm at least for a little while.' He didn't believe Aunty Nell's guff about the father selling them for drink. 'And Aunty Nell likes knitting, she's always at it,' he added defiantly to himself. Something of

the defiance must have leaked into his expression for Grandmother made her impatient noise, "Tshah!" and sent him
straight to bed from the table. Grand, at the other end of the
gleaming mahogany, had looked up as he went but had said
nothing. John wondered if he might have been listening,
might even have heard what he had done. He went to bed
comforted.

25

Dawn at Inchbeg was always spectacular as the sun burst through the low river mists. John paused to stare, perched on the Mains farmgate, the light levelling like spears over the mist dazzling him.

"Whitcher doin'?" demanded an irate voice. "Get doon off o' yon gate! Ye'll hae it affa the hinges."

John scrambled over hastily.

"Ootside, damn ye! You've nae business here!"

John made out the speaker with difficulty because he was standing between him and the sun, a squat, red-faced grizzled man with metal-framed spectacles.

"I was going up to the Mains," John explained.

"Whit wey?" demanded the man.

"To say hullo," John returned resentfully. "I always do, every holiday."

"Weel, ye'll dae't nae mair. I'll no hae bluidy weans aboot the doors rinning poonds affa ma stirks. Oot!"

He thrust the gate open and jerked his thumb at the road.

"Mr. Tait doesn't mind . . ." John began.

"Mr. Tait's awa'," interrupted the red face. "The Mains is mines, bought and paid for. Oot!"

"But . . ." John began to protest.

"OOT!" the red face repeated and shoved him roughly on to the road. "And dinna come back. I've nae need tae arse-lick the laird these days. The Mains is mines."

He slammed the gate and glowered over it at John who found himself breathless with surprise and dislike.

"And much good may it do you, you toad-faced, foul-mouthed shrivel-brain," he observed politely borrowing heavily from Davidson's vocabulary. Red-face went almost black in the face and spluttered.

"May I wish you swine-fever, fowl-pest and drought,"

John went on till he saw Red-face stoop for a stone and took to his heels.

"You come your foot-length on ma land, you pan-loaf, chance-come, gentry-get and I'll feed ye tae the dugs!"

The stone cracked viciously on the wall.

Ruby explained over the teacups in the kitchen.

"The farms is a' gone. The Mains was the last on 'em and a hard bargain yon Blackie drove. Turned off all the men, he has, and let the cottages out to townsfolk frae Dundee for weekends as they cry it. He's got twa loons frae Brechin as hard-nosed as himsel' and they're livin' in the hoose, batching it. Ower mean tae marry, the three on 'em."

"Why did Grandfather sell?"

"Money," said Ruby succinctly. "There's naethin' like as much as there used tae be. And this auld place fair eats money. You could drive a coach and horses through the roof."

"I wish they'd told me about the Mains."

"There's a fair bit they havenae told you, Master John," Ruby said grimly, "but it's no my place tae dae't for them. Awa' and get cleaned up for your breakfast, ye look a right tink."

Dressing in his bedroom, paying careful attention to nails and parting, he thought over what Ruby had said about money and other things occurred to him. The stables had been empty for over a year. Nowadays they contained only an elderly Humber which Aunty Nell drove, very badly, on the few occasions that his grandparents went out. And there used to be lots more people about the house, two maids cleaning the rooms and waiting at table, three gardeners, two kitchenmaids to help Ruby, a coachman and a groom to help him. Now there was only Ruby and a succession of girls from the farms round about who came and went and rarely stayed from one school holiday to the next. And the gardens were a wilderness now, he could see that for himself from his bedroom window.

At breakfast, the echoes of yesterday evening's row still lingered. His grandmother, plump and neat and severe, eyed him with disapproval before she said Grace. Aunty Nell smiled at him furtively, ingratiatingly as if to say, 'Never mind, I'm on your side . . .' John avoided her eye and looked down the table at his grandfather. As usual he was withdrawn, unaware of John or anybody else, listening to the sounds inside his mind. The four of them ate in silence until John gruffly asked permission to leave the table.

"Not for a moment," said Grandmother. "I wish to discuss this . . ."

She put a plump faultlessly manicured finger on an envelope. John recognised his school report.

"Yes," Grandmother observed in a sardonic fashion. "You may well look unhappy."

"Oh, come, Mrs. Lindsay-Innis . . . you know, I mean . . . it isn't as bad as all that . . ." interrupted Aunty Nell. "It's not . . . I mean he hasn't . . . that is to say, it all depends on what . . ."

Grandmother ignored her. She usually did ignore Aunty Nell.

"Is there no subject at which you excel?" she enquired disagreeably. "This is a most undistinguished document."

John said nothing. His results had not been brilliant but, on the other hand, they could have been worse.

"He does very well at games and drill . . ." faltered Aunty Nell.

"Games!" Grandmother said contemptuously. "John, you are nearly fourteen. What do you mean to make of yourself?"

John felt his face go hot and he hung his head.

"Dunno . . ."

"Speak up, boy!"

"I don't know, Grandmother," he said squeakily.

"Isn't it time you did know?"

"Yes. I suppose so . . ."

"Yes what?"

"Yes, Grandmother."

"You will have to earn your own living, you know."

There was a silence and John felt that he was rapidly becoming all knees and elbows and hands, huge knuckly hands. Grandmother had always had that effect upon him.

"Well?" she asked impatiently. "Law? Medicine? What? Surely you have some idea what you will be able to do?"

John said nothing. Silence, he found, was like an armour.

"Oh, run along!" Grandmother snapped and John did not delay. He heard Aunty Nell's chair scrape back and made swiftly for the back door. He did not wish to be sympathised with and probed.

He wandered aimlessly into the old kitchen garden. It was shoulder-high with grass and weeds: there were fruit bushes rioting along the walls and only one small area dug, a plot no bigger than his own room. Ruby obviously intended to grow a few lettuces and saladings again. He pushed his way along what was once a path, sniffing the smell of turned earth and decaying vegetation. He saw the garden with the eyes of a small boy as it had been not so long ago, with line upon line of green, rows of stakes, regimented fruit, glittering cloches and always two or three figures working somewhere with that air of leisure which seemed to be the mark of gardeners. He wondered if Jock the Garden could see what had happened to his old domain and if he minded or whether he had known what would happen after he died. Perhaps he was pleased. He was a cross-grained old man. The sacrosanct shed which had always been forbidden was half-hidden by weeds and ivy but behind the cobwebbed windows the orderly ranks of tools were still to be seen. The key was in the lock.

By lunchtime he had cleared one side of weeds. By dinner time it was rough dug and he surveyed it with vast satisfaction. The next day he did the same for the centre bed. The fruit bushes in the third bed he ignored: he did not know what to do for them. He hoed and raked the cleared beds and wondered what he should plant. He found enormous pleasure in the sight and smell and the feel of the turned earth. He never remembered feeling so pleased, so satisfied with anything he had done.

"My, but you've made a differ, Master John. If that isnae a real good job o'work."

Ruby was standing in the doorway and looking about her incredulously.

"I kent fine you was up tae somethin', but I never dreamed . . ."

"What'll we plant, Ruby?"

"Tatties," she said instantly. "Aye, and some carrots and onions and peas and beans. Ma certes, but it'll be like the old days . . .yon stuff Miss Scott brings from the greengrocer's in Perth is just rubbish . . . rubbish just. Oh, my! oh, my!"

Together they planned and planted under the warm April sky, day after day of sunshine and blue skies.

"We'll pay for this, you mark my words," prophesied Ruby, bent double over onion sets. "May month will be as cold as last week's porridge."

It was the fruit bushes which lit the train. Ruby examined them and shook her head.

"They're done, Master John. Done, every last one of them, done, and past praying for. There's to be a few berries, but few and far between. Never heed, we'll dae fine wi'oot berries."

John mulled it over and that night at dinner he broached the subject of new bushes.

". . . the old ones have been let go too far," he explained. "If we could get half a dozen of each and put them in this . . ."

"Just what are you talking about, boy?" asked his grandmother impatiently.

"Raspberries and currants and gooseberries," he said, "for the kitchen garden . . ."

His voice squeaked and rasped and he swallowed and fell silent.

"Johnnie-boy's been doing simply wonders in the kitchen garden," said Aunty Nell, "you ought to see what he's been . . ."

"The kitchen garden? You've been grubbing in the garden?"

"He's done such a . . ."

"It does explain the state of your nails, I suppose."

"Lots of seeds planted," Aunty Nell burbled on, "and all those potatoes . . ."

Grandmother's lips thinned.

"Very laudable, no doubt, but wasted work."

She rose and made her way to the door.

"Why, Grandmother?"

"We are leaving here in June," she said without looking at him. "Inchbeg is sold."

John could not take in the words for a minute: he stared after his Grandmother's neat rotund figure. Aunty Nell hovered around him, her eyes worried and pleading like a spaniel's and mouthing things he didn't quite hear.

". . . mustn't take it too hard, Johnnie-boy. It had to come, you know . . . we couldn't go on as we were . . . such a huge

259

place you know and everything costs so much . . . and now there are fewer and fewer people using gas . . . oh, dear . . . oh, dear!"

"Nell!" Grandmother called out and Aunty Nell shambled indecisively out of the room to pour the coffee, looking back at John with her eyes wet and worried.

"Grand! Is it true?" John demanded.

His grandfather nodded.

"When do we go?"

"They want possession by June."

"Who do?"

"A girl's boarding school. St. Biddulph's."

Grandfather poured out his glass of port and instead of drinking it, pushed it over to John.

"Drink that," he said gently.

John obeyed, not realising till later the step he had taken on the way to becoming an adult. He barely noticed the strange taste.

"Where will we go?"

"To Glasgow. She has bought a house in Kelvin Drive."

John heard the word Glasgow and he saw vividly the alley where Jinty sat at her closemouth, the dirty defaced stonework, the dingy, flaking paint, the cobbles and the grey, dirty pavements, broken and cracked, and above a slip of smoky sky between the high houses, papers blowing in the gutters . . . that was what Glasgow was like.

"Your Grandmother thought we could send you to the Academy there, then to the University if you wanted."

The horse stood in an alley too, heavy and patient and resigned, grass and trees forgotten; John could almost feel its nose under his fingers. He swallowed a great mouthful of port and felt it burn its way into his belly.

"Grand? Do you want to go to Glasgow?"

Grand did not answer at once and sat very upright and still, his pale eyes staring at the red wine in the decanter.

"Grand . . ."

"Time I went home, I think," said the old man, very quietly, and his fingers were moving on the cloth as if he was picking out chords on a keyboard.

"Will we be taking the piano? Will there be room?"

"There's always a piano," Grand said vaguely, "even at sea. But nowadays no one wants to listen."

John unsatisfied but unwilling to press sipped at the wine and the question which festered in him rose to his mouth like a bubble of gas.

"Grand, Aunty Nell isn't my mother, is she?"

He found himself for almost the first time in his life the object of his grandfather's concentrated attention.

"No," Grand declared and there was nothing vague about that. "How in the world did you come by the notion that she might be? Your mother was my daughter. Surely that was made clear to you from the start?"

John wriggled.

"Yes . . . I suppose so. It's just the way Aunty Nell goes on . . . hugging and stuff like that . . . as if I was hers."

"Well," Grand looked exasperated, "I expect she means well . . . but she is not your mother."

"Then who is she?"

"She is no relation to you at all. She was a friend . . ." Grand hesitated and fumbled over the word, "a colleague of your mother's. She was here when you were born. Afterwards . . . she stayed on. She had no one left of her own and your grandmother thought she could be useful here . . . helpful. We were neither of us very young. It was a daunting thing . . . a new baby."

He drew a quavering breath and John saw incredulously that Grand was really angry: never in all his life had he seen Grand angry.

"I cannot conceive," said the old man, "how you could be given such an idea."

Long-nourished resentments bubbled up irresistibly, released by port.

"Because no one ever tells me anything!" John blurted out. "I've no one I can ask. Grandmother scolds and sends me away if I ask her anything about . . . things. She says I will know when I'm older. I gave up asking her. Aunty Nell just hushes and gets weepy and hugs me if I don't dodge. And Ruby says it isn't her place. And you don't listen," he ended shrilly, his voice cracking, "you never do, you know you never do!"

Grand looked stricken and John pressed his advantage.

"No one talks about my mother ever . . . there aren't any pictures even. Plenty of everyone else but not one of her. I don't even know what she looked like. Why won't people talk about her? Did she do something awful?"

"No! Indeed, she did nothing of the kind!"

Grand's face was flushed and his eyes bright with indignation.

"Then why won't they tell me about her? Is it because she wasn't married to my father?"

Grand's colour faded. He passed his hand over his mouth and sighed.

"Sometimes people want to forget painful things. They push them from their minds. Your grandmother felt . . . what happened . . . very much . . . very much."

"What did happen?" John demanded. "Who was my father? Is he dead too?"

"We don't know," Grand said simply. "We never knew. Anna never told us his name."

"Not even you?"

The thin mouth trembled and tightened.

"I wasn't here. I was in London. I was too old to serve properly but they found me something . . . They didn't tell me that Anna was to have a child. Caroline just said she had been sent home from France. Anna didn't write. I got a telegram to say you had been born and Anna was ill, terribly ill. I came at once but she was dying. She couldn't speak . . . she didn't know me. I couldn't even say goodbye to her," Grand paused, staring unseeing into the glass. "It was a terrible time, John, and your grandmother was dreadfully grieved, not just by Anna's death, but because she had been so . . . so . . . unhappy. That's why she won't speak of her. I think about her a great deal. My dear, plain little girl. She was plain, you know, not like all the rest of the girls, and she felt it. We were good friends once. When she went away I missed her sorely."

"Why did she go away?"

"She wanted to train as a nurse."

"A nurse!" exclaimed John. "No one ever mentioned that."

"She and Nell trained together in Glasgow. When war came your mother went to France with the Q.A.s."

"Aunty Nell too?" asked John incredulously.

"No. Nell stayed here with your grandmother and they turned the place into a convalescent home for officers. Your mother was in France for three years. In 1917 she fell ill and they sent her home. She was ill because of you."

"So she must have met my father in France. Do you think he was a soldier?"

"More than likely. But we never did know."

They looked at one another across the shining table.

"Well," John said. "I just wanted to *know*. When you don't know, you think awful things sometimes. I think it's something to be proud of that she was in France all that time. Not something to not talk about and hide from a person."

"Be proud," said Grand. "I have always been proud."

"Why doesn't it say about her on the tablet in the Kirk? Her name ought to be there with all the others."

"Your grandmother . . . she didn't want it. She never mentioned her name after the funeral. That same day everything of hers was taken away and put out of sight. But I had no idea she had not told you. You had a right to know. I blame myself."

"I didn't think about it very much," John admitted. "Not till I went to school and they called me a bastard. I started to wonder then. But now I'll tell them a thing or two. Their mothers weren't in France at the war, I'll bet!"

Unexpectedly Grand's face, which had stiffened with dismay, relaxed into laughter.

"We've more in common than you might think, grandson John. From now on you and I will have a glass of port after dinner and we will talk about your mother."

In the morning John remembered that conversation before the knowledge that Inchbeg was sold settled upon him like a grey cloud. Unable to face his garden knowing that he wouldn't be able to see it in full bearing, he begged a lunch from Ruby.

"Where are ye aff tae?"

"Up the hill."

"Then mind that Inchbeg woods is let. There's a wheen folk got together frae Perth for the shooting. If you disturb the birds the keeper'll no be best pleased."

"I've a place I want to see. I won't be able to after . . . after . . ."

He felt his voice quaver.

"Ah well," Ruby said, "the Botanic Gardens and Kelvinside Park'll no be the same, so they'll no."

Inchbeg woods climbed high above the Carse, thick and ill-cared for, with fallen trees everywhere overgrown with bramble. The surviving trees were furred and distorted with ivy. The path was narrow and often disappeared under greenery but John knew it too well to lose it. Just under the brow of the hill the trees petered out and gave way to heath and moorland. John came out into the sunshine and turned north. There was a maze of sheep paths among the heather clumps and a scatter of wooden hivestands. A number of smallholders brought their bees up in the late summer to work the heather bloom. John followed the ridge until he found a tiny burn, no wider than a man's arm. It wound its way down the dip slope of the hill until it had carved out a miniature glen and began to jump and chuckle around the rocks. A stunted rowan leaned across the water and at this point John struck up the side of the glen towards a group of huge glacial boulders, each the size of a house which had lain there since the glaciers melted. Behind them, he knew, there was a crack in the hillside and this led into a cave. He paused beside the boulders, pulled out the candle-end which Ruby had found for him and lit it in the shelter of the cavemouth.

The cave was not so well-known as Wallace's cave which was further to the west near Kinnoul but some legends said that it had been the home of a notorious bandit during the seventeenth century. He had been remarkable for having had three wives all at the same time, innumerable children, and having practised cannibalism. From time to time refugees had found shelter there, Catholics from the Reformation, Jacobites from the Hanoverian redcoats. In 1931 it sheltered nobody but the occasional sheep. As far as John knew he was the only person who had rediscovered it. He crept in, bent double and then straightened and held up the candle to look about him. To his amazement the place showed signs of occupation. There was a wooden box with a candle in a jam-jar standing on top beside a tin plate and a battered spoon. In the middle of the

264

floor were the remains of a fire with pale smoke wisping up into the dark above. In the far corner was a shapeless bundle which might be bedding.

It might have been the wavering of the candle flame but it seemed to John that the bedding moved. John, petrified, his mind chasing after cannibals, stood and stared. There could be no doubt. The bedding heaved and a tousled head appeared, glowering sleepily.

"Who the hell?" demanded a voice.

Later, they ate rabbit stew and the sandwiches and scones which John had brought. John ate mostly stew and Hughie ate mostly sandwiches and scones.

"Rabbit's meat o' a sort but a body kin get fair fed up o't," Hughie said. "I don't get bread that much. I make a sort o' flat scone on yon stone."

"I could bring you a loaf. I'll get one from Dave the Baker," John promised.

Hughie talked while they ate, a steady monotonous flow which suggested that it was some time since he had had anybody to talk to.

". . . there wis nae work," he mused, "no the sniff o' a job. I'd been on the Burroo near enough two year. The wife left. Went hame tae her mither an' took the wean . . . aye. Ye cannae blame her, the lass. Nae money, nae fun, an' me like a blue-ersed fly aboot the doors a' day gettin' atween her fingers. Aye. Puir lass."

He ate another sandwich.

"Ye kin manage on the dole money, jist . . . but it isnae much fun. Her feyther's a polis . . . no much money but reg'lar and no likely tae be laid aff. I got real fed up and drank the rent four week running and the landlord pit us oot. We went tae Cambuslang tae her folk and her feyther chucked *me* oot. Mind, I kin see why. Aye. I dossed a few days in the lobbies nearaboot but I couldnae bide the dirt, aye, an' the cauld. Waur nor France it were for naebody's yer freend when yer dossin' an' ye've nae money. In France a'body was freends for ye had tae be."

"My mother was in France," John told him, rejoicing in being able to say it. "She was a nurse. She's dead though."

"Then she'll hae her reward, sure's death. I ken fine. I was hit twice. Aye."

He felt reminiscently around his hip.

"Efter the first time they made me up tae sergeant. There wasnae naebody left much efter the push. Twice wounded I was, and a sergeant afore I was one and twenty. Aye. They gave me a wee tin medal for my pains efter, but folk forget quick. There's better men wi' mair medals waur aff nor me. Aye. Times is hard, laddie. Awfy hard."

"Why did you come here?"

"My Grandda came from Deanston, upbye. He was foreman at the Mill. I came here a summer once. Och, it was a grand summer, I used tae think long for it whiles I was in France. We went fishin' an' berrypickin' an' that. Aye a grand summer. I thought on it one awfy bad morning in Finnieston and I says tae masel', I'll awa' tae the Carse. It cannae be waur nor Finnieston and ye never know there micht be work. So I walked oot the Great Western Road that very day. Three weeks it took walkin'. Aye. And ma feets wis like raw beef for ma buits was done. I says tae masel' it canna be waur nor the trenches and there'll be nae damn Jerries shootin' at me. Folk gied me a bite whiles an' the Sally Anne found me buits. Aye."

"I didn't think that anyone knew about this cave but me."

Hughie smiled.

"I found it yon grand summer. I'd be your age mebbe. Great, isn't it? Just great. Dry as a bone."

He stretched his arms up above his head to where the smoke hung in drifts of blue.

"There's rabbits," he said, "and neeps in the parks and whiles I get a wee job and buy flour and the like, I kin keep livin' alive. Just aboot, just aboot, aye."

"Winter will come, though," John said.

"I never died a winter yet, no even in France. Man, yon was wicked. Never right warm, never right dry . . . I'm fine and snug here. It would have seemed like heaven in France. Aye."

John wandered round the cave and found it was as neat and orderly as the garden shed at Inchbeg. He said so.

"Aye, I'm snug. Warm and dry. Better than any damned dug-out. Nae mud and nae stink and nae bloody whizz-bangs. Nae corpses neither. Aye."

John was conscious of a vast envy.

"You're lucky," he muttered. "I'd like to live in a cave up here. I've got to go and stay in Glasgow. There's a girls' school coming to be in our house."

"What'll ye dae in Glasgow, laddie?"

"I'm not clever enough to be anything like a doctor or a lawyer. I expect I'll have to go into an office."

"And you don't like that?"

"No!"

"What d'ye want tae dae?"

John hung his head and glowered.

"I dunno," he mumbled, "but not towns and offices and papers and stuff and stuck inside all day."

"Aye, aye," Hughie observed. "A job's a job, mind, and folks has got tae eat."

"You manage."

"For masel'. Aye. But I cannae keep my family an' yon's a blight on a man," Hughie remarked. "I keep hopin' things'll look up."

"I don't want to spend all my life doing something I don't like. It seems such a waste."

"You listen tae me, laddie . . . there's thousands and thousands dae just that. Folks has aye had tae dae't."

"Well, it isn't right," John said obstinately.

"Mebbe no, but folks is mostly in the same barra. There isnae one in a hunder' kens whit he'd dae, gi'en the chance. A' they're efter's tae be rich. An' even if they wis, they'd no be happy, the feck o' them, no they . . ."

"What would you do if you could do anything, anything in the world?"

"I'd like tae work at my trade," Hughie said simply. "Just that. Aye. Mebbe a touch mair money in ma poke at the end o' the week but tae work at ma trade."

"What's that?"

"Chippie. Foreman chippie. I served my time at Stephen's."

John looked at the wooden chest against the cave wall. On top there lay a bag of tools.

"Aye, them's mine. I got up here wi' naethin' but a shirt in my pocket and my tools. I found that wood upbye. There was a wee tumbledoon sheddie but some planks of it good yet. Ye need a wee boxie for yer bits and bobs here for there's rats whiles and mice an' that. I'll make a bed when I kin lay ma hands on some mair wood."

John admired the box.

"It's no bad, but."

"Can I come again?" John asked.

"Come and welcome. I like a bit o' company."

"I'll bring some bread."

"I'll be glad o't."

"Anything else I could bring?"

"No, no. A bit bread would be just fine," Hughie said and picked up the tin which had once held rabbit stew. "It's grand to have water so handy. I'll walk you down a piece."

In daylight, Hughie was a brawny figure, not tall but solidly built. His clothes were tattered and his flat cap worn to the extinction of the pattern. He went lightly down the path barefoot.

"I save the buits they gave me at the Sally Anne," he explained. "I just put them on tae gang doon the road. My shirt an' a' . . ."

He opened his coat and revealed a bare torso and hanging round his neck a knife in a sheath. At the stream he bent down and scoured the tin with sand and a handful of grass; John squatted beside him and watched, unwilling to go down again to Inchbeg. He longed to be able to stay up here beside Hughie. Even to stay up here by himself.

"Laddie," Hughie said suddenly, looking up from the tin, "you'll not tell on me?"

"No . . . not if you don't want . . . of course not . . ."

"They'd likely turn me oot," Hughie explained. "No for any harm I'm daein'. And they kin spare a rabbit or so . . . even a bird whiles . . ." he looked up and winked, "an' never notice. I'd no take frae folk who'd feel the want . . ."

"My grandmother says there are far too many rabbits."

". . . but folk dinnae like whit doesnae fit in wi' their notions and thae days folk doesnae live in caves. They'd pit me oot for sure."

"I won't say."

"There was a time when folks a' lived in caves," Hughie said. "They learned me that at the schule. Whiles I think aboot

268

a body like me a' those years ago, makin' dae, jist like me, wi'
nae lucifers an' nae tools . . . naethin' but stanes and the like.
I talk tae him whiles. He's company. An' compared wi' him,
I'm the lucky one."

John looked back up from the edge of the wood and Hughie
was still there, standing watching him. It would have been
hard to pick him out if he hadn't known just where he was, so
well did his worn and ancient clothes blend in with the heather
and the rocks and the hay-dry tussocks of coarse moor-grass.
He seemed like part of the countryside.

26

When John got back to Inchbeg there was a fuss of people talking in corners and hushing each other when he appeared. Aunty Nell was wearing her church hat and the tweed suit with the fur collar and inching the Humber jerkily out of the stable gate. She drove away with the sound of tortured gears and soft tyres spurting the sparse gravel aside. Ruby was trotting up the back stairs with an armful of blankets and sheets when John found her.

"A friend of your grandpa's," she told him. "A foreigner, puir soul. That Miss Scott's away to get him from the station. And that's all I ken, Master John, so there's nae use prig-priggin' at me . . ."

Grandmother was in the drawing room, sitting abstractedly crocheting among the faded chintzes. She frowned at him when he came in and told him to run along and find something to do and, as an afterthought, to ask Ruby to give him his tea in the nurs . . . schoolroom. Ruby's lips thinned at the message and she laid him a place on the corner of the scrubbed kitchen table.

"Ye'll dae fine there, Master John, and never mind three flights of stairs and a visitor and two trays a'ready . . ."

Grand was in the music room standing in front of the huge piano and frowning at the keyboard. The second of Ruby's trays cooled unheeded on the table. John looked at him and understood for the first time that Grand was an old man. He came in like a mouse, perched on the table and eyed the buttered scones.

"Aren't you hungry, Grand?"

"No, John. You eat them."

"I'll pour your tea, shall I?"

He put the cup, slopped in the saucer, beside the music rack of the piano and Grand removed it automatically.

"Nothing on a piano but music," he said and carried the cup

over to the wide window seat. John joined him with the plate
of scones.

"What's all the fuss, Grand?"

The old man didn't answer.

"Who's coming to stay?"

Grand put the cup down very carefully.

"My friend's son," he said. "Daniel Dominic Heilbron."

John was disquieted by the note in his voice. Grand fell silent
again, staring at the garden.

"Why is he coming?" John asked, as much to hear the sound
of his own voice as to find out.

"Because he cannot live in his own country any longer."

"Why not?"

"He is a Jew."

The scene behind the stables jumped suddenly into John's
memory. Davidson's saturnine face looked scornfully at the
gang as he asked, 'Have you heard what the Nazis do to the
Jews?'

"He told me that my friend was dead."

Grand swallowed convulsively, the wrinkled throat moving
under the old-fashioned high collars he still wore.

"I can't believe he's dead," Grand went on. "He was so
full of vitality that he could make other people live as well,
he shocked them like electricity so that they understood
they were alive and must make the most of something so
precious . . ."

'They beat them up . . .' Geogehan had said cheerfully.

"They dragged him from his house and beat him and kicked
him and trampled him . . . I wonder, did they trample on his
hands, my God those black boots . . . he had such hands. Oh,
God . . . help me to bear it . . ."

John stared. Grand had forgotten he was there. It was an
eerie uncomfortable sensation as if he was witnessing something which was none of his business.

"Why didn't he come to me? I wrote as soon as I heard what
was happening . . . and there were others who would have
taken him in gladly. He wouldn't leave Vienna. 'I will die
where I have worked,' he wrote, 'and I will hope that death
will come for me before the Nazis . . .' Oh, God above, death
might have left him a little dignity!"

The tears were running down his cheeks as he stared at the spring colours in the garden below.

"I've never known hatred," he said, so quietly that John had to strain to hear the words. "Never, never before. Grief, yes. When Anna died I thought I should wither with grief. But now, if I could raise this hand . . ."

He lifted his left hand, bony, freckled with age and tremulous.

". . . and know as I did it that his killers would die in torment . . . then I would. I would."

The hand dropped to his lap as if it did not belong to him.

"For Anna I could play . . . music always eased grief for me. I remember when my mother died. And there was the time when Caroline was ill and I thought I should lose her and the baby died. Then I could play or hear the music in my head and it was like a dressing on a wound. But not now . . . I feel as if I will never play again. I am eaten up with hatred . . . eaten hollow. There is no music left."

His voice faded away and John felt giddy and insignificant as if he was looking over a precipice into an abyss . . . He put the half-eaten scone back on the plate: there was a picture in his mind of Grand lying on a pavement being kicked and trampled by Brownshirts whose faces were all Luckenham's, glistening and greedy.

"They won't come here?" he asked in an uncertain bass.

Grand's attention returned to him.

"How old are you, boy?"

"Thirteen."

"Five years," Grand mused. "Heaven knows what will happen in five years . . ."

John sighed. Grand never quite answered a question. It was as if he responded to another one which he thought you might ask . . . or should ask. If you didn't know the question, he thought in bewilderment, you couldn't make much of the answer.

The car came into view at that moment and came to a jerky halt at the front door. A man stepped out. He was quite old, John thought in disappointment. 'The son of my friend' had sounded young. He was tall and thin and his hair was grey, sweeping back from his forehead in a great mane which touched his collar. 'Grandmother will think he should have a haircut,' John thought. His clothes were shabby but somehow grandiloquent, a fur-collared overcoat and underneath it a velvet jacket, braided and frogged. He stared about him at the peaceful spring-green countryside and then pulled out a huge bandana handkerchief and wiped his eyes and blew his nose. Aunty Nell climbed gracelessly from the driver's seat and groped for something on the back seat.

"Grand . . . he's here . . ."

Grand was looking down on the weedy gravel sweep but John couldn't be sure that he was actually seeing what was in front of him.

"He's brought two violins. That's all the luggage there seems to be . . ."

That was all the luggage there was. Dan Heilbron had fled from Vienna, leaving everything he possessed except his father's instruments. John, sent to bed after dinner, left the room reluctantly and lay awake remembering the stranger's stories; his adventures as he crossed Europe, the attempts made to recapture him and the shifts he had been put to. He had begun to explain why it was that the Nazis were so anxious he shouldn't escape them when Aunty Nell had coughed theatrically.

"Pas devant l'enfant, je pense," she had said. "Les petites cruches ont des oreilles longues . . ."

John snorted scornfully. If he couldn't understand that after three years of French . . . and Mamselle would find Aunty Nell's accent, 'affreux, affreux . . .' In any event, who tattled most, himself or Aunty Nell. It was obvious that Dan was a scientist of some kind. Perhaps he had escaped with the secret plans of something. What? Something the Nazis wanted badly. A new weapon, perhaps, a new gas . . . His mind dwelled momentarily on Hughie and he could see him as he must have been in the war, knee-deep in mud and filth, 'never right dry, never right warm', his groundsheet about his shoulders and his tin hat a little askew on his head, waiting in the dark for this new 'awfulness'. Tomorrow, he thought sleepily, he would go up to the cave again and take Hughie some bread . . . and maybe a scone or two. Suddenly, he wasn't sleepy any more.

Ruby had said in the kitchen, and he had taken it in only with part of his mind, that for two pins she would not be coming to Glasgow. She had this habit of grumbling aloud and he didn't always listen very carefully. She had said that this school would need plenty folk both inside and out and they'd not expect one body to see to the whole place and no more help than a pair of gormless blatherskites for two hours in a morning. Inside and out. Perhaps there might be a place for Hughie? He thought of the janitor at Springwood with his creaking artificial foot and the row of medal ribbons on his navy-blue coat. He mended this and mended that and made the other and grumbled at the mess the boys made. Hughie could do anything that Grumbleguts did, probably more because he wasn't lame. But perhaps girls' schools had lady janitors? If Hughie found a job here in Inchbeg the cave would be empty. He lay awake, making plans, staring up into the darkness. He could live there. No one would ever know and he needn't go to live in Glasgow. Tomorrow he would go up into the attic and find a trunk or a box or something to keep stuff in. Hughie said you needed something like that. He daydreamed the details of his life in the cave until they were as real to him as the furnishings of the room hidden by the darkness. He would make a garden and grow vegetables, he would take a swarm as Mr. Tait had shown him and keep bees; he might be able to find an orphan lamb and rear that . . . sheep could be milked and he would have cheese. If he took an egg or two from the kitchen, could he hatch out some chickens? He was planning in very confused detail the contrivance in which he would brood the eggs when he fell asleep and dreamed hideously of Luckenham in a brown shirt and black boots trampling on Grand's hands. He woke sweating and sick.

Next day Hughie welcomed him and exclaimed with pleasure over the loaf, all hot and fragrant, which John had bought from Dave Adamson's van. The suggestion that he should try for a post as handyman-gardener-janitor to St. Biddulph's was absorbed thoughtfully. John waited for a reaction and watched Hughie's face. It wasn't that he thought slowly, more that he thought very carefully and thoroughly.

"There's a sort of cottage place over the old stables," John explained. "When we had horses the coachman lived there. It's been empty since old Mrs. Arthur died. I thought your wife might like it. It used to look pretty, I remember. Grand made one of the hay lofts into a bathroom . . ."

"A bathroom. My, that's posh. A schule, eh?"

"St. Biddulph's School for Girls."

"If any schulemarm saw me in these duds she'd rin a mile. I look a richt tink thae days."

However, it was clear that he found the suggestion appealing.

"They'd mebbe need a wifie to clean?" he mused, "or to work in the kitchen? My, but it would suit us fine, just fine . . . and a schule doonbye for the laddie. But . . . these duds is jist no on. And the schulemarm, she'll likely hae a mannie in her ee. Aye."

John discounted all these things. In his mind the job was there and Hughie was doing it and after June he would have vacant possession of the cave. He came back down through the woods dreaming. When he reached the house Aunty Nell pounced on him and demanded what he was thinking about? Didn't he realise that in three days the term would start and nothing had been done about his 'things'! Next day they must go to Perth and do some shopping and this time he would please not give away half his wardrobe. John listened with half an ear and decided that he would have to find his trunk quickly. During the summer term Inchbeg would be cleared out and the furniture sold or packed up to go to Kelvin Drive. All the things in the attic would be sorted and probably burned. He went into lunch knowing what he must do.

At lunch there was an 'atmosphere'. Grandmother had a tight-mouthed look and spoke no more than she had need. Grand looked weary and grey and played with his food, chasing it round and round his plate. Dan ate in silence and asked permission to leave the table before the pudding was served. He had a letter to write, he said. While he was there Aunty Nell chatted brightly and incoherently: when he had gone she tried to continue, caught Grandmother's pale blue glance and faltered into silence.

"What happens if he is still here when we leave for

Glasgow?" Grandmother demanded suddenly as if she were carrying on with an argument.

"He will go with us," said Grand. "There is plenty of room."

"And if I don't want him to come?"

"Then I am sorry, but as long as he needs a home he will have one here or in Glasgow. He is Adam's son. And Adam is dead."

"He is old enough to make a home of his own."

"Doubtless, when he is able to he will. Meanwhile, for as long as he needs it, *this* is his home."

"You might have consulted me before you issued an open-ended invitation," Grandmother said angrily. "This is not a convenient time to have a house guest."

Aunty Nell coughed emphatically and looked theatrically at John but neither of them took any notice of her. Grand got up shakily and laid his napkin on the table. He looked down at Grandmother unsmilingly.

"I rarely insist, Caroline, as you know. But this time I will listen to no more arguments."

He left the room walking haltingly and there was a silence. John scraped his plate and crammed the last scraps of pudding into his mouth, chewed and swallowed hastily.

"Grandmother?"

She looked at him coldly.

"Kindly wipe your mouth . . . and your hands."

He obeyed.

"It'll be school on Thursday."

"I am aware of it."

"You said about going to Glasgow. Can I pack up some of my books and stuff?"

"Doubtless you *can*, whether you *may* is quite another matter. Most of the rubbish in your room will go on the tip."

"It isn't rubbish . . ."

"Don't argue, boy, it is very tiresome. If you promise not to take anything outworn or outgrown it might be useful if you were to pack up some of the contents of your room before you leave."

"I'll need a box or a trunk."

"There are plenty in the attic. There's the rubbish of years up there," she said impatiently.

"Four hundred years," said Grand from the door. "The family built the house in 1526. Miss Scott, if you are going to the village today, I would be obliged if you would take me with you."

"Why?" asked Grandmother sharply.

"Why not?" returned Grand and shut the door softly behind him. Grandmother's mouth twisted as it did when she was upset.

"Can I go and look?" John asked.

"What? Oh, yes . . . I suppose you *may*. If you're finished, you *may* get down."

The attic was an adventure in itself: it ran the length of the house and was lit only by a couple of skylights. When John was very small it was forbidden ground for part of it had been made into cramped box-like bedrooms where generations of servants had sweltered and shivered under the slates and another part was unfloored. It was the part above the gallery which was used as a store. It was entered by a low door which always made John think of Alice in Wonderland and, as Grand had said, the discards of four centuries were lying there: buckled shoes and swords, clothes and cooking pots, boxes and baskets and trunks. There was furniture, broken-legged or broken-backed, battered toys and nursery paraphernalia. Cobwebs hung thick from the rafters and buckets studded the floor. As Ruby had said, the roof was in a parlous state, with daylight leaking between the huge stone slabs which served for slates on the main section of the roof.

John straightened up in front of the door and blinked while his eyes adjusted themselves to the dim light. He had a torch but the battery was almost finished and he was reserving the light for when it was needed. He picked his way along the cluttered floor and saw what he wanted almost at once. It was a small tin trunk, japanned black with a rusty padlock fast in the hasps. The front was grey and webbed and dusty and on top of it were piled a number of flat mattress-like objects about two feet square. Any serviceman would have known them for 'biscuits' but they puzzled John. When he pushed at them they released a harsh, musty smell and slid back obligingly into the mysterious half-lighted clutter behind. The trunk lid was dust-less, shining black with white letters painted on it. A. SMITH, they proclaimed. There was a label, too, very neatly written, 'Perth Station. To be collected.'

John rattled at the padlock, wondering if the key was in what had been the butler's pantry where there was a drawer full of keys, the uses of which were mostly forgotten. To his astonishment it came off in his hand. A shower of powdery rust fell out of the keyhole and lay in the palm of his hand. He brushed it off and slowly lifted the lid.

The trunk was full of clothes. A smell of camphor and lavender and disinfectant engulfed him. He laid back the neatly folded blouses and dresses. A. Smith had been a woman. Not far away was a laundry basket with a broken handle and a disintegrating rim. John began to remove the clothes and lay them neatly in that. Underneath the top layers were blue cotton dresses and large white aprons. A. Smith, he decided, must have been a maid at Inchbeg. He wondered why she had gone away and left her clothes. Under the aprons were shoes, very small and neat, and wrapped in newspaper. There were a dozen or more pairs of black cotton stockings, rolled up into packets, the same size and shape as the buns on Adamson's van. They went into the basket too.

The books which lay in the bottom of the trunk made him change his mind. A. Smith had not been a maid. Ruby read the *Sunday Post* and the *People's Friend* and little storybooks with pictures on the cover which she stuffed under the cushions of the kitchen chair when the Minister came to call. A. Smith had read Milton's *Collected Works* and a massive tome entitled, *An Introduction to the Anatomy of the Human Body* by a man called Gray. Lifting it out John wondered what a full book on anatomy would have been like. Mr. Gray weighed nearly five pounds. There were nursing manuals of all kinds, booklets entitled *Post-operative Care* and *Ward Management*. A. Smith was evidently a nurse . . . a small leather case containing a gold medal suggested that she had been a very good nurse. An idea, a wild exultant idea, crept into John's mind like the light between the tiles and he sorted through the rest of the contents with a rising excitement. There was a battered shoebox, with Bayne and Duckett on the lid, tied up with string and he undid this carefully, picking at the knots. Inside were old letters tied together, not many of these: some brooches and bracelets in a wash-leather bag and at the very bottom a drift of photographs. The topmost one was of Grand sitting at his piano.

Convinced his idea must be right, John put the shoebox back into the trunk together with the books, and carried the trunk down to his room. There he spread the photographs out on the bed. There were two kinds: formal studio portraits, mounted in stiff cardboard which could have been displayed on a table or a shelf and a number of more informal 'snaps' blurred and faded and brown. The framed ones were of Grand, much younger and happier-looking, Grandmother, in the tightfitting formal clothes she still preferred, looking into the camera with an air of disapproving reluctance and a group outside a low rambling building, posed carefully and stiffly. John recognised it at once. Grand had the same one in the music room, much enlarged; it was of their relatives in New Zealand and the place was called Bennachie. There was one more, a blurred enlargement of a young man's head. He was laughing and his hair was blowing over his face but it was too unfocussed to be recognisable. This was framed in a tiny silver frame and was right at the bottom of the shoebox, the frame tarnished and the chain from which it hung almost black. John turned his attention to the 'snaps'. These were almost all of nurses: nurses in groups, in pairs and individuals. They smiled out uninformatively from under their high-piled hair and frilled caps. In one of them John saw suddenly a young Aunty Nell, tall and slim then, not clumsy and bony and uncertain. In another, there she was again squinting into the sun and beside her a small dumpy figure with short straight hair and a round face on which a pair of spectacles sat a little askew, small spectacles framed in silver. John had already found such a pair in the shoebox, the frame tarnished black and one lens cracked right across. The small dumpy figure was only to be seen in one other group, a bevy of cloaked and white-capped girls; there she was holding an open box with a medal in it and looking uncomfortably into the middle distance.

John bundled his finds back into their box and tore downstairs to the music room. Vaguely, he had heard the Humber returning about ten minutes earlier. Grand was still in his outdoor things. A bottle of medicine stood on the table, 'Horniman's Stomach Remedy' it said on the label. He had poured out a measure of the viscous pink liquid and was about to drink it when John dashed in with the box.

"Grand . . . it's my mother . . . I'm sure of it. In the attic. I found this trunk with clothes and stuff, a sort of little tin one . . . black . . . and the padlock was rusty . . ."

Grand stared and put the medicine glass down beside the bottle.

"Look! There are photos . . . one of you and one of Grandmother and the same one as that . . ."

He pointed at the photograph on the wall beside the fireplace.

"Bennachie!" said Grand and John felt his attention on him like a ray of sunlight through a shutter. "Yes, she would have had that one. Let me see!"

He leafed through them all while John watched him eagerly. The last things to come out of the box were the spectacles which Grand folded together with a tremulous hand and the little tarnished silver locket.

"Where did you say you found these?"

"In a black tin trunk in the attic."

"But we could never find the key . . ."

"The padlock was rusty. It just fell off."

"The Infirmary sent it here when she was ill. We put it aside because there was no key and Nell said it would be just clothes and books. What else is there?"

"Lots of books, nursing books and poetry and stuff. And some huge great note-books all filled up with writing. It's terribly hard to read . . . I'll fetch them!"

He ran out of the room almost cannoning into Dan who was coming in with a newspaper.

"You are in a great hurry, Jüngling."

"I've found something awfully exciting . . . I'm sorry."

He fled the stairs three at a time. When he came back more sedately with his arms full of books, Dan was examining the bottle of medicine.

". . . might as well be chalk and water and peppermint

drink," he was saying. "Have you the doctor seen, for such a pain?"

"No. It's just indigestion. No need to worry anyone."

"I must worry. I am physician . . . or I was once. I will examine you and soon . . ."

Alerted by Grand's look he broke off but John had heard.

"Is Grand ill?"

His voice scraped and squeaked but he didn't care.

"I have a little indigestion," Grand said, "but don't tell anyone or Ruby will pack her bags and leave us and that would be terrible."

"But Herr Dan said . . ."

"But I a doktor am and have no patients," said Dan and rolled his eyes in comic despair. "To keep my hand in I must on my friends make practice. Any excuse I will use. Are you well, Jüngling?"

He peered at John with exaggerated concern.

"You have not the *trombicula autumnalis*? A little touch of *medulla oblongata*? No? Coreopsis of the *umbellata*?"

John giggled uncertainly and put his load on the window seat.

"What a pity . . . never mind, I shall practise upon your grandfather who undoubtedly suffers from long-leafed streptocarpus . . ."

He broke off and lifted the picture in the little silver locket from the scatter of objects on the table. He frowned and peered at it in bewilderment.

"But here am I! I remember this. It was taken here, oh, many, many years ago. Long before the war. I had what? twenty-one years. Where found you this?"

"You?" Grand said hoarsely and took the locket. "But it *is* you . . ."

John's head spun and he stared at the man whose picture his mother had evidently treasured. Inevitably he wondered, 'is *he* my father?' and decided in an instant that he would like that.

"It was found among Anna's things," Grand said quietly. "She had a great regard for you."

To John's astonishment Dan's eyes filled with tears and he made a gesture as if he was asking for forgiveness.

"I knew . . . I knew well, aber wass kannst du . . . I told myself it was a schwarm . . . how do you say it . . . it would pass . . ."

"It did. In time."

"It must have done," Dan exclaimed and put an arm round John and hugged him. "For here is her son!"

Dan smelled of spice and tobacco and eau-de-cologne, a reassuring comfortable smell and John did not pull away as he would have done from most such gestures.

"And much as I would like to be," Dan went on, "I am not his father."

John knew a kind of sour disappointment. He pulled away and went to the table.

"I don't know who my father was," John said. "Nobody knows."

He thought he had come to terms with this curious circumstance and embodied in all his daydreams was the figure of his current hero who arrived, peered at him with incredulous joy and claimed him for his son. But he would have liked it if it had been Dan. He looked round at him and saw him stiffen.

"It cannot be true!" he exclaimed.

"It is quite true," Grand told him. "She died without telling anyone."

"I remember her," Dan said. "She was like a little round brown bird. She made me think of my sister Sari. She had a habit of silence, that I remember also. Like you, my friend."

"She was no talker," Grand agreed. "And John here keeps his own counsel."

"So!" Dan's attention turned upon John like a searchlight. "Sagst du mir, is it that you are silent because you have nothing to say or because like your grandfather you have much that happens in your mind?"

"Dunno," John mumbled and went scarlet. It was as if Dan could see into his mind to the picture of the cave, the growing things around it in the little glen and the sheep grazing nearby.

"And you are almost grown," Dan went on, "are you to be musician like your grandfather?"

"No," croaked John.

"He has a good ear," Grand said, "but we have found that he is no performer."

He smiled at John: Grand rarely smiled and at once John felt comforted and less inadequate.

"What then?" Dan demanded. "You have a rhyme with fruitstones, my father knew it. 'Tinker, Tailor, Soldier, Sailor . . .'"

John shook his head.

"And yet you may have to be soldier," said Dan. "In this world there is much evil . . . ah, well . . . you have time yet to decide."

"I like animals," John blurted out, "and growing things. I would like to have a farm."

If anyone had asked John when he got up that morning what he wanted to do or to be when he grew up he would not have been able to say. The dream of the cave was an escape from the threat of a life in Jinty's alley. It was as if the idea had grown in his mind like a seed under the ground. It was Dan and the intensity of his interest which had made him understand what he wanted. He looked as surprised as his grandfather at his sudden declaration and Dan, looking from one to the other, threw back his head and laughed uproariously.

"So it goes!" he chuckled, "so it goes! We have here one farmer. You did not know this?"

"No," John's voice squeaked. "I only just realised . . ."

Dan laughed again.

"It was so with me. Mine father, he taught me to play and to play well and we played much together but it was one day when he was discussing whether I should study the violin or the 'cello that I knew with certainty that much as I liked to make music it would not be enough for me. I should be Doktor. This I knew. And so I was. And so I am . . . or perhaps I will be no longer. Who can say?"

John did not hear much of what he was saying because he was looking at Grand and Grand was staring at him as if he had suddenly grown another head.

"Of course," he was muttering under his breath, "of course . . . I should have thought of it sooner. It's the best . . . the only possible . . ."

John suddenly wanted to turn the attention from himself.

"The books, Grand, don't you want to look at the books?"

283

he suggested, touching the old man's arm. "They're sort of diary things."

To his relief the two men turned away and began to examine the pile of shabby hard-backed notebooks. Grand picked up the topmost one.

"That one was at the very top of the trunk, Grand. The others were packed together at the bottom."

"I may?" asked Dan and picked up another. He leafed through it, nodding and pursing his lips approvingly. "It is a ward journal . . . so we do in Wien also. A private record of her cases and their treatment . . . it is useful, one learns much. She was a most careful nurse, your Anna."

Grand opened the shabbier, more battered volume which had been at the top of the trunk. A slip of paper fluttered out and John bent to pick it up.

"Why did my mother call herself Smith, Grand?"

"Because your Gran . . . because we didn't want her to nurse. We knew it was a hard life. But she ran away. She didn't come back for over a year."

Grand scanned the paper and frowned.

"Your eyes are younger than mine. Read it to me."

It was written in a smallish cramped hand, neatly spaced and pleasingly placed on the expanse of the paper. John cleared his throat and began to read aloud.

My dear Smithie,

News like yours travels very fast. It came with your belongings from France yesterday. Matron told me in a hushed whisper but I did *not* say I had heard from half a dozen people before she told me. She gave me the job of sorting things out. I disposed of the uniforms. I fancy you won't want them again. Apart from them there was only your box of photographs and some little bits and pieces so I put the bits and pieces in the box and put the box in your trunk. There were two books, your Milton and your diary. I never could understand what you saw in Milton. Opinionated old party in my estimation and not above playing on his blindness. Nell was in . . . now there is a female who would have pleased Milton. He would have thoroughly disapproved of you, Smithie. She said she would take anything I

284

thought you might want at once but I didn't think you ought to have Milton, such an apocryphal poet and much too depressing for someone in your condition. Nor did I think you would want her to have the diary. I always suspected Nell of reading everybody's postcards. So, I have locked them both in your trunk. Matron says it will be sent to your home as soon as possible.

Matron is being very tight-mouthed about your affair and obviously doesn't know whether to be shocked to the marrow or flabbergasted because it happened to you, of all people, the apple of her chill blue eye. In fact everyone is feeling a little like that. There were one or two whiffs of disapproval but Sister Theatre rose in her wrath and said that none of us had been in France and none of us had any right to judge and I felt like cheering. War changes even Sister Theatre.

Chin up, my lamb. It's bound to be a difficult time for you but you have a host of well-wishers here. We all wish you well and a safe delivery.

Your affectionate friend,
Alice Sloan.

PS I cannot find the key for your padlock anywhere but I expect you have a spare at home. I shall just click it to and hope for the best.

A. S.

John handed it back and Grand folded it carefully into its original creases.

"A pity she never read that," he commented. "Such a pleasant friendly letter. She had so few friends."

Dan was frowning.

"So that," he pointed at the notebook in Grand's hand, "must have been in France with her."

"She was sent home very ill," Grand mused. "A stretcher case. They called it nervous collapse caused by overwork. They didn't discover . . . about the baby until she had been ill for a week or two. When they did they sent her straight home."

"When was this?"

"In 1917. About a month after the end of Passchendaele."

They looked at one another and Grand turned to John.

"It'll take time to read this, boy," he said gently. "You shall have it, I promise, but I would like to read it by myself. Do you mind?"

John shook his head.

"Why don't you take Dan and show him around? It's spring and he's hardly been out of the house since he arrived."

27

Dan was a good companion for a walk. He watched birds and found insects and explained things: he appreciated John's preferences and made nothing of his complicated 'short cuts'. They found a fox's earth but did not catch sight of the occupants; they lay watching rabbits playing on the edge of the Inchbeg woods. Suddenly Dan drew in a deep breath and turned over to lie on his back and stare at the clouds scudding across the sky.

"Healing . . ." he declared, "the very air is healing."

The rabbits bolted for cover, white tails flashing.

"Have you any notion what is life under a shadow, Jüngling . . . a shadow of fear and hatred and violence?"

He pointed up at the sky.

"There will be rain before long. See that cloud swelling up from the west. Think what it would be if that cloud contained venom and when its shadow reached you you must die. You watch it and know nothing can disperse it or stop it. It spreads towards you always, always, always . . ."

He watched the cloud for a little.

"In this land the clouds bring only rain," he reflected, "and thank the good God for that grace. Over there . . ."

He pointed over to the east.

". . . men and women think of this country as Joshua and his people thought of the Promised Land, the land of milk and honey . . ."

Greenhalgh, McCaw, Geogehan and Luckenham popped into John's mind like characters in a Punch and Judy booth: he dressed them in brown shirts and jackboots and gave them weapons. They would create a cloud on anyone's horizon. He thought of Luckenham wielding a blackjack on some defenceless old man and shivered, not quite recalling his nightmare, but knowing that Dan's words had stirred something disquieting inside him.

"Why do some people like hurting people?" he asked.

"Because they know in their heart they are good for little and to be able to hurt another disguises that knowledge."

John chewed on that in silence for a moment.

"You mean they hit people because they know they're bad lots?"

"Not bad. Just not good. Just little people trying to feel big. This they will do. But there are some who are evil. They are perverted and to see others in pain it will give them pleasure."

Luckenham, thought John, thinking of that wet, red, smiling mouth. He smiled at the memory of his fist landing on that fat face. Luckenham's nose had been broken. His smile faded. Was he one of the evil people . . . the people who got pleasure . . .?

"Herr Heilbron," he began, "Doktor, I mean . . ."

"I am Dan. Call me that. No Herr, no Doktor. I am just a man running away."

"Dan . . . if a person hit a person who had been . . . well . . . baiting him, and he was in an awful wax and the other person's nose got broken and he felt glad and pleased about it does that mean that he is one of the . . ."

Dan bellowed with laughter.

"Was he bigger than you?"

"Yes, well . . . heavier anyway . . . and older . . ."

"Then, I don't believe you need worry," Dan told the sky above them. "To resist a bully is no sin. By me who runs away it is a virtue. Too much goes by default through cowardice . . . as I know."

There was a pause during which Dan seemed to find something hideously displeasing in the clouds.

"Dan?"

"Mmmm?"

"What you said about the Promised Land . . ."

"I recall."

"Everyone here doesn't get their share of that milk and honey and stuff."

Dan leaned on his elbow and paid attention.

"Joshua and his people were far away," he said. "Some of the honey was from ivy flowers and the milk must have soured from time to time."

"There's people in Glasgow without warm clothes. Kids. And people who can't find any work . . ."

Dan nodded and made a despairing little gesture.

"In my country also, there are many such. In all countries of the world. Even in the wealthiest the riches are not well distributed. This I know. The Brownshirts are the idle and the desperate as well as the evil and the cruel. And there are many now and will be more who will find work making guns and ships and aeroplanes for war. Better to be idle, I think, than prepare death for your fellows."

He nodded as if to approve of his own sentiments, as if what he had said had been said by someone else.

"I've got a friend . . ." John began, and then hesitated. Perhaps he had best not tell Dan about Hughie. If Dan knew of the cave he might mention it at home and then his plans would all be useless.

"Yes?"

"He can't find any work," John said, "and his wife has gone and left him."

"It is very sad," Dan agreed. "But consider that in this country no one will thrust him into uniform or into labour camps to work for a pittance far away from his family. Nor need he starve . . ."

"The dole isn't much."

"True. But it better than nothing at all."

"My friend . . . there just could be a job for him but his clothes are awful. They're in rags . . . and they smell rather . . ."

"There is a place in Perth which has clothes for such people. Your Aunt works there one day in the week. Did you not know this?"

John shook his head. He did not know very much about Aunty Nell. In fact he had not even known that she had been a nurse. It seemed to him that she would have been a funny sort of nurse even when she was young. And now he heard she worked in this place in Perth. Why did she mind when he gave his clothes away, then?

"Your friend could go there, could he not? I may have to go there myself if I do not hear soon from Wien."

He smiled resignedly at his elderly jacket.

"I'll tell him," John said. "I'll tell him before I go back to school. I'd have asked Grand for he's got lots of clothes which he never wears but Hughie's sort of short and thick. Not like Grand a bit."

"And your grandmother might have word to say too, nichts?"

"They don't know about things," confided John. "They don't seem to see the same things I do. They look away. Even Aunty Nell. She made it sound *wrong* to give away my socks and stuff. But Jinty *needed* them, she really did. She was *cold*. I had more and she didn't have any. I don't see why they should go on and on so."

Dan smiled sympathetically.

"And when I try to tell them they won't listen. As if what I had to say didn't matter at all. Grandmother calls me 'the boy' when she talks about me and thinks I can't hear. I'm not 'the boy' . . . I'm *me*."

He wrenched at a tuft of grass.

"I don't call her 'the woman'," he muttered. "*And* I'd get what for if I did."

Dan looked curiously at him.

"And Onkel Klaus . . . your grandfather?"

"Grand's O.K.," said John. "He doesn't always know you're around but when he does he knows who it is."

"And he is by me very much O.K.," Dan agreed. "I have loved him since a very long time when I was a small boy no higher than his knee and he took me on it to let me play the piano . . ."

"Me too," John said delightedly.

"And *my* father loved him also."

"Even in the war?" John asked daringly. He had wondered about the Heilbrons and the war ever since Dan had come.

"More than ever in the war," Dan assured him. "More than ever. When I was sent to the Front he told me that there were many like my Onkel Klaus over the Channel and I was not to let myself be dyed in hatred as so many others."

"You fought on the Jerry side?" asked John open-eyed. He found the idea horrifying, nauseating, incredible . . .

"I am . . . I was an Austrian," Dan said simply. "And I was a doctor. The army needed doctors, so I went."

John relaxed: doctors were different. There was something horrible and frightening in thinking that Dan might have been trying to kill Hughie or his father . . . or that Hughie or his father might have been trying to kill Dan.

"It's silly and disgusting!" he exclaimed.

Dan looked taken aback but only for a moment.

"All war is silly and disgusting. Me I know well. And you may yet find out."

"Me?"

"Yes. I think only war will rid us of what Hitler represents."

"But people said that we will never fight again. The war was a war to end war. It's in my history text book."

Dan smiled a little. "Not soon perhaps, but someday . . . someday . . . there will be war."

"What will you do?"

"I will fight."

"Won't you be too old?"

Dan made a face.

"There are plenty of ways to fight."

"Won't you be fighting against your own country."

"I will fight against evil. Country is no matter when there is evil. For a Jew, country is always a second loyalty. I will avenge my father."

He came to his feet in one movement.

"In any way I can I will avenge my father."

He went on talking, looking out across the Tay valley.

"You see, it should have been me. I made a speech. It was at a medical conference. I told the world what was going on and condemned research into chemical and biological warfare . . ."

He glanced down at John.

"I recalled what I had seen on the Front during the war. I begged my fellow-scientists to abandon such evil work . . . to refuse to continue. And I hinted at another kind of work which can chill my very soul to think of."

"What happened?"

"What I should have expected. I was howled down. Forced to sit down. Afterwards the Brownshirts came looking for me. The hunters set the dogs on the quarry. But they found the wrong man. They found my father. He, too, was Herr Doktor Heilbron. That was his name upon the door. He was Doctor of

291

Music. They found him in his study and killed him like a stray dog in the street for no reason except he was a Jew and had my name."

"Were you there?"

"No. I had gone into the country to wait until the noise died down. You see, I thought that the police would protect me. I was so innocent. I had a friend and he rang to warn me that my assistant had denounced me. Doubtless he has my place now. I ran that same night. I borrowed a bicycle and made for the border. I knew nothing of my father until the next day when I bought a newspaper and I read. At first I thought . . . they are fools and they look fools for telling the newspapers they have killed me before the event . . . and I laughed. I *laughed*. Then I bought another paper, one which the Brown-shirts had not yet got control of. I read details. The house . . . the street . . . the age . . . and then I knew what had happened. To die for a cause is one thing, but to die because of an illiterate gangster's mistake is quite another. My father would have laughed. I can hear his laughter in my ears, day and night, day and night . . ."

"What did you do then?"

"What could I do? My father was dead. I thanked the good God that my mother was dead and my sister Sari safe in France with her banker. My friend who was not a Jew went to the house. It had been looted, he said, but they had not found the violins. He brought them away and gave them to me and told me that I would have to leave for good. The Brownshirts don't care to admit that they have made mistakes. As far as they were concerned I was dead and if they found me I would be dead. I walked over the mountains to Switzerland. The mountains were my pastime and I can climb a little. Not much, but enough to take me over the frontier to safety. Almost to safety. Their arm is long. I thought to go to Sari, but she and her husband are gone to America. Bankers see very far into the future. So, I worked as a waiter until I had money to come here. And here I am. And my father is dead."

"You know what I think," John said, after a long silence during which he had cast about frantically to find some comfort.

"What do you think, my friend?"

"I think your father would be pleased. Pleased you got away, I mean. I haven't got a father but if I was in danger I think he would be pleased if I got away safe. I mean . . . he was old, wasn't he? Grand said about him saying that he hoped death might come before the Nazis."

"Old, but he enjoyed his life."

"But he wouldn't grudge what was left?"

"Ay, ay . . . you lay a heavy weight on me, Jüngling. What must I do with this expensive life of mine?"

"You're a doctor."

"Not the sort of doctor that heals, alas, I have not been that these many years."

"You could be again."

"Perhaps. Just now I am a refugee, penniless . . . not homeless, thanks to your Grand and not friendless, but I cannot just announce, 'Behold, I am a doctor. Consult me.' I am foreign. I am German in my speech and it is but a little while since all things German were anathema in this country. And I fear soon they will be so again."

John felt again that same helpless indignation he had felt in Glasgow: it must have shown in his face for Dan plumped down on his knees beside him and gave him a great hug.

"Ach, but you must not look so . . . you are too young to bear the sorrows of this bad world yet. I will survive. My race has always survived. Come, we must go back."

At the back door by Ruby's kitchen where they shed their muddy shoes Aunty Nell descended upon them, crying incoherently for Dan to come quickly for Mr. Innis was sick, terribly sick and the doctor at a confinement beyond the reach of a telephone.

". . . a seizure!" she cried. "He is such a colour . . . do come!"

Dan drew in his breath and ran up the back stairs two at a time with Aunty Nell panting behind and trying to answer his questions.

"It was just about an hour ago . . . I took in his tea . . . he was gasping and his lips quite blue . . . no, he was conscious . . ."

John came up behind them in his stocking soles and came

into the music room. Grand was lying flat on the balding deerskin hearthrug, his collar standing open and his face grey. Beside him knelt Grandmother, holding his hand. Her plump face had creased with worry as if the firm flesh had melted like candlewax.

"Cushions," Dan said urgently. "Sit him up. Brandy."

John ran to the drawing room and grabbed at the cushions which sat in ranks along the sofa, fat and satin and decorated with tassels. Grand was leaning against Dan's knee when he came back and John thrust the cushions behind him. Grandmother and Dan between them lowered him on to them.

"Brandy," said Dan again, his ear against Grand's chest.

"In the sideboard," said Grandmother. "Left hand side. Key in the box on the hall-table. Hurry. And don't forget to bring a glass."

John sprinted for the dining room, the sight of Grand's grey sweating face and the sound of the difficult breathing like his nightmare. He was back with the bottle in a very few moments and saw Grand with his head lolling sideways on Grandmother's shoulder while she smoothed the hair from his forehead and crooned wordlessly. Dan was watching but he jumped up when John came in.

"Good. Give it to me. So."

He moistened Grand's lips with the spirit and then gently persuaded him to take a sip, and then another. Aunty Nell was watching from the door, wringing her hands. It was hard to believe she had been a nurse. They watched the old man, willing him to respond. The breathing ceased to rasp and grate; the thin chest stopped heaving.

"Wie geht's?"

Grand looked at him from the refuge of his wife's shoulder and frowned.

"Not yet," he whispered. To John it sounded like a plea.

"Nein, my friend. Not yet. Certainly not yet. Drink a little more."

He put the glass against Grand's lips.

"Drink it, Nick . . . it's helping . . ."

Grandmother took the glass from Dan and held it as if she were feeding a small child.

"There, my lamb, there . . ."

"A blanket, Jüngling . . . bring a blanket . . ."

John ran upstairs and flung open the chest on the landing. There were blankets there, he knew, and eiderdown quilts. He grabbed an armful and ran down trailing them on the worn carpet. He tucked them round Grand's long thin frame while Grandmother watched jealously, ready to rebuke if he were clumsy.

"It goes better . . ." Dan raised his head from Grand's chest and put two fingers just under the angle of his jaw. "Jah, it goes much better."

Grand smiled faintly.

"Good."

He barely articulated the word.

"I still have something I must do," he said quite clearly after a moment and then his eyelids closed.

"He sleeps," said Dan. "This is good."

He stood up and began to scrawl upon a piece of paper.

"We need this," he declared. "You must fetch it. Go to the doctor and explain."

He thrust the paper at Aunty Nell.

"But surely I . . ."

"If you have to, go into Perth and find another doctor. But this we must have."

"Do as you're told, Nell," said Grandmother and Aunty Nell went out clumsily, bumping against the doorpost.

Dan stood looking down at Grand, frowning a little.

"You will stay here with him, gnädige Frau, and John and I will bring down a bed. He may not be moved. Not for a day or so."

Grandmother looked around the room as if she hated it.

"It was a small ward during the war," she said. "We put people in here when they were too ill to be in with the others."

She looked at John.

"You were born in this room."

He caught his breath at her expression.

When Aunty Nell came back with a small bottle from the doctor's house and the promise that the doctor would be there within the hour, the bed was down and Grand was lying upon it, propped high on a mound of pillows and breathing evenly. Grandmother sat beside him crocheting.

John did not return to school that week. The summer term started without him. At first this was because Grand was so ill. Once he was better and walking about again, very bent and slow, John still did not return. Gradually he learned that he was never to go back to Springwood. He was to go to New Zealand. He was to go to Bennachie. No one ever told him this, not to his face. The knowledge percolated through to him like water through moss.

For a boy who had travelled no further from his home than Edinburgh or Glasgow the voyage across the world was an experience beyond all his expectations. The very idea of it coloured all his waking thoughts for the months before Grand was well enough to sail. Even when they were approaching the huge white-painted vessel in the tender from Tilbury he still could not believe that it was really happening to him. None of the preparations had seemed real. He had helped to fill a huge packing case with items from Inchbeg. They had put in pictures, small pieces of furniture, dozens of books and various items which he had always taken for granted because they had always been there: the sabre over the dining room fireplace which his great great grandfather had carried in the charge of the Scots Greys at Waterloo, a carved chair made from the timbers of a ship, a teacaddy which had been in use at Inchbeg for two hundred years, a tiny writing-desk, no bigger than an attaché case which had already been to New Zealand and back with his great grandfather. Once in the packing case they looked so tiny and shabby. There were four crystal goblets in a wooden box which, so Aunty Nell told him, had been used by Prince Charles Stuart when he came to Inchbeg on his way south in 1745. There was even an unbelievably ancient christening robe, wrapped in layer after layer of worn linen sheet and tissue paper. He had chosen some of the items himself, like the ivory and ebony chessboard with its tiny men, and the minute 'dancing master's fiddle' which had been the first instrument he had learned to play, but for the most part Grand had chosen them and he had watched jealously while Cairds' men wrapped them up and packed them away in straw. This chest, so heavy that it took four strong men to lift, had been sent away even before the removal vans had come for the rest of the furniture. Some of the chairs and tables had been sent to Kelvin Drive, the rest, load after load, to the salerooms in Perth. When they had all gone, Inchbeg had been left like a vast echoing empty shell with the shabbiness of paint and paper ruthlessly exposed to the daylight. When they had climbed into the Humber and left the ancient house for the very last time. John knew he should be sad. He knew with his head that it was the end of a story more than four hundred years in the telling, but the more he tried to feel as he ought the more he thought, 'in three months time we'll be going to New Zealand.' And the shabby stone shell was no longer his Inchbeg. It was much more difficult to say goodbye to Hughie and Mrs. Hughie now installed as caretakers in the coachman's house until the workmen should descend to turn Inchbeg into St. Biddulph's School for Girls. Already the roof was aswarm with men stripping off the ancient slates. Ruby had left in the morning to be at Kelvin Drive when the furniture arrived.

Aunty Nell drove the Humber and she sniffed gloomily at intervals as they left but Grandmother sat very upright beside her in the front seat, wearing the round high-crowned hat with a spotted veil which she considered to be the correct headgear for a long car journey and did not even turn her head to see the last of the house. In the back, John sat between Grand and Dan and he noticed that neither of them looked round as he had done but Grand's hands on the silver-topped ebony cane he used now clasped and unclasped jerkily as they turned out of the gates. But that might have been Aunty Nell's driving. She was a dreadful driver, John thought. Nobody in the car said anything at all, but nobody had been saying anything for weeks.

Without the prospect of the voyage, life in Kelvin Drive would have been worse even than he had expected. The house seemed cramped and small after the spaciousness of Inchbeg: there seemed nowhere to be by himself except his tiny room with its view of the lane behind and the backs of other less prosperous houses. The garden was tiny, no more than a daisy-studded plot of grass with washlines strung across it. Aunty Nell planted annuals but they languished in the sour, sooty soil. Only the daisies flourished and Aunty Nell spent hours kneeling on a scrap of carpet and digging them up with a special little fork. Ruby found her new kitchen far more convenient than the vast offices of Inchbeg but John was no longer welcome in it. No matter where he stood or sat he would be in the way and Ruby would have to say to him, "Shift, Master John, till I reach this," or, "Move yourself, laddie, till I do that." Before long, he ceased to go there.

His only refuge was Kelvinside Park and he went there, rain or shine, all that wet summer. There was a gate at the bridge end just over the road and there he would go and walk among the sooty shrubs or watch the 'keelie' children in their comfortable tatters swinging on the swings which were forbidden to him or playing cowboys and indians. The river ran through the park but it stank of sewage and chemicals and swirled turbidly under the footbridges leaving swags of yellow scum along the banks. Those banks rose steeply and were seamed with neat paths where the gravel was retained by planks set endwise, making each path a series of long shallow steps. Before a month had passed John knew every inch of those paths and carried an adventure in his mind to fit each one. He had read stories of the explorers and on the steepest path he searched for Fawcett in the Amazonian jungle, pushing his way through the thickets of rhododendrons which smelled so strongly of cat. On the path which wound along the edge of a bare slope down to the river he would be Younghusband making his slow way to Tibet. Sometimes he ventured to the other side of the river and climbed up into the Botanic Gardens where he wandered round the vast greenhouse they called the Kibble Palace. There was a range of hothouses, too, and there he would examine the little metal labels under the plants and when he found one which said, 'native of New Zealand' he would stare at it and wonder if it was to be found around Bennachie.

He was forbidden to wander the streets: while he did not always obey this injunction he had no money and could not take the trams. The grim tenements so close behind the gentility of Kelvin Drive contained a swarm of yelling children as savage as the jungle dogs which hunted Mowgli and once they had set upon him. There were no Jinties to be found there.

Dan was preoccupied. He spent most of the day in his room and John could not discover what he did there. Some days he went to a place he called The Mitchell but did not take John. Once in a while, however, he would declare a holiday and he and John would set forth to view the great city. Once they went to the Kelvinside Art Galleries and Museums and John looked his fill at the stuffed animals and the ship models and once or twice they went to the Hillhead Salon to see a film. Dan looked at the screen but he never seemed to remember what they had seen and John found that the flickering images and trite stories palled quickly though they provided a talking point with Ruby who went regularly on her afternoons. They resented the habit of the management which sprayed its clientele at irregular intervals with a sickly-smelling disinfectant, rather as if they had been infesting the seats instead of paying for them.

Grand spoke less than ever: since he had been ill his movements were studied and economical as if he were rationing his strength. Grandmother, on the other hand, once the house was to her liking, 'had people in', a phrase John learned to hate. She had endless relations in Glasgow to whom she had written regularly from Perthshire and they all came to call. Once they had called and seen the respectabilities of Kelvin Drive they came by turns to tea: John, his hair slicked down and his shoes shining, was called in to hand round milk and sugar in the silver bowl and jug, carry the cakestand laden with the issue of Ruby's love affair with her new gas cooker or help Grandmother identify the figures in the photographs in the albums she deemed fit entertainment for such guests. There could be no escape. Kelvin Drive had no corners, no forgotten nooks, no refuges. After he dropped a Crown Derby cup on the brass fender, however, he was not asked to officiate again.

At night, once or twice, he thought of the horse he had seen in the spring of the year waiting its life away in the cramped, dank alleyway off Buchanan Street and he wondered whether it too felt imprisoned by little things and remembered open spaces and clean fields. When, one morning in September, Ruby dragged his old school trunk in from the boxroom he felt like a prisoner whose sentence was dwindling to an end. Gladly he packed with the meticulous attention to detail that

Ruby demanded, and when she cried a little over the bundles of socks and piles of underpants he felt wicked and cold-hearted for he could not wait for that day, the very thought of which made her weep. There had never been a time when Ruby had not been there and yet he could not regret leaving her if that meant leaving Kelvin Drive.

From the tender the SS *Bendigo* seemed to tower into the sky, a vast white wall, patterned with lines of rivets and line over line of portholes curving round the hull like an exercise in perspective. The companionway, up which they would soon have to climb, looked like a tiny fragile toy against that enormous expanse. Somewhere in that great structure lay that packing case, marked 'Not Wanted On Voyage,' and it seemed a marvel that it would ever be found again. Why, John wondered for the thousandth time, did they have to take all that stuff with them to New Zealand?

Later, their baggage bestowed and the cabins' position carefully noted, they went out on deck to watch the tenders fussing to and fro with the people who were to fill up the decks below theirs, E, F and G. Emigrants, Grand said, people going out to Australia to make a new life. As they watched, John wondered whether Jinty would ever get a chance to make a new life, to make a voyage like this. Grand shivered a little and said he was going back to the cabin but Dan and John watched them stream aboard, show their tickets and be sorted into groups for the white-coated stewards to escort below. They looked shabby and gaudy, both at the same time, and their faces seemed grim and apprehensive and didn't match the 'best' coats and the hats with flowers and feathers. The children clung to worn toys and looked bewildered. Many of them were crying, men, women and children alike.

"Why?" asked John for it seemed unbelievable that everyone aboard should not be able to share the bubble of excitement within him.

"It is hard to leave everything you know," Dan reminded him sombrely. "They are leaving their relatives, too. They may never set eyes on them again. It is a long way."

He pointed at the quay, crowded to the walls with tiny waving figures.

"It is hard," Dan said again and John felt ashamed and tried to feel regret that he was leaving behind everything he knew and Grandmother and Aunty Nell and Ruby and Hughie, but the sad feeling would not come. He looked sideways at Dan's grim face and the people swarming aboard and wondered if he was wicked not to feel sad.

"I'll see if Grand's O.K.," he offered and ran along to the cabins.

They had booked two, side by side, and John knew that they were the best on the ship because they had to be where Grand didn't have too many stairs to climb. There was a little door between them and a sort of step-thing which you had to remember to lift your foot over everytime you went in and out anywhere. There were two bunks in each cabin but Grand was to have one all to himself while Dan and John shared the other. He was to have the upper bunk which delighted him and he could not wait for night time when he could climb up by the tiny ladder. Everything he saw delighted him, the neatness, the ingenuity, the white paint and the shining brass, even the strange rubbery, salty, painty smell. In spite of anything he could do, the bubble of excitement swelled inside him again till he felt he might float up in the air. He pitied everyone who could not be aboard the SS *Bendigo*.

Grand was lying down, his polished black shoes placed tidily upon a folded rug so that he did not soil the white coverlet.

"We'll be sailing in twenty minutes. The man in the white coat said so. Do you want to come out and see?"

The excitement sang in his voice and Grand smiled at him.

"No," he said gently. "I said my farewells a long time since. Off you go. I want to rest a little before dinner."

He held out a scrap of paper he had been holding in his hand.

"A telegram," he said. "You can take it up to Dan."

It was from the Dalhousies and the Coopers. It said, 'Au revoir, good luck and the best of weather.' Dan frowned at it.

"Was that all?" he enquired. "No message from Glasgow?"

By the time the *Bendigo* moved majestically downriver in the hazy dusk, jewelled and girded with lights, there was still no message from Glasgow, though there were flowers from the Fillinghams and another telegram from friends in Perth. No one remarked on this but even the excitement of feeling the ship move under his feet in the slow Channel swell and climbing up the ladder into his bunk could bury John's consciousness that Grand was distressed.

28

John had his fourteenth birthday at sea. They were seven days out of Capetown and it was oppressive grey weather, grey sky and grey sea patterned with swell as far as the eye could penetrate through the grey haze. The only thing to be seen was the ship's wake, dying interminably behind them, bow wave, stern wave and then a silver trail as if a vast snail had traversed the featureless waters. The passengers were bored, even a little cross. The novelty of sea travel had worn off and the uncertainties of life in a strange country were beginning to loom large for most of them. The next port would be Adelaide and many of them would disembark there. Among the emigrants in the bowels of the huge vessel, the singing and the drinking and the impromptu concerts of the first leg of the voyage had given way to anxious speculation and the counting of what was left in their purses.

There were few children among the cabin passengers and none of them was the same age as John. The emigrant children swarmed all over the lower decks but they had been quick to form their own gangs and societies which necessarily excluded anyone from the cabin class. John, among over fifteen hundred people, was as alone as he had been during the holidays at Inchbeg. Grand, though stronger, had become more silent and withdrawn than he had ever been and Dan, when he was not attending to Grand, spent much of his time writing. He did not tell John what it was, and John did not ask. However, the crew were kind: once they had summed him up for a quiet, sensible creature which did not take them long, he was welcomed into the odd nooks and crannies of the ship which few passengers were ever allowed to see. He was allowed to steer *Bendigo* for a breathless ten minutes. He was taken to see the engines and marvelled at them. They seemed so massive compared to the puny men who controlled them. He was given cups of tea in the engineers' quarters and listened to their almost incomprehensible 'shop' and once he was permitted a glimpse of the stokehold where the boiler fires throbbed and pulsed and shone on the sweating firemen who fed the gaping square maws. 'Spike Row' the young third engineer called the stokehold and grinned mysteriously when John asked why.

"Because they've mostly been guests of His Majesty at some time," he said.

John had a wild picture of the stokers in top hats and morning coats moving among the guests in the garden of Buckingham Palace with their eyes shining blue out of their blackened faces. It was a long time before he understood that most of them had been in prison. At Capetown, under a huge moon, he had watched two of them being hoisted aboard, fighting drunk, in a cargo net.

He learned a lot: he learned to tell the time by bells, to know the watches kept by the crew, to call portholes 'scuttles', walls 'bulkheads' and floors 'decks'; he learned which sides of the ship were port and starboard, the difference between true and magnetic, and the meanings of words like gimbals and fiddles and binnacles. He even learned a little about navigation and could repeat the morse code, very slowly but accurately. Grandmother had not approved of the Scout movement so he had never encountered these mysteries before.

Before he went aboard he had realised that he was going to have a birthday during the voyage but the days and the weeks ran together so that it was hard to remember which day of the week it was, let alone the date. When he woke on his birthday morning he had forgotten all about being fourteen. He woke as he had done for weeks, saw that Dan was already up and dressed and writing, and slipped away silently for his bath. He liked to have a chat with the bath steward before all the other passengers came crowding in with their sponge bags and their towels and their gaudy dressing gowns. It was best to have a bath as soon as the water was on, at half-past six. The steward grinned at him and turned the water on in number eight and then went to the fresh water tap to fill his basin. It had fascinated John at first to find that all the taps on board were little brass wheels. He watched the steaming salt water gush into the bath like the falls of Lodore. It never took more than a couple of minutes to fill the bath. The steward adjusted the board across the bath and placed the basin on it. Hot salt water was a super bath but you needed to rinse off the salt afterward or you felt sticky. The steward went away and closed the door. John put one foot into the water, testing the temperature, and it was then, straddled over the side of the bath, that he remembered it was his birthday. The year before he had been taken to Perth Theatre as a treat to see *Lady Windermere's Fan*. Grandmother disapproved of the cinema as well as the Scout movement and John's visits to the cinema had been few. He stirred out of his trance and lowered himself into the water. This year, he decided, he would say nothing about having a birthday. Birthdays were for babies. But he was conscious of a slight pang that no one had remembered.

He had reckoned without Grandmother and Signor Marconi. Grandmother disapproved of the telephone which she regarded with severity as a means whereby one might be constrained to talk to the oddest people, but she had no objection to the telegram. At breakfast, the dining room steward handed him an envelope from the radio room and winked. The slip of paper inside said, MANY HAPPY RETURNS OF YOUR BIRTHDAY STOP LOVE TO YOU AND YOUR GRANDFATHER STOP GRANDMOTHER. At the bottom, his friend the Radio Officer had scrawled, 'Happy Birthday from me too! Come up and see me sometime!'

Grand and Dan looked at the form a little disconcerted by the news it gave. Grand had always depended on Grandmother to remind him about things like birthdays and of course Dan had never known when it was. It was strange to think that at his last birthday he had never even heard of Dan.

"Well," Dan said, "surely we must a party have. I will discover what can be done."

He went across the dining saloon to talk to the Chief Steward.

Grand sat folding and unfolding the paper, clearing his throat from time to time.

"Grand," John ventured and it was a question he had not dared to ask before, "why didn't Grandmother come with us? She likes sea voyages. She told me once what a fine time you had going to New Zealand."

Grand didn't answer at once and when he did it wasn't a proper answer.

"There was the new house," he said, "she felt she had to see to that."

It was a lame excuse for John knew very well that all that had to be done to the house in Kelvin Drive had been done long before their train had drawn out of Glasgow Central Station, leaving Aunty Nell weeping bitterly on the platform. It didn't explain the raw and terrible antagonism which had poisoned the last days in Glasgow, the more terrible for being, as far as John was concerned, unvoiced. All he had heard of the argument which he sensed to be raging between the grown ups had been through a door. When Grandmother was angry her voice became shrill.

"If it is true, and who is to say it is, they won't welcome the news. How could they? How would you feel?"

But he couldn't make out Grand's reply. All he knew was that Grandmother had watched Aunty Nell packing up their trunks in a sour silence broken only when she saw an omission or disapproved of an inclusion. And she had ignored Dan with point and determination, never looking at him, or speaking to him. When they left she had bidden them farewell in the parlour without embraces or good wishes and had not even come to see them into the taxi. This radiogram was the first word they had had from her, although John had written conscientiously every Sunday, just as he did at school and posted the letters in a bunch at Las Palmas and Capetown.

"Grand, please can I send her one back?"

Grand looked up.

"*May* I," John corrected himself. "Just thank you and love and we're all well."

"A good idea," Grand said, "yes, a very good idea. We'll go along now."

The radio cabin was manned by John's friend, a cheerful young Ulsterman.

"So, if it isn't our birthday boy," he grinned. "How many bumps is it? Fourteen? That's a man, near enough."

He had thumped him heartily upon the back fourteen times before he sat down again and got to business, taking down the text of the message.

"Thank you for cable stop all very well here stop love from all stop John."

"I'll have that winging its way in a jiffy," he said and began to put on the headphones.

"Wait," Grand said, "just a moment . . . would you add to that . . ."

He hesitated for a long time, frowning, and then shook his head.

"No, I don't know how to put it," he sighed. "I had best write . . ."

"Och, surely not," the young man said, "you'd be surprised how much you can get in a few words. When it comes down to it most news is one of four things, birth, marriage, death and send me more money. And all of them can be put down easy enough."

Grand smiled.

"Make it a separate cable," he said, "and put, 'I do not remember our parting just our life together, all my love Nick.'"

"Now there's a grand message," approved the youngster, "says a lot that does."

But John supporting Grand back up the stairs found the message disquieting: it stayed with him for the rest of the day, even during the party. To John's immense surprise the party was huge. Lots of people joined in, passengers and crew; paper hats appeared from somewhere, and crackers and streamers and squeakers. The galley (John had made the acquaintance of the chief cook) produced a large iced cake with fourteen candles and if the icing was still a little soft over the fruit cake which usually appeared in chunks with the teacups at four in the afternoon, no one mentioned the fact. At dinner everybody round the table and at the neighbouring tables sang 'Happy Birthday to You' while he blew out the candles and cut the cake. Presents appeared on the table, recognisably from the stock of the ship's shop or souvenirs from Las Palmas and Capetown. After dinner was over a concert and a dance was arranged and the ship's band, an amalgam of talent from the crew and the passengers, assembled in the saloon. John, red-faced and stumbling over his own feet, waltzed off to open the dance with the prettiest of the girls, carefully selected for him by the younger ship's officers. He listened to several songs and danced the 'Dashing White Sergeant' before he thanked everybody in a mumble and fled below to bed.

"Why?" he asked Dan later, bemused by the occasion. "None of them knew me. I'd only ever spoken to about half a dozen and yet there's all this . . ."

He indicated the pile of presents on the compactum.

"Ach, it is natural enough," Dan shrugged. "We had become traurig, melancholy . . . for it is a long voyage. My friend has a name day and they seize the chance to rejoice a little. And they are pleased to have the chance."

"Grand and I sent a cable to Grandmother," John announced. "I said thanks and love and we're all well and Grand said . . ."

"Well?"

It was not a casual enquiry. It was plain that Dan wanted very much to know what Grand had said.

"It sounded O.K.," John told him, "but it made me feel funny in my inside . . ."

He repeated Grand's message. Dan sighed and put an arm round him.

"Do not disturb yourself. This is a good message. Your grandparents parted in anger which is not good. Now all is mended. Now she is sorry and she sends a message to say so."

"But the cable was to me."

"Again you the occasion are. The dove to carry the olive twig. Your grandmother is proud and not used to being defied. She is too proud to say, I was wrong, I was unkind and I am sorry. Your grandfather knew at once what she meant and he answered that."

"But why were they angry? If only people would tell people things. It's beastly knowing there's something up and not being told what or why or anything."

Dan sat on his bunk and nodded.

"Ja, by me it is wrong to leave you in ignorance."

"Then tell me what was wrong."

"I can not tell all," Dan shrugged. "It is not my secret. But I will explain what I may. Your grandmother did not wish you to go. Also she thought your grandfather too sick to go so far. But he was set upon it and I thought it would not be good to stop him and I offered to go with him and care for him. This angered her much because she thought if she would not go, he could not. He would not wish to be ill with only you."

"Why didn't she want us to go?"

"This I must not tell you. In time you will know for it concerns you."

John looked at him for a few moments and then climbed up into the bunk and pulled the blankets up to his chin.

"When we get there," he asked, "what are you going to do?"

Dan shrugged.

"I will work. I am strong and healthy. I will finish my book and discover if anyone would care to publish it."

"What is it about?"

"Men and war."

"People always like to read about war."

"Sad but true. If I make some money I will to America go."

"America?"

John sat up and bumped his head.

"Ja, America. There I have many friends. There may be some will listen to what I have to say. There I will work and fight against Herr Hitler. In time we all must fight, I think. Perhaps after that when I am an old, old man I may be able to go home again."

"You won't go right away?"

Dan stood up and stood by the bunk looking at him.

"As long as your grandfather has need of me, so long I shall stay."

"He needs you an awful lot."

"Ja, this I know. For the sake of my father I stay and for his own sake . . . and yours. Now, it is time you were asleep."

"Did Grand want to come here because he didn't want to go to Glasgow?"

"I am not sure your Grand cares very much where he lives," Dan said with an undercurrent of amusement. "If he has a piano, he is quite content."

"When he heard about your father he said, 'there is no music left'."

Dan drew in his breath sharply.

"Said he that? Then to travel eleven thousand miles is but a very small thing to do for him."

In the darkness John lay and thought about what had been said. It came over him that Dan had told him, as gently as he could, that Grand had not much longer to live. He had known that in a way, but now he knew properly and it was desolating. Whenever he thought of his birthday afterwards it was that he remembered, and not the cake or the party.

After the birthday the days seemed to speed up. The rest of the voyage passed very quickly. The most vivid memory for John was the great ship listing at Adelaide when the emigrants came flooding up to the port rail to see the first glimpse of their new country.

"We've used up most of our coal and our water," the young fourth officer explained, "so we're a bit short of ballast. Don't worry, it happens every time and we've never turned turtle yet."

At Melbourne they transferred to the New Zealand ferry and went to the baggage room to look out some warm clothes for winter was only just beginning to lose its grip on those southern waters. Grand seemed to have benefited from the voyage. He was less shaky, more energetic and his face was a better colour. Both Dan and John hovered about him but he laughed at them gently and told them not to fuss.

"I was born in New Zealand," he told his fellow passengers with pride.

On the night before they reached Dunedin he played the tinkling piano in the saloon for a sing-song. Dan looked on smiling but watchful.

However, Dunedin to Bennachie was an exhausting journey for a sick man. They took the train up the Taieri valley and it stopped and started its way up river until the foothills came into view and it began to climb, slowly and painfully. John stared open-mouthed at the peaks in the far distance, still capped and caped with snow.

"They make the Grampians look pretty silly," he said to Grand who smiled.

At Cromwell they left the train and Dan was obviously concerned. Grand looked grey and weary.

"For now," Dan said firmly, "we go no further. Two days we will rest."

"What will they think at Bennachie?" John asked.

Dan said an astonishing thing.

"Unless your grandmother has written to tell them, they don't know we are coming."

John's mouth fell open.

"Why not?"

"Your grandfather thought it best. In spring, he said they will be lambing and that is no time to send anyone down to fetch in visitors."

A friendly fellow passenger recommended a boarding house not far from the station and commandeered his own friend to drive them there. They were made very welcome. Grand was put to bed in a bare ugly room with a stone hot water bottle and a coverlet of patchwork: the landlady brought in his supper on a tray.

"My mother's work," she told him proudly. "She brought it from Home. I was born here, but only just. She was carried off the ship into the hospital. I'm a proper Kiwi by thirty-five minutes."

"So am I," Grand told her and smiled. "I was born on Bennachie, upbye near Inchture."

"Inchture!" she cried, "why, my man is from thereabout . . . he comes from Ellangowan. Do you know it?"

"Christie's," Grand said at once. "He'll be James Christie's boy."

"In the name! Wait till I tell him . . . though he's no boy any more . . ."

She fussed about him, overwhelmed by a simple delight in such a coincidence. Joe Christie, home from his work at the sawmill brought the scent of new-cut timber into the room when he climbed the stair to speak to this special guest. He remembered Dominic Innis for they had met when Grand was over before the War. His father had known Hannah and Hector. Indeed, Hector had built the Christie homestead. And he had news of Bennachie. Dan and John listened spellbound to Grand's talk of people and places unknown to them as people do when an old acquaintance displays an unsuspected talent.

Ian Angus still ran Bennachie, Joe said, but it wasn't the place it had been under old Hector. The price of wool and meat was low. Mind, things were bad all over, and getting worse and the blam'd government wasn't no help. Bennachie wasn't no worse off than hundreds of farmers in the back-blocks. As far as he knew Ian Angus wasn't in debt like half the ex-servicemen who'd taken up sections after the war, poor sods. But he'd a job to get men and when he got them they wouldn't stay or their wives wouldn't. These days folks wanted to be able to drive everywhere and you couldn't get a lorry into Bennachie. It was still horse-and-cart country and a full day from the tarseal. And in the winter you'd need to be a bird to get on and off the place. If they was heading up that direction they'd best make haste. The roads was open just at the moment but there was usually a late snowfall . . . just to make lambing more interesting, he said grimly. Ian Angus was running the place pretty well on his own. Young Hector, that was the grandson, he wasn't cut out for the boo–ay, a lazy cuss by all accounts. Didn't know nothing about sheep and didn't want to learn. His mum was Chrissie Esslemont as was, used to be barmaid at the hotel in the town, she was worth ten of him, so they said.

Grand revived hearing this gossip, revived like a watered plant, but Dan, a wary eye on his patient, cut Joe short after an hour and went downstairs with him, leaving John to make Grand comfortable. He threw out little items of information.

"Ian Angus must be twelve years younger than me. He was the youngest. I saw him last when your mother was born. He was the image of his father then. He was huge. He used to make me think of that picture of Samson in the little parlour at Inchbeg."

"What happened to his son, Hector's father?" John asked.

Grand had looked at him frowning. He hesitated a little before he answered.

"He was Hector too. Ian Angus only ever had one son. He was killed in the war."

"Was he at Gallipoli?"

John had read a story about Gallipoli and knew that the ANZACs had fought there.

"No. He joined a Scots Regiment. It was in France."

312

He lay back against the pillows and his eyes closed. John turned the lamp down to a glimmer and followed Dan downstairs. He found him, not in the stiff parlour which was kept for the guests but in the cheerful shabby kitchen discussing earnestly with Joe the difficulties of taking an old sick man to Bennachie.

It proved as difficult as expected. On Sunday, Joe borrowed a rattletrap of an elderly Ford lorry from a friend and with Grand in the cab and John and Dan sharing the tray with their luggage, two piglets in sacks, a crate of hens ('chooks' Joe called them), a barrel of paraffin oil and the other assorted hardware, they drove over one of the worst roads John had ever seen. It remained that until they came to a battered sign, INCHTURE 17m, at which they turned on to a gravel track over which they bumped and rattled for about eight miles with Dan peering at intervals through the tiny rear window to see how Grand was faring.

They drew up at last at a farm which had proclaimed its preoccupation with cows for several hundred yards downwind.

"The cockie here's a chum of mine," Joe announced. "I reckoned if I brought his traps up for him . . ."

He jerked his head at the assorted load in the tray.

". . . he'd give you a bed for the night and loan of his jinker to get over the hill."

The bed for the night proved to be a shakedown in the kitchen for Dan and John while Grand, stoutly refusing to take the only bed, slept on a broken-down settee in the parlour. But the hospitality was heartfelt. The cockie who was called Eck beamed broadly at them and his wife came in from the shed obviously delighted to have company.

"They're Bennachie's folks," Eck proclaimed. "Ian Angus's brother . . . the one that went Home all them years ago. My word but they'll be pleased upbye."

Mrs. Cockie whose red hands and damp handshake suggested that she had been scrubbing out milk pails smiled in delight.

"I ken a' aboot ye!" she cried in the broadest Scots. "We sing your sang in the choir at Inchture. The Minister tell't us it was wrote by a body frae here. Sic a bonnie sang."

"She's just about crazy on music an' that," her husband apologised. "She was at me to buy a pianny when she first came. Fancy, eh? A pianny!"

He laughed uproariously.

"Just you bring a pianny, next time you're this way, Joe, and we'll have a musical swaree."

Mrs. Cockie flushed.

"I doubt I'll no be able for it, noo," she said regretfully and looked at her red and swollen hands.

Her husband put a great arm across her shoulders.

"Never mind," he told her, "you can still sing. Got a voice like a bell–bird," he added proudly. "You'll have some supper with us and she'll sing for you."

Which she did. They drank tea as strong as ink and ate boiled eggs and home–made bread spread with syrup.

"Milk cheque don't run to much once I've paid interest and the feed bills," said Eck cheerfully, "but there's good times just around the corner, so they say, and even if there ain't, it ain't a bad life. Give us *Annie Laurie*, Hilda."

She gave them *Annie Laurie* and the *Wee Couper o' Fife* and *Leezie Lindsay* and then she sang *The Empty Cradle*, standing before them like a good child, her hands folded in front of her. She had a clear true soprano, as appealing as a boy's treble. When she had finished there was silence and to John's astonishment he saw tears running down Eck's face.

"Comes a mite near the bone, does that," he said, wiping them away unashamedly with the heel of his hand. "We lost our littl'un six months ago."

Nick rose and took Hilda's hands in both of his.

"I must have heard that sung a thousand times," he told her, "but I will never hear it sung better."

"I never thocht tae meet ye," Hilda said, "but I'm fell glad for yon sang was an awful comfort efter . . . it said whit I felt here . . ."

She pressed her hand to her chest.

". . . but I couldnae say it . . . no even tae Eck, here."

They were lucky to reach Bennachie alive. In the morning there had been a curious arched cloud formation over the mountains to the south west and a chill damp feel in the air.

314

When they set out in the borrowed jinker there was no more than a breath of wind. The jinker was a sturdy two-wheeled cart drawn by a stolid cartmare called Jess. The baggage provided a seat behind for John and Dan drove with Grand beside him, pointing out the track. At the start this was necessary for it led over featureless tussock-grass pasture till it forded a trickle of water in a vast expanse of pebbles. Nine-foot pole markers showed the way across. Dan looked at these as the mare splashed her way across, barely fetlock deep. There were twelve on one side and fifteen on the other. The water ran turquoise-coloured and milky, barely chuckling over the pebbles.

"A cannon to kill a sparrow," Dan commented.

"Oh, no," John heard Grand reply. "That can rise six feet in a very short time after the snow melts. Tomorrow it could be impassable. Look up there."

His arm indicated the white topped mountains: above them the cloud had thickened.

"That means rain . . . or snow," he told them. "Best not to dilly-dally."

Later on, the track was easier to find because it was the only possible way a cart could go. There were traces of some attempts to improve it: stones had been rolled aside, holes roughly filled in, or a bank partly dug away. In one marshy place a corduroy of logs was laid with the rank marsh grass thrusting up between them. Across a chuckling hill burn a plank bridge had been set, so rickety and narrow that Grand took the reins from Dan's inexpert hands and drove the jinker across, leaving Dan and John to follow on foot.

At noon they ate boiled eggs and the bread and syrup which Hilda had provided, but Grand ate next to nothing and was restless. He looked apprehensively at the clouding sky. The wind rose and sang about them mournfully; a few drops of rain hit them on cheeks and brows. They paused to put on mackintoshes and when this was done Grand took the reins again despite all Dan's protests.

"You're no driver," Grand said. "It's going to take us all our time to make shelter before the storm."

"What storm?"

315

Grand didn't answer but gestured over to the south west where the mountains had been blotted out.

"Snow," he said.

Dan jumped up on the seat and didn't argue any more.

When the snow began they had about four miles still to go. These lay through a narrow defile, steep and stony, barely wide enough for the jinker. Afterwards, Dan was to say that had the snow been on their faces they could not have come through. As it was, the wind and the snow howled and beat upon their backs, lightening the weight of the jinker for the mare. Even though the visibility ahead was reduced to a few yards it was still possible to keep one's eyes open to peer through the dancing snow and see the hazards.

Twice, Dan and John jumped out to clear a way through the clinging drifts for the high wheels and at the very head of the pass where the path was steepest Dan went to the mare's head while John plodded at the side of the cart ready to bear a hand upon the wheel when it stuck fast. The last mile was easier going, downhill and in the lee of the storm, but it was hideously dangerous because the track zigzagged down the hillside and the snow lay so thick it was hard to see where the bends were. It was all too easy to find a wheel over the edge and a long steep drop beneath. Here they were dependent upon Grand and his memory did not fail them, though there were some moments when they wondered whether they might not have to leave the jinker behind.

John kept plodding through the snow, his head bent, conscious of nothing but the need to keep moving, the crunch of snow under his boots, the wind leaping at them and worrying them and his charge, the wheel, slow-turning and creaking by his ear, the spokes clogged with snow. When the wheel slowed and stopped he put his shoulder to it automatically.

"We're here," he heard Grand say breathlessly.

John stared ahead and saw a shape looming out of the dusk and a honey-yellow light streaming towards him. He smelt woodsmoke and the warm byre-smell of cows which made him think of the Mains at Inchbeg. Somewhere close by there were dogs barking frantically. Another light bloomed as a door opened and the light framed a huge man coming out to greet them.

316

"John!" Dan yelled urgently. "Catch . . ."

Grand slithered down from the high seat of the jinker and John only just managed to break his fall. He laid him flat in the snow while Dan plowtered desperately round the mare's head to reach him.

"We're here . . ." Grand whispered. "This is Bennachie . . ."

29

It seemed a long time afterwards that Dan stood back from the bed and said,

"Now he will sleep."

Grand's face in the lamplight was still ash-pale and he hardly seemed to stir the covers with his breathing but the blue shade was gone from his mouth.

"There was a moment," Dan said quietly, almost to himself, "when I have thought, this must the end be . . . but it is not yet. He has something still to do."

They left the lamp burning low and the door open and returned to the kitchen. There Ian Angus was waiting for them and the table was laid for a meal.

"How is he?"

"Not good," Dan said. "He has trouble here, you understand," he tapped his chest, "his heart is very sick. Had I known that this weather was to come we should not have set out this morning. But it was a fine spring morning . . . He knew, I think, that there was a storm to come but he said nothing until it was too late. He was set upon reaching you. It was something he must do."

"I wonder why?" Ian Angus asked. "He is welcome of course but I cannot think what should bring him all the way from Scotland when he is a sick man."

"He has reasons," Dan said sombrely, "he will himself tell you. To me they seemed good or I would not have come with him."

Ian Angus looked at him beneath the heavy white eyebrows.

"Are you a doctor?"

"I was. Today I have no country and no profession. But my father and his were friends."

Ian Angus nodded.

"This must be Anna's boy," he said and looked at John.

"Your mother was born in that very room. Did you know that?"

The woman standing behind him was looking at John so intently that he felt uncomfortable.

"This is Chrissie," Ian Angus said, turning to her. "She was my son Hector's wife. And this . . ."

He turned round to indicate the youth who was sitting at the table staring at the newcomers.

". . . this is his son, my grandson, Hector after his father . . . and my father."

Hector was about four years older than John but he was small and dark with very black eyes and a mop of curly dark hair. His expression was sullen and unwelcoming. He was staring at John too. The woman came forward with her hand outstretched and shook both Dan and John by the hand.

"You must be starving," she said. "Sit down and eat. It's all ready."

They both realised as she said it that they were so hungry they were hollow. They sat down and she brought bowls of broth, thick with carrots and turnips and peas and leeks and scraps of mutton. Afterwards, there was cold mutton and baked potatoes with lumps of butter melting into the floury interiors. Then there were slices of cake and cup after cup of tea. It was the best meal that John could remember. The others did not share it. They had eaten before the jinker stopped outside the door. All the time John was eating he was conscious that the three of them kept looking at him. Ian Angus made no secret of his staring and when John caught his eye, he smiled benevolently at him. Chrissie's gaze was more furtive; she would look and then look away and she had the expression of someone who was normally smiling and good-humoured but had been shocked into solemnity. Hector glowered and said nothing, plainly resenting their arrival.

Dan did most of the talking: he explained about the sale of Inchbeg, described the voyage and answered the questions which Ian Angus asked. John, once the edge was off his appetite, was conscious of a certain constraint, as if there was a question which everyone wanted to ask and did not.

For the time being John was told to share Hector's bed while Aunt Chrissie, as he had been told to call her, made up a campbed for Dan in the same room as Grand. Ian Angus chased them both to bed as soon as the meal was eaten.

"We'll be up at first light," he said. "After this snow there'll be plenty to see after."

Hector showed John the hut across the yard which was the privy and the basin in the scullery where he could wash. John, weary beyond telling, stumbled through his preparations in silence, grateful that Hector had nothing to say. In the wide bed was a stone hot water bottle wrapped in flannel and its warmth was a blessing like the honey-yellow light from the window had been when they arrived. Hector stared scornfully at his striped school pyjamas. Hector appeared to sleep in his woollen underwear. He said only one thing before he put the lamp out.

"You're Great Uncle Nick's grandson, isn't that right?"

"Yes," John agreed sleepily. "His daughter was my mother. I don't remember her. She died when I was born."

Hector said nothing but stared down at him stonily.

John slept late into the cold blue light of the next morning but he woke suddenly, with no interval of drowsiness, instantly conscious of being at Bennachie. He dressed rapidly in shorts and thick woollen socks and the sleeveless Fair Isle sweater which Aunty Nell had knitted for him as a farewell present. It was the first time he had worn it. He pulled it down over his head wondering why he had not thought of her since he had seen her on the platform at Glasgow Central Station, her face pink and tearstained. He felt guilty because he had not thought of her, except to send love in the letters to Grandmother and it was a guilt which he resented. He could not think why he did not love Aunty Nell; she had mothered him as much as he had permitted, which was not a great deal. At one time he had thought that she could be his mother. She had shown him more affection than Grandmother and he still thought of her with a sort of irritation. His thick, warm, grey socks were more of Aunty Nell's work and as he turned the tops down over the red tie-garter he wondered rather helplessly why he should think so much of her this first morning in a new place. What had she to do with Bennachie? Wasn't he glad rather than otherwise to be free of her cloying, demanding love; was it

320

love, that Aunty Nell felt for him? Love should feel different. Aunty Nell would be in Glasgow now, in the new house in Kelvin Drive which looked out unseeingly across the brown and stinking river and the caged park which bordered it. She would shop vaguely and fussily in that row of shops in Queen Margaret Drive, buy sweets in R. S. McColl's (sweets were her vice, if she could be said to have a vice), buy fourpence worth of teabread from the flyblown baker and eat it with strong tea in the parlour. Grandmother would read the *Glasgow Herald* as she always had, even at Inchbeg, and Aunty Nell would read little paragraphs aloud out of the *Bulletin*. John stared out at the mountains, sharply white, the little lake and the cruel, beautiful snow that smothered the growing things beneath and he found them less alien than that house in the city and the people who lived in it. He was glad to the very soles of his feet not to be there and because he was glad he felt eaten up with guilt. He felt obscurely that it was unfair. He looked about him for a looking-glass in which to make sure that his parting was straight. It was over the wash-stand, just too low for him to see easily. Hector was four years older but he was not so tall as John. He bent his knees and performed the morning ritual with the comb: suddenly he remembered that no one would say to him, 'Go upstairs and part your hair properly, boy. I will not have ruffians at my table.' Nor would Aunty Nell waylay him in the hall and say, 'Let Aunty Nell set you to rights, Johnnie-boy, before your grandmother sees . . .' He stared at the face in the mirror as if it were that of a total stranger, long and bony, it had become, the soft outlines of the boy seemed to have dissolved on the voyage. His eyes were deepset, more grey than blue, under brows which seemed to have become thicker, more prominent. His hair was still the same, thick, straight, unruly, light brown hair, which had called down his grandmother's wrath so often. It was a new face to him, in a way, for it was a long time since he had really looked at it. In the strong pale snow-light he could see down glinting on his jaw and his upper lip.

"I'll need to be shaving soon," he told the stranger in the looking glass, "or I could grow a beard like my half-uncle . . . great half-uncle . . . half great-uncle . . . Lord, what do I call him?"

Above the fireplace was a photograph in a home-made frame. It caught his eye as he was about to leave the room and he went to look at it. It was of a man, a man about twenty-two or three, in uniform, a kilt and tunic and a glengarry. It struck John that the man looked like himself. He might be looking at his own photograph in ten years time. The brows were the same, the long jaw. It was not surprising, he supposed, in Bennachie. The Bennachie people were his people. It was uncanny though, even a little frightening, like a prophecy. Perhaps he would be in uniform in ten years time. Dan seemed to think there would be war. 'If there is,' he thought defiantly, 'I'll join the Air Force.' Hughie's tales of death in the mud and of the filth and squalor of the trenches were vivid in his mind. He tidied his things away as Grandmother's rule demanded and wondered whether Hughie liked the coachman's quarters, whether he was happy. He cared more about Hughie, he realised, than he did about Grandmother and Aunty Nell. He felt guilty about that.

The kitchen was warm and neat; bread dough proved fragrantly on the rack above the range and there was a brave smell of meat and onions stewing together. The room was empty but he could hear the clatter and swish of washing-up and he found Aunt Chrissie in the scullery.

"You're up!" she exclaimed. "I thought you'd sleep longer after yestiddy. The others is out on the hill after the sheep. Want some breakfast?"

"How is Grand?" he asked.

"Better. Had a bite of breakfast. Your friend . . . the foreigner . . ."

"Dan."

"Dan says he oughter sleep all he can."

"Can . . . may I see him?"

"Help yourself," she said, "but mind you don't wake him."

Grand lay still and flat under the sheepskins. He seemed no more than a head on the pillow, his breath was so shallow. He looked so frail, so ill, that John could not believe that here was the same man who had brought them over the Pukeatua. It was not till that very moment that John understood that, some day, he himself must die. An icy hand grasped at his guts.

There was tea waiting in a shabby brown pot, boiled eggs and buttered scones.

"He looks ill," John said. "Is Dan out with the others?"

"No. He said there was nothing more he could do for him. Just time and luck, he said. He's trying to make the Craigies' place. They got a phone."

"Why does he want a phone?"

"He wants to send a cable to your Grandma," she explained gently. "See?"

It was a curious sensation to be in two places at once; in the bright snow-lit kitchen eating scones and in the parlour of the house in Kelvin Drive. Six weeks had etched that house into his mind; it represented everything he had escaped with guilty rejoicing, the tiny sooty garden, the malodorous river in the park, the prams paraded along the paths, the contrast between the warm, well-clad children of the Drive and the swarming, yelling 'keelies' from Maryhill at the swings on the hill. The doorbell of the house was brass and the stone around it stained black with the years of polishing which had softened the angles of the knob. When the Telegram boy in his round cap and tight tunic pulled at it, the wire would grate in the tube and in the kitchen above the dresser the biggest bell of the long row would stir and jangle flatly. Ruby would go up the two stone steps, through the hall over the red and blue carpet and open the door to him. It was unbelievable that something which Dan did here could ring that bell in that house.

Ruby would be dressed in blue if it was the morning and if it was the afternoon she would have changed into her black dress and have a little white apron and a white cap worn down over her eyebrows. On the hall-table was the enamelled silver tray with the inscription, only just visible, 'To Captain Dominic Innis of Inchbeg on the occasion of his marriage to Miss Amy Pollock of Wetherpark from his fellow-officers in the 65th.' It had stood on that table for nearly a century and during all that time cards and letters and telegrams had been carried on it. Grandmother would take the yellow envelope and open it . . . at that point his imagination failed. Would she come at once, hoping to be in time, or would she wait, with Aunty Nell red-eyed and lachrymose on the other side of the fireplace, for another cable to be brought in on that same silver tray? No one ever quite knew what Grandmother would do. Had she known, at that stiff, miserable leavetaking in the parlour that she would never see her husband again?

". . . much too cold," Aunt Chrissie was saying above the cup of tea she was holding in both hands in a way that Grandmother would not have allowed, "I've laid out an old pair of my husband's."

John, uncertain what she was talking about, followed her meekly into the room above the kitchen. There on the crocheted afghan lay a pair of heavy, dark-brown breeches.

"They were too thick for me to cut down for Hector like I done with the rest of his stuff," Aunt Chrissie said. "But they'll fit you, I reckon."

They fitted as if they had been made for him. Aunt Chrissie brought out a thick leather belt and said that shorts were no wear for a grown man, especially in winter, no matter what his age was. She broke off suddenly, her fist at her mouth.

"My gawd . . . it's like having a ghost in the house. You're his spit an' image . . ."

John looked over his shoulder, alarmed at the note of hysteria in her voice. She sat down on the bed, staring.

"I'd forgot," she muttered. "I'd forgot him. Folk do. It's natural. It's sixteen year, near enough, since he went off. It's not as if Hector was like him. He's like my side. He's like my brother Sim. He's a preacher, my brother Sim. He don't have nothing to do with me because I worked in a bar before . . . before I was married. Set against drink is Sim. Sometimes I think it's a sending that Hector's that like him. His Dad didn't want to marry me . . . you know that . . ."

She dropped her head in her hands and began to laugh, her plump shoulders shaking. John stood in her dead husband's breeches helpless in the face of these revelations.

"It was his Dad. When he heard . . . about the baby, I mean . . . he came down and brought me up here. Not Hector. Oh, he'd have seen me right, but I wasn't . . . he wasn't . . . oh, hell . . ."

She had looked up and seen John's horrified embarrassment.

"Oh, forget it, son. It's just that you're like him. Like enough to bring things back. I'm sorry, straight up, I'm sorry . . ."

However, it was impossible to forget what she had said and it stayed with him during the rest of that cold bright difficult day when Grand lay dying in the room off the kitchen.

"The lying-in room, that's what it's called but there's as many have died there as've been born. Old Hector and his wife, a tartar she was by all accounts, Hannah she was called. Their daughter Judy, too. She never married. Elspeth died last year in Auckland. There was a letter from her Minister. She never had no children. But there's been a few births there. Your own Ma. And Dad's three."

"Hannah, Hector and Jess," John said.

"Right," she agreed. "Hannah's in the North. Married a music teacher in Wellington; they'd sent her down there to a boarding school. They got a daughter, Ruth. I never seen her. She'll be about twelve. Jess is married in Dunedin. He's a big bug, pots of money an' that. She don't come here much. Never took to me, that's the truth . . . or me to her. She got two boys, twins, right little devils. When Dad's wife died four year back she stops coming here. Though she writes regular."

"What was my Great Aunt Gretl like?"

Aunt Chrissie thumped the shirt she was ironing as if she hated it.

"Don't ask me," she said bitterly. "I never found out. I lived with her. I was her son's wife. I had her grandson. I nursed her like a baby when she was dying. But I never knew her. I think she hated me. But I don't know. She'd never let on what she felt. Sweet as ice cream she were, polite as pie. But you couldn't never get near her. I couldn't talk to her like I'm talking to you. Hector was like her. Looked like his grandpa, the old Hector, but he was like her other ways. Never knew where you stood, you didn't. You knew where you lay . . . oh, yes . . . but not what he thought, never that."

John had realised by this time that she wasn't really aware of him except as a pair of ears. She had spent so much time on her own, she probably talked to herself when he wasn't by. He helped her with the things she had to do, fed the beasts and the hens and swept the snow from the paths. All the time she talked and he listened and learned about this place. At intervals they went in to see Grand but he lay there, sleeping, motionless, his breathing very fast and shallow but his face peaceful. At midday he woke briefly, smiled at them and swallowed some soup which Chrissie spooned for him. Then he fell asleep again between one spoonful and another.

At dusk Dan returned, exhausted and grim.

"They'll send word if there's an answer," he told John, "but she cannot be in time. I will not lie to you, John. It is a few hours only."

He looked at the sleeping face.

"I am surprised he reached here at all. His will was stronger than his body."

John was startled by this comment. He loved Grand, in fact if he were honest he knew that Grand was the only person he loved, but he had always thought that he was, not weak, precisely, but prepared to let Grandmother go her own way and take him along with her. In his mind he could see Grandmother and Aunty Nell, one on either side of the parlour fireplace, waiting for the front door bell to ring again, for the message to come in on the enamelled silver tray. Suddenly, there was something he had to ask.

"Did Grandmother know how sick he was? Did she know when we left?"

"Yes," Dan said. "I have myself told her. But I do not think she believed me. I am a foreigner, you understand and not reliable. Also, I think she believed he would not go. That he would turn back before the ship sailed. But this cable she will have been expecting. It will be no surprise."

Ian Angus and Hector did not come home that night. They slept in a whare on the far side of the property where there was hay stored for just such an emergency. It was a cold, clear, frosty night and the light in the whare could be seen easily. Messages were exchanged by passing a piece of card in front of the lamp. John, sent to bed, stood at the bedroom window looking at the light and wondering what his half-Great-uncle (if that was what he was) and his cousin were thinking and saying. He did not know what was going to happen after Grand was dead. Was he to go home again? He understood that he did not want to go. Almost without conscious thought he knew what he meant to do. If they could not let him stay here on Bennachie he would try to find a job on another station like it. This was the place for him. He blew out the lamp and fell asleep almost at once.

The next day Grand seemed to get weaker. The cold was ringingly intense so that the tiniest sounds could be heard for miles. At dusk which was as blue and transparent as a sapphire Hector and Ian Angus plodded up on their tired horses with three tiny lambs in their saddlebags. They were cold and wet and weary. Aunt Chrissie let John serve them the huge hot meal and fill the tub of hot water in front of the kitchen fire while she cared for the lambs. She came in as they were finishing and said that they had eaten and were sleeping. Ian Angus told her of what they had found, the survivals and the losses. He seemed to accept both. Hector said nothing and it was plain that he was too exhausted to speak.

Ian Angus rose from the table, ready to strip and have his bath, just as Dan came in from the sickroom.

"He wishes you to come," Dan said. "It is important. He has been asking for you today. He must speak tonight and he has much to say."

John understood that the time was coming very near. Ian Angus nodded for Hector to take first go in the tub and he followed Dan into the sickroom, sweeping John with him. Grand was propped up on pillows, his face fallen in and his ears curiously prominent. He looked like another man, not like himself at all. On the sheepskin under his hand was a book. John recognised it as the diary from A. Smith's trunk; his mother's diary. He had never seen it since the day he had found it and when he had asked Grand if he might see it, Grand had put him off, saying 'Soon, soon . . .'

Dan stood by the head of the bed watching. Ian Angus sat down on the chair on the other side with John still in the curve of his arm

"Well, Nick," Ian Angus said. "So you're well enough to talk, eh? I've been wondering what brought you all this way."

"The boy . . ." Grand said. His voice was faint but it was clear. "It was because of the boy."

"John, here?"

"I found out who his father was," Grand said.

"Ah," breathed Ian Angus.

"She never told us. But there was a diary. The boy found it. He doesn't know. Anna was in France . . . you knew?"

"Hector wrote that he had met her," Ian Angus said. "Just the once. It was the last letter we had from him. He said he had gone over to Bethune to see her."

"They . . . they . . . spent some time together . . . a week . . ."

Dan looked anxiously at his patient. He had the flaccid wrist in his fingers.

"Let me explain a little," he begged. "Rest a moment."

He turned to Ian Angus and John.

"John here was the outcome of that leave. It was something sudden and I think unexpected for both. The war is not as newspapers describe it. War is a monster. Anna had spent three years pulling victims from his jaws and she was lonely . . . forlorn. She felt her place in her home had been taken. She had few friends. She had, Nick has told me, a great feeling for Bennachie. She wished all the time when she was a little girl to learn about Bennachie. And suddenly here was someone from that dreamplace. It is all in the diary. The ward journal had become a confidant, you understand. In it she has disclosed her despair and her sick horror which for the sake of others she must conceal. And she meets someone from this place. Poor child . . . poor child . . ."

There was a long pause.

"The diary says," Dan went on, "that he was stationed not far away. He was given leave and found her with leave also and unwilling to go home. He felt compassion and they went together to Brittany, to the country."

"They had six days," Grand murmured. "Six days."

"In such times, six days can be more than a lifetime," Dan interrupted harshly. "After that leave he was sent up the line and was killed in the first battle of Passchendaele."

Again there was silence. John felt curiously apart, as if he was hearing about something which had nothing to do with him.

"Read . . ." said Grand, and his voice was hardly more than a whisper. Without hesitation Dan picked up the journal and found the place.

. . . tonight, Hector went back to billets. We said goodbye
outside Michel's. I won't see him again, I know. We both
know he has very little chance. He said that he hoped he
would be killed outright, that was as much as he hoped for.
But even if he survives I won't see him again. He has a wife
and a son. He must go back to them. I suppose I should feel
guilty about what we have had together, but I don't. I have
taken nothing really. I pretended Hector loved me but inside
myself I know he doesn't. He never pretended to. He was
sorry for me, I think, and he was able to talk to me about
Bennachie. Really, he has just hidden his head against me for
a little because he doesn't want to die. No one could grudge
him that.

Dan's voice faltered a little and silence filled up the room.
Into that silence came a sob. Chrissie was standing by the door
and the tears were running down her face.

"He was cruel, your son!" she accused. "Cold as bloomin'
charity. A lie wouldn't have hurt him. She was that unhappy I
can't bear it! God knows I wouldn't have grudged her what *I*
never had . . ."

Ian Angus's face was like granite but his arm tightened
round John. Dan was giving Grand a drink for the blue shade
was back and his breath was rasping again, the only sound in
the room except for Chrissie's sobbing.

"Money . . ." Grand gasped, pushing Dan's hand aside.
"Not much. For John."

"Peace," Dan begged him, "let me tell thy tale. Inchbeg is
sold. He has brought John's share. He knows that John wishes
to be a farmer."

"Unless you help . . . "

Grand's breathing worsened and Dan pulled him up to lean
against him, his head on his shoulder.

"He spent his life to bring you his grandson," Dan said.

"And mine," Ian Angus said. "And mine. Listen to me,
Nick . . . can you hear?"

Grand's eyelids rose, slowly, as if they were made of lead.

"I'll do my best for him, Nick, I swear it."

"Good boy . . . John . . ."

His eyes closed again. Ian Angus bent over him. John was

watching Dan. Dan laid down the thin, bony wrist and the hand which had played for the passengers on the ferry.

"Home . . ."

The word was barely articulated. It was the last he spoke. After a very few minutes Dan shook his head, and nodded at Ian Angus to remove the pile of pillows before he laid down Grand and folded his hands over his chest. The rasping had stopped.

A long time later, it seemed, they were all together in the kitchen. John still felt as if he was watching a scene which had nothing to do with him. He did not see Hector glaring at him.

"Well," Hector said, "what a thing! Welcome, little cuckoo, welcome to the nest! Talk about chickens coming home to roost!"

He began to laugh, harshly, without humour.

"So much for my sainted father, my hero, without flaw and without stain!"

His laughter increased until Ian Angus slapped him sharply on the side of his head.

"This is no way to behave," he said disgustedly.

"Don't touch me!" snarled Hector. "Don't you try to tell me how my father would never have behaved like that. You can't trot that one out at me any more, can you? Can you?"

"Out," said Ian Angus softly and it was enough. Hector flung out of the room.

He was in bed when John came upstairs. The blanketed hump looked hostile. He undressed as quickly and quietly as possible and crept in at his side of the bed. He lay on his back with sleep very far away. He couldn't quite take it in. He couldn't be sure how he felt, even how he should feel. Grand was dead and that should matter more than anything except that he knew at last who his father had been. He only had to light the lamp to be able to see his father's face in a photograph. Now he could fit that face to his daydreams but Grand was dead and he was not even sure that he liked the face. Grand was dead but he had a whole new host of relatives, he even had a brother . . . a *brother* . . . or a half-brother at all events. But Hector wasn't in the least like the brother he had dreamed of having and he wasn't at all sure whether he would like having one. He had been an 'only' for a long time, all his life really. Grand had been the only person he had reached out to: other people had been there, Grandmother, Ruby, Aunty Nell, teachers like Mr. Davidson, some boys at school and they had been all right but they hadn't come near; only Grand ever came near enough to guess how he felt about things. Now he had a brother and a father and found he didn't like either of them. There had been a sense of utter misery and humiliation in that bit of the diary. It made him ache with distress for the girl who had been his mother. Aunt Chrissie (she had said to call her Aunt Chrissie) had cried for his mother and that made him like her better than his father or his brother and, if it was like in the books, she should hate him. Grand was dead and he had no one really and yet he had all these new people. Dan would go away soon, now. He had said so.

John lay and stared up into the dark. He began to sweat a little, to feel sick: new people, a new place, a new life which he couldn't even guess at . . . and no Grand, no Dan. He felt like the time when Luckenham shoved him into the swimming pool. He had the same sense of having lost touch with everything familiar, of being in a hostile place where there was nothing to hold on to, nothing near. He moved distressfully . . . .

"Aw . . . whassit . . ." grumbled a sleepy voice. "Shurrup."

"Sorry," John muttered.

The warm presence at his side grunted, heaved at the covers and stilled into sleep. John lay quietly, the chill creeping in at his uncovered side. Gently, John pulled back enough of the covers to keep out the cold. His brother stirred but did not protest. He could hear movement below in the kitchen. He had heard Aunt Chrissie come up to bed not long after he had done. He wondered what Dan and . . . as he hesitated over what to call Ian Angus, the understanding came over him, like the warmth of the blankets, that he had another grandfather. He still wondered what they were doing down there. Dan had closed Grand's eyes, folded his hands and pulled the sheet over. What more was there to do with that stillness which wasn't Grand any more. Soon they would bury him. And what then? Those stories he had learned, heaven and all that, angels and harps and golden pavements, all above the bright blue sky . . . they didn't seem to have anything to do with Grand. Lift up your heads ye gates of brass . . . it didn't seem the sort of place that Grand would like. Aunt Chrissie had hugged him, her tears smearing across his cheek and promised him that he would meet Grand in heaven . . . but he didn't really believe her, he couldn't. If there was a heaven it shouldn't be like that, like a huge railway station with gold and crystal platforms with everybody meeting and not knowing what to say. He almost wished there were ghosts. He couldn't be afraid of Grand, even as a ghost.

"Won't it be nice," Aunt Chrissie had said a little while afterwards, "he'll lie beside his mother."

But Grand had never talked very much about his mother. If there was that sort of railway station kind of heaven, perhaps he had met her there and they were wondering what to say to one another. What could it matter to bones where they lay or what other bones lay near them. Meeting the dead was scaring. How would he know his mother? How could he have anything to say? He wasn't even sure that he wanted to meet his father. And if there was heaven there was the other place to think about. There had been a boy at Springwood who had nightmares about hell. He was certain he was damned, certain he would burn for ever and ever, because someone had told him he would if he went on 'playing with himself' as matron called it. The boys had laughed at him but those nightmares had been real enough, full of torment and hideous monsters . . . surely Grand wasn't there . . . Grand was good, good, *good* . . .

A sliver of light outlined the door.

"John," a voice said, barely a sound at all, "are you awake?"

"Yes," he whispered back.

"Come," said Dan. "It is not good to lie so. Come and talk to your grandfather."

Downstairs there was a bottle on the table. Dan brought another glass. John sipped gingerly at the golden liquid and found it strange that people chose to drink such stuff: he said nothing, remembering Grand letting him have a glass of port after he had heard that Inchbeg was sold.

"Now," Ian Angus said, "grandson John . . . how do you think you'll take to sheepfarming?"

For ever afterwards John was to link the taste of whisky with comfort, the feeling of belonging, of being part of something he loved. Before that moment he had always felt as if he had to prune himself, the real self inside the awkward, clumsy, gangling schoolboy, in order to fit inside the life he led, just as Jock the Garden had pruned the roses and the fruit trees at Inchbeg to fit the places where they grew. At Bennachie he could grow unhindered like a tree in the park and take his true shape.

30

John, in the years which followed, was to identify himself completely with Bennachie. They were not easy years for they struggled along on the verge of financial disaster but they were still years which he was to look back upon as utterly happy: flying Hurricanes above the lush, flat, green fields of Essex, he was to crave for the tawny hills around Bennachie, for the tussocks and the snow-grass; no flowers in English gardens could compare with the mountain lilies and no birds with the bell-bird or the graceful banded dotterels which haunted the little lake. In all that time he rarely gave a thought to Scotland, to Inchbeg. It was on Bennachie that he had become John Innis Macadam and it was Bennachie which was his home. For him his real life had begun there, everything that was in him was channelled into it. When later he fought, he fought for Bennachie. It was a headlong love affair.

It was on Bennachie that his real education had taken place: school had not begun to scratch the surface of what he needed to know in order to outwit the weather, the harsh country and the isolation in order to raise sheep: to win the harvest of their fleeces and their meat. It was a harsh life, a constant battle to stem the tide of work which had to be done despite everything which conspired to make it difficult, but it was, without question, the life for him. It wasn't often he had time, as he took more and more of the work upon his shoulders, to stop and think, 'I am happy'. But there could be no doubt that he was. In the eighteen months after Grand's death he topped six feet, in two years he was taller and heavier than Ian Angus himself. It was a quiet pleasure for him to go into the little-used parlour from time to time and look at the photograph of the first Hector. He and Hannah had taken advantage of the visit of a travelling photographer in the late seventies. They had been posed with Hector sitting on the bench outside the front door in his 'best' clothes, a dark suit which buttoned high. Doubtless he had worn a clean white shirt and cravat but his thick hair and beard obliterated all sign of them. Hannah stood behind, her hand on his shoulder, looking as if she could not be done with this tedious nonsense soon enough. Her 'best' had been ten years out of date, a vast fringe-trimmed, tiered skirt over a crinoline and a tight bodice, buttoned high to her throat with crochet lace disposed over her shoulders. She wore it with an air, unbecoming as it was. Her hair was drawn back into a tight chignon which made her look severe, even forbidding, though there was a quirk about her mouth which hinted at a readiness to laugh. John used to go in to look at Hector because he was supposed to be so like him but he always ended by staring at Hannah. Her face drew him and he could not hear enough of her from Ian Angus who was willing enough to pass the long winter evenings talking of the old days and the old ways.

"She never had much to say, my mother," IA said, "but she had a laugh I can hear yet. And how she worked. I never saw her idle. My father said she was as good on the hill as any man and she was aye at the knitting or the sewing or the crocheting even when she was sitting down."

He jerked his head at the beautiful rosewood chest which stood gleaming and graceful between the parlour windows.

"Yon's full of her work. My wife Gretl, she treasured it."

"Did she ever meet your Gretl?"

"No. She never did. The Königs came the year she died. They took the old Mackenzie place in the next valley. The Ellershaws went into it after the war."

And then the talk would leave Hannah and range round the stations and how they had fared over the years and how the grim post-war world was treating them.

IA was delighted to find that John could play the piano. John, accustomed to measure himself against Grand, was astonished to find his limited abilities so much in demand. He played the harmonium at the little kirk at Inchture and when the Minister came on a visitation he played hymns. 'A peely-wally creature,' IA called the Minister and treated him with the careful chilly politeness he reserved for people he did not much like. He spoke to Hector like that sometimes and it distressed John. From time to time there were shearing-shed dances and

John was in demand to play the waltzes and the Scottish country dances which were in favour for these occasions still. His ear was quick and he soon picked up the syncopated rhythms of ragtime and jazz. IA liked to sing old-fashioned ballads, like *Just a Song at Twilight* and *A Bicycle Built for Two* for he had a splendid bass voice and John learned to accompany him.

"In the old days we all used to sing," he told John once after there had been an argument about the purchase of a wireless. "My mother had a bonnie voice, not strong ye ken, but clear and pure and she'd all the old songs by heart. *The Piper Cam' tae oor Ha' Door* and the *Wee Couper o' Fife* and *Leezie Lindsay*. Och, there's nothing like the old songs . . ."

Hector sighed ostentatiously and left the room.

"My sister Judith played the piano and we'd all sing round the fire on winter nights with my father rumbling away in the bass. I can hear him yet. He made the china rattle in the cabinet."

"Was it this piano?"

"Oh, aye, this one. Nick, your Grand, chose it and bought it and had it shipped out. I mind fine the day it arrived with the carrier cart and the whole household wild with excitement out to see it brought in in a storm of rain heavy enough to drown you. We found a rick cover and spread it out over the top of the case like a king's palanquin and brought it inside. None of us had seen such a handsome piece before for the old school piano had seen better days. My mother was fair lit up with pleasure. Judy'd learned her pieces down at the school and as soon as it was in place she sat down and played *All People that on Earth do Dwell* and we fairly lifted the roof singing. Aye, it was a grand day, yon, a grand day . . ."

Once, after Hector had cut himself and Dan had dressed it out of the big first-aid box which stood in the porch, Dan asked about doctors. IA got up and opened a drawer in the rosewood chest. He came back with a tiny booklet, bound in a cotton-covered card with 'Sickroom Hints' embroidered across it in faded cross-stitch.

"This is all my mother had," he told them. "She'd cut it out of a book of Etiquette for Ladies, she told me once, and she used all the rest of it to stuff the chinks and keep the wind out of the house. The nearest doctor was in Cromwell then and it would take a good deal to get him to come into the boo-ay. You'd go to him and lord help you if you were too sick to go. My mother could set bones and sew up cuts and deliver babies as well as any doctor. She'd a little garden, the lake's covered it over now, and she called it her physic-garden. She'd herbs and stuff in it and she used to brew medicines, and fell nasty some of them were."

"She'd her first baby all on her own," Chrissie put in. "My Mum told me that. There was no one around at all. Your Grand that'd be, John."

"Right enough. There was an old Maori woman around for the rest of us. Maraea."

"Is that the one on the stone upbye?"

"Aye. She died when I was five or thereabout. My mother missed her sore."

"Your mother used to deliver other folks' babies," Chrissie said. "She was well-known for it. My Granma told me that half the folk around here were helped into the world by Miss Hannah. She was one of them, she said."

"Miss Hannah?" queried John.

IA chuckled.

"Aye. She was Miss Hannah to the end of the chapter. You take a look at her stone, laddie. It's Hannah Lindsay that's on it."

"But I thought it was like at home. Women have their own names on their stones and then it says 'beloved wife of . . . of whoever'."

"No. My mother was never right married."

John stared and Dan laughed deep in his chest like a stream underground. IA grinned mischievously.

"It's right enough," he assured John, "Hector here's the only Macadam born the right side of the law, and he . . ."

He pulled himself up and looked apologetically at Chrissie.

"Don't mind me," Chrissie put in, "the whole district knew it was a race between the parson and the midwife."

Dan laughed again at John's expression.

"Your grandfathers both and now you. So what is strange? Or shameful?"

"I never knew . . . no one said . . ."

"Your grandmother preferred to forget such a thing," Dan said drily.

"My Gretl too. Anyway, laddie, it's of no consequence," IA said, lighting his pipe. "It's the intentions that matter."

"It's of consequence to me," Hector interrupted angrily. "I'm legit. He's not. He can't prove he's one of the family."

IA glowered at him and stabbed at the picture hanging over the mantel with the stem of his pipe.

"You've mebbe got a bit paper," he said, "but John's got proof enough for anyone with eyes in their head . . . isn't that right, Chrissie?"

Chrissie nodded, her eyes on the heel of the sock she was knitting.

"His voice is different," she remarked, "softer, sort of, but every other way he might be . . ."

"Bloody Pommie," Hector snarled and slouched out, leaving an uncomfortable and irritated silence.

"I mind when my mother was dying," IA said after a pause. "Nick arrived with your grandmother and a whole cartload of trunks and such full of everything she thought she might need when your mother was born. My father had planned to have a grand wedding at long last, with Nick there and everything. He'd kept it all a secret and got the licence from Dunedin and the Minister arrived. He was that put about he didn't know where to look. Mother wouldn't hear of it. She said she'd chosen the way she'd lived with all her wits about her and to wed now would be as good as saying she'd chosen wrong. The Minister tried to persuade her . . . I mind, he began, 'My dear madam . . .' and she turned on him, just . . ."

IA rumbled with laughter.

"My word, but my mother had salt under her tongue when she was roused. She said she was no madam and never would be and she obviously had more faith in God's mercy than he did. And given the choice, she said, she'd rather be disreputable than uncharitable and if he wanted to preach morality there were plenty respectable folk with a skeleton hidden in their closet for him to preach it at and she threatened to name one or two round the district and he didn't know where to look. It's my firm belief he was one of them. Lord, but I can hear her yet, and see her, sitting in that very chair . . ."

He pointed at the carved rocking chair where Chrissie was knitting.

"She glared at the poor wee cratur until he just crept out of the room without another word and then she was sorry that she'd given him a red face but he'd never fill McVean's breeches and he was stupid to think he could. McVean was the minister before this one. The first to come to Inchture. He'd died a year or so before, smoored in the snow on his way over to Ellangowan."

"What happened?" John asked.

"The end of it was we'd a grand party but no wedding."

"Did the Minister ever come back?" Chrissie asked.

"Och, he was a good soul enough. He did. When she'd need of him at the last. But even then she floored him . . ."

He heaved with laughter again.

"It would take my mother to make ye laugh at a death-bed," he said. "He sat with her a wee while, I mind, and she took ill with something he said. I canna just remember what it was but I can hear her yet saying that she'd once been tokened to a minister and the banns cried and she'd left him standing on the wedding day. She didn't regret it then, she said, and she didn't regret it now. He looked as if he'd been stung by a dead bee. And it must have been true for she never lied by ordinar'. My, but I felt sorry for the wee man. But this I'll say for him, he took her funeral and told my father that she was a woman whose price was above rubies. And I heard after he fairly trounced the guid folk in the kirk who'd not come to the burying."

IA was always ready to tell tales of Hannah. About the first Hector he was more reticent, though it was clear that he both loved and respected his father. Only once did he mention something other than Hector's prowess as farmer and builder and doyen of the scatter of stations around Inchture, something which arrested John's attention. They had been talking about Grand.

"Whiles I thought himself was more taken up with Nick than he was with any of us," IA said. "He missed him sore after he left, always on the watch for a letter. When he died I found every letter that Nick had ever written to Bennachie, and Nick wrote like a religion, every fortnight. They were in the back drawer of yon desk, all in order and tied in bundles. Aye, and they were read to rags. And in the same box were newspaper cuttings with the dates with what folk had said about his music. It must have been your grandmother sent them for he'd kept her letters as well, right from the beginning."

"Did you mind?" John asked, greatly daring.

"Aye and no . . . aye and no. I was there and I was his right hand and he knew it. But when I was around your age it angered me and I laid it on him one day out on the hill. He didna deny it, just said Nick needed more support than most folk and I wasn't to grudge it him. After, when I was older and had troubles of my own it came to me that mebbe my mother had been more taken up with the girls and me than she was wi' Nick and my father knew this."

John didn't ask more. IA shyed away from such matters. Instead he took the matter to Dan.

"Would he be right, Dan, do you think?"

Dan had been busy with a lame ewe and hadn't answered at once.

"It might be," he said slowly, "it might be. It is plain to me that Hannah loved her Hector much. She might reproach herself that she had a son by another man and this must affect what she felt for that son. This Hector would know and he might wish to atone for a fault in the beloved one. It is not strange. I think Nick knew. I think he knew."

Grand had been buried for nearly six months before the packing case from Inchbeg arrived with its curious assortment of treasures. Amongst them was a box, a tea-caddy of the eighteenth century and in it, in neat bundles, John found all Hector's letters to Nick. They were quiet, workaday letters but when John read them he felt uncomfortable as if he were eavesdropping. He locked them away again and said nothing to IA. The rest of the things were absorbed into the household until after a while it seemed that they had always been there. They blended with Hector's sturdy chests and chairs and Hannah's treasures and even the heavy Edwardian furniture which Gretl had brought with her, solid, ugly things, bought in the emporium in Dunedin and carried in laboriously by horse and cart.

About Gretl, John learned very little except that she had been a housewife of renown. When he visited round about people regaled him with her recipes and tales of her expertise: but none of them claimed to have known her, or to have been her friend. It was Chrissie's outburst which was as near as he ever came to knowing what she had been and what lay behind that rather forbidding pudgy face crowned with thickly plaited hair which stared from a large over-coloured photograph in the parlour. IA rarely spoke of her.

"The children left," Dan said once. "That tells its own tale. They write but seldom and come never at all."

"It's a hell of a trip," John said.

"Postage is cheap," Dan rejoined. "And there was much love waiting for you. Much love. When I leave I will remember this and be easy."

John, hunting for a pair of snowshoes in the attic that first winter, found a tiny doll's carriage on sledge-runners with a rag-doll still in possession, her woollen hair in thick plaits and a comically smug expression embroidered on to her grimy face. IA grinned ruefully at it.

"My father made it for Judy," he remembered, "and my mother made yon doll. Lucinda they called her. But Judy aye wanted to push me in the pram, not Lucinda. A tomboy, she was, a right wee terror . . . but she was good sister to me."

"Chrissie said she never married."

"She was tokened to the Minister's son, McVean's boy, but he died of the consumption before they could be married. Aye, there was a lot of it around in the old days. Judy was like my mother, never one to parade her feelings, but I doubt she never looked at anyone else. After Elspeth went north to be married Judy stayed on to keep house and look after my mother. She was ill a weary long while."

He patted the handle of the absurd little toy.

"After mother was dead I met my Gretl and we were married and I brought her here. I never thought but that they'd agree, Judy and Gretl, but they did not. No, they did not. It came to the point when I was looking around for a place of my own but one afternoon I came in off the hill and Gretl told me that Judy was gone. She went to Dunedin and learned the typewriter and found a job in the weaving mill there."

He stared down at the rag-doll smugly ensconced under the faded patchwork quilt.

"I felt badly about it for it was her home and my father was grieved. Maybe it was for the best that she went . . . but it put between Gretl and me. I couldna feel the same as once I did. Judy was a good sister to me."

John said nothing.

"But young Hector was just starting to run and Hannah new-born so I put it behind me as best as I could."

"What about your father?" John asked.

"He died that same winter. It wasn't just Judy going, he missed his Hannah sore and he had a bad fall out on the hill there . . ." he nodded towards the high pastures, gleaming under the first snowfall. "You have times like that, John-lad, times when you think you'll never be happy again."

"But Judy came back?"

"She came home to die," IA said harshly. "She was taken ill in her lodgings in Dunedin and the wifie who kept them sent for me. They were good folk but they'd family of their own and they couldn't be nursing her. She wanted to go to the hospital but I brought her back here. I thought she'd pick up again when she was home but she died. It's my belief that she took the consumption from Alec McVean. And for all that lay between them Gretl nursed her like a real sister, as if she was sorry. But if she was she'd never say it."

John put the little sledge-pram away carefully in a corner where it would be hard to find. After that he didn't ask about Judy or Gretl. IA, he began to understand, had had a difficult time of it. His own father, the young Hector, was another subject on which IA was not readily to be drawn unless it was to tell of his exploits in the sports field. What John learned about him he could not like much. Chrissie talked of him once.

"His mother thought the world and all of him," she said once over a vast tub of potatoes which John was helping her peel for the shearers' tea. For years afterwards the smell of roasting mutton would make John remember his father.

"She found him a wife. He was engaged when I met him. He didn't tell me and no one else did. She was one of his Ma's grand relations. She was the niece of a Graf or some such thing. She was to come out and marry him. His mother was set on the match and everything was arranged for him to be married up north. But I never knew anything about it. We were going together quite a while but he never talked much. Deeds not words . . . that was my Hector."

She smiled rather wrily.

"My oath, I thought the sun rose and set on him, so I did. When I told him about the baby he said he'd pay for it, give me money to raise it somewhere else. I couldn't believe it at first but my Missus at the hotel told me about his fiancée and I had to believe it. It was a pill."

"Poor Chrissie," John murmured.

"That's just what I thought," she said and pulled a funny face. She peeled another few potatoes.

"Sometimes I think it would have been better if I'd taken the money and gone to Aussie the way he wanted. But I couldn't bear the thought that I'd never see him again. But she never forgave me and he never forgave me . . . neither did Hannah or Jess. There were times I wished I'd never been born."

She smiled at John.

"Never mind," she said, "we all make mistakes. The great thing's to keep going, isn't it?"

Dan had done what he said he would do: in the autumn of 1933, after eighteen months at Bennachie he sailed for America with a wad of manuscript in his baggage. In 1934 a luridly jacketed copy of *The Threatening Cloud* arrived at the station, together with a wad of reviews alike only in the violence with which they praised or berated the author. Dan had found a publisher. The book warned the world about the dangers of Nazism and Fascism. When John opened it he found a brief note. Dan either wrote thirty words or thirty pages:

It will not sell, and those who read will not heed. Cassandra has a hard road though they will believe her when it is too late. However, it has found me a job. D.H.

John wrote to Dan whenever he had something other than sheep to write about. Dan had made it clear before he left that he found John's liking for sheep incomprehensible. It was his view, often repeated, that the young David slew Goliath and joined the army of Saul because he could not abide sheep rather than because he had any spite at the Philistine. For all that, they had missed him when he went. During the lambing he had been as good as a vet and had taught John much that was to stand him in good stead.

"As far as you will be from a doctor," Dan said, "there are some little things that you must know."

He did his share of the work while he was there and explained his dislike of sheep by saying that they reminded too sharply of the human race.

"Once they are in a mob they will over the cliff run shouting with delight. In Europe there are many, many woolly sheep, woolly in their minds. I must go herd them to run in the right direction, like Moss here."

Between Dan's departure and 1938 there were three events on which John could enlarge at some length in his letters. The first was a breach in the isolation. The Government, which was attempting to use the unemployed to fill some gaps in amenities at a very low cost, offered to split the cost of making a road over the Pukeatua with Bennachie. In September the welfare gang arrived and by the end of the summer were camped in sight of the homestead. John wrote to describe what had happened in the hot February days:

It was very hot and oppressive all day and we hadn't had rain for weeks. It happened just before sunset. I thought I heard thunder. You must remember the tremendous thunder-storms we have. Then the house began to shake. It wasn't much, really, just the china tinkling and the windows rat-tling. I realised then it wasn't thunder it was a shake. They get them here from time to time though this is the first since I came. They said afterwards that it wasn't bad as shakes go. I never even thought about the camp though I should have done because they had set it up under the cliff which IA calls Salisbury Crag. The ganger came galloping down on his wall-eyed brute and asked had we got a place where the men could shelter for the camp was squashed flat under a landslide and there was the father and mother of a storm brewing. I hadn't been altogether wrong about the thunder. I said we could probably squeeze them all into the shearing shed. He went back up to tell them and I went to tell Chrissie. She is a topper. She had things going in no time. Remember how she set to and fed the shearers? But this time it was forty gangers, not a handful of swaggies. When they arrived they were carrying a stretcher in the middle of them. The gangers' cook had been in the camp when the slide hit and they had had to dig him out. I never saw such as mess as his right leg was in. I didn't know whether to bless you for what you'd taught me or curse you for not being there. We did what we could. Chrissie was a brick and didn't turn a hair. Hector took the mare and went for the doctor but there'd been a slip over the road from Inchture and it was ages before he could make it.

We've put him in the room off the kitchen where Grand died because it's easier for Chrissie and the gangers are still in the shearing shed. It isn't long now before they'll be finished. Another thirty yards or so. Lord, but they're a mixed crew . . . swaggies and factory hands from the wool mills at Dunedin and clerks all bunched together. IA's taken on one of them as a rouseabout. Prices are a bit better and we reckoned we could afford it. He was glad to get the job though we can't pay a lot. He says the gangwork's worse than prison from which I gather he's been inside. Lucky (that's the cook who's hurt) says he's a good bloke. So is Lucky. He insists on doing what he can to help Chrissie and the day after the doc left he was sitting up peeling potatoes and stringing beans in his bed.

However, we'll soon have a road. Imagine being able to get lorries and cars right up to the very door. It will make a difference. IA's away to Cromwell with the postvan next week to buy a Ford van. Mind you, if the river's up, you remember that wee trickle you were so scornful about when we crossed it in the jinker? If that's up we'll be cut off till it goes down.

Afterwards it was hard to know which was the greater blessing for Bennachie, the new road or Lucky. Lucky stayed on with them. Even when his leg had healed he was still too lame to find another cook's job with the gangs. From what they could discover his wife was dead or departed with someone else and he had no relatives and no home where he could go to convalesce. Before a month was past it had been taken for granted that he would stay. Lame leg or no he found plenty that he could do and he was ingenious in finding ways in which he could do it. He was something of a gardener and something of a carpenter and it wasn't long before they were all wondering what they had done without him. Lucky's readiness to attempt jobs to free the people on Bennachie for the main job of caring for the flock and the tempting presence of the road winding up the hill from the front of the house between them brought the tension between Hector and his grandfather to a head.

The tension was not new: it had been in existence long before John appeared on the scene but John's presence had made matters worse. Hector hated farm work. He would have liked IA to sell the place and invest the proceeds in a business near a town. The kind of business Hector had in mind was a garage which could be shut at five and on Sundays and leave him leisure to pursue his own pleasures. He had been waiting impatiently for IA's age and falling prices to bring this dream about when John and Grand had arrived on the scene. John's money and his own innate ability and liking for the work had made this possibility ever more remote and Hector was bitterly resentful. He was jealous of John, too, because of his size, and the way IA treated him as an equal and because his mother had obviously taken a liking to him as well. As the months passed and Lucky throve Hector did less and less about the place and took every chance he could to be off to town. He fell foul of IA more and more often. One time during a difficult wet lambing he went off to Cromwell once too often. He took the van and stayed away with it when it was needed badly.

. . . there was the most awful row [John wrote to Dan]. IA told him his fortune twice over because we lost the sheep and her lamb and they were the new pedigree stock and worth a bit and then some. Hector answered back like an ass instead of holding his tongue and just taking it. He said he wasn't a kid any more and he'd come and go just as he liked. IA clouted him and I had to stop Hector from clouting him back because IA would have knocked him cold and Chrissie

346

was frightened. He started yelling at me then. He's got a nasty habit of calling me the bastard when IA can't hear and he did then and a bit more . . . quite a bit more . . . about his father and all that. IA grabbed him from me and kicked him right down the verandah steps and told him not to come back until he was ready to apologise and do his share of the work instead of just wasting his time and IA's money in the pub. Then he slammed the door and Chrissie wept a bit because it was coming down in buckets. IA said she had made a mess of bringing him up but he could come back in the house as long as he didn't set eyes on him in the morning, and that was his last word.

Well, it wouldn't have been. IA always simmers down though he does get into the most fearful waxes. But Hector was gone in the morning. He took the van and all his gear and a lot of mine and was well away before daylight. He didn't even leave a note for Chrissie and she was horribly upset. That was bad enough but he made matters even worse because he sold the Ford, and it wasn't old at all, to a dealer from Wanganui and went off with the proceeds which left us without transport except for the horses. And this in the middle of lambing! IA says now that he's never to set foot in the place again. I told Chrissie not to worry because he'll come round after a bit but Chrissie seems to think selling the van was the last straw and I must say he couldn't have done it at a worse time.

They heard nothing from Hector till nearly a year later when he wrote to Chrissie saying he had a job in a garage near Dunedin and was doing well and had a flat over the business. IA drove her to Cromwell to visit him. She never came back. They had a letter saying that Hector needed her and could Lucky carry on doing her bits and pieces. Lucky could, quite easily, but IA worried about Chrissie.

"He'll marry," he said. "And what'll happen to Chrissie then?"

But it was Chrissie who married. Within six months she had met and become engaged to an hotelkeeper in a good way of business in Dunedin. The Bennachie folk were all invited to the wedding and it became the occasion for what was, on the surface at all events, a family reconciliation. IA and Hector shook hands.

   . . . and such a relief [John wrote], because Hector and Chrissie blame me and when you think about it I am to blame. Without me and the money Grand left, IA would have had to sell out. None of the others would have come to the rescue. They wanted him to sell. Hector never liked the place. Once I came Bennachie got a new lease of life. That was really what the row was all about. Funny the way people never really *say* what they're angry about. IA does of course, but he always says what he thinks . . .
   Little as you wish to hear about the 'woollies' I must tell you that this year promises very well. What with the pedigree stuff and the improvement in the pasture and having the rabbiters in we have had a decent wool-cheque this year. This means we can have the rabbiters in again and try to keep the brutes down now we've reduced the numbers. They are a problem, though.

Dan replied on a postcard from Washington State where he had a post with some Government Department. He had never explained to John what work he did.

   I am pleased that you prosper [he wrote], though alas I fear much of that fine wool goes to make shirts, brown, black and red and uniforms, uniforms, uniforms. Yesterday I have married a wife. If ever I prosper too I will bring her to see your lambs and my own gangling lamb. No son that I have will replace you in my heart. D.H.

John smiled when he read that and put it in his pocket before IA could see and scoff. When Dan wrote something like that you knew he meant it and envied him his readiness to say what you found so difficult. If John wrote to him that he was the nearest thing to a proper father he had ever known, he wouldn't have been able to find the words and it would have sounded stiff. All he could do was write the sort of letters that a father might like to get.

348

In 1936 John had his eighteenth birthday and IA shocked and terrified him by presenting him with the deeds of Bennachie, made out in his name, to become his own absolutely when he was twenty-one.

. . . I couldn't believe it. In fact I was scared at the thought. I mean I don't know a quarter of what I ought to know yet. But IA said he wasn't getting any younger (he'll be seventy this year but he still gets about the hill faster than I do) and when he died he wasn't going to have the vultures descend and carve the place up and throw me off. He said it was mine for as long as I wanted it, all my money was in it anyway and I'd worked like a black for the rest. But for the meanwhile if I thought this meant that I was the boss and not him I could think again and he scowled at me as if I was going to start giving him orders right then and there. I didn't know what to say. I never do know what to say. He gave me a great buffet on the shoulder and sent me out to feed the calves, birthday or no birthday.

He described the party they had had with the Duncans over for the night and the huge cake which Lucky had baked and kept secret in the parlour.

IA has bought a gramophone too and Mrs. Duncan tried to teach me to dance. She's got two daughters but the eldest is only twelve and she doesn't come up to my waist. I felt like Gulliver. Mr. Duncan heard what IA had done and said he thought it was a good idea but warned me later after he'd had a couple of drams from IA's bottle that he thought there might be trouble . . .

Mr. Duncan was perfectly correct. There was trouble. It was heralded by a number of letters which IA snarled over and then dropped into the fire without telling John what was in them. At Christmas that year the family converged upon Bennachie for the first time in years, straining the still primitive facilities of the station to the utmost. Their object, apart from a free summer holiday, was, as Jess's husband Gerald put it, to reason with IA. IA, however, was not easy to pin down for a reasoning session, especially at a busy time. John invited their two sons to come out on the run with him and did his best to avoid all the conclaves. Aunt Hannah left her husband and daughter in Wellington and arrived with a trunkful of curtain materials with which to make over the homestead. While the others were trying to find IA on his peregrinations round the run she stayed behind and drove poor Lucky to profanity by trying to teach him new and involved recipes from magazine cuttings, sniffing suspiciously into his store cupboards and professing herself horrified by his methods. She told her father that what they needed was a decent housekeeper.

"Leave Lucky be, girl," IA told her bluntly when she complained that the dishcloth was never boiled and the cold store needed a good scrub and as for the privy she couldn't understand how anyone could use such a place and why didn't he have a proper bathroom and lavatory installed instead of spending all that money on a new shearing shed.

"Leave us alone too. Let me tell you, we manage very well as we always did. And Lucky's the best thing which could have happened to us. We'd have been in Queer Street without him when Chrissie left."

"Oh, Chrissie!" she said and sniffed. "She was no better than that Lucky. If ever I met a slattern. How you put up with her cooking for so long I'll . . ."

"Chrissie did fine," he snapped. "She'd mebbe none of your airy fairy notions of fancy this and fancy that but I'd like to see you produce a hot meal for thirty hungry men twice a day for a fortnight. If you'd like to try you're welcome to come along at the next shearing."

After that encounter Hannah confined herself to making curtains and cushion covers which she did with a martyred air on the ancient treadle sewing machine which the first Hector had brought into Bennachie on a packhorse before IA was born. Things might have continued in this way without the 'reasoning' ever taking place but for the arrival of Hector and Chrissie on the day after Boxing Day. They had heard of the gathering of the clans and guessed at the purpose. If there was to be a dividing of the spoils she thought that Hector ought to be there. IA saw them arrive in a shiny new Morris and snorted faintly before he went out to welcome them.

After supper that night, battle was joined in the parlour under the faintly amused eye of the first Hannah. The arguments were trotted out in the most reasonable way by the portly prosperous Gerald, Jess's husband. They had heard what IA meant to do with the station and they felt that before it passed finally into . . . he cleared his throat . . . other hands they ought to have some say in the matter. Bennachie was a family property after all, surely it wasn't the right thing to do to pass it over completely to a . . . well . . . a newcomer. They (Gerald meant Hannah, Jess and himself) had talked it over and thought that the best thing to do would be to turn the whole concern into a family company with John as a minority shareholder and manager. This would be fair to all parties and everybody would have a say in the management . . . Hector interrupted, lounging back in his chair with his hands in his pockets as he had seen Jimmie Cagney do in a film when he had attended a meeting of the gang, and demanded that the place be sold and the proceeds divided 'properly' among the real heirs so that they could all have their rightful share. He for one could do with the money, not like some he could name and he cast a bitter look at Gerald. And what about John? asked Hannah. John could go back to Pommieland with his blasted fancy accent, Hector said. He wasn't wanted. Gerald cleared his throat and reminded IA politely that he had other grandsons . . . and a granddaughter, Hannah put in . . . all these things ought to be taken into account. Surely IA could see the strength of their argument . . .

IA's silence as he listened to all this reminded John of the day before the shake which had injured Lucky. From his seat by the window he found Gerald's arguments at least reasonable, even convincing. He wondered with a slight sinking of the heart whether IA might not find them reasonable as well. He was, as Gerald had pointedly *not* said, an interloper. He might carry his birthright in his face and in his build. It would be hard to deny that under the picture of the first Hector. No one could really doubt that he was a Macadam but the fact was that there was no legal proof of his paternity, unless it was the entry in Anna's journal and the idea of having that read out in court for the papers to fall upon made him shudder.

Gerald's familiarity with board meetings permitted him to

drone on uninterrupted about the procedures of company formation and registration and proportional holdings up to the third and fourth generation until he was interrupted angrily by Hector.

"Listen to me. I've got a stake in this. You and your companies. I want my share. I don't want a dividend doled out to me by the bastard!"

Hannah and Jess exclaimed in horror.

"I want the bastard off the place altogether. He's no right here. The bloody place ought to be sold. And let me tell you I'm entitled to a third share at least. I'm the only one of you that's had to work their guts out on it. And I don't mean to be done out of it by the bastard. There!"

There was a confused angry reaction to this and an embarrassed protest from Chrissie which was silenced by IA's great gnarled fist coming thump down on the table so that the teacups jumped in their saucers.

"By God," he said and John knew he was angry for IA swore very little. "I'm not dead yet and I mean to let you know it. I'll tell you all a thing or two . . ."

"Tell the lawyers!" Hector snarled. "I'm not going to be diddled out of my rights by *that*!"

He jerked his thumb over his shoulder at John.

"If you don't divide it properly I'll splash it all over the papers. I'll take you to court!"

"You do that," said IA, "and I'll prosecute you for the theft of a Ford van. You may have forgotten that you stole it. I haven't."

Hector abandoned the Cagney pose.

"For Chrissake!" he said, "a measly fifty quid . . . you wouldn't . . ."

"Just try me," IA told him.

"You chucked me off without a penny . . ." Hector shouted, his voice rising, "I was entitled to something . . ."

"You've all been using that word a lot," said IA. "Just you listen to me. None of you is entitled to anything. Not a penny piece. Bennachie is mine. It was left to me outright. No strings. I can do what I like with it and I mean to do what I like with it."

He glowered round at them.

"Father," protested Hannah, "I do think you ought to listen to reason . . . I mean we have reason to think that we might well . . . after all why not . . . we are . . . I mean more than . . . well, aren't we?"

"It's your turn to listen to reason. You're all very set on your entitlements as you call them, and your company and your dividends which is a fancy way of saying getting money from something for doing no work. Tell me, how much did I see of you two in the bad years? Damned little. You both had money from me when you got married. I borrowed to give you that and it was at the worst time and it took me years to get out of debt. But that didn't worry you, did it?"

He pointed at Jess.

"You married a wealthy man. Your tocher was a drop in the bucket to him. He owns half the Southland by all accounts and he's lent money on the other half. Did either of you offer me help when prices were rock-bottom and I wasn't even making my expenses and had to borrow from the bank again? No, you did not."

"I did offer to find a buyer," Gerald said pompously.

"A buyer," IA almost spat the word. "You were ready to do a friend a favour at my expense. Do you think I'm a fool? And now you come sniffing around like dogs after a bone when prices are high and the station's beginning to pay its way and a bit over. You're entitled to nothing, for none of you's put anything into the place. Except John, of course. He's put everything he had into it. Work and money. Everything his other grandfather left him. Now, you can put that in your pipes and smoke it and you can light those pipes with *that* . . ."

He twisted the sheet of paper headed 'Bennachie Enterprises' which Gerald had used to show how the company should be formed and thrust it back to him. Gerald looked at it and then at his wife and decided that he would keep his peace.

"Didn't *I* work?" Hector demanded. "Didn't I work? You kept my nose to the grindstone all right. I earned my share."

IA turned on him.

"You've forfeited anything you've earned and that wasn't much for if ever there was an idle little shirker it's you, you always were and you always will be."

"You were happy enough with what I did till *he* came along!"

"I put up with you because I could get no better. You're a drunken fool. If I gave you anything you'd squander it in a year on drink . . . and other things. I know why you're so keen to get money and let me tell you I'd marry this one instead of paying her off. Poor Chrissie paid off the last one didn't she? You're a fine one to talk of bastards. Do you think because I'm forty miles from the tarseal that I don't hear anything of what goes on? You make me sick. Get out of here and don't come back. Chrissie, you're welcome to stay. John'll take you out whenever you like. But I won't have that one here making his foulmouthed slaver about John."

"If you stay, I'll never speak to you again!" Hector snarled at his mother.

"Her husband will be glad to hear that!" IA thundered. "Or can you beg for money in dumb-show?"

Hector turned on John, his face twisted with hatred and jealousy.

"This is all your fault. We were all right until you came. I'll be even with you, see if I don't. It isn't fair! Why should the bastard get it all and we get nothing!"

"If you will fling that word about," Jess said angrily, "I might remind you that there's some of us think that there might be two of you. If you're a Macadam you don't look or act like one!"

This sharp observation resulted in a loaded silence which Chrissie broke by bursting into tears.

"Every time I see them," she wailed, "it's always the same . . . always . . . and it's a lie . . . it's a lie . . . a lie . . ."

IA got up and put his great arm round her shoulders.

"If there's any one of you apart from John who's earned their share of Bennachie, it's Chrissie here. She's done more for the place than either of you. You'll be civil to her or I'll know the reason why. Gerald . . ."

He glared at Jess's husband.

"You'll take that viper-tongued daughter of mine out of here and I'll thank you to be off the place first thing in the morning."

"I don't need you to defend my mother," Hector said

sulkily, trying to pull Chrissie away from IA. "I can deal with any of these toffee-nosed . . ."

"John," said IA wearily, "I'm an old man and I've had enough of this. Put Hector out. Jess, you apologise to Chrissie or you'll not set foot on Bennachie again."

"Do you think this is Buckingham Palace?" Jess demanded angrily. "I don't care if I never see it again."

"You were keen enough for a bit out of it a moment ago."

"I won't apologise! Chrissie knows what Hannah and I think. She always has."

"Apologise!"

"I will not apologise to that slut! She always was a slut. You forced Hector to marry her in spite of anything mother could say to you! That creature there could be anybody's. Anybody who had the price!"

Gerald, his prominent eyes popping with dismay, was trying to drag her away but she shook him off without trouble.

"My mother knew," Jess shouted, "she told me that Chrissie was no better than a trollop. She slept with anyone who came to the hotel . . . not just Hector. That's what she told me and I believe her before I'd believe Chrissie! So I won't apologise!"

"But it isn't true," Chrissie sobbed. "It isn't! It isn't!"

Hector twisted free of John's grip and flew at his aunt. Gerald interposed his not inconsiderable bulk and gave Hector an unpractised blow which knocked him off balance for long enough to let John get an arm-lock on him. Hector struggled to free himself but John was much too powerful and he had to content himself with glaring. Chrissie meanwhile had put her face down on the table and was crying as if her heart was breaking.

"I never knew they really thought it was true," she sobbed. "I never knew . . . I should never have come . . . I should never have come . . ."

"Lucky!" bawled IA suddenly.

Lucky appeared with suspicious speed for one so lame.

"Mrs. Chrissie's upset. Take her to the kitchen and give her a cup of tea with a dram in it."

Lucky accepted the weeping Chrissie with a flood of Irish endearments and a glare of dislike which he shared between Hannah and Jess in a way which made it plain he had been listening. He bore her off in a torrent of alannahs and mavourneens. IA looked at Hector, helpless in John's huge embarrassed hands.

"Well . . . it's the best thing I've learned of you yet that you'll defend your mother. She's worth twenty of you . . . any of you . . ."

He favoured his family with a scowl.

"Take him inbye, John, and give him a dram as well. I want a word with these two."

Hector and John left the parlour gladly and gratefully if for different reasons. The row continued to rumble on while Hector lowered the level in the whisky bottle.

. . . I had to put him to bed [John wrote], and the only place was the shearers' quarters. He and Chrissie left first thing the next morning. Chrissie was driving. I think Hector had a head because he didn't have very much to say for himself except that he'd like to see me get my comeuppance, whatever that is. Aunt Jess and Uncle Gerald left next day because I'd promised the boys to go fishing with them and they would have been disappointed. Everyone was very polite to everyone else but the boys must have known there had been a row. It would have woken Rip van Winkle while it lasted. That left Aunt Hannah who got into IA's good graces again by telling him that on mature reflection she thought she understood why he had done it. She told him that he would have to be careful to see that I got the right sort of wife and wasn't snapped up by the first little flibbertygibbet I saw. She thought I didn't hear this. She told me when I drove her down to the railway that I was a fine upstanding young man in spite of everything and a credit to the family. After that episode I'm not sure whether to take it as a compliment. Lord alive, what a Christmas! It's been so hot, too, which didn't improve things. We're badly troubled with fly on the cattle for all we can do to stop it. I did tell you we've decided to use the home paddocks to raise steers for fattening.

Dan was not John's only correspondent though he was the only one who received such confidences, nor was he the most regular. From Kelvin Drive came two monthly envelopes, one white with Grandmother's elegant looping illegible handwriting and the other pale blue with Aunty Nell's, small, back-sloping and faint. Ruby wrote too, not so often, but her letters were much more illuminating than the contents of the white and the blue. These contained much the same thing every time. Aunty Nell's contained news of Grandmother, she was well and very active for her age, they had had a bridge evening with friends and had been for a drive to Loch Lomond. On Sunday they had been to St. Silas Church and heard a very good sermon and she was his very devoted and affectionate Aunt Elena. Until the letters came John had never realised that Aunty Nell was really Elena. The white envelope had a more astringent flavour: Aunty Nell, Grandmother wrote, was vaguer than ever, though very devoted of course, she could never remember all her errands and always had to go twice to the shops which was a sinful waste of time. They had had friends in to play bridge and would not be doing this again. No one could play a decent game of bridge these days. They had driven out to Luss for an airing and Nell had dawdled for miles behind packs of cyclists. Cyclists simply did not dress decently and it ought not to be allowed, all those bare thighs going up and down like a machine, and as for those newfangled low handlebars, if the cyclists knew what they looked like from behind they would not buy them. She strongly suspected the new vicar at St. Silas of being a socialist. And she was, with regards, his Grandmother. When John wrote back he told them of the minutiae of the station and the weather. He did not tell them of the rows and the unpleasantness. Their letters were like flashes of light from distant lighthouses indicating the fact of presence and little more. Once Grandmother said, '. . . of course we always buy New Zealand lamb and butter.' That 'of course' said, as the Americans would say, a mouthful and John's next letter was the warmer for it even though he was fairly sure that Grandmother had not been inside a shop for forty years. Then it occurred to him that New Zealand lamb and butter were comparatively cheap. He wrote to Ruby then, asking outright if she thought that money was short. He got a swift answer: Ruby knew her mistress's affairs inside out.

. . . shorter than it was, Master John, but we're no on our last legs for all that business is bad and our dividends haven't been what they should. The money'll last our time, I reckon, though that Miss Scott will be ill-left. I've a bit put by, though, so no need to concern yourself for me.

In 1938 Bennachie bought a wireless and kept abreast of the Munich crisis and a card came from Dan. 'Have a new son and we have called him Nick. War is close, very close. We have a year, perhaps.'

That same year from Kelvin Drive came descriptions of the trying on of gasmasks.

. . . not for your grandmother. She says that she will not make a guy of herself at her age for any jumped-up little house painter. They gave me a list of things to do to the house in case we have an air raid. I must buy net stuff to stick on the windows. Paper would be cheaper but your grandmother says she will not look out through bars like a monkey in a cage. I have bought buckets and filled them with sand and water and put them on the landing but how to black out the lantern window over the staircase I cannot think. The man who came said that we should paint it with two or three coats of black paint and put a blue bulb in the stairlight but I do not know how to get out there and in any case your grandmother will not hear of it. She says she does not mean to go upstairs on her hands and knees. Oh, dear, sometimes I just do not know what to do for the best!

John grinned a little at this cry from the heart and opened the white envelope.

Nell appears to think we are going to be gassed or bombed any minute. Balderdash. As if the Germans would dare after what happened to them last time . . .

Around midwinter IA listened to the news of Poland one night, shook his grizzled head and switched off the set.

"In a month we'll be at war," he said grimly. "No way out now. Will you go?"

"I must, I think," John answered and wondered in the silence which followed what he would say if IA asked, as indeed he might, why he must go. In his mind was the picture which he had first seen in the music room at Inchbeg when he was only thirteen, of brownshirts, grinning like Luckenham, kicking an old man to death. A system which could allow, even encourage someone to do that, must be fought. He had known that since he talked to Dan on the hill. In fact it had been knowing that someday he would have to fight which had made his days on Bennachie such a joy.

"I think I'll join the Air Force," he added. "If they'll have me."

"They'll have you," IA said drily. "Though how they'll fit you into a plane, God knows. There's a man over at Watson Downs I used to know. He'll come as manager. He lost an arm in the last lot but he can do wonders with the one he's got left and he knows the high country . . . none better. I'll write to him."

And that was that. John had been dreading the moment when he would have to tell IA he was going. It had been simple after all. Next week he left for a training camp and learned to fly. It seemed he had an aptitude for it for he learned fast. After the war, he told himself, he would buy a plane and make an airstrip at Bennachie. What a difference it could make. The outbreak of war passed almost unnoticed. In December he heard he was posted to the U.K., seconded to the R.A.F., and he went back to Bennachie to spend his embarkation leave shearing the flock. At the end of it he took a silent leave of IA knowing that he might never see him again. It was bound to be a long job and IA was well into his seventies, however strong and healthy he might be. However, the new manager had arrived and John liked him. Bennachie would be all right, and that was important, more important than anything. But all during the long voyage to the north he carried a picture in his mind of the old man standing at the station in Cromwell, not waving, just looking.

In Wellington he found that the trooper had not yet arrived. The town was packed with young men like himself waiting for transport to England and there was not a bed to be had. Rather than trudge vainly round the hotels he decided to telephone his Aunt Hannah.

"John! In Wellington! Whyever didn't you let us know you were coming? Allan will come in for you right away."

John left the number with the Transport Office and stood outside in the steamy heat waiting for the car. When his uncle arrived in the shiny new Austin his daughter Ruth was sitting beside him. John, who never did anything by halves, took one look at his cousin and fell in love. Fathoms deep in love, deeper than ever plummet sounded.

31

It was a mistake, a hideous, almost irretrievable, mistake. In the normal way of things they might have met, exchanged a few exploratory sentences and then relinquished the acquaintance thankfully. If they had been two men or two women it would have ended there. John had nothing in common with Ruth, they had nothing to base a friendship on, no common experience, no common interest, nothing at all. When they spoke to one another it was almost as if they were talking different languages, but of course they did not talk very much. John looked upon the world as men do who live far away from it. It was vast, it was full of a 'number of things' and he was eager to examine them, grasp at them, experience them and 'to be as happy as a king' that he was able to do it. For John, all the world's creatures, human and animal, were interesting and valuable. On Bennachie where people were scarce every person encountered was an individual, someone to be valued according to what was in him: distinctions were drawn and sharply drawn, but they were based on real criteria. Bennachie was a touchstone which revealed people clearly. Ruth had no touchstone and her criteria were those of a middle-class suburb in a provincial town: even in democratic New Zealand there were people one knew and people one preferred not to know, things which were done and things which were not done: thinking was retained behind a high wall of preconceptions and ill-founded certainties. People were fitted into procrustean categories and were expected to behave accordingly. Ruth's world revolved around Kauri Villa and its confines were narrow compared with those of Bennachie. What 'other people' thought was intensely important. One had to be, as far as possible, like 'other people'. The people that Ruth and her parents wanted to be like were interested in games, tennis, swimming, golf and they took them seriously, turning first to the sports page of their newspapers. The arts they regarded as their prerogative, their responsibility in a curiously Presbyterian way, and they attended exhibitions, plays and concerts dutifully and returned to their radiograms and their dance music with guilty relief. They took out the latest novels from the library as they were bidden by the reviewers but they read mainly thrillers and 'nice' stories. Ruth differed from her friends only in that she was a surprisingly good pianist. Her father taught music, was in his undemonstrative fashion a true musician, and her mother sang in an amateur way so Ruth's talent was not unexpected. People didn't like unexpectedness. Ruth's friends admired her talent: 'Ruthie's a dab at the old joanna, aren't you, Ruthie?' but they kept a wary eye upon her in case she should show symptoms of 'long-hairedness', a propensity they despised, and they were quick to qualify and excuse such a quirk as musicality: '. . . but she's an absolute whizz at tennis, of course . . .' as if that excused their knowing such a person. Music might have been common ground between John and Ruth but even here their attitudes were utterly different. For John, music was like bread, a staple part of the diet. He thought that he was no performer but he would perform rather than have no music. A gramophone and records had been the first of the luxuries to be imported into Bennachie. Music was a part of life there. For Ruth the music was less than her ability to perform it to other people's approbation: what she could not play did not interest her. Her ability was almost a freak for she knew very little about music.

If John had been a girl introduced into her circle Ruth would have looked upon her with nervous contempt and avoided her as far as possible because she would have been too outspoken, too eccentric, too 'common' in her likings and tastes, too ignorant of the things which Ruth respected and valued. If Ruth had been a man John would have put him down tolerantly as 'rather a weed' and thereafter ignored him.

As it was, they were married after they had known one another for a week.

When he first saw her she had been in tennis kit which made her look angelic and athletic all at the same time. She was a small slender girl with a rounded face, dark brown eyes and a mass of dark wavy hair. John promptly endowed this pleasing specimen with every virtue and fell in love. Ruth in her turn saw a vast young man, older than his years because of the responsibilities he had undertaken, six foot three, with shoulders like an ox and his eyes curiously bright in his brown face. He fitted into her category of 'eligible male' because he was good-looking, and it was gratifying to be seen with him, because of his lack of a Kiwi drawl, and because he owned, so her mother told her, a large property. She was nearly twenty and her best friend (and rival) had been married for six months. Her current young man had gone to a new job in Auckland and his letters had diminished to an occasional post card. She was a little bored without his attentions and perfectly ready to be persuaded that she, too, had fallen in love at first sight. There were certain other pressures. The week before John's arrival she had had an audition with a visiting concert agent and this had been well-known among her circle. The agent's low, albeit gently phrased, estimate of her potential as a concert artist hurt her less than the worry that her friends might come to hear of it and laugh at her behind her back. Marriage was a universally accepted excuse for pursuing a musical career no further. And, to do her justice, the idea of John's going overseas to fight touched her emotions. She had been brought up on the nostalgia and pride of ANZAC Day. To marry John would be like all the books, it would be romantic . . . her friends would envy her.

If IA had been there he might have been able to keep John's feet on the ground and he would certainly have tried to do so. Ruth and John were first cousins and John himself was the result of a liaison between first cousins. From that point of view the match was inadvisable. It was even more inadvisable from other points of view but he would have had a hard time persuading John of this. For John, Ruth embodied all his vague imaginings about women. She was a symbol for him of love, of summer, of the immense burgeoning of feeling within him, a love for all humanity because he was going to defend it. There was also his consciousness that his life could be short for he remembered all that he had heard and read of the last war. He did not grudge that but wanted to experience all he could of living. Moreover, he was ready to fall in love with someone, at the peak of his physical splendour and starved for years of female company: Ruth crossed his path at a moment when almost any girl would have become the object of this enchanter's brew of circumstances and emotions. IA would have understood this. But IA was not there and there was no one to make any objections. Aunt Hannah was delighted. This match had been in her mind since she knew John was to have the property and she was delighted that her wish should come true in this romantic fashion. She thought that John was a little uncouth but the property made up for that: when he came back, she had decided, he should sell up and settle somewhere nearby. John could find something more . . . more gentlemanly to do than messing about with sheep. Her nose wrinkled at the memory of her childhood, the noise and the smell and the rough shearers. If John did not come back . . . well, Ruth would, of course, inherit and there would be no question of not selling. Meanwhile, her dearest little Ruthie could stay at home with her mother and still possess the desirable and respected status of married lady. Ruth's father made no objections either. He never did object to anything his wife approved because he respected her judgments and her acumen. If he wondered dimly about how John might feel about selling the station he didn't mention it. He liked a quiet life.

John and Ruth were married a week after they met and two days before John had to sail. They spent those two days in a seaside cabin borrowed from friends and found even in that short time a degree of physical rapport. If Ruth was more than a little overwhelmed by John's passion she was young and she was healthy and ready to respond to him in bed . . . and they spent a considerable portion of those two days in bed. However, even two days was long enough to demonstrate that out of each other's arms they had very little to talk about. John's attempts to express in words his physical content and the pleasure he took in lying with her were hushed in alarm: one did not *talk* about sex.

"Why not?" John asked. "If we enjoy sleeping together why not talk about it?"

"It's not the sort of thing nice people talk about," Ruth protested. "It isn't nice to talk about . . . that."

"Didn't you enjoy . . ."

"Oh, do be quiet, John. People might hear, out here on the beach . . . and don't do that. People might see."

"Come back to bed, then . . . I want to do that . . . I want it more than ever . . ."

Ruth looked at him appalled.

"In the morning? In daylight? Whatever will people think?"

John overcame this caveat by carrying her off and making love to her until lunchtime but he was aware that she had been self-conscious when he undressed her in the half light of the bedroom. Lovemaking was something to be done in the dark.

Ruth was not interested in Bennachie. John tried to describe it to her and found little response and no desire to know about his home.

"Mummy says it's absolutely miles from anywhere," she said. "And the road's frightfully rough. The car was a wreck after she visited. She said you don't have electricity, even, and no phone or anything like that. And the toilet doesn't flush."

John admitted all this.

". . . but the price of wool's going up fast," he observed. "We're going to buy a petrol generator. I want to use electric shears. We could run electric light from that. And I am going to build on a proper bathroom. You could be planning things like that while I'm away. I'll leave a plan of the house . . ."

Ruth looked at him blankly.

"You don't mean we're going to *live* there?" she blurted out, "hundreds of miles away from all my friends and Mummy and Daddy and everything?"

John sat up, feeling cold round his midriff despite the hot sun and the warm sand.

"Where else would we live?" he demanded. "Bennachie's my home and my livelihood. You knew that."

"But I thought now we were married you'd sell it and live in a proper house with electricity and a bathroom and things and get a proper job somewhere. I never dreamed you'd be going back to that place."

John swallowed hard.

"I'm going back to Bennachie," he told her. "There was never any question of my leaving it."

"I don't believe you. You're teasing me again."

Her voice rose, almost to a whine.

"You wouldn't make me live out there . . . you wouldn't . . ."

"I wouldn't make anyone do anything they didn't want to," John said quietly. "I leave that to people like Hitler."

She smiled in relief. John lay back on the sand and fell silent. It had never occurred to him to ask if she were willing to be an up-country sheep farmer's wife. Bennachie was so much part of him that it had been axiomatic that if she accepted him she accepted Bennachie. But it seemed that it had not been axiomatic. The rosy vision of their life together after the war, the children coming with him out on the run, coming back to find her in the house, faded very suddenly. Even then, at the very height of his physical infatuation with Ruth he understood that if it came to a choice, he would choose Bennachie. He smothered the memory of this exchange in one last night of frantic lovemaking and carefully avoided all talk of the future. It was easy enough: both of them knew that there might be no future for them, to discuss it was almost to tempt fate. Neither of them realised as the distance widened slowly between the ship and the quay and they waved interminably and smiled across the distance that part of the future, at all events, was already waiting in the wings.

The summer of 1940 was one of the most beautiful that people could remember. It lasted for week after week, as if the gods felt that Britain and the British had troubles enough without rain over the harvest period. It was sunny and hot, too hot to stay indoors in the baking confines of tin-roofed huts. John and the rest of the squadron dragged the mess-chairs outside and sat under the arch of blue which was their battle-field. To anyone who did not know what was happening it must have seemed slightly comic to watch these young men in their flying-gear sprawled in the delapidated basket chairs which had been begged from the nearby pub, reading or talking, playing chess or simply basking in the sun like the sailor in the rhyme. While they waited, John usually wrote letters; there were always letters to write and he had acquired the habit of writing them at Bennachie. Now, in the middle of a desperate battle, 'somewhere in England' to write to IA brought back the shape and look and scent of the high country in a way which let him believe that some day he would return in spite of the odds against it. He didn't hint to IA of these odds but he was still aware of them. He would look up from the airmail form and look at the chairs scattered over the sparse brown grass and wonder who would be missing from the company tomorrow and whether it would be his turn. Each day he survived seemed to him a miracle, but it was a miracle like the summer weather which must break some time. He had been with this squadron since the last week in July and that day, the fourth of September, he was the longest serving pilot, bar one. The rest of the July faces had gone, some dead, some grounded, some burned . . . he flinched from the memory of Jimmie's face, blunted, shiny and blind, with nothing of his friend left, but the voice emerging from the distorted mouth. By tomorrow he could be like that, or crippled like Peter, coming to terms with a wheelchair somewhere in Yorkshire. Or he could be dead, entangled in a heap of red–hot wreckage. Before long the hooter would go which was the signal to scramble and they would sprint across to the Hurries which were waiting under their netting, each with its lazily moving attendant figures, making do, repairing, checking once, twice and again . . . without the ground staff they would all be dead.

The letter on his knee was to Grandmother. Aunty Nell had written that she had had a slight stroke and while fairly well was unable to write yet, or to walk very far. He had written cheerfully to her, promising to come and see her on his next leave and giving her the news which had arrived last month, that there was a baby due. Mail from New Zealand took months to arrive. He looked up from an uncompleted sentence, '. . . my wife tells me that she is to have a baby and it is due very soon . . .'

He found the idea disquieting and comforting at the same time. His marriage had come to seem less and less real as the months had passed: he looked back on it rather shamefacedly as he looked back at the drunken parties which studded the life of the Mess. It was frightening to know that out of that interlude was to come a new human being: he tried to visualise being a father but found that he had little idea how fathers behaved. He decided that he must write to Dan and tell him. He put the letter to Glasgow into the envelope and then found another airmail form. Dan was working in America still. 'Dear Dan,' he began, 'I heard two days ago that I am going to be a father and I find I don't know what . . .'

The hooter went as he reached this point and he dropped his writing case and ran towards his plane. All the Hurries were stripped and waiting like boxers by the time the flight reached them. Routine enfolded him and swamped his thoughts about death and marriage and procreation. Once they encountered the 'bandits' they had been sent to intercept there was no time to think about anything but dealing out death and destruction and avoiding them in one's turn. The R.A.F. had discovered in John an instinct for aerial fighting, an ability to foreknow his opponent's moves and counter them, to direct his flight as he directed his dogs on the slopes of Bennachie. This operation differed in no particular from any other of the dozens of similar sorties he had flown since July. The Hurries gained height in the blue September sky, were directed on to the bomber formation and dived at them out of the sun. After that there could be no coherent plan, just a series of situations which formed and reformed with lightning speed. A fighter pilot needed to meet these and deal with them and still be conscious of his aircraft and of his fellow-pilots and of the ultimate objective of destroying the bombers which had sent them scrambling into the sky. There was no time to follow-through on a hit, no time to watch the smoke-trailing bomber to the ground because there was a Messerschmitt on the port side and he must be dealt with before he dealt with you or with anyone else in the flight. When time and ammunition and fuel began to run out he recalled them, as he recalled the dogs at home and they banked away for the airfield that was home now. John checked to left and right and found a gap.

"Blue Leader to Blue Three . . ." he said into the confines of his mike: it was always a marvel to John to speak this way as if he were sitting beside his pilots in the same plane, to demolish space in this way with a word, "any news of Blue Two?"

"Blue Three to Blue Leader," Pilot Officer Parker drawled, he affected a pose of imperturbability which had become almost second nature to him, "two got winged. I saw him peel off and lose height but after that I was ra-ather busy . . ."

At base the debriefing session revealed no more than that

368

slight observation. They had all been rather busy. Blue Two's fate remained a mystery while the Ops Room phoned round the other airfields asking questions which increasingly expected the answer, 'no'. At dinner no one mentioned Blue Two though the quirks of the day's battle emerged in anecdotes. After dinner Blue Two walked into the Mess, none the worse for a forced landing in a harvest field two counties away. A party began to develop. Pilot Officer Parker's party piece was a parody of the Western Brothers and he had contrived a long, improbable rhyming saga about the adventures of Blue Flight to which he could add almost ad lib. John's role was at the piano, improvising an accompaniment. The return of Blue Two, a shy, almost silent youngster from Newcastle who was called Denton gave immediate rise to a series of libellous verses describing Denton's fate at the hands of the landgirls who had pulled him out of the plane. He endured this in scarlet grinning silence and when Parker was finished with him, weighed in with one of his own, limping but pointed, which referred to Parker's little whirl with the barmaid at the Swan. There had been better additions to the saga which was Blue Flight's pride, but this one was so unexpected that the party reached a height of hilarity and camaraderie. John was left stranded at the piano as the tide receded to the bar. He turned round on the stool and thought that these people meant more to him than Ruth. He knew them better, loved them more, the relationship with them was more real, more true . . . and yet he and Ruth had a child. He could not even conjure up Ruth's face into his mind's eye, or, what was more important to him, the sound of her voice in his inward ear. She had faded away, become no more than an unformed rather childish handwriting on an envelope, the sight of which made him feel, not loving, but impatient, for he knew, almost to a word, what she was going to say and none of it ever seemed to have anything to do with him, John. But by now, this faint memory might have given birth to his child and yet the return of Denton, unscathed, meant more to him than either Ruth or the child. And before long the child could be fatherless as he had been. It was not a good thing to be fatherless. A wave of dismay struck at him and he ducked his head almost as if it had been a real wave. His child would have a mother . . . but he did not know what sort of a mother . . . he looked up because someone was tapping him on the shoulder, a WAAF from the Ops Room. He knew her in a vague sort of way, Caroline somebody; he remembered the name because of Grandmother . . .

"You O.K.?" she was saying.

"I'm fine . . ."

"Telephone."

He looked at her, frowning in bewilderment.

"Telephone?"

"Yes," she said with an elaborate show of patience. "Telephone. That black thing out there in the glass box . . ."

"But who would . . . oh, God, Grandmother . . ."

But it was not the expected voice of Aunty Nell. A faint and blessedly familiar voice sounded in his ear, as if it had been conjured up by that unfinished letter.

"John? It is Dan. I am in London and I would see you."

As he answered, rejoicing, his voice leaping with pleasure, and explained how to reach the nearest town and which hotel he should go to, John's mind was working on a number of levels. Sheer gladness that Dan should be so close swamped them all, but there was curiosity as to what had brought him to beleaguered London and underlying it all a prayer that they should both survive to meet. London was under bombardment every day and his own life was hardly worth a day's purchase.

"I may be a father by now," he blurted out suddenly. "I don't feel qualified at all, Dan."

Dan's chuckle at the other end was comforting.

"Fatherhood brings its own qualifications," Dan said. "Just love, plenty of love. That will come, have no fear. You have great potential for love."

Dan could say these things and they did not sound sloppy or sentimental but like remembered truths. He wanted to pour out to Dan all his doubts and regrets.

"I can barely remember Ruth," John admitted. "It was so quick . . . so short . . ."

Why, he wondered, did Dan have this ability to call forth confessions of things he had barely admitted to exist even in his own mind.

"I am afraid," he went on. "If it was a mistake it will be so hard on the child."

370

"Be tranquil," Dan advised. "All may yet be well. War brings more than death in its wake. I, too, am Papa again. I have a little girl who will be the delight of my declining years. She is in New York with my wife."

They exchanged news for a few minutes and with their meeting arranged rang off. John lingered for a few seconds in the call-box, unwilling to go back into the Mess.

"Not bad news?" asked Caroline Something, making him jump.

"No. Not at all. A good friend of mine has arrived from the States. He is in London."

The sky outside the open front door glowed and pulsed with the fires below, thirty miles away. The bombers had left their mark.

"Not the best place to be," Caroline Something said harshly. "My people are there. My mother won't leave Father and Father's in one of the Ministries and can't leave."

John could think of nothing to say.

"I wonder every day what's happening to them. If the blitz really gets going there it will be like hell in London. I have to come out here and look every night, it's compulsive . . . sometimes I think I'll go mad," she added matter-of-factly.

"Don't they phone?"

"When they can. I was waiting for a call when your friend rang. But it isn't easy. Mother always says the same thing, 'It's the Old Bad Penny, darling . . .' It's being in that Ops Room and seeing the bandits come, thousands of them, and wondering all the time if one of those things you're shoving around like a croupier is *the* one . . ."

John put his arm round her because she was shivering a little and she turned her face into his uniform jacket.

"Sorry," she muttered after a moment, "didn't mean to blub all over you. Things get on top of you after a bit. It seems to have been going on so long."

She fumbled for a handkerchief and blew her nose.

"And you've got your own worries . . . like staying alive and in one piece. Mine are borrowed, second-hand really. I don't know why I said anything, except that you're so, well, sort of solid . . . I don't know why I picked on you. Unless it was because I was bloody sure that you wouldn't say, 'Cheer up, chicken, it may never happen, have a drink and forget all about it in my arms.' That doesn't work. I've tried it."

"Pick on me any time," John assured her and remembered suddenly that she had been Reeves' popsie.

"Don't worry. I won't cling and weep all over you every night . . ."

"I mean it," John told her, "it helps to talk. All this strong, silent stiff-upper-lippery is all very well until things start happening and you need to be able to say something which isn't flip. I never can. I just go dumb. Come on outside and have a Harry Wragg."

The armchairs of the morning had been taken inside but there were a few ancient tattered deckchairs. Caroline sat in one but John chose to sit on the ground beside her.

"Those things are not calculated for someone of my bulk. I'd hate to do a Laurel and Hardy and sit right through. Now, talk . . . or not, just as you please. If you don't want to perhaps you'll let me bore your ears off talking about my home. I'm a Kiwi, you know . . ."

"Yes, I knew. Tom told me. He called you the wild colonial boy."

"Are you town or country?"

He didn't want to talk about Reeves.

"Neither," Caroline said. "Suburban. Betwixt and between. A pseudo-sophisticate. Plenty of half-baked convictions but not much courage."

She fell silent and John said nothing because he sensed that she meant to go on. The red tips of their cigarettes glowed and died, died and glowed.

"It's not just that I'm afraid for the parents," she said suddenly. "I feel I've betrayed them."

"Why?"

"Because I feel like a whore."

John was startled into an exclamation.

"Rubbish!"

"I looked it up, you know. It's the sort of word that people throw around and don't know what it means. One who permits the use of her body to men for money or other reward. Tom had the use of my body. It helped him to sleep. He was scared you know, he was scared all the time."

John did know. He knew very well.

"A lot of them are scared. Some of them drink but Tom thought it was stupid to fly when you had a hangover. I was his glass of whisky. No aftereffects, you see."

"Did you know this?"

"No . . . oh, Lord no . . . I dressed it up in all kinds of fancy dress. None but the brave deserve the fair and all that. Doing my bit for our brave boys in blue. I really did think like that. It was all those war stories we read at school. I was defying convention, breaking out of the suburban mould . . . oh, I was chockablock with reasons for sleeping with someone else's husband. Then, when he was killed, I saw how much I had meant to him. Precisely nothing. He left a letter for his wife, one for you . . . so they told me . . . nothing for me. Not a message, nothing. So now I feel like a whore. Without any reward."

She had taken out another cigarette and when John lit it he could see her eyes were dry and her expression grim.

"It's stupid when you try to explain how you feel. I've done something which ought to be punished and the worst punishment would be if anything happened to the parents. If anything happens to them it'll be my fault."

"But you must know things don't work like that . . ." John began, horrified.

"Knowing's not good enough. It's what you feel that drives you round the bend."

John lit himself a cigarette and drew in a great lungful of the smoke.

"I wonder," he murmured almost to himself, "just why you chose to tell *me*?"

"I don't know . . . the time had come to tell someone before I borrowed a razor and cut my throat. And you knew Tom. There aren't many left who did. And you knew about us. Not that Tom kept it a secret, exactly. It made him feel better that he had a mistress right on the station. Made him feel less of a coward."

The word hung between them.

"Nobody said anything," she muttered, "but I guessed. He nearly killed you, didn't he?"

"Nobody said anything because nobody really knows," John said. "Only Tom knows exactly what happened and he's

373

not telling, poor blighter. No, I wondered why you told me for quite another reason."

He thought of his mother and the entry in her journal and decided not to tell the whole of the story. Coincidences happened all the time and Caroline's situation was not unusual. He could think of half a dozen current liaisons. They weren't supposed to happen, but they did. What made Caroline unusual was her feeling of disgust and guilt. Most of the others were light-hearted enough: he had had a veiled offer or two, himself . . . and one or two not so veiled. He had taken no advantage of them, not so much because he felt a loyalty to Ruth, though there was that, but because he felt very much as Caroline did, that such a transaction was wrong, that death or the fear of death should have no part in it and the presence of death debased it to something subhuman, panic copulation such as occurred in disasters like earthquakes.

"What reason?"

"You'll never guess. It was just that I was a war baby. A bastard. My father was killed at Passchendaele and my mother died when I was born. These things do happen you know. My father was married too. I have a half-brother older than me."

"Good Lord," she murmured. "I would never have guessed that."

"Not that it makes any difference to know that it happens to other people. I suppose in some ways it might help to think that you were unique."

He was trying not to think about Ruth. He had realised that his marriage was no different to the affairs around the station. Because it was legal, had parental blessing and now, as the lawyers would have it, issue, didn't make it any less sordid and subhuman. He suddenly felt desperately ashamed. Did Ruth, he wondered, feel like this girl, that she had been used for a final fling? No. He could be fairly sure she did not. Perhaps, the thought crept into his mind like a cold draught under a door, he would be able to like her better if she did.

"Unique?" Caroline was saying and laughing a little. "Even at my most dramatic I never saw myself as unique. In fact I suppose if I were honest I would admit that I was a little piqued that such a damned commonplace thing had happened to me, marvellous me. We all think we are a cut above the common-place."

John heard the phrase, 'happened to me' and smiled slightly in the dark. Confession had already set the sin at one remove.

"If it's so commonplace, surely the fates won't visit it upon your parents . . . or upon you through your parents," he suggested.

"What you are saying," she said after a short pause, "is that what I've done isn't important enough to merit that sort of attention."

"Take your choice. Either you feel it's important enough to be guilty about or you shrug it off as unimportant. No one was hurt by what you did . . . except you."

"Tom's wife."

"You don't need to worry about her," he assured her.

"But I . . ."

"Not to worry," he insisted.

She gave him a sharp look and then ground out her cigarette underfoot.

"I do feel a lot better," she admitted. "Thanks."

"Just part of the service," he said lightly.

When she had gone away he stayed outside for a little, thinking about Ruth and the baby who might be born that very day. It was as if he had taken on Caroline's burden. He got up at last and went inside to make his Will again. There was always something one could do to safeguard the future.

Dan arrived four days later: he was little changed, thinner, greyer, a trifle stooped, maybe, but he still had the trick of turning the searchlight of his attention on anyone he met. John saw him at the bar of the hotel in the village where he was hearing of the difficulties of running a hostelry in wartime from the landlady. One might have thought he was going to write a thesis on the subject, John thought with amusement.

Later it felt as if they had never been apart. They did not talk much about themselves because in some strange fashion what had happened to each of them was on the surface and irrelevant to the relationship between them. Over the deplorable dinner they discussed, of all things, etymology. Dan had his usual effect upon John of forcing him to voice opinions and ideas which he had not known he possessed. Only as they drank the unspeakable coffee did Dan touch on the reason for his visit.

"I am here for a year at least," he announced, "but I may not tell you why. It is hush hush as they say. But I can tell you that I will live in the lap of luxury and in complete safety in the depths of this beautiful countryside while you and those like you hold the hordes at bay . . ."

He leaned forward and touched the new, bright, purple and white ribbon over John's breast-pocket.

". . . very effectively it seems."

"Came up with the rations," mumbled John.

"That I do not believe. There are times when I wish myself young again to hold the pass beside you. As it is, I must do what I can, little as that may be. And perhaps we may meet from time to time?"

He had brought a walletful of photographs and John looked at the dark, intense woman whom Dan had married and the gangling schoolboy who was Grand's namesake.

"He will be an All-American boy, this one," Dan said. "He learns at school what he must be. I find it a little disquieting that he will never know his inheritance. But such things happen in this world and in this time. Me, when I can I will return to Vienna: it is my home. But whether they will wish to come or wish to stay when they have seen it . . . who can say? I would not wish to uproot them. People are like plants, I think. They reach their full growth only in their native soil. In alien soil they will be stunted or distorted. After this war there will be many such. That will be a damage which will outlast all that shells or bombs can do. Nothing can mend such damage. God send that it does not destroy us all in the end."

John stirred his coffee.

"Wasn't I transplanted?" he asked.

"No!" Dan exclaimed. "Never. Bennachie was your native soil from the very beginning. You know it. I knew it and so did Nick. If we meet in heaven, Nick and I, it will be because we brought you to Bennachie. Tell me, how is IA?"

John gave the news which he had had from the one-armed manager. IA was failing, slowly but steadily. Dan nodded.

"He pines for you."

John felt as if he had been slapped.

"But I had to come," he muttered. "I had to . . ."

He could not tell Dan why. The nightmares about Luckenham and the black boots trampling on Grand's hands came only seldom for these days brought other nightmares, but they came still.

"But of course," Dan sighed. "It is yet another item on Herr Hitler's long account with the Devil that an old man should grieve himself to death on the other side of the world. All of us have had to make such choice. I have left my wife and my son and the daughter of my old age."

He frowned.

"But you too have left a wife. Tell me about her."

He listened to John's halting account of his marriage with intense interest and then held out his hand for the photograph.

"She is young," he observed when he had studied the bland prettiness in his hand, "she may grow to match you. If not, you have your continuity whatever happens and that must be a comfort. We are arrogant, we humans, and do not care to see the waters of our being lose themselves in the sand."

He handed the photograph back. John buttoned it back into his tunic pocket and wondered how it was that Dan could say such things without a blush. He considered the idea of continuity but took no comfort from it.

"I shouldn't have done it," he exclaimed. "IA was always telling me not to go at things like a bull at a gate. It wasn't fair to Ruth . . . or the child . . ."

"It was natural," Dan comforted.

Just then they were offered more coffee and the expression of horror on Dan's face dissipated the moment in amusement.

"Come on back to the Mess," John urged. "The beer's not bad and there are a few who've got billets in the village. You'll get a lift back."

They walked back to the station between the dusty hedgerows with reaped fields stretching away on either hand into the hazy dusk. At the guardhouse there was an atmosphere of suppressed amusement as they examined Dan's identity papers and produced the form for John to fill in.

"Is Flight Lieutenant Jenkins still on the station?" enquired John as he signed. "I was rather hoping he would give Doctor Heilbron a lift back to the Feathers"

"Yes, sir," said the young pilot officer in charge and coughed. "No one's gone home yet. They're all there."

Someone chuckled in the group behind the desk and John looked up in surprise.

"Flap on?" he asked.

"No . . . nothing like that. A quiet night," said the pilot officer. "So far."

There was another smothered guffaw at this response but no one volunteered to explain the joke. As he left with Dan, John saw the Flight Sergeant lift the phone.

The Mess was about three hundred yards from the gate. As they went in through the double doors which kept the blackout intact John thought that things seemed to be unusually quiet for the time of night and wondered anxiously on whose account this might be. He was bracing himself to hear the news when the door of the bar was flung open and Westy Parker advanced to meet him with a silver salver on which was a bottle of champagne, a vast cigar and a cable. Along the wall of the bar was a streamer which offered, CONGRATULATIONS DADDY DEAR! in daubed capitals and below this was a sheet of brown paper on which someone had painted a stork wearing a flying helmet with R.A.F. roundels on its wings and a baby dangling from its beak in an inverted parachute. A confused chorus broke into *Sonnie Boy*.

The cable read, SON BORN EARLY 8TH SEPTEMBER STOP BOTH WELL STOP DOMINIC JOHN STOP LOVE UNCLE ALLAN. John read it and passed it over to Dan who shook him solemnly and ceremoniously by the hand before he popped the champagne cork with impressive expertise and the party really got started.

"Where's Caroline?" John asked at one point.

"London," someone shouted over the racket. "Parents' flat went for a burton last night. Think they've both bought it. They're still digging . . ."

Continuity, he thought, Caroline is their continuity and what the hell comfort had that been when the bomb hit? Would he find comfort in Dominic John's existence when he was hit? One thing was certain, he was likely to find out sooner rather than later.

32

He was diving, diving, out of control, the controls loose and meaningless. His ears popped and crackled and his eyes bulged against the forces which were breaking the plane apart . . . now he was turning, turning in the dive . . . nothing answered . . . spinning like a toy on the end of a thread . . . the ground was rushing up, the lines and squares and blotches blurred as it circled like a record on the turntable, nearer, nearer . . . behind him was the roar of fire, kept from him by the speed and the rush of the air which fed it . . . in a moment he must strike the ground . . . go in, go right in, nothing answered . . . just a second left to live . . . a second . . . a second . . . nothing to be done . . . helpless . . . screaming but never a sound . . .

"Wake up, mate! Come on . . . wake up! This train don't go no further . . ."

John started awake and stared at the face bending over him.

"We're here," it said. "Time to rise and shine, matey-o."

It was a real face, lined, unshaven. It belonged to an elderly man in a shabby uniform. His teeth were broken and stained brown. He was alive. He was in a train. The train had stopped. This must be a station . . . heaven was a station and people would be here to meet . . . but he was alive, he was on leave. Dreaming . . . he had been dreaming and he was alive. The man shook him by the shoulder again.

"Glasgow Central," he announced, "and a real bastard of a fog. What a hole!"

John stumbled to his feet and reached for his case. The man stood back and nodded.

"If yer back wiv us, matey-o, I'll be getting along . . . you put more water in it next time . . . that's my advice."

John, still dazed with sleep, the shreds of his nightmare clinging to his mind, got himself on to the platform and shivered convulsively as a bitter raw cold bit at his flesh through the uniform. Quickly he shrugged himself into his greatcoat and buttoned it high. The air stank of sulphur and smoke and the foul waters of the Clyde which lay, oily and ice-fringed, a hundred yards away under a pall of fog. Even in the shelter of the great curved roof of the station it wasn't possible to see for more than a few feet. Dim figures streamed past him, the merest shapes. A trolley, piled high with luggage trundled towards him and he moved aside hastily; pushing it was the porter who had wakened him.

"Glasgow," he grumbled as he stumped by, "you can keep Glasgow. Give me the South. Freeze the balls off a brass monkey, this would. You O.K., mate?"

John nodded because his teeth were chattering too much to speak.

"*That*'s hunky-dory, then," he said and vanished into the fog. John followed the sound of the wheels, squealing and rumbling on the uneven concrete of the platform. Footsteps kept pace with him. It was like being a ghost in an army of ghosts, half-heard, barely glimpsed. It occurred to him that he might be dead after all and they would all be waiting for him at the barrier. He slowed his pace, appalled at this thought and someone stumbled into him and cursed. There would be such a crowd . . . IA, Grandmother, Aunty Nell, Grand, his mother, his father . . . He swallowed and, shifting his grip on the suitcase, walked tentatively into the murk. Once through the barrier the fog was thicker that ever, a figure in khaki as large as himself loomed out of it and confronted him and John felt his heart beating up high in his throat and hardly dared look at the face for fear it might be his own . . .

"This Platform Twelve?" enquired a voice. "Christ, it's like a madhouse . . . can't see your hand in front of your face . . ."

An exasperated stranger grinned at him and pushed past and vanished as if he had never been. John walked on trying to get a grip on himself. He was safe, he was alive, he was unharmed, he was on leave . . . on *leave*. This was Glasgow. His parachute had opened. He had floated down. He had not gone in. He was not dead, he was alive and he was in Glasgow and he had an appointment at eleven. He needed a bath and a shave and breakfast. Perhaps he could get these in the Central Hotel. He dredged up his memory of the station and headed towards the hotel entrance . . . he hoped.

Outside the station the fog was even worse. The great city was hushed and muffled under a stinking blanket of yellow-grey. The lawyer's office where he was due at eleven was in St. Vincent Street, less than a quarter of a mile away, but it might have been on the other side of the Atlantic. Yellow lights blazed up suddenly in the murk, crawled past, clinging to the kerb and then slowly vanished, the vehicles outlined blackly against the halo of reflected light. Somehow, he would have to cross the road. He waited for a moment when no lights loomed and moved tentatively out on to the slippery setts, only to jump back hastily as a cyclopean monster clanged and whined and charged out of the fog: it was a tram, grinding past down to Argyle Street, its passengers peering through the gaps they had rubbed on the steamy windows. When it had passed he tried again and this time found the opposite pavement outside the Corn Exchange, canoning into a bowler-hatted man, feeling his way along the kerb with an umbrella. Once he was across it was easier to move. He felt his way uphill, never out of reach of the walls and the shop windows, encountering people coming downhill in the same fashion. There was a spirit of camaraderie abroad; people could be heard laughing, cursing cheerfully and commiserating with one another. He felt his way over Waterloo Street and Blythswood Terrace and knew that St. Vincent Street must be next. The higher he climbed, the further he could see. The fog was lying thickest in the Clyde valley. His fellow pedestrians appeared like figures in a dream: H. G. Wells might have described such a scene in another world or another time. He paused to let a trio of office girls pass, giggling and exclaiming, and thought that for once the weather fitted his mood.

In spite of everything he was early for his appointment. The office was luxuriously uncomfortable, all the furniture expensive and solid and polished and inhospitably slippery. The waiting room was full of leather; a leather-topped table ready for board meetings with inkstands ranged about it; leather-seated chairs which were damp and clammy to the touch; leather-covered volumes peered dispiritedly through a high glass-fronted bookcase as if they were hoping that someone might be kept waiting long enough to let one or two of them out. There were no magazines or papers. John looked along the gilt dates on the spines of the books, 1890, 1891, 1892, 1893, 189 . . . It seemed to him that the books floated out through the glass in order, in line ahead and made a graceful curve over the table, swinging high and climbing up under the moulding of the cornice where wisps of fog floated like clouds . . . they moved into formation, each flight above the other in the far corner and the nearer flight began to dive . . .

"Squadron-leader! Squadron-leader!"

For the second time that morning he woke, unsure of his surroundings and stared into a strange face. This time it belonged to a woman, rather an elderly woman with her white hair bobbed in the style of twenty years before. Aunty Nell had worn her hair that way. She wore a tweed skirt with a bulge in the seat where she sat and a shabby, mud-coloured cardigan.

"Mr. Stewart can see you now," she told him in the well-remembered accents of Kelvinside. Her gaze sharpened. "Do you feel quite well, Squadron-leader? If I may say so, you're an awfully poor colour."

"I've been in hospital," he said, and saw her face soften with concern. "I had ear trouble," he added hastily, "so far this war, I've escaped without a scratch."

"There are wounds which don't show," she said astonishingly. "I must say you look very tired."

"I came up by the night train," he explained. "I didn't have a lot of sleep."

"I'll go and make a nice hot cup of tea," she decided. "Will you walk this way?"

She bustled ahead of him, dowdy and comfortingly real.

Stewart's office was quite unlike the waiting room. It was warm and shabby and a bright fire in the high grate kept the fog at bay. The carpet was worn but it had once been a rich red and the chairs were upholstered in moquette, with the sharp angles and deep comfort which had been fashionable in the thirties. Mr. Stewart was behind a desk, overladen, overflowing, overwhelmed with papers. The room felt cosy in a strangely impersonal way. It said wordlessly, 'This air is thick with secrets, one more will make no difference, nothing can shock in here, anything you say is safe . . .'

Mr. Stewart was just as he remembered. Lawyers bore the

mark of their profession more than any other men: they seemed to take on the qualities of the paper which was their main tool. He waved John to one of the angular chairs, made a few enquiries about his health and his intentions.

"I knew I ought to see you about things," John said. "I've been grounded. They may send me back to New Zealand. And I wanted to see some real hills. The south is terribly flat, I find."

"And whereabout do you mean to go?"

"I haven't made any plans. Just somewhere in the hills."

"Well, I might be able to make a few suggestions later. But now, to business."

His chair was an ancient swivelling desk-chair and he swung round to the desk.

"First, the graves. I have arranged for them to be cared for. The stone was set up last month. You know they are together?"

"You wrote at the time . . ."

"Miss Scott was no relation but we felt, in the circumstances . . ."

"Of course."

How else could it have been? They had been inseparable for as long as he could remember; dominator and dominee. Neither was whole without the other. A younger voice said in his head, 'What does it matter to bones which bones lie near?' and his own voice replied, 'It makes a difference to *me*. I didn't do enough for them when they were alive, I like to think that this is something I can do for them when nothing I can do makes any difference. Everything we do for the dead is to comfort the living.'

". . . a sad business," Mr. Stewart was saying, "a stray land mine. They were after Clydeside that night. Or maybe they hoped to destroy the B.B.C. I was so shocked and distressed to hear what Miss Wilson had to say."

Miss Wilson must be Ruby. Only Ruby had survived the land mine.

"Your grandmother would not go to the country. That night she had another stroke: it was very severe. We got her into the nursing home as soon as we could next day but she never recovered consciousness. I am only thankful she never heard what had happened to Miss Scott."

Aunty Nell had died under half a ton of masonry which had fallen from the terrace wall above the telephone box where she had been attempting to call the doctor to Grandmother. The landmine had exploded only yards from her.

". . . to visit the grave," Mr. Stewart was suggesting. "It is in the Western Cemetery. A bus from Buchanan Street will take you right to the gate."

John was not thinking of graves.

"Is Ruby all right?"

"Oh, yes, she was perfectly all right and a tower of strength as always. She stayed on till we closed the house and stored the furniture and then she went back to her sister in Errol."

"Is she provided for?"

Mr. Stewart shook his head.

"No. You must understand, Mr. John, if I may, that there is very little money. Your grandmother's annuity died with her and her other income had . . . dried up, as you might say. Your grandfather left what he had to you. And of course, Miss Scott had nothing at all. What there is, has been left to you. There is the house and its contents, a little jewellery, a few items of silver . . . I imagine a good deal was sold to defray expenses over recent years. Money was short. And your grandmother did not like to do without things to which she had been accustomed."

"I wish I had known," John said. "I did ask from time to time but Grandmother never answered and Aunty Nell simply said that everything was all right."

"These are difficult times," Mr. Stewart said, and he sighed. "One sees it in my profession. Difficult times, especially for the elderly."

"Ruby must have something," John declared. "When the house is sold . . . can something be arranged? Could you sell it and arrange for the proceeds to be invested to give her a pension. Will it run to that?"

"It is damaged, very much damaged, I fear. Not an inch of glass left and the roof in a bad state. But it is sound in other respects. They built well in those days. A modern bungalow subjected to the same blast would have collapsed like a house of cards. And it is still a desirable area, and a good site. Your grandmother bought very shrewdly. Yes, I daresay we could arrange what you wish. And I must say I am very pleased that you should want to do such a thing."

He nodded several times in succession.

"Ruby was very good to me when I was a boy," John said and remembered her bending over the garden bed he had dug all those years ago. That was where he remembered her always, not among the linoleum and stove-enamel modernities of Kelvin Drive.

"The plenishings," Mr. Stewart continued, using the quaint word with relish, "the plenishings of the house are all in store. Ruby packed them all up just as your grandmother would have liked, she said. What would you wish done with them?"

"Well, I hardly know," John said rather helplessly. "Should they be sold too?"

"Well, it's not for me to say, of course, but there might be items which you would wish to keep . . . family silver . . . items of sentimental value . . . or of family interest. There are a great many photographs, I understand. I think you should look through it before you decide . . ."

"I would like my grandfather's piano . . ." John began.

Mr. Stewart shook his head as rapidly and as emphatically as he had nodded it.

"Smashed," he said, "broken beyond repair. It was a lamp-standard blown in through the window. Landed right across it."

It was that news which ended his childhood, not the deaths which had crowded on him in the past two years. It had seemed too ironic that he, who expected to die, who put his life at risk should survive without a scratch and IA and the others should die. But people died every day; it was something which you might dread, but you did expect. The piano was all that was left of Inchbeg and the room where he had been born.

". . . advise you not to be too hasty. They can stay in store for as long as is convenient. Some of the things will be very hard to replace. You should perhaps consult your wife be-fore . . ."

He paused at the expression on John's face.

". . . you are married, are you not? I seem to recall . . ."

"I had a letter yesterday," John said, and pulled it out of the pocket where it had lain during the endless train journey when the words had passed in front of his eyes over and over again. "She wants to marry an American. She wants me to divorce her . . . she wants to divorce me, that is . . ."

"There is a difference," Mr. Stewart said drily. "A very considerable difference."

'I'm sure you won't have been all you should have been,' she had written. 'Daryl's parents are very nice and I would rather you did it all, and it's more the sort of thing Daryl's people would expect.'

"There was issue?"

"I've never seen him."

"Do you want custody?"

Mr. Stewart had become a different man, much sharper and shrewder.

"I don't know. She says she wants to take him to the States with her."

"He is your son."

It was a statement which hinted at a question.

"Yes," John said. "He is my son. But I don't know him. How can I take him from his mother? He's only four."

"Do you want to lose him?"

It was as if the fog of uncertainty and distress which had enveloped John since he had read that letter began to thin and to lift.

"No. No . . . Bennachie is his heritage if he wants it."

"Offer a divorce on her terms in return for custody."

"How can I? Who would look after him? Lord knows when I'll have a home for him. In any case . . . I can't just drag him away from everything he knows . . ."

Mr. Stewart looked at him compassionately.

"I begin to understand, Mr. John, why you're looking so peely-wally."

John smiled at the old phrase.

"Away and have yourself a holiday and leave the letter with me, if you like. Don't answer it, yet a while. Nothing was ever lost for a little thought. Come and see me before you go back. Try to forget everything for a little while and maybe things won't seem to be in such a tangle. Are you going to have a look at your old haunts?"

"I hadn't thought of it."

"Well, think of it now. Eat and sleep and walk and just *be* for a week. You look as if you needed that."

The fog was thinning out under a drizzle when he left the office. The temperature had gone shooting up. It was possible to see across the width of the street and the traffic was moving with more confidence. The prostrate city was beginning to come back to life. John walked towards Buchanan Street. He had decided that he would go to see the graves before he did anything else. He didn't really see the point of looking at a lump of stone. It didn't make up for not having gone to see them the Christmas before the Clydeside blitz. When he turned into Buchanan Street he remembered the horse in the alleyway and before he had passed more than one side street, there it was, huge and patient and smelling nostalgically of stable. He paused and looked at it and it scraped a hoof on the cobbles and tossed the beautiful heavy head so that its bridle jingled. The man came forward to quiet him.

"Does he ever get out to the country?" John asked.

"Whiles," said the traceman. "Whiles. Jeez, but you should see him roll!"

John gave him a note.

"Get yourself a pint and get him a bag of sugar or apples or whatever he fancies."

"Right! But, here, mister . . . sugar's rationed, there's a war on!"

John walked on, smiling at the crack, and felt cheered at the idea of that huge creature rolling on the soft green grass, his vast hooves in the air. He saw in front of him, blurred by the fog, the entrance to Buchanan Street Station and went in to see whether he could take a train out to Milngavie. He did not care for buses.

The names on the arrivals and departures board sang in his memory, like a song; Campsie Glen, Milton of Campsie, Killearn, Buchlyvie, Gartmore, Aberfoyle; on another he read KIRKTON OF LANGMUIR . . . it jumped out of the board at him like the blow of a fist or the shape of a fighter in the corner of his eye . . . Instantly he was back in the kitchen at Bennachie listening to tales of the first Hector and Hannah while the third

Hector yawned and made faces at his mother. Hannah had come from Kirkton of Langmuir. Within quarter of an hour he found himself in a cold First Class compartment chuntering over the points with a ticket in his pocket to Kirkton of Langmuir. There was bound to be an hotel, he told himself, and he could walk in the country round about and find out where the smiddy had been . . . perhaps it was still there . . . the kirk would be there and the manse.

The Kirkton was not at all what he had expected. The journey was slow and the train stopped at every station. He arrived at dusk. The station was tiny and delapidated and no one got off the train with him. Outside he found, not a little farming village but a dingy, depressed, little manufacturing town huddled in mean, narrow streets and mean, shabby houses around the high brick walls of a huge Works. A chimney towered above the angular pattern of long roofs and belched out thick smoke. Over the gate was a metal arch with letters worked in it: S AND L TUBES AND PIPES. As he was looking around for an hotel a siren began to blow, the gates under the iron arch swung wide open and a multitude came swarming out, dirty-faced and cheerful, calling out goodnights, mounting bicycles, making for the pub on the corner: a sharp acrid smell came from the working overalls they wore under their raincoats. Nearly all of them wore knitted scarves and the flat cap, the 'bunnet'. John stood still like a rock in the river as they swarmed past, the works siren still whooping behind them. One or two looked at him curiously for there were few there who would have come up to his shoulder, he heard the inevitable comment, 'Brylcream Boy'. There were women, too, their heads tied up in scarves, and with overall trousers, too short and too wide, showing under the shabbiness of a once 'good' coat relegated to everyday, some with worn and matted fur trimmings, buttons hanging by a thread or missing. The women eyed him with even more interest than the men and one or two of the bolder ones wolf-whistled and were acclaimed by gales of giggles from their friends. 'Got a date for the night, handsome?' one of them called. John turned away smiling and peered through the growing dark for a pub of some sort. There was nothing in view. A shop, its windows covered with cards offering items for sale or rooms for rent, seemed to be open. He went in and was confronted with empty shelves, a litter of newspapers and magazines on the counter and a boxlid with NO CIGS scrawled on it. A smell of frying was so strong as to be almost visible. An old man peered up at him from behind a newspaper folded into a tiny wad.

"Uh-huh?" he enquired.

"Is there a hotel or a boarding house," John enquired, "somewhere I could get a bed for the night?"

The old man stared at him and grinned around a short pipe.

"In the name o' Gawd wha's likely tae want tae stay here? Mair like tae fecht their wey oot. But I'll ask Maw? MAW!"

Maw was fat, slatternly, gap-toothed and helpful. There was no hotel, never had been and the pub didn't have bedrooms and she for one wouldn't stay in any bedroom in yon pub but there was a widow-body who let lodgings to folk. The works had visiting workmen whiles. She was that pernickety but a great cook, so she was, and had a daughter married on a farmer so there was aye eggs and a bit butter. Maw would see had she a room.

"Jeannie!" she bawled into the back. "Awa' spier at Mistress McKenzie has she a bed for a visitor?"

Jeannie, unexpectedly trig in school tunic and white blouse, hurtled through the shop pulling on a raincoat. She cast an admiring glance at John and was gone.

"Oor granddochter," said the old man proudly. "She's go' a bursary to the High. For the Higher Eddication. She's a clip, Jeannie."

"They're learnin' her French," Maw said, "je soo an' that . . ."

"And the Mathymatticks . . ."

They listed Jeannie's timetable with pride and said she was coming out for a teacher and it was grand that she should have a chance like her brother.

"You got folks hereaboot?" asked Maw. "Sit doon while yer waitin'. I'll fetch ye a wee fly cup."

She disappeared into the back but it seemed that this was not held to be any barrier to conversation and John raised his voice to reach her as she put water in the kettle and lit the gas with a resounding bang.

"I don't know whether there's any left. My great great grandmother was born here. Her father was the blacksmith. Lindsay was the name."

"Lindsay? Never heard o' nae Lindsays here. No in ma time."

"Awa'!" cried the old man disgustedly. "Nae Lindsays! Whit aboot Saunders and Lindsay?"

Maw appeared briefly in the doorway with a battered metal teapot.

"The Works?"

"Aye, the Works. Lindsay sterted it up nearaboot fifty year back and Saunders was a Glesga felly pit money in during the war . . . the first ane."

"You mean that Works, out there?"

"Aye. There's just the one."

"Any Lindsays left?"

"Na. They sellt oot tae Stewart and Lloyd in the bad times. Auld Lindsay deed and he'd nae family. Deid in France, the baith o' them."

"That's right enough," Maw agreed and handed him a huge mug of black tea: she dolloped a spoonful of condensed milk into it from a long-opened tin. "Nane left. They'd a great big hoosie upbye on the Campsies but it's a hospital for weans noo."

"There wis an auld wifie but she deed mebbe twa year syne and she'd no been in her richt senses for a whilie," Paw added. "Would they be your folk?"

"I don't know," John said. "After my great grandmother died I think they stopped writing and my grandmother said she never met any of them."

"Where do you stay?" Maw asked.

"New Zealand."

"There's a fair few hereaboot wi' folk oot there," Maw said.

"Aye, aye," mumbled Paw, "but it's an awfy distance New Zealand."

"Ken whit ye should dae?" Maw declared. "Awa' up tae the Carnegie the morn's morn an' hae a word wi' the lassie there. She's an awfy yin for the auld days. Her folks has been here syne Paw wis a boy and afore that and she's aye spierin' at folk aboot their granddas an' that. She'll ken for sure."

This being translated as advice to visit the librarian in the town library in the morning, John agreed to do just that.

"Puir lass," Maw confided. "She's this mither winna let her in nor oot. Keeps her trotting at her apron string, day in day oot. Wouldna let her gang tae the war wi' the ither lassies, na, na . . . you mark my words, Paw, when yon yin kicks ower the cairt it'll mak' a fell stushie!"

Mistress MacKenzie proved to be as pernickety as Maw predicted. His bed was short, all beds were short for John, but it was aired and clean and warm and his breakfast was the best he had had since he left Bennachie; boiled eggs, fresh baps and farm butter. He thanked her fervently and won a slight, rare smile. Mistress McKenzie concealed a weakness for a braw lad and John was surely a braw lad. She directed him to the library and watched him down the road, planning his evening meal with an enthusiasm she would have died rather than admit.

The Carnegie was a dingy place. It was an abandoned chapel, built at a time when architects favoured vari-coloured bands of brick and light-coloured windows and edging. After half a century of soot and sulphur dioxide it had the air at once raffish and depressed of an aging whore. Inside, it was painted buff in an attempt to smarten it and the walls were lined with shelves, but brooding over it was the thought of hell fire. John went in and saw in the centre of the room a circular desk with a queue of children waiting under the eye of a teacher to take out books. He waited till the last boy handed over his pile of Biggles books to be stamped and then he moved to take his place. The girl behind the shining mahogany expanse looked up at him, startled to see a stranger. She was small, rather pale with a cloud of dark hair and eyes of a startling blue under fine tilted eyebrows. John held his breath for to breathe, to speak, to move, would spoil the moment. He fell in love for the third and last time in his life.

33

The borrowing days are those three sunshiny days which winter borrows from early summer and often pays back with interest at the beginning of May. When John next approached the office in St. Vincent Street, winter was displaying one of those borrowed days. The sky was blue, decorated with little fat fleecy clouds, the air was still and almost balmy and sunlight glinted on the dusty winter-grimed windows. It might have been spring except that winter's lease had another month and more to run. John and Lucy walked along the dignified, slightly shabby, street on the generous wide pavements looking about them as people do who are on holiday and relish seeing the work-a-day world go by. If the world looked on them it was to smile at their air of being absorbed in one another, and it was mostly the female world which looked. Where John, huge and handsome, took their eye, Lucy attracted few glances unless they were those of frank female envy. She was small, dowdily dressed in nondescript clothes, a brown tweed skirt, a faded, much-washed, knitted jumper and over those a tweed coat with a deep fur collar which had first seen the light twenty years before and which the clothes shortage had retrieved from a mothballed retirement in a trunk. Neat, mended gloves and oft-repaired leather brogues agreed with a shabby leather satchel. Over her splendid cloud of fine dark hair she wore a woollen Fair-Isle tam o'shanter. Dozens dressed as she was emerged every day from suburban homes and vanished into schools and offices. There was nothing remarkable about Lucy at first glance unless it was held long enough to see the vivid blue eyes and the silky long lashes which framed them. At a second glance the understated delicacy of her other features became plain, the small but perfectly proportioned body under those drab clothes and the grace with which she moved. At a third glance . . . but only John had taken a third glance and seen at once what he had been looking for.

At the bottom of the flight of foot-worn stone steps which arched discreetly over the sandbagged area below they paused and smiled at one another in the delighted and inconsequent fashion of new lovers before they walked up, hand in hand. Miss Dalrymple in the front office looked at them over the venerable Royal typewriter which had delivered so much human life reduced by the process of law to typescript, wills, contracts, conveyances, and she recalled the young clerk who had sat where she was sitting and laboured with a pen before he had shouldered a rifle and left for France. Thirty years before Miss Dalrymple had taken his place and he had taken her heart to his grave at Messines. These days she remembered him seldom, and then with a guilty start, for the years and the paper had overtaken and smothered that summer, the first summer of the war and Miss Dalrymple, well-versed in the pitfalls of married life, often thought that she might have had a narrow escape. But now she saw John and Lucy in the sunshine and with a pang of that long-forgotten agony she thought that she would never know what they knew or feel what they were feeling. A fountain of resentment arose in her, a bitter longing for what had been snatched from her. It took her by surprise and she stared at the neat typescript on the roller fighting for the cheerful composure which had been the armour of thirty years against the shafts of pity and contempt.

John noticed no difference in the figure who emerged from the door of what had once been the dining room of some prosperous Glasgow baillie, his broadclothed belly well-lined with Highland beef and French claret. Miss Dalrymple smiled at him and then at Lucy.

"Mr. Stewart can see you right away," she told them. "If you'll just follow me. Can I have the young lady's name?"

In John's mind a ghostly voice said, 'Of course you *can*, but whether you *may* is quite another matter . . .'

"Miss Lapraik," John said and lingered with loving amusement over the alliteration, "Miss Lucy Lapraik."

They followed Miss Dalrymple up the shallow stone staircase with its elegant iron bannisters and she saw with a kind of despair that they scarcely knew she was there. In the shabby cosy office which John remembered, Stewart rose and shook hands fervently.

"Now . . . that holiday's done you a power of good, Mr. John . . ."

For the first time John noticed the delicate compromise which avoided the use of the discarded name Lindsay-Innis as well as that of Macadam which he used with every justification except the legal one.

"My word, but you're looking more the thing. Was it the hills or was it this bonnie lass, here . . .?"

He took Lucy's coat and hung it on the bentwood hatstand and then waved them both to the fireside chairs.

"Come to the fire, the sun's out but it's winter yet. Sit there . . . fine. Miss Dalrymple, tea, if you please, and mebbe a biscuit if the points'll run to it."

Miss Dalrymple shook her shingled head at him and withdrew into a minute apartment in which the Glasgow baillie had had his hair powdered for civic occasions. There she could be heard running water hollowly into a kettle and clattering cups and spoons. Stewart turned his desk-chair to face the fire and beamed upon them, his head a little to one side.

"Eh, well," he said, "I don't suppose you're here for the pleasure of our company. What can I do for you?"

"There's one or two things," John said. "May I start with the bits and pieces?"

"Of course, of course."

"First, could you arrange for us to see the stuff from Kelvin Drive?"

Stewart scribbled in a notebook.

"As soon as you like. This afternoon? About three?"

John nodded.

"The sooner the better. We'll decide . . ."

He saw Stewart's attention sharpen at that 'we'.

". . . after we've seen what's there, what to sell and what to keep," he went on, "and the stuff we sell is to go towards Ruby's annuity. And I've a note somewhere of one or two items she'd like to have for . . ."

". . . for a wee minding," Lucy mimicked and they smiled at one another.

"You went to see her?" Stewart asked. "My, but she'd be fine pleased about that. She'd a soft spot for her Mr. John."

"She is not to know about this annuity," John warned him, "not till we've gone home. After that she'll have you to deal with and you can tell her what a devil I am to have my own way."

Stewart winked and tapped the side of his nose.

"Rely on me."

"And that really winds up the Glasgow end," John said briskly.

"The capital to revert?" asked Stewart.

"Yes, I think so. The children might be glad of it some day."

Lucy went a little pink. Stewart smiled to himself.

"Now, there's the other thing," John said briskly. "Would you write on my behalf to Mrs. Macadam in Santa Monica, California . . ."

He consulted a letter which he had in his pocket.

" . . . I've the address here. I want you to request custody of my son Dominic John . . ."

Stewart began to scribble again at greater length.

" . . . if she will agree to this, she may divorce me on whatever grounds the American courts accept. If an American divorce is not valid in New Zealand or in Britain . . ."

"I'll ascertain the position."

"She may bring proceedings over here. We . . ."

He glanced at Lucy who nodded agreement.

" . . . we will not defend the action. But this is only if she relinquishes all claim to Dominic."

Stewart scribbled frantically, slashed a line under his scrawl, looked up and grinned.

"Well, now, here's a change," he observed, "there's a sight more decision about you, young man, than the last time you sat in that chair."

"Well," John grinned, "you've only yourself to thank. I took your advice. You were right. I needed a holiday."

"Where did you go?"

"Kirkton of Langmuir."

"Kirkton of . . . *Kirkton*! You're codding me. There's nothing there but a tube works and a tangle of dirty wee streets. No one in their right senses would go there for a holiday! Whatever came over you?"

John chuckled and Lucy laughed aloud at his expression.

"Well . . . you could say it was my great grandmother. She was the blacksmith's daughter there a century ago. I thought I'd go and have a look at her old home."

"She'd be birling in her grave if she could see the place now. What did you find?"

"Oh, the kirk she attended, her mother's grave and her father's and one of her brothers. There were quite a lot of entries in the register. There's none of the family left there now. And there was the works itself, of course."

Stewart stared.

"The works? You mean Saunders and Lindsay?"

"It was her nephew started them. Alec Lindsay."

"Saunders and Lindsay . . . well, I'll be hanged. Your grandmother never knew of that."

"No. She would never have any truck with Grand's own people," John said.

"Well, well, I would never have thought it possible."

"I visited the farmhouse that she was going to live in."

"We found out that she was engaged to my own great grandfather," Lucy put in. "The engagement was broken off for some reason and he married someone else but it can't have been a great quarrel because they were great friends afterwards. My great grandmother used to write to her. And there were stories about her . . ."

"My favourite was how she bathed her stepmother before she'd let her in the house," John remarked.

"And there was another one about how she was going to marry the minister," Lucy added. "It seems that she left the Kirkton on her wedding day and used her tocher to sail to New Zealand and just left them all standing."

"I can see you didn't waste any time," Stewart observed.

"I found the local librarian very knowledgeable and helpful," John said with a straight face. "She made a hobby of local history."

"Aye, doubtless. And doubtless I don't have to look far for this knowledgeable librarian," suggested Stewart, looking from one to the other.

"No," John agreed. "It was Lucy."

"And I don't suppose for a minute that it's a puckle family

history which has set you up and put the gleam in your eye, young man?"

"No," agreed John.

"And I don't suppose that all you came to tell me was the story of your great grandma giving her guidmither a bath."

"No again. We came to see whether we had got ourselves into hot water. You see Lucy's mother . . . Mrs. Lapraik . . . is threatening to have the law on me."

Stewart's benevolent smile faded.

"You make me shake in my shoes," he said. "Whatever have you been about?"

John looked at Lucy and hesitated.

"Go on," she said. "He's got to know. Show him."

John unbuttoned the breast-pocket of his tunic and produced a letter. He handed it to Stewart who examined it as if he expected it to contain a bomb. It was addressed in a wild, spiky, sprawling handwriting which sloped sharply down at the end of the lines to, Squadron-Leader Macadam, c/o McKenzie, 7 Ramsay Macdonald Row, Kirkton of Langmuir. *Please Forward Immediately* was scrawled across the top. It had been readdressed, neatly and soberly, to the Station Hotel, Perth. Stewart opened out pages of the same wild, spiky writing which he read with an expressionless face.

"Mmmm . . ." he observed when he had finished. "Dear me."

"She can't really do anything to John, can she?" Lucy asked anxiously.

"It seems that she accuses you, Mr. John, of seduction . . . forcible seduction no less . . . and abduction of her daughter . . . that's yourself, Miss Lapraik . . ."

"It's haivers," Lucy said indignantly, "absolute haivers."

"That's not all . . . she says you are guilty of theft of property, damage to property, breaking and entering, mercy me . . ."

"It's all haivers," protested Lucy.

". . . and contamination of her premises . . . what can she mean by that?"

Lucy went bright pink.

"Well, that's true enough in a sort of a way."

"She accuses you of exposing her to public scorn and humiliation . . ."

"She ought to know about that," Lucy cried. "She humiliated me often enough."

"She intends to have you arrested and put in jail and made to pay," Stewart finished. "My, my, but she was in a right paddy when she wrote this. Dear me, dear me!"

"Most of it's plain hot air," John said, "but we wondered whether she could do anything?"

"Well, I'd need to hear the whole story," Stewart declared solemnly. "In fact if I don't hear it, I'll perish with curiosity. What in the name have you been about, the pair of you?"

"But that abduction and seduction bit . . . can she put John in gaol?"

"Well, well," Stewart said indulgently, "let's see. How old are you?"

"Twenty-four."

"Over the age of consent and no longer a minor. Did you want to go with yon wicked seducer?"

It was John's turn to blush.

"More than anything I'd ever wanted," Lucy assured him.

"So you weren't carried off kicking and screaming."

"Certainly not."

"Giggling, more like," John added.

"And did you do any damage during this . . . er . . . abduction?" Stewart asked John.

"No. Not a scrap. I even padded the top of the ladder," John explained, "so that it wouldn't make a noise."

Stewart's eyes bulged a little.

"Ladder!" he ejaculated much in the style of Lady Bracknell and added hastily, "no, no, you can explain that later . . . did you take anything which wasn't yours?"

"No. Everything I brought with me was mine. Clothes and some bits of jewellery my grandmother left me," Lucy said. "I couldn't take much . . . in the circumstances."

"And I wasn't even in the house," John added.

"Then how the hell could you contamin . . . never mind, I doubt Mrs. Lapraik hasn't a leg to stand on. You're of age, lass, and your own mistress."

John and Lucy leaned back and smiled at one another in relief.

"Such wild and whirling words," Stewart murmured, turning the sheets of the letter backwards and forwards in his hands. "By jiminy, I can't wait to hear the whole story."

Miss Dalrymple came in with a tray spread with an embroidered cloth and set with tea and biscuits.

"Ah, Miss Dalrymple, I have excellent news for you. Romance is not dead."

"Is that a fact, Mr. Stewart? Sugar, Miss Lapraik?"

"It is indeed. Romance has blossomed in the unlikely purlieus of Kirkton of Langmuir."

"Where? Oh, my! Whoever would have thought it! Sugar, Mr. John?"

Stewart took his cup from the tray and stirred it mightily and then removed the spoon and pointed it at John.

"Miss Dalrymple, meet the young Lochinvar."

She shook her head reprovingly and held out a plate of biscuits.

"Rich Tea or Osborne, Miss Lapraik? You take no notice, Mr. John. He will have his little joke."

"No joke," said the lawyer and began to laugh, softly at first and then so hard he had to put down his cup. "By the Lord Harry . . . if your grandmother knew about this, she would be black affronted. Now, suppose you tell me just what did happen."

Miss Dalrymple retreated to the powdering closet but, being human, she left the door open a crack.

John began, a little hesitantly: it was not at all easy to explain how it had all begun. How could you explain something which was neither logical nor reasonable. He had known before he had even spoken to Lucy that 'this was it' and she admitted that it was the same for her; 'like the sun rising,' she had said, 'as if the whole landscape had been newly made.' But, at first he had tried to be sensible, to remember his disastrous impulsive marriage to Ruth, to hold in check the certainty which possessed him and which was so different to the wild torrent of feeling he had experienced before. For two days they had behaved like two unexpectedly compatible strangers; they had enquired together into the local records of the Lindsay family, visited in stolen lunch-hours and tea breaks the visible remnants of the Kirkton which Hannah had known and discussed what they had found. The discussion had had nothing to do with what they were really saying to one another. They were not the strangers they appeared to be and they never could have been. It was as if they had taken up an interrupted friendship. The third day was Saturday and Lucy, heedless of her mother's instructions, slipped away and came with John in the bus to Stirling. There they had spent an afternoon wandering round that rather dull little town, talking, though not yet of themselves. John described his home, he remembered and Lucy remembered the passion with which he had recalled it. They had eaten an early and dreadful dinner among the brass hats at the Golden Lion and caught the bus back to the Kirkton. Not until then had he told her about Ruth.

"It was a terrible blow in a way," Lucy admitted, "but at the same time I knew it wasn't going to make any difference . . . it was just another obstacle to be got over. Like my mother was. I knew John wouldn't lie to me . . ."

At that point she had missed the expression on Stewart's face.

"I knew I ought not to feel like that but knowing didn't make any difference. I had made up my mind long before, that if he asked me I would go with him and it didn't matter where. That was that. It wasn't as if it would hurt anyone."

"Your mother?" queried Mr. Stewart.

"I didn't think that I owed her any more," Lucy said quietly. "She was angry already. I'd gone without telling where I was going or who I was going with and she was waiting up for me. She never let me go out, you see. Not even with girl friends. I just wasn't allowed. If I did it was never worth the scene which followed so I had stopped going anywhere. But John was worth any scene. When I got home she said I would make her ill and did I want to kill her. She brought up about my father and how she had had to bring me up all alone and that I owed her something for that. I'd heard that again and again. This time it sounded different, sort of hollow and false. I can't explain. It was as if I was seeing her plainly for the first time."

Stewart nodded, pursing his lips.

"I hadn't realised just what she'd had to put up with," John interrupted. "Mrs. Mackenzie told me. She knew everything about everybody. Lucy hadn't said much, just that she was going to be in trouble."

Mrs. Mackenzie had been outspoken.

"She's been sair hudden doon, yon puir wee lass. There was aye trouble in that hoose. Her mither is a doer's daughter frae the Borders and she thought she'd done Dougal Lapraik a favour marrying a working farmer and a rare life o' it she led him. Aye. Six month after wee Lucy was born he lit oot wi' the barmaid frae the Langmuir Arms and he never cam' back. Sma' blame tae him. Yon wumman made a right speak o' him, screechin' and flytin' if he just looked the road o' anither lass and makin' a show o' him, fetchin' him oot the pub afore the hale toon. Ach, he was weel rid o' her. Mind, she's never wanted. There was a fair bit o' siller for hauf the Kirkton's biggit on Dougal Lapraik's parks. But, fegs . . . has she no ta'en it oot o' yon wee lass?"

After he heard that, John admitted, he hadn't felt quite so bad: but his leave was slipping away and he was desperate to make sure of Lucy somehow. He decided to face Mrs. Lapraik and try to explain.

"I told him it wouldn't be any good," Lucy said. "She'd no law for men . . . any men. She'd never have given us her permission even to be properly married, let alone to go off with him to New Zealand and wait for his divorce to come through."

"I'm a father, myself," Stewart observed.

"But you'd listen," Lucy said. "However, John insisted we had to try. He wanted everything to be above board, he said."

"I did . . . and I do," John declared.

"On Sunday afternoon he arrived at the front door . . ."

"And she wouldn't listen?" asked Stewart.

"She never even let him start . . ." Lucy shivered. "She just yelled at him and shouted abuse, horrible words, I never heard her use them before . . ."

"She told me to get out and never come back and never to speak to Lucy again or she'd have the police on me . . ."

"She was spitting," Lucy said, "her chin was wet and her

eyes were staring. She frightened me. I thought she really was going to be ill. I begged John to go."

"So I did. She said she was going to try to calm her down and reason with her. I didn't sleep much, that night, I can tell you. On the dot of nine I was on the doorstep of the library. But Lucy never came. I waited and waited. Then the milk-boy delivered a note to the head librarian saying she wasn't coming back to work."

"I heard he plucked it out of old Porteous' hand," Lucy said. "Without a by-your-leave . . ."

"I was worried out of my mind. I went along to the house and knocked and rang but no one answered. I knew she was still there because I could see someone moving behind the curtains. I didn't know what to do for the best for, when you come to think about it, I didn't have a leg to stand on. So . . . I went back to Ramsay Macdonald Row and asked Mrs. Mackenzie what she thought had happened . . . I told her the whole story. She said she thought that Lucy would be locked in her room in the attic."

"What!"

"I couldn't believe it either. But she said it had happened before. Twice."

"The first time was when I wanted to go to the university," Lucy explained. "I'd won . . . anyway, I was wild to go. She locked me in then. The next time was when I wanted to join the Wrens. She locked me up on bread and water till I gave her my promise not to go. The doctor wrote a note to say I should be exempt. That time it was nearly three weeks before she let me out."

"When I heard that," John said grimly, "I reckoned she'd be better off with me, however little I could offer."

"I'm tempted to agree," said Stewart.

"So I set about trying to make some plans," John went on, "and Mrs. Mac was right there. You know, to look at her you'd think she was as prim and proper as a pin, but she was like a schoolboy. I'd need a ladder, she said, and she'd a nephew, a housepainter. Round she went that instant to his house and brought him back. She didn't say what she wanted it for but he hadn't the nerve to ask, just agreed to leave it along the hedge at the back of Netherbiggin where it wouldn't be noticed and I was to put it back there after. Mrs. Mac said, aye, I'd find it fell hard to swim the Esk River with a twenty-foot ladder. She didn't crack a smile when she said it and the nephew just swallowed hard and edged out of the house. Lord knows what he thought I wanted a ladder for."

"Well, he knows now," Lucy reminded him.

"And what were you doing meanwhile?" Stewart asked Lucy.

"Seething with rage and plotting to catch her with the key when she brought my food. But she always waited until I was asleep. I think she sat outside and listened. Lord, but I felt such a stupid *lemon*! Having to sit there like Rapunzel except that my hair wasn't long enough and waiting for someone to ride up on a big white horse. I knew John would try to do something, but I didn't know what or when."

Her expression of disgust set them both laughing and the ghost of a giggle was heard from the powdering closet.

"Meanwhile, back in Ramsay Macdonald Row, Sir Launcelot was saddling his snow-white steed," Stewart suggested.

"Well, no, actually . . ." John said, "the horse was being yoked nearly two miles away. Mrs. Mackenzie had a daughter married to a farmer in Langmuir Mains."

Lucy giggled.

"You see," John persevered, "Mrs. Mac had decided that what we really wanted was a diversion. And she was quite right, we did. Quite apart from the fact that Lucy's mother spent her time sitting outside her door there were other difficulties. You try putting up a twenty foot ladder unobtrusively . . . even when you know which window to put it at . . ."

"What did she come up with?"

"You'll never believe this . . ."

The army had lost a general in Mrs. Mackenzie. Her son-in-law, the tenant of the Mains, had been instructed to deliver a load of manure to Netherbiggin the following day. Obediently, and with a certain glee, he had despatched a malodorous cartload in the charge of his one remaining male farmhand, an Irishman who combined almost total deafness with an extraordinary degree of bloodymindedness. He arrived at dusk when the road was thronged with homeward bound workers from the S and L. A crowd gathered. Mrs. Lapraik's angry and incredulous refusal to accept delivery was completely ignored by Ignatius who, despite all protests and gestures, opened the gates, backed the cart up to the entrance of the old stableyard and then prepared to tip his load. Mrs. Lapraik's protests became shriller and shriller and more and more vehement but Ignatius's head had room for only one instruction at a time and he had a low opinion of women at the best of times. This was not the best of times either for the pubs were open. Inexorably, half a ton of best, well-rotted, farmyard manure descended upon the oft-swept flags of the Netherbiggin stableyard. Ignatius then directed the horse in the direction of the Langmuir Arms where he intended to spend the pound note in his pocket.

After the worst had happened Mrs. Lapraik had rushed off to the phone box on the corner to protest, first to Mrs. Mackenzie's son-in-law and then, when he had stolidly maintained that he had the order in writing (which he had, John having delivered it that morning on the housepainter's bicycle), she had slammed down the receiver and dialled 999 and summoned the police.

Sergeant McCaffrey arrived, moved on the much entertained crowd at the gate, and then firmly and amiably refused either to fetch Ignatius to remove the manure or to arrest Mrs. McKenzie's son-in-law. Mrs. Lapraik was an old acquaintance of the Sergeant's for she was prone to send for the police on trivial occasions. He walked about the slow-steaming heap in the stableyard and made notes in his notebook which were unlikely to please Mrs. Lapraik had she been privileged to read them.

'Practical joke,' the Sergeant had written, 'and serve the old bitch right.'

He interrupted her reiterated threats of legal action against all concerned by congratulating her rather wistfully on the excellent quality of her unwanted acquisition. Sergeant McCaffrey was the guiding and the shining light of the Kirkton of Langmuir and Bonnyburn Horticultural Allotment and Garden Association. Mrs. Lapraik babbled with fury at this irrelevance.

"I could mebbe manage to find somebody to take it off your hands, mistress."

"When?" Mrs. Lapraik's squawks ceased abruptly.

"The morn's morn . . . early afore folks are about . . ."

"I'll not pay a penny piece!"

Sergeant McCaffrey shrugged and buttoned away his notebook.

"Och," he said regretfully, "then nae doot you'll can spread it on your ain garden. It's grand stuff for this Dig for Victory caper."

"Me!" she spluttered. "Me? File my hands with yon filth?"

"Filth," protested the Sergeant, "good muck's not filth, mistress."

He stirred the heap lovingly with the toe of his boot and the aroma arose in its might.

"Five shilligs," offered Mrs. Lapraik with her handkerchief to her nose, "nod a peddy bore . . ."

"Done," Sergeant McCaffrey said and smiled.

While all this was going on John had been staggering about all among the thorny fruitbushes with a twenty-foot ladder, trying to attract Lucy's attention by throwing handfuls of gravel at her window. After that there had been the business of bringing her down together with a hastily packed suitcase. However, the following day there had been a number of versions of the exchange circulating the neighbourhood, each one more lurid than the last and Mrs. Mackenzie had gleefully included a selection in her letter.

It had not been until long after Sergeant McCaffrey had cycled away, the ancient bicycle squeaking and clanking under his bulk that Mrs. Lapraik discovered, much as Shylock had done, that her daughter had departed. The Sergeant, torn a second time from his tea, was less tactful than before.

"I canna see that's it's any business o' the polis, mistress."

"Abduction isn't police business! . . . kidnapping! . . . rape!"

"There's nae evidence o' any o' they things," he said stolidly and, because like Mrs. Mackenzie he heard most of what went on in the Kirkton sooner or later, he added, "If you'd the lassie shut up, mistress, you've only yourself to blame."

Sergeant McCaffrey spoke for the Kirkton which was quick

405

to hear of the elopement, gloated to hear that Mrs. Lapraik had been outwitted and wished Lucy well. This too, Mrs. Mackenzie had put in her letter. More ominously she also included the news that Mrs. Lapraik had been away into Edinburgh to see her lawyers.

"They'll not touch the case with a bargepole," Stewart assured them chuckling. "Folk would never be done laughing at them. Mind the papers would like it fine. The Young Lochinvar . . . man, I can just see it all over the front pages. But Lochinvar would never have thought of a cartload of dung . . . compared with you he was a rank amateur. And I take it you nipped down yon ladder spry as a speug with all your duddies done up in a spotted hankie?"

"Yes," Lucy agreed, with a grin like a schoolboy.

"Then what?"

"The bus to Stirling and then the train to Perth," said John succinctly. "Then we spent a week looking about the Carse, seeing old friends and so forth . . ."

"Mmmm . . ." commented Mr. Stewart and made a church-and-steeple of his fingers. "Am I to understand that you two babes-in-the-wood have . . . er . . . thrown your caps over the windmill, so to say?"

"Yes," said Lucy firmly.

"As you've reason to know," John added, "in my family a wedding's not always essential for a marriage."

Stewart shook his grey head at them but they sensed he was more amused than disapproving.

"Well," he said, "I propose we proceed in this fashion . . ."

As he proposed and disposed John listened with only half an ear because he was remembering those first few days at Bennachie, the sense of peace and security which had permeated all the hours and which even the grief for Grand had not been able to affect. He felt the same way now. There might be storms ahead, something would have to be done about Lucy's mother, the war was still to finish, but some day, not too far in the future he would bring Lucy down Lucky's road and show her his kingdom, their kingdom. His mind ranged over the paddocks and hill pastures, recalling each stream, each hollow, each patch of bush with loving particularity as if it were a present hoarded up for Lucy.

". . . and now we have to consider the child," Stewart said. "I understand he has been taken to America . . ."

"No. He's in Wellington with his grandparents," John interrupted. "There was a letter waiting at the hotel, forwarded from the hospital. Ruth decided to leave without him."

"Ah ha! Matters may not be as difficult as we expected. Possession is a difficult circumstance to overcome and hard on the child. Now, with a competent housekeeper . . ."

He darted a twinkling glance at Lucy.

". . . and a settled home, I think you may put up a very strong case."

John nodded contentedly and smiled when he thought of the letter which had been written by his Uncle Allan. He could never think of him as his father-in-law. Hannah was a born mother-in-law, but Uncle Allan was Uncle Allan.

. . . the truth was that young Nick did not take to Daryl. Ruth felt that perhaps it wouldn't be right to take him with her. I have to say I agreed with her. Daryl, while perfectly happy to take the kid on, as he put it, did not strike me as the ideal stepfather for a boy like Nick. Ruth appears to think that Nick may see things differently when he is a little older and want to come to America. I suspect this is unlikely and I suspect she knows it. In any event, he is still here with us and will be until the war ends. Daryl has been posted to California where he is to work for the Douglas Corporation. Ruth suggests that we take him out to them after the war is over. However, like Nick, I did not take to Daryl. Nick will be better with you.

When you come home, and we all wish it will be soon, you will find that your son is something of a prodigy. He has perfect pitch, can already play a treble recorder very well, and is learning to play the piano. Music is a consuming interest with him. I know it is early days, but I feel he must have a musical future. Between us we have composed a tune for you; he can read simple music already . . . in fact he was as quick to learn his notes as his letters. He calls this, *For Real Daddy* and I enclose a copy which he made for you. This tells its own tale. I must add that for Daryl he refused to perform at all. In fact his behaviour was most regrettable and probably prevented his being taken to the States. I cannot disguise from you that he is a difficult little boy, with a mind of his own and no inhibitions at all about speaking it. Ruth doesn't pretend to have any control over him and Hannah who has had charge of him for much of the time is divided between pride in his ability and his liveliness and exasperation at his stubbornness. She says he is like you, but he reminds me very much of IA.

It was the first time that Dominic had come alive for him. The photographs of the wiry dark-haired little boy busy in the Wellington garden and impatient of the takers of photographs had not become his son for him in the same way as this badly-behaved, outspoken little boy who was passionately interested in music and reminded Uncle Allan of IA. He conjured up a picture of him playing the sweet-toned upright piano which Grand had bought and sent to Bennachie while Lucy was in Hannah's chair, curled up with a book in her lap. He wanted to touch wood, to avert the eye of the jealous gods from his happiness. He would tip-toe into his future to avoid their attention. How rare it was to be happy, he thought, even for those who recognise the condition: so many people never knew what would make them happy or believed that happiness was just the negative of unhappiness. He had always thought of himself as untalented, Grandmother had sought for talent in him and found it wanting. He had accepted her verdict as children do. He had discovered an aptitude for shepherding but knew all too well that Grandmother would never have accepted that as a talent. Nor would she have accepted his outlandish ability to fight in the air. He understood at last that she had been wrong: he had a talent, perhaps the rarest of all talents, he was able to accept happiness, to recognise it, and he did not despise it or himself for accepting it. It was a curious thing to discover about oneself in the middle of a war eleven thousand miles from home.

"John . . . John . . ." Lucy said and tugged at his arm, "Mr. Stewart wants to know . . ."

"Sorry . . ." he said hurriedly, "I was miles away . . ."

"Eleven thousand miles away, as usual," suggested Lucy.

"Well," Stewart observed, "to judge by today's news it'll not be long before you're there in the flesh as well as the spirit. The Americans have crossed the Rhine at Remagen. A matter of time now, all the papers say."

"When we do reach home," John said, "be prepared for a long stay, Lucy. It'll take a hell of a lot to winkle me out of Bennachie again."

FINAL CURTAIN

34

It had taken a World Première to bring him back, John was thinking, as he listened to the applause beating on the walls of the theatre like breakers on the rocks of the north coast. The noise pressed on his ears coming and going, louder and louder and louder still as the blood had beaten in his ears when his plane was spinning down. On the stage, in the centre of the bowing, smiling cast was his son: dark, thin, heavybrowed, accepting this acclaim with calm. John was not clapping, he was experiencing a kind of vision. The cast lost reality and were like pale ghosts around that dark, glowing figure in the centre of the stage: instead he could see ranged rank on rank behind him into the dark recesses of the dim world behind strange figures who had nothing to do with the opera. Hannah was there, and her brothers and behind them anonymous blue-bonnetted figures, happed in plaids and bowed with service to the land. Hector was there and behind him the flash of grey water and a shadowy snarling prow and grey helms. Grand watched with Grandmother at his side and behind them were other figures in sober black and white and rich crimsons. The whole stage swarmed with shapes and shadows of men and women, their faces and hands pale against the gleam of steel and silk. As the waves beat ever more strongly in his ears he saw himself in his wide-brimmed hat and the ancient sheepskin jacket he wore upon the hill. His heart beat thickly like a muffled drum and the waves thundered in, higher and higher. The auditorium swam with open cheering mouths and moving hands. The only steady point was the figure on the stage looking up at him while the rest of the world whirled and swung . . .

He came to with Lucy kneeling beside him, the torturing collar undone and a blur of faces behind Lucy's.

"Oh, John," she said reproachfully. "You gave us such a fright."

His heart had steadied to a laboured thud in his chest.

"Just a faint, Mrs. Macadam, "said a quiet voice on his other side. "He'll be fine in a few minutes."

"Damned collar," he heard himself croak, "too tight . . ."

"Very likely," agreed the quiet voice. "Drink a little of this."

'This' was whisky, thin and sharp and shocking and tasting of comfort, blasting the shadows aside, clearing his vision. When the door of the box was flung open he could see it clearly and the figure which stood in it. Nick, his face twisted with concern, plunged down beside Lucy.

"A simple faint," said the quiet voice, "and not surprising. A long journey, hardly any dinner, a tight collar and a lot of excitement . . ."

Nick's face cleared like the sky after rain. He smiled down at John and shook his head.

"Well," John said. "It was well worth the journey . . . well worth it."

Lucy giggled briefly and put her hand to her mouth.

"I never thought to hear him say that . . . damn festivals, damn operas, damn planes, damn shirkers, damn weather, damn hotel, damn shirt, damn stud, damn taxi, damn . . ."

There was a ripple of laughter and Nick grinned down at him.

"I get the picture."

He looked across his father at the possessor of the quiet voice.

"Can he sit up?"

"Not too quickly," said the quiet voice.

"Come on, Man Mountain, upsie-daisie and take it easy . . ."

Nick always looked thin and slight but that frame was surprisingly strong. John sat back in the chair.

"The Infant Phenomenon strikes again," he observed acidly. "Now, what's this surprise you have for us?"

"It was you sprang a surprise," Nick reproached. "Sure you're fit enough?"

"It'll do him more harm to keep in suspense," Lucy said indignantly, "not to mention me . . ."

"I don't suppose you'll be surprised really . . ."

"Come *on* . . ."

"I got married last week," Nick said. "I mean, I know I'm thirty-odd and it shouldn't be a surprise, but in view of the fact that you still haven't given me permission to ride my bicycle on the tarseal yet . . ."

"Less of your snash," John retorted. "When can we meet her?"

"You have," said the quiet voice, "though you weren't taking a lot of notice at the time."

John turned his head and saw that the quiet voice belonged to a tall, rather plump woman with a short crop of wavy dark hair and an unnoticeable face distinguished by a pair of dark bright eyes.

"Welcome to the family," he said, rather feebly and thought of the variegated series of luxurious beauties which had faced the photographers beside Nick over the past decade. He chuckled and held out his hand.

"Obviously a case of mild shock," observed Nick's wife and shook it.

"The best kind," John replied, "definitely."

"Sheep we got," Nick began, "music we got, bookworms we got . . ."

He hugged Lucy.

"Teachers we have acquired, a vet we married . . . now Bennachie will have a doctor. Jane and I want to come out for a while."

"Super!" Lucy said. "I was hoping that was it."

John remembered the curious vision he had seen and looked from one to the other.

"So," he murmured more to himself than to the people round him, "the story goes on . . . for a little while longer, the story will go on . . ."

He felt that if he really tried he could see into the future as he had seen into the past; his body felt light and hollow, like a vessel. Consciously, he turned the future from him. There was too much in it that he had no wish to know.